We Are Made of Stars

"With characters so real you'll feel like you just vacationed with them, *We Are Made of Stars* is at once a page-turner and a story that makes you slow down and examine your own life. Rochelle Weinstein's latest absolutely sparkles with warmth and wisdom."

—Camille Pagán, bestselling author of *Good for You*

"*We Are Made of Stars* is a work of art—suspenseful, intricate, and completely redemptive. It explores the brokenness and misunderstandings between us and the healing that happens when we acknowledge our connectedness."

—Annabel Monaghan, bestselling author of *Nora Goes Off Script*

"Incredible cast, splendid setting, and more than one story to keep you turning the pages!"

—Penelope Douglas, *New York Times*, *USA Today*, and *Wall Street Journal* bestselling author

What You Do to Me

"Good music vibes and compelling characters make this good for public libraries."

—*Booklist*

"Bestselling author Rochelle B. Weinstein had me at *mixtape*. Her nostalgic new page-turner, *What You Do to Me*, hits all the high notes: a strong, determined female protagonist, a dreamy love interest (ahh, the lead singer in a band), forbidden love, family drama, journalistic pursuits, suspense, and second chances. *Rolling Stone* reporter Cecilia

James has committed the cardinal sin: she has become emotionally involved in her story, as she deep dives into finding the truth behind a hit love song while trying to detangle her own messy love life and family secrets. I sang, I wept, I laughed, and I applauded—holding my lighter high for an encore performance. Weinstein's latest must-read gem doesn't miss a beat."

—Lisa Barr, *New York Times* bestselling author of *Woman on Fire*

"Warm, witty, and as lyrical as a love song, *What You Do to Me* is Rochelle Weinstein at the top of her storytelling game. A tale of broken dreams and second chances, this insider's look into the glitzy, gritty world of the music industry captivates—and, like a favorite melody, will stay with readers long after the final page. Five huge stars!"

—Kristy Woodson Harvey, *New York Times* bestselling author of *The Summer of Songbirds*

"Weinstein had me at *music*. Throw in a retro timeline that brings back all the '90s feels, and I'm a forever fan. *What You Do to Me* has everything I love in a story: romance, mystery, and suspense—the trifecta of an unputdownable read. Weinstein savvily crafts not one but two love stories, each with a heart-tugging emotional end; wraps them both in some of my favorite tunes from the best decades (IMHO), plus some new ones; and adds in a mystery detailed so visually I could easily picture this on screen. Fans of *Daisy Jones & the Six* and novels with music themes and persistent protagonists both flawed and edgy will obviously love this book, but I think Weinstein's novel packs an extra punch for us romantics who grew up falling for a rock star or two, even if he was only a poster on the wall above our bed."

—Kerry Lonsdale, *Wall Street Journal* bestselling author of *Side Trip*

"Long a master of the family saga, Rochelle Weinstein now turns her formidable talent to a passionate and playful love story. *What You Do to Me* is the story of star-crossed lovers Eddie, a musician, and Sara, his muse, and Cecelia, the journalist who is trying to rewrite their ending—and her own. Fans of Taylor Jenkins Reid's *Daisy Jones & the Six* will flock to this sweet and soulful book about first love and second chances, and will be moved and inspired to revisit the playlist of their own lives."

—Pam Jenoff, *New York Times* bestselling author of
Code Name Sapphire

"With a deft hand, Rochelle Weinstein has crafted a fascinating, multilayered tale expertly weaving between then and now. She introduces not one but several intriguing elements from the past and how they shaped the present, and I desperately needed to know how everything would end. And all I can say is, what a wild and wonderful ride."

—Tracey Garvis Graves, *New York Times* bestselling author of
Heard It in a Love Song

"I love everything Rochelle Weinstein writes, and I am still swooning over *What You Do to Me*, a story brimming with suspense, rock music, forbidden love, and a heroine who is determined to uncover a decades-long secret. Sexy, sweet, and ultimately so satisfying—you need to read this one!"

—Maddie Dawson, bestselling author of *Matchmaking for Beginners*

When We Let Go

"An emotional tale of mothers and daughters, loss and acceptance . . . A fully entertaining and at times thought-provoking read from first page to last."

—*Midwest Book Review*

"Poignant and heartfelt, this one truly shines."

—Allison Winn Scotch, *New York Times* bestselling author of
Cleo McDougal Regrets Nothing

"Rochelle Weinstein creates compelling, authentic characters I didn't want to let go of in this deeply heartfelt novel about love, loss, and the family ties that can break us—and make us whole. I absolutely loved it."

—Colleen Oakley, *USA Today* bestselling author

This Is Not How It Ends

"Readers who enjoy watching a protagonist's journey to emotional truths will appreciate this story of a woman struggling to determine how hers ends."

—*Booklist*

"The journey to the inevitable ending still manages to take some fascinating turns along the way."

—*Library Journal*

"An immediately and exceptionally engaging novel by a writer with an impressive knack for the kind of narrative storytelling style that rewards the reader with a story that will linger in the mind and memory long after the book is finished."

—*Midwest Book Review*

"In Rochelle B. Weinstein's latest, *This Is Not How It Ends*, Charlotte Myers is caught between two love stories—neither of which she expected, both of which come with great loss. Poignant and evocative, Weinstein has crafted a story that draws you in and won't let go. Keep the tissues nearby, especially for the heartbreaking yet gratifying conclusion. A wonderfully moving read!"

—Karma Brown, bestselling author of *The Life Lucy Knew*

"A beautifully written tale about love and the unexpected choices we are forced to make. Full of rich description and soulful characters, Weinstein's original story will have you turning pages quickly."

—Elyssa Friedland, author of *The Floating Feldmans*

WE ARE MADE OF STARS

OTHER TITLES BY ROCHELLE B. WEINSTEIN

WE ARE MADE OF STARS

A NOVEL

ROCHELLE B. WEINSTEIN

LAKE UNION
PUBLISHING

Text copyright © 2025 by Rochelle B. Weinstein
All rights reserved.

No part of this book may be reproduced, or stored in a retrieval system, or transmitted in any form or by any means, electronic, mechanical, photocopying, recording, or otherwise, without express written permission of the publisher.

Published by Lake Union Publishing, Seattle

www.apub.com

Amazon, the Amazon logo, and Lake Union Publishing are trademarks of Amazon.com, Inc., or its affiliates.

ISBN-13: 9781662520884 (paperback)
ISBN-13: 9781662520877 (digital)

Cover design by Lisa Amoroso
Cover image: ©Slanapotam / Alamy; ©David Lichtneker / ArcAngel

Printed in the United States of America

*For the people of western North Carolina and
eastern Tennessee.
Your strength, resiliency, and sense of community are as
beautiful as the land.
You are forever my home and in my heart.*

The darker the night, the brighter the stars.

—*Fyodor Dostoevsky*

SUNDAY
Day 1

First Course: Salade d'endives au roquefort

Second Course: Croque monsieur bites

Main Course: Roasted leg of lamb with brown butter and jus

Dessert: Highbush blueberry clafoutis

Veuve Clicquot champagne

Château Pavie-Decesse Saint-Émilion

CHAPTER 1

JEAN-PAUL

He tells himself it's going to be an extraordinary week. The trumpet mushrooms he chose at the farmers' market are bulbous and brown; their nutty flavor fills his nose. Leafy greens glisten under the faucet. He whispers it aloud. *An extraordinary week.* Because if he says it, it must be true.

Shutting the water off, he reminds himself the inn is an extraordinary place, and the guests about to converge are spices on his shelves, a medley of flavors. A thrill courses through him as he towels his hands, his eyes lingering on the fresh cheese they picked up for the croque monsieur bites. For the roasted leg of lamb, he swapped out the cauliflower cream for classic French jus, his wife's favorite. These little gestures please Renée, earn him a nod.

The guests will arrive soon, traveling up the lengthy drive that winds through the wispy grass lined with spruce and hemlocks, toting their individual tales. As he prepares meals in the gourmet kitchen, Renée coaxes those stories out. Jean-Paul and Renée are a formidable team. They've turned their brainchild from all those years ago into a charming bed-and-breakfast nestled in the rolling hills of Vilas, North Carolina, where each week eight guests check into the stately farmhouse. They named her *Vis Ta Vie*, French for "live your life," because they were living theirs. Could this really mark the end of an era?

Renée finds him in the kitchen, the evidence of their sleepless night marking her hazel eyes. Delicate strands of silver thread through her brown curls, but she's as beautiful as when they first met. She catches him staring, and they exchange thin smiles.

When she slipped the blanket off their tangled bodies this morning, she was careful not to disturb him, but he was awake, replaying their difficult conversation into early dawn. The decision weighed heavily, more so on him, the guilt another ingredient in a famed dish. Subtle. A pinch. But you could taste it. Renée has always been the beating heart of their collaboration. He hates disappointing her.

He watches as she stuffs recipe cards into envelopes and seals them with gold foil stickers. They choose the dinner menus carefully, each dish satisfying a discerning palate with eclectic, seasonal flavors. In his opinion, the world has grown overly complicated with the gluten-free, vegan, Paleo craze, but these are trends and demands the proprietors of a popular inn must adopt if they want guests to return.

They work quietly, the disappointing conversation hovering close. She wipes the line of sweat forming along her neck, cramming her thick curls into a hair tie, confirming what they already know about the air-conditioning system—it needs to be replaced. The worry climbs inside his chest, and he swears the cookbooks that line the floor-to-ceiling bookshelves mock him.

Jean-Paul belongs here. And the antiques staring out from the glass cabinets, the ones they collected on their trips to Italy and France, remind him so. Vis Ta Vie is home, and he has poured everything into her upkeep and refurbishing. Entering the glass doors is like slipping inside a cloud swaddled in sunlight. He wants their guests to feel the same buoyancy, a sanctuary in which they can escape the pressures of life. Recharge. Reboot. But now he feels it all slipping away. Building a life around a passion for food, wine, and breathtaking scenery once seemed romantic. Creating a place to unplug and restore diminished reserves now feels terribly foolish.

Bach's "Toccata and Fugue in D Minor" plays on the sound system, which sends an ominous shiver down his spine. His niece, Simone, pops her head through the open door. "*Bonjour, tante et oncle.* Our guests have arrived."

He catches Renée's expression. The excitement mired in disillusion. She unties her apron, dons her best smile, and together they greet the cars lined up on the gravel driveway.

He breathes in, repeating the phrase so it will be true. *This will be an extraordinary week.*

CHAPTER 2

CASSIDY

"Wake up, Rosalie, we're here."

The car winds up the unpaved road through the towering trees and rolling hills before coming to a stop in front of the two-story inn. Cassidy jumps out, already calculating the number of miles she'll have to run to offset the hours spent behind the wheel. She's not sure why she agreed to drive from Chicago, two full days of sedentary torture, but apparently Rosalie expected a road trip adventure of some kind. Cassidy jogs in place to get the blood flowing as Rosalie steps out of the car.

She wavers, taking in the pale-gray building trimmed in white.

"What is it?" Cassidy comes around, noticing the dullness in her daughter's cheeks. "You're the one who chose this place. I've heard nothing but 'Vis Ta Vie' for the last nine months."

Her daughter doesn't meet her eyes, though this and her colorless cheeks are nothing new.

Cassidy has made it abundantly clear how she feels about Rosalie's selection for their annual summer trip. Given the choice, she would have headed west to Tucson's Canyon Ranch. Nothing is as satisfying as portioned meals, round-the-clock wellness, and calorie counts. But this year was Rosalie's turn to pick their summer getaway, and Cassidy couldn't argue, not when her daughter had been such a champ last year while biking through Croatia before landing in the hospital with a broken arm. Okay, two broken arms.

Today Rosalie's gloominess suggests something else, and there's a hesitation in her step. Well, let's be frank here, there's *always* a hesitation, except when it involves slathering herself with charcoal makeup and dark lipstick, or scrolling through TikTok and devouring stacks of novels. For those activities, her energy level is at a remarkable high.

Cassidy has felt an apprehension mounting in recent weeks, and now her daughter rubs her belly in a tender, circular motion, which reminds Cassidy of the young expectant moms in her downtown spin class. Like any other neurotic single mother with a fifteen-year-old daughter, her mind wanders to that forbidden place, where she quickly vanquishes the thought. *No, impossible.*

"You were so excited to come here." Cassidy drapes her arm along Rosalie's shoulder, snagging a strand of purple hair. Her daughter is both familiar and foreign. It's anyone's guess what's spooling around her brain.

When Cassidy found out she was having a girl, she imagined spa days and movie nights, shopping trips and Bravo TV. Cassidy had that closeness with her own mother, and she expected the same with Rosalie. Yet the kinship never developed. How could someone who took refuge in her belly for nine months grow to be so alarmingly different from her? Rosalie hides herself beneath the harsh tones of Glam Goth Beauty, her favorite cosmetics brand, and regularly refuses invitations to join Cassidy at the gym. Didn't all mothers and daughters have an affinity for shared workouts?

Instead, Rosalie keeps to herself, her nose in a fantasy novel, closed off in her room with headphones. She prefers documentaries and dark, ill-fitting clothes that match her smoky eyeshadow, her features obscured by rebellion. She's smart. Straight As in all her classes. For reasons Cassidy doesn't understand, Rosalie aspires to be the antithesis of her *feminine, active* mother, though some would say Cassidy has other qualities. *Irresponsible. Careless.* She's heard people call her *ditzy.* She stops herself from continuing the freight train of negativity. Raising a daughter, alone, is hard. And their annual trip is nonnegotiable.

Rosalie inches closer to the inn, calling over her shoulder, "Don't forget your suitcase in the trunk. And take the keys out of the ignition." Caught, again, Cassidy circles back to the car, reaches in, and lunges for the keys. Slamming the door, she scours the property. Trees. Grass. Pond. *Dullsville.* Why couldn't they have gone somewhere else? Another car approaches, and a life-size Ken and Barbie hop out. Her long blond hair floats down her narrow shoulders; his ass is impeccable in fitted joggers. Cassidy winces at their youth. She's been trying to replicate the woman's smooth, dewy skin with a truckload of serums and creams. Their hands and arms coil together, so it's hard to tell where he ends and she begins. They'll eventually get to be her age. *Life won't be so kind.*

An older couple exits the building. The woman's got noticeable crow's-feet and dimpled cheeks, and Cassidy inwardly smiles. Someone closer to her age. They make their way over, pride bursting from the woman's greenish-brown eyes. "You must be Cassidy and Rosalie." She smiles broadly. *Could use a little filler.* "I'm Renée De La Rue, and this is my husband, Jean-Paul." Behind her, the door swings open, and a woman carrying a tray of champagne emerges. "That would be our niece, Simone."

The man looks vaguely familiar. Thick salt-and-pepper hair matching a neatly trimmed beard. And then it hits her. A chubbier George Clooney. Renée De La Rue smiles while Simone hands out flutes. Simone looks to be in her twenties. Cassidy can tell by the flawless texture of her skin, the wavy brown hair. Simone attempts a conversation with Rosalie, but her daughter's nervously biting her lip, eyes darting back and forth. Cassidy's lost count of how many times she's had to remind Rosalie of the importance of eye contact.

Renée and Jean-Paul make their way toward Barbie and Ken, and Cassidy overhears their names: "Adam and Sienna." Charming, cute names. If she's being honest, she didn't accidentally overhear them. She craned her neck so she could eavesdrop while Rosalie pelted Simone with one-word responses. Cassidy brings the champagne glass to her lips, pausing as she assesses Sienna embracing the inn owners with her trim body. *Pace yourself.*

Renée makes a quick introduction, and Cassidy smiles—no teeth, her specialty. Renée motions for them to head inside. To the young couple she adds, "Your friends have already made themselves at home."

Ken and Barbie skip ahead, disappearing inside the building, and Cassidy's anxious to follow. "C'mon, Rosie."

But her daughter hangs back, her black booties planted in the rocky driveway. "I can't." Her heavily made-up eyes land on the ground. "I think this was a mistake."

"You're just figuring that out now?" Cassidy's annoyed but does her best to disguise it. "We could've been transforming ourselves, hiking the Sonoran Desert."

"That's not what I meant." She turns, stricken. "I made a mistake. This was all a mistake."

Cassidy sidles up to her, gripping her shoulder. "Rosie, what's going on?" Rosalie is on the verge of tears. And Cassidy doesn't do tears, can't take people crying—the whole empathy thing coupled with drippy noses and flowery soliloquies. "Please don't cry," she whispers.

Rosalie stiffens at her mother's touch. Stopping short of full-blown tears, she begins to count. Fast, consecutive numbers. "One. Two. Three. Four . . ." Cassidy finds it almost as puzzling as the crying. The counting is a door that Cassidy can't pass through, and she eventually stopped trying. When Rosalie reaches a comfortable number—today it's one hundred and twenty-seven—she lets out a deep breath. "Mom."

This stops Cassidy dead in her tracks. Rosalie has always called her *Cassidy*. It was a term of her arm's-length endearment, and her quivering lips forming this foreign word—*mom*—means *strap in*. "I'm sorry . . ." She struggles to get the words out. "I'm sorry I made you come here."

A swearing woman might have asked her what the hell she was talking about. Cassidy is a swearing woman, but this isn't the time or place. "You're not making one iota of sense, Rosie." But her daughter has already picked up her suitcase and marched toward the glass doors. The De La Rues wait nearby, smiling, and Cassidy silently prays Rosalie's smiled back. Just because her daughter doesn't make any sense to her doesn't mean she hasn't taught her manners.

"Ms. Banks," Renée says softly as Cassidy enters the threshold. "I think being here will be good for both of you."

Cassidy sees no hidden agenda on her face, but Renée's eyes hint that she knows how to read people. And even though it's a balmy day, a chill finds its way up Cassidy's leg and spreads up her spine. She's sure Renée doesn't mean to sound foreboding, but she does.

CHAPTER 3

ROSALIE

When Rosalie's nervous, she counts. The consistency of numbers provides structure and routine, assurances she's lacked for most of her life. The digits slip off her tongue as she follows Jean-Paul through the doors, catching a glimpse of the cozy interior. She picked the bed-and-breakfast for a reason, and not because the website promised a mountainous escape. Well, that was part of it, but she has other news to share with her mother. Big news. And when her count reaches one hundred and twenty-seven, she exhales, assuring herself she made the right choice.

Rosalie had done her research. Lots of research. She had her pick of destinations, but Vis Ta Vie made sense. Back home, Cassidy would peer over Rosalie's shoulder while she tapped away at her computer, tossing out baseless opinions, but Rosalie stood firm. She had thought long and hard about her decision, from the location to the activities to the master chef. Actually, Rosalie didn't really care about the activities. That was Cassidy's area of expertise. Zip-lining, tubing on Watauga Lake, hiking the Blue Ridge—none of it mattered. What mattered was that Rosalie would finally get to tell her what she'd done. And it didn't hurt that the place sounded perfect: peaceful and balanced, so unlike her life in Chicago.

It would be good for them. Just like Renée said.

CHAPTER 4

HENRY

Henry Rose-Wall peers out the second-floor window of *Blanc d'Ivoire*, watching Adam and Sienna exit their car. Little has changed about the couple they've known since college. They capture attention wherever they go for more than their striking good looks. He watches the other guests stare, how Renée beelines in their direction, arms outstretched. This summer marks their thirteenth trip to Vis Ta Vie, and the number strikes Henry as an eerie premonition. What will Adam and Sienna make of their decision?

He and Lucy have argued about the timing. Henry feels an announcement on their annual trip will be disruptive, a stain on mostly enjoyable memories, but Lucy insisted. Arriving hours earlier and separately from their friends was part of her strategy. Lucy is wired for preparation, always a step ahead.

When Henry and Lucy checked in earlier that day, Renée greeted them warmly, chatting amiably with Henry about recent cosmic activity and his work at Atlanta's planetarium. "What does the sky have in store for us this week?" she had asked. One of the reasons they'd chosen Vis Ta Vie as an annual summer destination was because there is no light pollution, the sky a blank canvas easily read by the trained eye. Renée De La Rue shares Henry's affinity for the galaxy, and they've spent hours discussing stars or how when the moon is at its fullest, behaviors change and tensions brew.

He was pleased to see the cycles still interested her, and when Lucy passed through the doorway, she waved a hand in the air. "Don't get him started, Renée. He'll monopolize your entire morning with his celestial talk." Which reminds him of that tension. Perhaps they should postpone their news until a new moon.

Henry should have known it would come to this. For years he tried to interest his wife in the rhythm of space, the marvel of an infinite galaxy, but it was a language that flummoxed her. In their early days, Henry would take her to the fifth-floor balcony of his college dorm, where his telescope sat. He'd talk endlessly about the stars, his dark eyes brightening, coaxing her to peer through the lens at the vastness of the universe. She couldn't comprehend what she was seeing. She saw darkness and disarray; he saw light and patterns. That's when she'd pretend, oohing and aahing, which gave Henry momentary satisfaction. Wasn't that what you did for love?

While Henry spent hours in the sky, Lucy rooted herself to Earth through the patients in her therapy practice. In some ways, their careers are similar: searching for answers, assessing a larger picture. But then that business with his father. He shakes his head, wishing it away, though the shame of the headlines burns his cheeks. The tentacles of scandal stretched wide, and not even Lucy's training could save them.

She joins him by the window, and Henry catches a whiff of her scent. Her fresh fragrance reminds him of when they last had sex. Despite their recent issues, she was hard to resist. There had been a strawberry moon that night, bold and beautiful and taunting. Like Lucy.

"We don't have to tell them tonight, Henry."

"I'm not sure why we have to tell them at all."

She cocks her head. "What are you saying?"

"I meant here," he corrects himself. "We don't have to announce it here. This week."

Her gaze lowers to the gray oak floors, and Henry's eyes follow. Renée loved reminding them how the floors are French oak from Provence, rich with history.

"This is about us, Luce. I don't know why . . ." His voice trails off, but then he can't stop himself. "I just don't understand how we got here." He catches her eyes with his. "Weren't we good together?"

"We were great together." Her voice rises when she says this, as though she's trying to convince herself, to salvage what's left. And when that doesn't work, she takes a deep breath and straightens. She reminds him it's okay to make this leap, that they haven't failed.

When she spews this sort of psychological jargon, it goes one of two ways for Henry: a direct miss, or some form of resignation. "When a marriage doesn't work, Henry, admitting it's best to move on isn't defeat. Defeat is staying. Defeat is wading through a loveless union where children grow up believing that's the norm."

He loves her. That hasn't changed. But there's still the matter of telling Adam and Sienna.

"I think we owe it to them," she says. "They're our closest friends—they're practically family."

After college, the Rose-Walls made their home in Buckhead while the Kravitzes moved to New York City, but the friendship has continued through holiday trips and milestones. Lucy and Sienna were there for the births of each other's children and have spent hours on the phone confiding in one another. During their visits, the men bonded over their college antics with golf and cigars and discussed the evolutions of their careers. As a sports agent, Adam always has tickets to the best sporting events, which is a definite perk. They are a close-knit bunch, an effortless family, and their annual summer trip to Vis Ta Vie has been a highlight.

"It's going to be okay." She drops a hand on his. "These are the best types of divorces. Amicable. Both sides in agreement. We're in agreement, right?"

But he can't be sure. He doesn't like the superlative, hasn't witnessed any "best divorce," which is a glaring oxymoron. They've had these conversations before, but somehow, whenever he thinks about the dissolution of their marriage, saying *divorce* out loud, his throat tightens, and the words stick. *Fight harder. For the kids. For who we used to be.* Except he isn't sure he has the strength, or if that's what she wants.

"Henry? We're in agreement, right?"

"Sure."

The word is barely audible, but she nods, eyes stuck on Sienna and Adam. "I don't think this is going to come as a surprise to them."

He steps back, dropping onto the window seat. "Did you discuss it with her?"

She doesn't look at him. "God no."

Lucy and Sienna are kindreds. They used to speak no fewer than ten times a day and didn't make a single decision without consulting the other, but recently things have changed. "Did something happen between you two?"

She turns around, failing to meet his eyes. She's in her head, where she often is. "It was just too much noise."

She's never referred to her best friend as noise. They were like sisters.

"I'm confused," he finally says. "You said they wouldn't be surprised."

"I don't know, Henry. Maybe you're confused because your head's stuck in the clouds." She pauses. "Or maybe, maybe you're just a little broken."

CHAPTER 5

CASSIDY

"Are you sure you don't want to switch rooms?" Cassidy asks when she checks to see how Rosalie's doing. "I know you relish your bath. *Belledonne* has a French tub that looks out onto the pond."

"I like *Le Beau*." She's perched beside the window, staring out. When Cassidy nears, she sees Jean-Paul and Renée lugging buckets of flowers from a delivery truck. Jean-Paul pulls out a pale-pink flower and sticks it behind Renée's ear. Then he kisses her.

"They seem to really like each other," Rosalie says.

Cassidy chalks up her daughter's hasty assessment to idealistic longings. "Appearances can be misleading. You know that."

Her daughter sighs, playing with a strand of hair with her black fingernails. She licks her dark lips, reminding Cassidy of the day she was born. She had fallen in love with those heart-shaped lips. When they'd rolled Cassidy into the delivery room, the first question they asked was if her husband would be joining. "A friend? Family member?"

Cassidy's mother pops into her mind. "Parenting won't be easy, Cassidy," Ann Banks had said. "You'll always have me, but it's hard to raise a baby on your own." Which was exactly what ended up happening when Rosalie turned two months old and Ann, Cassidy's only living relative, died.

Now Rosalie mostly hated her mother, making it her life's mission to prove how much. Granted, the dislike wasn't entirely unfounded. Cassidy had forgotten permission slips over the years, leaving Rosalie to miss out on school field trips, and there was the time she showed up to Rosalie's class with cupcakes laced with alcohol meant for her spin instructor's birthday. The teacher wasn't very happy about the mix-up. And maybe she had once fallen asleep with a cigarette burning in her fingers and almost torched the house. Rosalie had screamed, accusing her of acting like a child. A child! Begging her to "grow up."

Fortunately, Ann Banks had left them a tidy sum of money and her house. Rosalie was never without food and clothing, and the home was big enough to entertain guests, though Rosalie never brought anyone home. This baffled Cassidy—she knew the kids in the neighborhood called her the "fun" mom.

In between the arguments and hostility, Rosalie periodically asked about her father. And as she grew, so did her curiosity. Cassidy wasn't forthcoming. The pregnancy had been a triumph, but it also symbolized her greatest failure—an inability to find a life partner, to love and be loved.

Rosalie kept asking about her father, the question that could never be answered. The years passed, and as her classmates brought their fathers to school and Rosalie met her friends' dads at sleepovers, her quest for understanding deepened. And she was relentless.

At one point Cassidy, with little guidance and a serious case of impostor syndrome, sat her ten-year-old daughter down, prepared to tell her the truth, but upon staring into Rosalie's clear, blue eyes, she abruptly changed her mind. "Your father died, Rosalie. Right after you were born." It was simple, a finite resolution to put an end to the questions. But this was Rosalie. She wanted evidence. She wanted details—what he was like, how they had met. "Don't I have grandparents? Where are the wedding pictures?" She had questions upon questions.

Cassidy remembered feeling a little sick inside when she made something up about a flood in the basement. "All the pictures were ruined." But not sicker than when she told Rosalie that her father's parents were dead too.

"Oh" was all the young girl could muster. "You don't have a single photo?"

"Rosie, it's just so painful." Cassidy did have a flair for the dramatic. But once, when Rosalie had managed to wear her thin, she'd pulled a picture from her high school album, which happened to be in the attic with all Cassidy's presumably ruined pictures. She told Rosalie that Gene was her father. It was true that Gene had been Cassidy's boyfriend at one time. Heck, he was the young love of her life—the only love— and she had enough pictures to satisfy any level of curiosity. The two of them, big-toothed and big-haired, smiling at the prom. Swimming in Lake Michigan. And suddenly, Rosalie had a dad.

Blinking away the memory of that lie, Cassidy sits in front of the mirror and applies another coat of lipstick. "Let's try to have a good week." She smacks her lips together, and Rosalie turns from the window. The girl has globs of mascara on her lashes. "What was that about earlier? You said you made a mistake."

"It's nothing. I'm about to get my period."

"Phew."

"What's that supposed to mean?"

"For one, you're not pregnant."

"Funny."

"You know there's nothing funny about me, right?"

Rosalie picks up the welcome packet left on the end table beside a modest vase of cream-color roses. She skims the pages detailing their stay. "There's a schedule. Please try to follow it."

Cassidy glares. "Excuse me?"

"You know exactly what I mean." She throws on a light jacket. "I'm going for a walk—"

"Great idea!" Cassidy stands up. "Let me get my sneakers."

If a gaze had bullets, that would describe Rosalie's stare.

"No worries." Cassidy sits back down. "I'll just finish unpacking and . . ." She's really not sure what she'll do.

"We have to be downstairs at six. We're going to meet the other guests then." Cassidy starts to say something, but Rosalie continues. "Please try not to embarrass me."

Cassidy wants to make a face, but she stops herself, simply nodding.

"They want everyone there for a welcome picture, and then that Jean-Paul guy cooks dinner for us. Three courses, plus dessert."

Rosalie looks triumphant, knowing how it will kill Cassidy to eat more than a piece of lettuce. "Too bad there's no young people for you, Rosie . . . But that Simone seems lovely . . . Maybe you'll make a new friend."

"Maybe." But she doesn't sound entirely optimistic.

CHAPTER 6

HENRY

Lucy isn't wrong. He lives in the clouds. And maybe he's a little broken. But he hasn't always been that way. Like most great stories, there was a before and there was an after. *Before* appeared shiny and lacquered; *after* was dull and lifeless. In some ways, Henry preferred the latter, if for no other reason than the honesty of it all.

His phone pings, and there it is: another message from his mother.

You can't ignore him forever.

Of course he can. That's the plan. His hard-earned self-preservation.

Please talk to him.

Lucy catches the strain on his face and moves closer. "What is it?"

"Just the usual spammy politicians."

"Henry."

Lucy wouldn't be too pleased if she knew what had transpired the last few weeks. The frequent letters from his father he ripped in half rather than opening. The repetitive calls from across the country he's declined. She has never fully understood his knee-jerk reaction in cutting him from their lives, and none of her well-meaning lectures could sway him. His father is a criminal. His actions hurt people. He didn't pull any triggers, but people wound up dead. An early release doesn't change any of that.

"Please, Luce. Not now."

"You think I don't know what's happening? Don't shut me out. He's my family too."

Henry spots the frailty in her tone that wasn't there before. How could he have missed it? He takes a closer look. Her hair is styled differently. Instead of the slicked-back ponytail she wears with her patients, the dark-brown strands fall loosely down her shoulders. He once loved when she wore her hair down, especially when they had sex and the wisps would graze his chest. But it's her eyes that give him pause. They're their usual blue, Neptune blue, named for their deep, dark, and sometimes cool undertone. Today they're lighter, and he can almost make out the faint glitter circling the iris. Henry understands gravitational forces, and despite agreeing to the imminent divorce, he feels himself being pulled in.

Quashing the urge to gather her up and drop her onto the fluffy white duvet, he remembers when she first brought him home to meet her parents. The elitist, scholarly psychiatrists came right out and said, "You didn't tell us your boyfriend was Black."

Later that night, after he was inside her, she said, "Why would I have to announce the color of your skin, Henry? When I brought Daniel Miller home for the first time, they didn't expect me to hold up a 'He's white!' sign."

He had loved her for that. He still did. So when she used the word *family*, and he saw vulnerability slip from her eyes, it was hard to turn away.

"It's him." Her voice is wistful.

Henry isn't very good at pretending, especially with her. When you're married to a therapist, you're perpetually on a couch. Every word, every nuance laid out bare, your mind an open book. Motives are carefully examined. Answers magnified for deeper meaning—similar to how Henry uses a telescope at work. In her field, Lucy is the telescope, and Henry and the people around her are the stars she analyzes.

"The kids miss him." She finally says it. The thing that's been sitting between them. And before he has a chance to process, she says the other thing. "I miss him."

Lucy and his dad had been close. When her father died unexpectedly, his took over, swooping in—never overstepping—and providing enough paternal love to ground her. And what she held most dear was that at every holiday, every dinner table, any opportunity, Henry's dad pulled her aside to talk to her about her father to keep his memory alive. He'd tell her how their boys had his eyes, his sense of humor. While Henry disappeared in the constellations, Lucy and his father shared a love of ice hockey and regular chili cook-offs. They were close.

He knew what his dad's absence meant to Lucy. She'd lost another father. And when she told Henry she wanted to visit him, he cautioned against it. They told the kids Grandpa was away on business . . . traveling. Sometimes he'd allow them a quick phone call, but there was a missing piece in their lives. No matter how hard they tried to pretend, it was gone.

It has been three years since the world toppled over. Since the stars dipped erratically from the sky. Most of the time, he has felt as though he's floating in space. They decided to tell no one. That's how deep the shame is. And before he can languish in the downward spiral that is his personal hell, there's a knock, and Sienna's face peeks around the door.

"Hey . . . you guys hiding from us?"

Sienna's voice is lyrical, like Sienna herself. She moves in rhythm like a bouncy song. In Henry terms, Sienna could easily be the sun, radiant and bold, tough to look at directly, but you always feel her presence. Henry had bestowed Sienna with the title *Sirius*: luminous and sparkling like the brightest star.

Today she's as shiny as ever. Her blond bangs land just above her brows, framing her large hazel eyes. She doesn't wait for them to answer;

she waltzes in, wrapping first Lucy in her arms, then Henry. She smells like Sienna, a mixture of sunscreen and citrus perfume, and she steps back, taking them both in. "You ditched us!"

Sienna is the embodiment of summers spent beneath this roof. She's the campfire glowing under the night sky, the pink tube floating in the New River, the steady stream of a waterfall. For the last dozen years, the couples have met at the Charlotte airport and shared the two-hour drive to the inn. Their decision this year to travel separately made a bold statement.

"Things got chaotic with our schedule . . . and the flights . . . but we're here!" Lucy says, tripping over her words.

Henry observes the exchange, a history and a future about to unravel. Maybe they were foolish to think this annual trip would be anything like the others. "Where's Adam?"

"You know him. He's already out for a run. Can't sit still for a minute. Oh, you'll never guess who called me today—literally on the way to the airport: Syl Farmer. That woman has an eerie sense of timing."

"No way."

Syl and Sy. They had all met during year five at the inn. The eccentric couple had disrupted the table on night three with *Let's throw our keys in a bowl and play a little game.* Lucy and Henry were shocked. Adam and Sienna pretended not to hear.

"What did she want?" Lucy asks.

"What do you think? They're getting divorced." She tosses her hair back. "You know those types of games just cause problems in a marriage. You can never go back. Did you see the other guests?" Sienna talks in a rush, one fast sentence running into another. "So far, there's only two of them. You'll have a field day, Luce. Renée said they're a mother and daughter. Mom's obviously done a number on the kid. She looks pretty miserable."

Sienna jumps on the bed, wriggling her tiny body into the folds of the cozy down. "I'm so happy we're back together again." She stares at the ceiling, her blond hair fanning across the comforter. "I love our kids.

I love our house, but there's something about being here with y'all that just makes me giddy inside. It's like college again. Everything's simple. Just us. It's my favorite trip of the year."

Henry doesn't know what to do with himself. Lucy eyes him warily.

"Us too," Lucy says, breaking her silence to join Sienna on the bed.

"What's wrong?" Sienna rolls onto her side to face her. "You don't seem very excited."

"Just thinking about how many years we've been coming here. Makes you wonder how much longer we can keep it up."

"Rubbish," Sienna says. "We made a promise. We're growing old together."

CHAPTER 7

JEAN-PAUL

Jean-Paul's in the kitchen slicing fruit and cheese with the precision of a trained surgeon. He takes great pride in arranging the colors and shapes into art. A quiet calm has descended upon the grounds as the sun tiptoes across the sky, bathing the property in amber hues. The hour provides a respite from the guests' full day of travel, and he relishes the laughter filtering through the doors, the creaky footsteps signaling life.

Renée is nearby, dropping gray cloth place mats on the table. He sneaks up behind her, brushes the hair from the nape of her neck, and tastes the sweat on her skin. They debated long into the night whether to replace the air-conditioning, whether it was even necessary in the mountains, but that was to avoid the bigger issue—their diminished savings—and how it was impossible to keep up with the exclusive guesthouses sprouting around their quiet town, trendier establishments luring VIPs and elite spenders. The monetary loss wasn't entirely their fault—they had thought they were being prudent, investing how they did—but the conversation remains off-limits, the details too painful to discuss.

She drops her head and lets him massage her shoulders.

"You're tense."

"Disappointed," she says.

He spins her around. His wife is petite, barely reaching his chin. "We've had a great run, *mon amour*. We must be practical."

"Selling's the only option?" she asks.

"I think it is best."

The letdown's there in her eyes, and he knows she's restraining herself. He also knows better than to fool her with false hope. "Remember our first year when the guests arrived, and the anticipation we felt that first night, the magic we were about to create? Hold on to that, *mon amour*. For tonight."

He brushes a wispy curl from her face. Her head falls into his palm.

"It's going to be an extraordinary week." If he says it, it must be true.

"You're right. You always are."

He laughs. "I will remind you of that later." He's back at the sink, towel-drying the lettuce. She's setting variations of white and cream plates on the place mats. "Now tell me about our guests. How's everyone settling in?"

She tells him of the somber voices coming from Lucy and Henry's room earlier. "I have a champagne toast planned later in the week for his birthday and to celebrate their thirteenth year. Maybe you can prepare the *mousse au chocolat* they loved so much."

"I believe it was the flambé, *mon amour*. Things got *très chaud* the evening we served that, if I recall."

She thinks about this, gently nodding. "You're right. Better to serve something crisp and cool. A berry tart or carrot cake."

Jean-Paul isn't expected to remember names or faces or what makes a particular guest tick. That's her job. But he understands the effect of his food. How tenderloin sprinkled with the right amount of pepper makes guests feisty, or how oysters are an aphrodisiac, and when served with flaming hot sauce, they bring forth tears. His food sets the mood for the evening, elicits hidden desires.

If he is the magician, she's the wizard behind the scenes, the puppeteer—coordinating, coaxing—the one who brings the inn and its inhabitants to life. There's nothing cursory about his wife. Long before guests descend on the property, she knows their tastes, how they take their coffee, their favorite snacks and sleeping habits, the introverted extroverts, and (for lack of a better word) the assholes.

And while Jean-Paul performs his nightly cooking experience, showcasing his culinary expertise, she does what she does best. And it isn't merely ensuring that glasses are topped off with the best wines. Their table has power. Careful planning facilitates connection, the kind that delves beyond manufactured personalities. Renée's superpower is stripping strangers of their facades, digging deep inside their cores. Everyone at the inn has a past, a story. And when they gather, they become pieces of a puzzle, fitting together to make a much bigger picture.

"Who else?" he asks.

"Other than Adam and Sienna and Leo and Penny, it's the mother and the daughter."

"The one with the purple hair?"

She nods. "I feel for her."

He grabs a clean knife and begins chopping the lettuce. "I see where this is going."

"This feels different."

"You say that every time, *mon amour*."

Again, she tells him he's not wrong.

"The strays gravitate toward you." What he doesn't say is how she gravitates toward them. If wistful longing were an eye color, it would be hers.

"I spotted her walking the path. I'm not sure she wants to be here."

He disagrees. "That's impossible—impossible for anyone not to want to be here."

"I don't know, Jean-Paul. We don't typically have teenagers."

The inn was a labor of love. They spent years renovating floors and ceilings, choosing tiles and paint swatches. The pale furniture is timeless, the bedding plush and luxurious, and the monochromatic color scheme—five shades of gray—warms the clean, open space. But it's the kitchen he's proudest of. When guests descend the nine steps into the intimate space, with its high ceilings and natural lighting, they're transformed. The T-shaped dining area showcases a Carrara marble table, white with gray veining, that connects to his stainless steel chef's counter. From there, guests have a front-row seat as he prepares savory meals surrounded by top-of-the-line appliances he and Renée poured their life savings into.

He can already hear the buzzing around the room, the place where seeds of conversation sprout. Connections. Secrets. Truths. Heat flares from his range. Tempers and emotions spring from their seats. In their twenty-six years, they've witnessed walls tumbling, relationships deepening, and unusual trust creeping in. One guest, a renowned psychologist, described the experience as the stripping away of masks, a metaphorical undressing. He wasn't wrong.

Whatever reason guests landed at Vis Ta Vie—the decor, the beauty of the grounds, the food—the rare vulnerability felt in a private enclave made magic. And as Jean-Paul makes his way toward the antique cabinet that houses the fine china, he does his best to hold on to the belief that the magic still exists.

CHAPTER 8

CASSIDY

From the window of her room, Cassidy watches Rosalie scurry along the path leading to the small pond. Well, *scurry* is a stretch. It's more like dragging her feet. What she wouldn't give for her daughter to take up even a moderate form of exercise, anything to clear her head and make her less anxious and defiant. Whenever Cassidy suggests a gym membership or fitness class, though, Rosalie interprets it seventy-seven different ways. None of them complimentary. Granted, there's a noticeable difference in their bodies. Cassidy is grossly underweight. But as a forty-five-year-old woman, she feels it's important to maintain her college weight. Even if it kills her. Rosalie doesn't feel the same way, so any mention of the Peloton Cassidy recently purchased or a suggestion to take a walk or join a SoulCycle class is met with derision, an immediate insult.

Which usually leads to Cassidy bringing up Rosalie's rigid personality. Or Rosalie's anemic social life. Or Rosalie's choice of hair color and dress. The list is endless. Conversations are battlegrounds where benign statements turn into dangerous land mines. Is Rosalie depressed? Maybe they should discuss medication or therapy. Or boarding school? Maybe she would thrive away from home? But then it clicks in Cassidy's mind: Without Rosie, who would remind her when bills need to be paid? Who would make her favorite oil-free egg-white omelet for breakfast? Rosalie is an excellent cook. No, boarding school is not an option.

But what did she mean earlier, when she said she was sorry for making her mother come here? Cassidy has no idea. Is Rosalie planning to do something foolish? Cassidy's heart quickens. She doesn't know what to make of it, and it makes her yearn for her own mother.

Like Rosalie, Cassidy was an only child. And Cassidy and her mother were more than mother and daughter: they were close. Fine, maybe they were a little too close. They weren't as bad as the women on that show *sMothered* in that they never shared bathwater, but there were some similarities. Dressing alike, vacationing together, the two had been inseparable. When Ann died, it broke Cassidy. Little Rosalie was a newborn. How would she manage motherhood without her own mom? She didn't like to think of that time.

Instead, she prepares herself for dinner, slapping on blush and a fresh coat of mascara. She'll have to do something about the thin threads that used to be her lashes, but for now, she's stuck here for the week, determined to make the best of it. And as she walks downstairs, she has no idea that making the best of it is never going to happen.

CHAPTER 9

SIENNA

Sienna's preening at her reflection in the mirror of *Miel* as Adam thumbs messages into his phone. "I thought you were going to take a break this trip," she says.

He glances up, long enough to appraise her outfit. "You know I don't like when you wear tops that are so . . ." A hand lands on his chest.

He means high necked. Covering her modest cleavage. It's not half a second until he's back on his phone. "You know I'm brokering this deal with the Cowboys."

She nods, acquiescing. She's good at that. They step out the door and make their way through the old house, the floors creaking with each step. "Something's up with Lucy and Henry. I still don't understand why they didn't meet us at the airport. The drive is one of the best parts of the trip."

He drops his phone in his pocket. "What does it matter? We're all here."

"She's been weird. I don't know. There's this thing between us."

"*Thing.* Can you elaborate?"

"I've been telling you this for months."

This is the moment when she has to check herself. Lately she's had a hard time connecting with Adam about things that matter. His erratic hours. The endless traveling. The missed chunks of the kids' lives, their life. And now this business with Henry and Lucy.

She's not sure when it started, but there's been a noticeable shift in their relationship with Lucy. Unanswered phone calls. Excuses for not getting together. They usually see each other during the year for a long weekend, but they haven't since last summer, and it's the most time they've spent apart since college. Lucy, her ride or die, felt miles away even when they FaceTimed while the guys watched Sunday football. Lucy blamed it on her practice, patients spilling over into the weekend, and for a time Sienna understood. Lucy is dealing with real people with concrete problems to fix. She knows how it goes. She was once a high-powered attorney working seven days a week, but then Adam's business took off, and the kids arrived, and they moved to Westchester, and she quit the practice. Admittedly, she misses working. She misses the fast pace, the law, the stimulating conversation. She wonders about going back, if it's possible to strike a balance, to feel empowered and multidimensional again.

But she's distracting herself from the real issue. Adam's never around. If he were, he'd remember the times she's brought up her concerns about Lucy's distance, wondering if she's done something to upset her. His absence and lack of interest hurt. She hesitates to quote Henry, but he could be right: she might be Sirius, but the galaxy spins around Adam.

Taking the first round of stairs toward the kitchen, she shifts gears. Adam has no interest in continuing the conversation about their friends, which is fine, because what she really wants is to talk to Lucy about the thing that's been keeping her awake at night. Literally. Wide awake.

At first, Sienna felt stupid for succumbing to a childhood phobia, but when she looked it up online, she found other adults have the same fear. The first time the anxiety hit, she thought she was having a heart attack. Her heart raced, and she broke out into a sweat, her body filled with dread. The severity has only worsened in the last year.

Voices drift up the stairs from the kitchen below, interrupting her train of thought, and Adam draws her in close, wrapping an arm around her waist. "Why don't we skip this part and head back to the room?" There's a twinkle in his blue eyes, and she lightly touches the dark scruff on his chin.

Her husband is adorable, but as in most marriages, cuteness doesn't get you laid. If he really wanted to get her in the mood, he'd try a different approach. And she understood—oh, how she understood—how his work was a priority and afforded them a certain lifestyle. But lately she's been feeling adrift. Lonely. Even though they appear "perfect," thanks to Adam and his overt displays of affection. The doting I-can't-keep-my-hands-off-my-wife, isn't-she-the-hottest-woman-you've-ever-seen shtick makes a lot of miserable women in miserable marriages green with envy. She knows she should be grateful to be part of *The Adam Show*. She knows she's "lucky" to have a man who worships her, who still wants to have sex after two babies stretched her vagina apart. But here's the truth: at times, she feels like an object, and when it's your husband doing the objectifying, it's even worse.

Then there's the business of her newly developed phobia. She's determined to find the time to talk to Lucy. Just the two of them. Lucy will help her understand what's happening, help her make sense of it all. What she needs is her best friend.

Right on cue, she and Adam step down the stairs, and everyone turns. She holds her head high and takes it in. The admiration. It's there. It's always there. She smiles until her face hurts.

CHAPTER 10

PENNY

The car pulls up to Vis Ta Vie, and Penny's heart ticks in her chest.

Already she regrets following through on the stupid promise they made all those years ago. What was she thinking, coming back?

"We're here," the driver says.

"Can you give me a minute?" she asks. She needs more than a minute, but she's already delayed her arrival long enough. She sat in the airport's crowded bar with a tequila, deliberately stalling the reunion. They haven't seen each other since their daughter Cody's thirteenth birthday in January, and if she was going to be honest about anything, it was this: the thought of seeing Leo again has her jittery. The delay and alcohol were means of survival.

It hasn't been that long, but Penny has already forgotten what it's like to be Leo Shay's wife. There was a time when her face adorned magazine covers, and she couldn't step foot in a crowded airport without being trampled by a gang of paparazzi. But then a year ago, a trip to Palm Springs turned tragic, rocking their once solid marriage. They couldn't recover. And it didn't help when Leo returned to set, leaving her to wade through the grief alone. Left with no other choice, she fled Tinseltown for Coral Gables, Florida, the place where she and Leo had grown up, the place that shielded her from that other world, and could, perhaps, do it again. But she was wrong.

They've traveled to the inn many times before but never like this. Their storied marriage has turned into another clichéd Hollywood breakup, and returning is complicated. This is where they were married. And other than their three children, that afternoon was her most prized possession. Twenty-five years have passed, and though she couldn't hold it in her hand, the memory was priceless. Which explained how horrible it felt when everything fell apart.

The engine hums, and the driver waits patiently. She resists delving into that long-ago history, but it's hard. Leo. Leo and Penny. They were fifteen when they fell in love, paired together over a frog dissection in biology. Leo hung back as Penny assaulted the meaty creature with her gloved fingers, forgoing the tweezers and forceps. His fragility warmed her; her fearlessness impressed him. She was fascinated with the critter's inner workings and sympathetic to its sacrifice for a tenth-grade science class. When she relayed this to Leo, tugging the heart from the frog's chest, he shot back, "Your empathy's astounding."

Back then, neither of them had any idea how their own hearts would come into play, twisting their lives in a way that made Penny's radical dissection seem tender.

"He's dead," Penny replied.

The brown-haired boy cocked his head. "How do you know he's a he?"

She dug a finger inside the frog's abdomen and waved Leo closer. She pointed at the testes, located by the kidneys. "Your proof."

Penny gazed from the lifeless frog to Leo's face. His tanned cheeks turned a bright pink, and that's when she first noticed his eyes. One blue. Another brown. *Heterochromia,* he had called it.

She slaps her cheeks and draws a deep breath. *Don't go there.*

"I'm ready," she says, reaching for her purse. The young driver comes around to open her door. He grabs her suitcase from the trunk.

She hands him a few bills, and he carries the bag to the front step, where she hears the group gathered in the kitchen. Renée expected guests to check in by four. Dinner at precisely six. Penny normally makes it a point to be prompt. Today's delay was intentional, a brew of second thoughts. But now it's time.

CHAPTER 11

HENRY

The clinking of glasses and aroma of Jean-Paul's cooking have Henry believing that things are normal. They're in the gourmet kitchen, where Jean-Paul holds court behind the cooktop, slicing and dicing. They spend some time talking with the Cassidy woman and her daughter, Rosalie. Henry hears Lucy's therapist radar blaring—the mother knocking back two glasses of champagne in under ten minutes, the daughter cloaked in layers of black clothing and dark makeup.

He scans the table and sees the envelopes that greet them each year with the menu and accompanying recipes. "Can I peek?" he asks Renée.

She smiles, though it's more subdued than usual. "Anyone else, I'd say no," she says.

Lucy's lost in conversation with the mother-daughter duo; her red-rimmed glasses match the deep color of her lips. When he picks up the envelope, his phone rings. He should decline, but his mother has progressed from texting to calling, which means something, and he steps out of the room.

Before he can greet her, she's rambling. He sucks in his breath and smooths a wrinkle in his linen pants. "I understand." He doesn't, but he's trying to remain calm. "But we're away. It's hardly the time or place—"

"You're going to have to face him at some point," Dominique Rose-Wall replies. She is nothing if not blunt. "You can't hide away forever."

He's been trained to compartmentalize. His life has two distinct sides—only a handful know about his father, and nothing about his unexpected release. "Please, it's really a bad time." It will never be a good time. His father betrayed them in the worst possible way. His hero, his mentor, the man he had trusted most in the world. He clenches his eyes shut, banning the hurt from coming closer.

Lucy finds him, her hair pulled back in a dark braid, emphasizing the blue of her eyes. Her gaze grabs hold of Henry, telepathy kicking into high gear. Like a pit bull, she sniffs out any situation.

He should hang up, but Lucy's probing stare is worse than any conversation. This is what ultimately tore them apart: his father's deception and the layers of humiliation they were left to wade through.

"Are you there?" Dominique asks.

He's there, but he isn't. His work at the Fernbank Science Center's planetarium means feet planted on the ground with a head hitched to the sky. The sky means comfort from an antagonizing world, this embarrassing problem. With an eye trained on the stars through the lens of his Celestron telescope, he can disappear.

"I'm here."

"He's waiting. Please do this, Henry."

Lucy's eyes sear his skin, but it's his mother's voice that draws him away. The shakiness reminds him of a time when they were a family, and conversations centered on philosophy and finance, the Panthers and the Hornets. They were once so close, playing chicken in the pool or shooting baskets in the driveway, but now his mother's plea reeks of desperation, all they've lost.

"I can't."

He gently taps the screen to end the call, his mother's last words muffled.

"What was that about?" Lucy asks.

He gives her a sidelong glance. "Nothing."

If he wants to avoid an argument, *nothing* is the worst possible response. *Nothing* has upended seemingly pleasant afternoons, initiated multiple blowups, and slammed several doors. He waits for the canned responses, the ones she uses on her clients. *It's never nothing. This is why you're here—to talk about the nothing.* But this time, she only laughs. If Henry were a betting man, he'd say the chuckle was a white flag, a small sign of defeat. Or maybe she, too, is nervous about what waits for them at the table.

To drive that point home, they enter the kitchen as Sienna and Adam waltz down the stairs. Seeing them, all smiles and affection, it's hard not to feel as though he's failed, that the expectant life that once stretched ahead has gone astray. It's impossible not to compare.

What do they have that he and Lucy didn't?

CHAPTER 12

PENNY

Penny collects herself, listening to the sounds and laughter coming from the kitchen. She's come this far; there's no turning back. If the tequila was meant to stave off buried feelings, it had the opposite effect. Leo is front and center in every thought, in every cell in her body. She catches a glimpse of her reflection in the floor-to-ceiling glass doors—the long blond hair she just spent a fortune getting cut and colored, the jeans that flatter her generous ass, and the white cotton button-down that provides the right amount of cleavage.

When her mind latches on to Leo, time stops, skipping back to the past. They were once teenagers frolicking on the beach, nothing more pressing than his lips against her mouth, his fingers trailing up her blouse and skirt. Everything between them had been intense. A look across a crowded room meant, *I want you. Now.* His hand across her back said, *You're mine.* He had ruined her for any other man.

And then a sunny Saturday last August ripped them apart.

When they first met over the frog dissection, after Leo had resolved his skittishness, he grabbed his own scalpel and nudged apart the layers of thick skin. They had worked side by side, their hands brushing, and the chill that slithered down her back became the start of a long line of sensations. He stared at her with his peculiar eyes until she turned away. He told her that day she'd never see the world the same.

Leo walked her home after school, and without pretense, he reached for her hand. The gentle squeeze whispered, *Do you feel that?* And she let his hand curl around hers, memorizing his smooth fingers. Like the scalpel, he peeled her open until he was deep inside.

It was no surprise to any of them that Leo Shay became a famous actor. Everything about him was bright and shiny. Long before he was spoon-fed the perfect line or taught to perfect the piercing gaze or the flirtatious smile, Leo had that magnetic quality that set him apart. And for a time, Penny was enough. They were enough. But then that fateful summer day, followed by Claire a few months later. And before the director paused production on Leo's most recent film, they were fractured in two.

She peers inside to see if Leo has arrived, but she can't get a good look. They made the foolish promise that they'd spend their silver anniversary at Vis Ta Vie, but neither of them could have predicted that they'd be on the cusp of divorce. Yet here they are. Another Hollywood failure. She should turn around and leave, but she promised Renée and Jean-Paul this week—and Leo. Even the kids were in on it; Cody had circled the date on her calendar in bright red. Penny didn't want to let them down, not more than she already had.

She searches inside her bag for a cigarette. It's her emergency cigarette, the one she's been saving for moments like this. Inhaling, she decides she won't let Leo under her skin. Exhaling, she won't let the hovering memories cloud her better judgment. She'll remember the disappointment. And if she can't manage all that, she'll keep her legs crossed exceptionally tight.

She hears the car before she sees it. A cherry-red convertible Mustang with its top down. As it approaches, the sunlight glares on the man behind the wheel, hair mussed from the wind.

Leo.

She studies his profile as he comes to a complete stop. He's late too. Damn. He looks good.

Penny drops what's left of the cigarette onto the rocks, crushing it under her sneaker. She reminds herself to stop looking, stop obsessing over the hair that hasn't lost its luster, or the smattering of gray that makes him stupid sexy. As he puts the car in park and turns off the engine, she waits for him to spot her, to feel the physical pull.

Leo turns, and their eyes meet with a tingly ripple. Even when he confused her, she loved him. She nears the driver's side, where he sits, and she takes him in.

"I swear this wasn't intentional."

"Bullshit," she says. He knows what a red Mustang symbolizes. The virginity she lost in its back seat. "I'm going out on a limb here by saying this isn't the same car."

They appraise each other. *Stop falling into those eyes.*

"I swear, Pen. I had nothing to do with the car. Lily ordered it."

Penny steps back.

"My assistant. And, no, I'm not sleeping with her."

And because she doesn't know if entering the inn will be a colossal mistake, she steps around to the passenger side and sits beside him. The long-ago memory rests between them, and Leo reads her as he always does. "I promise I won't try for a home run, Penny. Maybe I'll try to get to first base, but not all the way."

She has always enjoyed Leo's humor, but today she's conflicted, and she crosses her arms and stares out the window. Taylor Swift's singing about a cardigan, and Leo continues, "Whatever's going on in that head of yours . . . it's good to see you, Pen."

Her fingers reach for her blouse. One of the buttons keeps coming loose, and she could swear it's from his words. They're brushing beneath the fabric, touching her skin. *Oh, Leo,* she thinks. *Look at you going "all Leo" on me.* He has no idea of his boyish charm. How he reels her in, back to the sensations of those early years. Starting with the day he walked her home from school after the frog dissection, when he pressed her against the tree in her front yard. His inhibitions gone. Their faces were practically touching, her heart slapping hard against her chest. She waited for his kiss, but he ever-so-slowly traced her cherry lips with his finger. He told her he was memorizing them. When his mouth found hers, the kiss was an explosion. After that, they were as tangled as the massive tree's roots. Gone was the boy who cringed at the dead frog. When he told her he was going to Hollywood, not the city north of Miami but the one across the country, and how he was going to be a star, she believed him.

"Sixteen years," she says. "That's how long since we've been back here."

"That long? I'm sorry, Pen."

She's not sure what he's sorry for. Which part. She trains her eyes on the trees and the pond off in the distance while slowly crumbling. She didn't expect to feel this much so quickly. She would have to protect herself from his shine.

"I wasn't sure you'd show up," he says.

She wasn't sure he'd show up.

"We have a week. You can't ignore me the whole time."

"I can try," she says.

He fiddles with the radio as his scent fans her face. Fuck if she'll let him break her. The perfect profile, the David Beckham scruff. She pinches herself, Taylor disappears, and in walks Morgan Wallen. She knows the song. Everyone knows the song. She can feel Leo's eyes boring into her cheeks, Morgan telling this woman that their relationship isn't over.

Six minutes, and Leo's already gotten under her skin. She feels herself weakening. She should call an Uber. The airlines. Hell, she could start walking toward the highway and throw a thumb out to the wind. Anything to get out of here. Too much has been lost, too much broken. And Leo is a cheat. Leo is a liar.

"This was a stupid decision," she says, but he's quick out of the car, grabbing his duffel from the back seat, making his way toward her luggage. Before she has a chance to argue, he's carrying their bags through the glass doors, and she has no choice but to follow.

CHAPTER 13

JEAN-PAUL

Jean-Paul likes the periphery. He likes the way his cooktop serves as a border from the fuss of the table, how he can slide in and out of conversation as he wishes. The guests like it that way, too, every so often lobbing him a random question about how something is prepared. They feel the comfort that comes from knowing someone's taking extra care in feeding them.

They're gathered in the kitchen, sipping wine and champagne as he mixes olive oil with spices. Renée fusses with the already perfect charcuterie board. She's probably wondering if Leo and Penny changed their minds, and when he spots his niece gazing out the window, he knows she's wondering the same. Simone has always had a massive crush on Leo Shay. She's holding her Nikon (a proper camera, she calls it), because on the first night, she always photographs the guests on the steps leading down to the kitchen. Simone makes a big deal of this ritual. She says she likes to capture those first moments, relishing how much is about to change, how guests arrive as strangers but rarely leave as such.

Renée checks her watch and eyes Jean-Paul. She signals to Simone that it's time and taps a glass with a silver spoon. "If I can get you all together for a welcome photo."

They set their wineglasses on the table, and Simone directs them toward the stairs. On the highest step in the back row are Lucy and Henry. Sienna and Adam are one step down, and Adam wraps an arm around his wife's shoulder. The mother-daughter duo stand on the front step, a noticeable distance between them, and the mother is the only one in the group still holding her drink. The daughter stands with her arms crossed. They're awkward, not yet at ease, and Simone waves them in closer. And just as she's about to snap the shutter, there's a commotion at the door.

"Sorry we're late!" Leo shouts, making his way through the hallway followed by Penny.

Jean-Paul hears Renée's sigh, the pleasant sound of relief, and before they can greet the actor and his wife, Simone gestures them toward the others.

"Oh my goodness, is that you, Simone?" Penny asks. "You were, like, five the last time we saw you!"

A collection of eyes dances as one of Hollywood's greats saunters across the room, some hiding their surprise beneath curious smiles. Penny and Leo Shay. Jean-Paul's mantra has worked. Sure, he notices the hesitancy of their steps, but their presence swells through the room. It will be an extraordinary week after all. How could it not? Leo is as handsome as ever; age has only made him more distinguished—at least, that's what Renée said when she saw him in *People* magazine. And Penny: she is a sight with that long blond hair and generous smile. Leo Shay is nothing without his lucky charm, the shiny penny he vowed to love, honor, and cherish.

The guests pose, hopeful and hungry, when Simone presses the button. Click. A few more times. He hears the sound, sees the smiles. Possibility. It's all there. When she finishes, the guests scatter toward the table, searching for their wine.

For now, they have a full house, and after Jean-Paul plates the salads, he joins Renée in properly greeting Leo and Penny. She takes

Penny's hands into hers as Jean-Paul pulls Leo into a bear hug. "It's been too long," he says.

"It's good to be back," Leo whispers, nodding at Penny. "I'm not so sure she'd agree."

Jean-Paul brushes him off, well aware of the scandalous headlines. "That'll change. Trust me. Renée will have it no other way."

"What are you two whispering about?" Renée asks, holding Penny's hand. "Whatever it is, we'll work it out." She isn't wrong. They've witnessed Penny and Leo's love in full bloom, and they know the inn's transformative power. "Sit!" she orders them.

When everyone's seated, Renée reintroduces herself and provides a brief history of her and Jean-Paul's time in France before moving to the area and purchasing the old farmhouse. He slips away behind the counter, returning to tonight's meal. It's the same speech she repeats every week. "We knew very little about Vilas, but after visiting a bunch of properties, we stumbled across Broadstone Road." She glances lovingly at him. "It took us forever to convince the owner to sell."

"Two years," he says, carefully shaping the croque monsieur bites. He feels their eyes on his fingers.

"Jean-Paul tends to this magnificent building the same way he tends to the menu. With care. Patience. Mostly everything you see was brought in from Europe, and Jean-Paul worked tirelessly on the restoration."

He notices Lucy and Henry aren't paying much attention. Adam's texting beneath the table, thinking he has everyone fooled. He doesn't. They've heard her speech a dozen times before, but Cassidy and Rosalie are new to the table, and Renée continues, sharing the week's activities, the house rules, and responding to questions as though it were the first time.

He listens. Fading in and out. He's on a precipice between doing what he loves and waiting to fall off the cliff, watching his life's work stripped away. And worse, living with the fact that it's probably his fault.

"Is there a gym nearby?" Cassidy interrupts.

Renée holds up both hands. "These mountains are your gym. There's tons of activities that'll get your heart racing."

From there, Renée turns the night over to Jean-Paul, and he describes the evening's menu and wine pairing. The table at Vis Ta Vie has a sterling reputation; the reviews describe Jean-Paul as a culinary genius, a master chef who carefully executes every detail. From the edible flowers adorning each course to the grades of meat and the years of certain wines, his selections are purposeful, the presentation exact.

The conversation among the guests begins simply, as it always does, with a greeting across the table. "We're Lucy and Henry Rose-Wall from Buckhead. And that's Adam and Sienna Kravitz. We've been friends since college," says Lucy.

Sienna sips her wine. "How's it possible that was eighteen years ago?"

"I'm Cassidy Banks." The mother drops a hand on her nearly exposed breasts when she says this. "And this is my daughter, Rosalie. We're from Chicago. Deerfield."

The daughter offers a weak smile. In the light of the kitchen, her features look dark and clunky.

Leo and Penny don't require an introduction, and someone asks what's brought the famous actor to these parts. "Same thing as you," Leo responds, praising the food and the peacefulness of the mountains. Unplugging. Renée pours wine, a bottle of red in one hand and white in the other. Leo points to the red. "We'll have our usual."

But Penny shakes her head. "White for me."

Jean-Paul lets them do their thing as Simone serves the first course. Lucy's chatting with the mother and the daughter, trying to draw the young girl out by asking her age and what grade she's in. "How nice you have this time with your mom," she says, to which Rosalie shrugs, gulping down a glass of water.

They dive into their salads as Simone and Renée circle the table refilling glasses. The chatter grows. The laces begin to knot together; the threads intertwine.

"We have friends who live in Deerfield," Lucy says to Cassidy. "The Pollocks. They have three boys. Do you know them?"

"Nope. Don't know any Pollocks."

"Yes, we do," Rosalie says with a scowl. "Billy's parents."

"Fordham," Sienna answers when Leo asks her which law school she attended.

People at their table do this. They prod each other in search of the connective tissue that affirms commonality. Mutual acquaintances provide context, and pedigrees are baselines in summing up strangers. He's heard the back-and-forth a million times. College is a tiny flag of victory, unless you attended an Ivy League. Bonus points for graduate school. The pecking order of who is who in the hierarchy of the world is decided on day one. But in twenty-four hours, maybe less, it will change. They'll all be on a level playing field.

"Thirteen," offer the two couples when asked how many years they've been coming to the inn.

"We've got you beat," Leo chimes. "Twenty-five."

"Not consistently," Penny corrects him. "We haven't been back in a while."

Jean-Paul remembers their first trip. It coincided with the inn's inaugural year. They were all so young, their futures bright and full of dreams. In light of the news, Jean-Paul is as surprised as anyone that they actually showed up.

Cassidy reaches for her wine and slurps what's left in a single swig. "I can't imagine we wouldn't want to come back." She says this between clamped teeth and a forced smile, fooling no one.

After the salads are cleared, Jean-Paul announces the second course: "Buttery French grilled cheese." He can tell by the expression on Cassidy's face that she wants to refuse them, but he doubts she'll be able to.

"We have three girls," Penny says when they're asked about their children. She then glances at Leo. "Leo's outnumbered."

Henry gushes about their two sons, and Adam tells the story of the time some famous quarterback carried his two girls onto the field when they were two and four. Being the only men in female-dominated houses bonds Adam to Leo, and the two swap stories of soccer catastrophes and waking up from naps with their cheeks painted in lipstick.

Jean-Paul takes careful note of Renée as the subject of children dominates their table. She's good, his wife. Practiced. And when Henry veers off toward his fascination with space, she follows right along, listening intently. Henry's a pleasant-looking man. Tonight, the green of his shirt matches the green in his eyes. Nothing excites Henry more than the solar system. When he talks about it, he becomes expressive and animated. Who knew there were multiple stages of twilight? Or how a *meteor shower*, as he describes it, resembles a burst of bright fireworks?

"I can't top what Henry does," Sienna says, adding, somewhat disappointed, that she gave up her law practice to stay home with the kids. "My kids are my world, but those days in the office were at times easier than child-rearing!"

"Mothering's next-level work," Lucy chimes in. "There's no such thing as nine-to-five. It's twenty-four seven. And you're consistently challenged mentally and physically by a tiny hellion. It's much more taxing on the brain. There's no on-off switch."

Jean-Paul studies Renée's expression. Vague. Unreadable. But he knows what lies underneath.

"What's it like to be famous?" Rosalie quietly asks Leo.

Penny snorts. "He's not really that famous. Anymore."

She's the first to touch on their very public scandal, but no one bites. Not yet.

"Can I get a picture with you?" Cassidy asks, standing up, phone in one hand, wine in the other. "The girls in my spin class will plotz." But then she yelps, and the glass slips from her hand and cracks on the table. "Ouch!" She bends over as the guests all leap to her aid, but

Jean-Paul saw it out of the corner of his eye. He saw the girl kick her mother in the shin.

"I love your movies." Sienna breaks the silence. "I watched *Andres and Sharita*, like, a hundred times." She pauses, licking the cheese from her lips. "Did you learn Spanish for the role?" And before he answers, she's already moved on. "It's really cool you're here . . . both of you."

Lucy adds, "It's good to see you've worked things out." Which is met with silence as Leo turns to Penny, and she stares straight ahead before stabbing a fork into the tiny sandwich.

Cassidy's tending to her shin. "Just banged into this leg here," she says, loud enough for them all to hear. Simone replaces her glass, and Renée replenishes her wine. There's one in every group, the one who drinks wine like water. This week it's Cassidy Banks.

Adam recounts Leo's infamous car chase with Dwayne Johnson in *Night Ranger* in excruciatingly long, dramatic detail. One of the women asks if he really threw himself out of the van on the Los Angeles freeway and jumped onto the moving train below, which has Leo downplaying the feat, his skin flushing. He encourages Adam to sum it up for her, and Adam doesn't need to be asked twice. Leo may be a star, but a quiet shyness eclipses his on-screen persona. Jean-Paul appreciates that kind of humility. The gilded world hasn't changed him. Jean-Paul wants to believe that Leo stayed true to himself and his family, that he's one of the good guys. That's why this stuff with his costar doesn't make sense.

Henry mentions a notable political figure. "One to watch," he adds. "Could be the candidate this country needs."

Not at Jean-Paul's table. Politics and alcohol don't mix. The minute he hears the mention of anything remotely political, he interferes. "Would anyone like to assist with the main course?"

The young girl, Rosalie, raises her hand, and there's something endearing about it. She must be getting used to the place. She jumps to his side, and in this light, he catches a glimmer in her heavily made-up eyes. She follows his lead, grabbing the wooden spoon and stirring the butter until it's browned. "How do you know the right amount of ingredients to use?" she asks. "I'm a decent cook, I think. But without a cookbook and exact measurements, I get lost."

He's preparing the lamb jus, and he hands her a bottle of red wine, motioning toward the pot of lamb gravy on the burner and nudging her to have a taste. "I want you to add the wine." The table looks on. Panic fills Rosalie's eyes.

"Can you be more specific?" she asks.

He presses her to trust her senses, but she's closing her eyes, lips moving as though she's counting. Counting? When she opens them again, the counting stops, and he holds a spoon out to her. The table falls silent, and she takes a taste. He can tell she's nervous, but he likes how she trusts him. How she will soon trust herself. She reaches for the bottle and pours the wine into the pot.

He dips a spoon in the sauce, smacking his lips. "Not bad."

She musters a half smile as he adds more wine to the jus.

"Rosie's a great cook," Cassidy says.

"She will be," he corrects her. Then he turns to Rosalie, who's either embarrassed or proud (he can't tell which). "You're welcome in my kitchen anytime."

This seems to please her, and she blushes. "Thank you so much, Mr. De La Rue." And he doesn't have to look at his wife to know what she's thinking. That old, familiar pang creeps up on him too from time to time, the one they buried many years ago. He finds Renée staring across the room, across the clinking of glasses and muffled conversation. Back then, she would say it aloud, but then he told her to stop. It was too upsetting. Now he can tell by the flicker in her eyes, the washed-out sadness. The hazel color says just one thing: *You would have been an incredible father.*

The moment passes, and Rosalie returns to the seat beside her mother.

Simone weighs in, sharing with the table how Jean-Paul taught her to cook. "Every summer I'd visit from London, and he'd have me spooning and tasting and marinating." She smiles when she adds, "Food is his love language."

His niece has grown into a decent chef, but she prefers her camera. Her plan is to move on from Vis Ta Vie to pursue a photography career, and he already knows how much he'll miss her.

The conversation continues as he serves the main course, each bite of his tasty meal uncovering another layer. The degrees of separation fan out, and commonality and mutual interest form. The camaraderie echoes the politeness found in friends and strangers, but there are still undertones of silent judgments, like hidden flavors, both sweet and sour.

Someone asks about past guests. This is always an entertaining subject. Renée and Jean-Paul describe the time someone sneaked in a puppy (pets aren't allowed), the bride who spent her wedding night on the sofa, the couple who hit it off and eventually married. "It's a great story but for the fact they were married to other people when they met."

There's laughter, and he loves laughter. He loves the joy the inn evokes in people.

When it's time for dessert, Simone and Renée pass around the French custard dotted with berries and powdered sugar. Someone holds up a glass, toasting the host and hostess and toasting each other, and there's the sound of clinking glasses. Renée finds him, threading an arm through his, and he takes it in, breathing in every nuance. The air feels cold, her skin, too, which defies their recent air-conditioning issues and the number of other reasons they should sell. But he won't let that get in the way of this week. No matter what happens, he's determined to make it a week they will never forget.

MONDAY
Day 2

First Course: Bitter green apple beignets, garlic confit, local charred goat cheese

Second Course: Salt-baked striped bass with ratatouille

Main Course: Beef Wellington, Carolina mushroom duxelles

Dessert: Grand Marnier soufflé with melted chocolate

Château Miraval Côtes de Provence rosé

Domaine Robert Chevillon Nuits-Saint-Georges rouge

CHAPTER 14

CASSIDY

Maybe she drank too much last night.

She throws the covers off, then stands, loses her balance, and falls back onto the bed.

Yes, she drank too much.

Mouth parched, she attempts to get up again, dipping her toes inside her furry slippers, wooziness padding her brain. There. She rights herself, pleased that Rosalie isn't here to witness her indignities. The eyeball rage Rosalie inflicted on her last night was plenty. She should have known to stop after the third glass . . . or was it the fourth? They pour wine here like water. That Renée, always with a bottle in each hand, insistent on filling and refilling. Normally, Cassidy doesn't mind an endless stream of good wine, but she's been trying to curb her consumption around Rosalie. Rosalie, who kept count. Rosalie, who begged her to slow down, implored her not to make a scene.

Appealing to her daughter's stubborn, willful personality exhausts her.

Cassidy definitely has a bruise on her right shin from when Rosalie kicked her under the table, but she doesn't understand the big deal. They're on vacation! She wasn't driving. What's wrong with having a little wine, a little fun? But when she asked Leo Shay for a selfie, you'd think she asked him for his phone number. Rosalie kicked her so hard that her drink flew out of her hand, shattering on the table, a rivulet of red wine staining the white marble.

When Rosalie wasn't kicking her under the table or inhaling her food with the suction of a Hoover vacuum ("It's not going anywhere, Rosie, slow down"), it was like pulling teeth to get her to talk. Granted, she brought the median age down, and she had little in common with married couples, but Cassidy's highly competent daughter knew what she had signed up for, and she had only herself to blame for once. Not her mother.

Cassidy was grateful for that Jean-Paul guy taking pity on Rosalie, inviting her behind the curtain like some culinary wizard. Rosalie was nervous, but she did whatever the chef asked of her. And she smiled, which Cassidy had been encouraging her to do for years.

Mercifully, the Simone girl also had taken a liking to Rosalie, and when dinner ended and the guests scattered to their rooms, Simone invited Rosalie to join her in the library to watch an episode of *The Bear*. "Our kitchen's a lot different," Simone said. Rosalie's face lit up, and Cassidy sighed with relief before sneaking off to her room with an unattended bottle of red, unloading face creams and astringents, and spending an inordinate amount of time sucking in her cheeks, stretching her neck, and wondering what she'd look like if she succumbed to the facelift her plastic surgeon recommended instead of pumping her cheeks with Restylane and Botox. Which conjured up an image of a younger Rosalie and her plump cheeks.

She was such a sweet baby. She burped on cue, quickly slept through the night, and rarely fussed. Cassidy took her everywhere—the grocery store, Cubs games, the hair salon, even her exercise class, where they had a childcare suite with a one-way mirror for the mothers to spy on their offspring. Maybe this was where Rosalie's aversion to physical activity took root. Cassidy saw nothing wrong with attending classes seven days a week. Seven days of little Rosalie watching her mother squeeze into Lycra pants and a skimpy sports bra before being carted off to the brightly lit space painted with colorful rainbows and farm animals.

As her daughter grew, so did her disdain for the gym, sending Rosalie into a tailspin anytime she saw a woman in Lycra. This made shopping excursions to Lululemon, Cassidy's favorite store, a real challenge.

The defiance continued. Cassidy would stroll her through Macy's, and she'd refuse clothes in soft, muted shades, gravitating toward dark, shadowy tones, a contrast to her fair skin. Rosalie would find the most oversize, shapeless pieces in a dark and menacing palette that swallowed her up. At the time, Cassidy reminded herself that at least Rosalie had those eyes. They were effervescent blue, clear as a cerulean ocean, framed by sleek, long lashes. But soon, in her next phase of rebellion, she hid those beautiful eyes beneath globs of thick, black eyeliner.

"Don't you want to be seen, Rosie?"

Which was the wrong question to ask a girl hiding under a shield of makeup. Rosalie gave her the once-over. "Why would I want to prance around town half-naked?" She might have used the phrase *like someone desperate for attention.*

Rosalie was ten when Cassidy told her that Gene was her father, and that he'd died. Rosalie, way beyond her years, still had questions. Resourceful as she was, she managed to find Gene's sister, Robin. Cassidy was minding her own business, trying to get their bills out on time, when she spotted a letter to Buffalo in the mailbox bearing Robin's name in Rosalie's scrawly handwriting. Heart pounding, she tore open the envelope.

Aunt Robin,

I am so very sorry about your brother Gene. It must have been very sad all these years without him and your parents. I'm writing because I was hoping maybe we could meet. Or let me just come right out and say it: Can I come live with you? Losing Gene so young, I never had a chance to know him, and my mother and I, I'm sure there was some sort of mix-up. My thesaurus says we're "incompatible." I think I must be more like your side of the family. I saw pictures of my mom and dad from high school (the wedding album got ruined in a flood), and even though I don't see a resemblance, I just know we could be friends. I see you're a librarian. I love books too.

Please write back. I'd really like to meet.

Sincerely,
Rosalie Banks

The argument they had that night was epic, the two of them hurling insults, neither backing down, a resolution far from reach. Cassidy could not have Rosalie sending Gene's sister secret letters, nor could she chance that her crafty daughter would end up in Buffalo and learn the truth.

Hence the day arrived when Cassidy was forced to admit that Gene wasn't Rosalie's father. Cassidy really had no other choice, and the confession rolled off her tongue. "If you insist on clinging to this ridiculous fantasy of a dad, Rosalie, you should know your father was a one-night stand. Does that compute? I barely knew his name. There're no pictures of him because we didn't take any." She paused to let it sink in. Cassidy may as well have slapped Rosalie. Her pasty cheeks flamed red as her dream of a family evaporated.

"I'm sorry I didn't come up with a better story. When I told you about Gene, I thought it'd be easier for you to hear that your dad died rather than the truth. But that's it. Your father meant nothing to me. I don't know who he is. I don't know anything about him . . . other than . . . we had a moment."

Rosalie's face fell, the crimson dissolving beneath a sheath of thick, dark hair. She composed a response, then quickly stopped. Her fingers knotted together. "That actually makes more sense."

Another jab at Cassidy's lack of responsibility, her carelessness.

After that, there was no repairing the damage. The relationship was broken, a dream given and then swiftly taken away. Cassidy, rather than mending the rift, surrendered. Instead of proving to her daughter how badly she wanted her and how her love was enough for two, she fell inside Rosalie's disdain. She lathered in Rosalie's scorn. Rosalie wasn't wrong. Cassidy was selfish at times, and her diet took precedence over everything else in her life. And maybe she popped a pill every now and then to calm her nerves or had too much to drink, but she was lonely. She missed her mother and the closeness she couldn't replicate with Rosalie. She ached for the thrill that came from her compulsive habits. And in the process, she had become the kind of woman Rosalie believed her to be. Horrid.

CHAPTER 15

HENRY

Henry rolls over and instinctively wraps his arms around Lucy until they're spooning, his face buried in her hair. It takes him a millisecond to realize that they're naked, and the stirring under the covers confuses him. Did they have sex last night? The memory is grainy. He braces himself for Lucy to find them in this intimate position, but she's warm and still, and he relishes her nearness.

When his hand glides down the side of her body, Lucy stirs, letting out a deep sigh. She's soft and curvy, and his hands know where to touch. He waits for her to wriggle away, to fling his hands off her, but she does neither. Beneath his palm is a balmy heat as her breaths rise and fall. She remains calm, feigning sleep, but he's shared a bed with her long enough to know she's awake.

"Was it as good for you as it was for me?" It comes out awkwardly. Henry has never been dubbed funny.

"Did we?" She pauses. "Because if we did . . ." Her voice trails off.

"I don't think we did." He has no evidence to prove otherwise, but if he made love to his wife, he thinks he'd remember.

She sighs again. It's slight, and her body relaxes beneath his fingers.

"What happened?" she asks, still not facing him.

"I'm not sure."

Maybe it was being back at their favorite place. Maybe it was habitual. Maybe there were some things, like space, that would forever remain a mystery.

Lucy seemed to think he hadn't noticed their distance—how she turned away from him, refusing his touch—but he had. In the beginning, the rejection hurt, but then things snowballed, and their sex life (or lack thereof) turned into one of those rubber band balls: messy and complicated and bound together tightly, rolling away from them at a speed neither of them could catch up with.

She slowly turns around; their noses are close enough to touch. His dick is definitely awake, and he wonders if he could give her that last hurrah and make it the very best.

"Are you sorry we came?" she finally says.

And when she realizes the double entendre, she smiles. A smile that still brings him to his knees. The thumping in his chest gets louder, or it's a pull somewhere else. He feels himself growing hard again.

"What is happening here?" she asks.

"You're naked against me." And then: "We're defying gravity."

"Or a divorce."

Her familiar eyes seem different. It's been a while since they last looked into each other's souls this closely. Does she see his shame? He likes to think he knows everything about his wife, but there's a universe behind those eyes filled with her own stories and secrets.

He doesn't remember first agreeing to the divorce, but he doesn't remember fighting against it either. In some ways, it was easy to relinquish control. If she left him, he could wade through his misery alone, save her from being dragged down alongside him. "If we love each other, and we want each other . . . which I think . . . maybe we do . . . why are we doing this?" He regrets the pathetic, desperate words as soon as they leave his mouth.

She presses a finger to his lips, and he smells the flowery scent of her lotion.

He stares into the blue of her eyes. "Lucy."

He wants her to fight him, to admit this whole divorce charade is just that, but she doesn't. And when he changes the subject, any lingering desire burrows into the white sheets.

"How'd it go with Sienna?" he asks.

"I'm not sure how much longer I can avoid the conversation. She knows something's up."

"Why don't you just talk to her? She's always been your person."

"I don't know. It just doesn't feel . . ." She pauses while a bird squawks outside their window.

"What?"

"I don't know . . . By the way, I think Adam did something to his face. He looks different. Or maybe it's his hair. Do you think he's coloring it?"

He laughs. "That guy gets better and better looking. It's annoying."

She waits a beat. "Yeah, but he's still intolerable."

Henry's ears perk up. So he's gotten to her too.

"Did you hear him bragging about flying private? Does he think that impresses us? It doesn't," she says.

Henry treads lightly. "He's worked hard. Let him have his glory." But he's surprised it's taken her this long to notice how Adam has changed and how it has become more and more difficult to inhabit his orbit. He almost laughs at his own joke. They aren't near his orbit. At least not anymore.

When the four of them first met, their lives fit together so easily. Adam went to a nearby community college, and the girls were roommates—immediate best friends—and they ended up in line at Coffee Break the first week of school. His connection to Adam was instantaneous. He was friendly and funny. People were drawn to him. And his *eyes on the prize* mentality made him seem light-years ahead of their peers. His ambition was contagious; his silly pranks and antics added the right touch of levity. He and Sienna struck up a subtle flirtation. Somehow he coaxed her to write all his papers, and their combined grit, smarts, and looks turned them into a supercouple.

As much as it pains Henry to admit, he owes Adam. He was the one who insisted Henry get out of his head. Adam drew him out and forced him to pay attention to what was here on Earth. That's how he finally came to see Lucy as more than a friend. "The girl's in love with you, Einstein." Adam had meant Galileo, and Henry didn't correct him. "Do you see the way she looks at you?" He hadn't. But the next time they were all together, on that first day of spring, when students lounged on the lawn by their dorms like a beach, he fell inside Lucy's ocean-blue eyes. They'd been inseparable ever since.

"They're so darn sweet together," Lucy continues while he commends himself for holding back on a wisecrack. "Did you hear what he's planned for her birthday this year? The boat trip to the BVIs?"

The whole table had heard what Adam planned for Sienna's birthday. And this was what Adam was known for: grand romantic gestures, all eyeballs on him, whispers of praise for his lavish displays. He ate it up like berry clafoutis.

A moment passes, the idea sinking in that they won't be on that boat.

"Leo Shay," she finally says, ending the silence. "That was unexpected, but he and Penny seem like a nice couple, don't they?"

Henry had thought a lot about the Shays being at the table, not because they're famous but because they've endured a very public scandal.

"Good for them for coming . . . I wonder what this means. You know Leo's presence will play miserably on Adam's psyche," she adds. "He's going to have to share the spotlight. And that mother and daughter. Those two are ripe for the picking."

He listens as she rattles off her observations, leaving no time for him to comment. "I suspect the mother might struggle with body dysmorphic disorder. Did you hear her complaining she's put on weight? And that Rosalie, she's clearly the adult in the relationship. It's no wonder she hides behind that mask."

Henry's amused at how she quickly sums up those around her.

"There's a collection of buried dreams hiding beneath that girl's makeup."

"Black hole," he says, one of his scientific terms. "I feel for her."

"Of course you do, Henry. You're too good for the earth."

When she doles out these hefty compliments, he wonders why he wasn't enough. And yet, they're naked, still close enough to feel each other's breath on the cusp of divorce.

Strange things happen at the inn. Being here gives the illusion that things are normal. Exceptional food, cups always full. Last night Jean-Paul and Renée were as welcoming as ever, inquiring about their lives and their kids, having no idea it's all about to change. The whole notion seems surreal, and he feels unsettled, as though there's something he's missing too. During their dinner conversations, he had smiled and pretended everything was fine. But when Renée announced their financial troubles and the possibility of having to sell the inn due to some bad decisions, he had a hard time keeping his focus after that. It always came down to bad decisions.

And as if reading his mind, Lucy weighs in on Renée and Jean-Paul's situation. "They'll work it out. They have to. This place is too special to let go."

He wants to tell her that their relationship was once special too.

Seemingly done with the short trip down last night's memory lane and nowhere close to figuring out how they ended up undressed, Lucy rises from the bed, oblivious to her nakedness, and strides across the room. She's complained about the changes in her figure, but his friend tugs at him again as she sweeps toward the bathroom.

"Let's go on the Crab Orchard hike," she shouts from behind the door.

Which is the signal for him to tell his friend to stand down so he can rise up.

CHAPTER 16

PENNY

Penny rolls over in bed, the sound of footsteps rousing her from a deep sleep. Surveying the room, *Lavande*, she knows she shouldn't have come. Every nerve, every instinct in her body screams at her to leave, to go home, but she wipes her eyes of sleep and reminds herself of promises. Vows. She's nothing like him.

She'll admit, dinner was nice. More than nice. She enjoyed being at the table, ignoring Leo, meeting new, interesting people. She's traveled the world, but no place has felt as comfortable or grounding as here. Renée and Jean-Paul hold their history, and they are gracious hosts. When you step through the doors, a calm takes over; you know you are about to get spoiled.

Penny has always enjoyed their time at the De La Rues'. Even in the early years, when Leo was considered "famous," they never imagined going elsewhere. Leo prided himself on living as normal a life as possible. Sure, the guests they'd met at the inn were always surprised to find America's heartthrob in their midst, but Vis Ta Vie had a reputation of being discreet. If you were looking for a pretentious playground for gossip, the inn was not it. Vis Ta Vie was about grounding yourself, quieting the noise and chatter.

Most people shed their pretenses at the inn, though that guy Adam didn't get the memo. What a sleazy name-dropper. She detests guys like him: wealthy and entitled, needing to be the center of any conversation. And then he carried on about the movie Leo made with Dwayne Johnson as if he'd starred in it. Didn't even notice how Leo handed him the mic. Because that was Leo. His star might be bright, but he prefers a steady dimness away from the shine.

As she watched Adam describe the infamous speed chase, arms in the air, hands waving, the annoyance crept in. The scene showed off Leo's daring athleticism. Refusing the stunt double, he'd charged across the screen, making audiences gasp. Listening to Adam drone on irritated her. Leo could have been killed, and it was a source of contention between them. She hated the story.

That Cassandra woman was interesting, but she kept inching closer and closer to Leo as the night progressed. The neckline of her top crept lower and lower, and the whole table had a clear view of her pumped-up breasts. The daughter looked close to blowing a gasket.

After dinner, Penny slinked out the back door to the firepit, where they used to roast marshmallows and sing Garth Brooks. Leo brought her jean jacket out for her. She hadn't wanted to accept any of his kindnesses, but she took the jacket because she was cold, and he took that as a sign she'd accept more, so he sat in the empty seat beside her.

Leo patted his stomach, going on and on about the little grilled cheese sandwiches, superficial conversation to avoid falling into the abyss. She nodded. "Croque monsieur." He used to love when she talked to him in French. A chilly wind blew through the air, and she pulled the jacket tighter. If she looked closely at the bench crafted from a fallen tree, she'd find their initials carved in the wood.

"Tell me about the girls," he said.

That's how he'd begun every phone call from set. She'd replay their daughters' girl drama, the secret crushes that weren't so secret, the goings-on at their schools. They'd laugh, and then he'd ask about her, and she'd tell him she missed him, to hurry home. Now they live on opposite coasts, embroiled in tabloid fodder. The drama and crushes pale next to their goddaughter slipping under the raft that August day. Then the second act with Claire, the coup de grâce.

She tried to update him, but what could she say? Kayla, their oldest at seventeen, was angry and bitter. For the last year, she refused to discuss college applications because of her broken-hearted cynicism. "College is a waste of time when we're all just going to die." And then the photo of Leo with Claire went public, and Penny tried to convince Kayla it was a scene from one of Leo's movies, but Kayla was no idiot. And it didn't stop the bullies from teasing her at school.

"She refuses to talk to me," he says.

Duh, you idiot. But Penny doesn't say it out loud. "She needs time." She doesn't know why it's her responsibility to make him feel better.

"It's been weeks."

It felt like yesterday to her. Raw and burning.

"Amelia's back with Dr. Cammerota." Their fifteen-year-old had just left therapy only to go back in. He kicks the dirt with his loafer. *Good. Let him think about what he's done.*

"There's a boy in the picture, I think. She's on her phone twenty-four seven, holding it like she's in love."

They used to be like that.

"And Cody?" Cody was their baby, and at thirteen, she still seemed like one.

"You know Cody. She's hoping for a miracle." She was the one who had circled their anniversary on the family calendar in bright red. Mom and Dad's twenty-fifth.

Then he asked about her. And there it sat, that thing between them that reared its ugly head no matter how hard they tried to fight it. After that August day in Palm Springs, there was no going back to normal. They managed to keep the incident out of the papers, but then Leo, with the producers breathing down his neck, had to return to work. They couldn't comfort themselves, let alone each other, and the kids were scared and confused. Grief and regret swept in like a desert breeze, and Penny had to prioritize, making the decision to move the girls to Miami and enroll them in school. She told him they needed to be closer to her mother, and by the time the bell rang that first day, they were living separate lives.

Claire was the freight train they didn't see coming. And that's when the images appeared in Penny's mind. Images of Leo with Claire. And then Ellie. Little Ellie on the ground. Because everything is mingled together. Her tiny limbs, the big brown eyes. All the grief that followed. The gap widened, their relationship weak and untenable, and with one swift kick, Claire pushed them over the edge.

It was so easy to hate Leo. Blame him for all of it.

She pulled the jacket tighter and finally answered his question. "I'm great."

She told herself it wasn't their fault when the nightmares woke her from sleep, when she lay drenched in her sweat. And she repeated it when the girls had sleepovers or birthday parties that involved pools or oceans or bays, which was basically all of Miami. Her grip on her daughters had tightened. It was easier for Leo to block it out, to step on set and assume another role, but she couldn't. She lived the nightmare daily.

The silence between them closed in against the backdrop of insects croaking and buzzing.

"Maybe it's time we talked about it."

She didn't ask him to clarify if he meant Ellie or Claire. It's all so draining. She's tired of feeling this way.

"How is Claire?" It was a jab, and she didn't care.

"I'm not with Claire."

"The whole world saw you. With Claire."

"That's not really fair, Penny. She and I have done six movies together."

They were like Clooney and Roberts, Lawrence and Cooper: audiences had watched them in dozens of scenes in cities across the globe. It was one thing to watch your husband have sex on a movie screen with America's most recognizable actress, but the kiss Penny referred to was different. A few weeks ago, he and Claire were caught clasping hands under the table at *their* café. Claire's lips on Leo's, her other hand draped along his neck.

"If you had let me explain . . . if you'd given me a chance."

"I don't recall much talking since Palm Springs, Leo. And what does it matter anymore?"

He raked a hand through his hair, his shoulders hunched. "It's been really hard, Penny."

His voice was thick. Like the way it sounded when he first told her he loved her. When he'd whispered those words in her ear and her whole body flamed. She knew how hard it had been.

He hesitated. "I don't know how to do this without you. I'm not a cheater. That's not who I am."

No, he wasn't. He was nothing like the others. But she had seen the picture with her own eyes. And she had promised she'd never put herself in a position to feel that way again. She had filed the papers; it was time to end the charade. The cicadas chattered, and the fireflies sailed through the air like tiny fairies. The wine made her woozy.

"Claire is the one who kissed me. She corroborated my story. I didn't kiss her. She kissed me."

"Look at you playing the lawyer."

"Nothing happened," he said more insistently. "She made a public statement."

That little blip on E! News? Was that what he was talking about? "Claire's one of the world's most talented actresses," she argued. "She makes a living telling lies."

He taps his chest. "I've never lied to you. We've always trusted each other."

Until that summer day.

She hated how she felt simultaneously hot and cold, remembering the sweat that dripped down her face as they tried to revive their goddaughter, how the sun blazed on their backs, stinging more than their skin. She wouldn't let him chip away at the fortress she'd built. He'd betrayed her. In the worst possible way. Publicly. They had three daughters. If she forgave him, what kind of example was that? She didn't care that her mother thought it might be a worthy lesson for the girls if she forgave him, that sometimes the best marriages are tested, and forgiveness is for the strong. The weak held on to rage.

She stood up, using all her strength, remembering the stab of his betrayal, their marriage a depressing video playing at high speed. "Good night, Leo."

And that's why she's lying in *Lavande* this morning, alone, sharing a wall with Leo in *Beige de Lin*. Her phone has a pile of notifications. Amelia asking to borrow a dress from her closet, Kayla sending a video of their dog chasing his tail, Cody telling her she misses her and Daddy. The last text is from Leo. She has changed his name in her contacts as a form of self-care.

DON'T ANSWER: I've made mistakes. We both have. But I still love you. I'm not giving up.

Penny's thumbs move over the keys, his words reminding her of what used to be, the sensations trailing down her skin. She starts and stops several responses but sends none.

Rising from the bed, she throws on workout pants and a black sports bra. Rummaging through the dresser drawer, she finds a long-sleeve T-shirt and tosses it over her head. Today's schedule has them going to Crab Orchard Falls, and she likes that activities are optional, because today's lends pause.

While brushing her teeth and fixing her hair (and before giving up and throwing it back in a ponytail), the memory of her and Leo's first visit to the falls closes in. How she and Leo were as tangled as vines. How she'd worn a similar outfit. How they'd stopped at a giant rock near the water's edge, and Leo pulled a picnic lunch out of his backpack. He'd brought a variety of crackers and cheese, plus wine from Erick's, a shop they'd passed on their way from the airport. The water was cool that day, and they took off their shoes and dipped their toes in the crisp stream. The sun burst through the trees just as Leo pulled her to her feet and got on one knee, a waterfall cascading behind them.

He was on the cusp of greatness, still straddling the line between local boy and rising star, when he stuck his hand in his pocket and fished out a modest diamond. The rock was slippery, and Leo wobbled. Looking back, she should have known it was a sign that he couldn't ground himself.

She had loved him. Fiercely. Protectively. And he loved her with an earnestness she couldn't quantify, as though he could swallow her with his affection. It was never enough to be side by side: he needed to be closer, deeper. And she innocently believed their devotion would withstand any test, even the pressures of fame.

She said yes. Of course she said yes. Leo was the love of her life. And he wrapped her in his arms, lifting her up in the air, twirling her until they fell in the water, a cold rush pricking their skin. Leo was going to be a star, and he'd take her to California with him. When you're young and hopeful, those seem like the best kind of dreams. But she was wrong. She knows that now as she blots the memory and applies cream to her puffy eyes.

Entering the kitchen, she grabs a muffin and makes her way toward the coffee station for a fresh cup. The mother and daughter are there, and Penny has clearly interrupted an argument. Cassidy—not Cassandra, as the daughter confirms (and not in a very polite way)—implores the young girl to join them on the hike, gesturing at Penny as if she's an ally. The girl's put on the spot, and Penny feels a sliver of empathy.

"It's really a beautiful hike," she says. "Short. Not too difficult. And the payoff—the waterfalls and the swimming pond—is great. You'll enjoy it."

The mother spins around, showing off her neon-yellow leggings. "You see, Rosalie. I told you. It'll be good for you."

The contempt on the young girl's face is unavoidable, but then Jean-Paul enters the kitchen, and the conversation ceases. He greets them warmly, and Rosalie asks him if he has time for that lesson today. Jean-Paul looks confused, and the girl seems upset. "I'm sorry," she says. "Maybe I misunderstood . . . I thought . . ."

"The cooking lesson! Yes, of course. You can help me prepare the dough for tonight's beignets . . . and perhaps more."

She turns toward her mother with her legitimate excuse to miss the hike. "Sorry, I can't join you today, Cassidy. I'm really looking forward to this."

The next few minutes are uncomfortable and weird for Penny as mother and daughter dive into a conversation about the purpose of the trip. "You can't spend the whole time in the kitchen," Cassidy argues.

"If you knew where our kitchen was at home, I wouldn't have to," Rosalie complains.

To which her mother replies, "There's nothing wrong with a healthy salad." She pauses for effect. "From True Juice."

That's when Jean-Paul intervenes. There's something actually very sweet about his concern. "I like having a student. Simone's tired of my lessons . . . more interested in her camera. Rosalie's wonderful company." This only embarrasses Rosalie further, as evidenced by the blush that fans across her cheek. "As long as it's okay with you, Cassidy," he adds.

The women come to an agreement, and Penny spies Cassidy sipping her coffee, avoiding the plate of fruit and a single muffin. She knows women like this. That quote "You can never be too thin or too rich" is misleading. Cassidy Banks appears borderline sick.

Renée enters with one of the other couples. She makes her rounds, asking how everyone slept, refilling coffee, and brandishing freshly baked chocolate croissants from the oven. The couple seems strained; the wife hides beneath a baseball hat. She wields a large backpack and asks if she needs a jacket.

"It's gorgeous out," Renée replies. "A cool sixty-five."

"I just don't have any room left in this thing."

Penny gestures at Adam. "That's what husbands are for."

The woman turns and replies matter-of-factly, "He's not my husband. I'm Lucy. Henry's my husband." She hastily unleashes her brown hair from the hat.

"Oh gosh. I'm so sorry," Penny stutters. "The hat . . . the two of you . . . I just got confused."

Adam laughs, biting into a croissant, flakes of buttery bread sticking to his lips, but Lucy doesn't seem to find humor in Penny's error. She attempts a smile, but it's more like a snarl.

Penny wonders if it's her or if everyone's cranky. And then Leo waltzes in. Leo in his powder-blue sweatshirt and navy joggers. Leo with the famous eyes. Leo with his big, cheerful smile. And the room transforms.

Leo has always had this quality about him. At one time she might have said it was his good looks and charming personality, and then she would have chalked it up to his stage presence, but now she understands that certain people have magnetic auras. The astronomer, this Lucy's actual husband, was talking about energy fields at the table last night, gravitational pulls that keep planets orbiting the sun. "The bigger the mass, the stronger the gravitational pull," he had said. It's the only way to explain Leo's effect. Everyone around him feels the tug.

He comes up alongside her, and she catches a whiff of his soap or some new cologne. It's light and breezy, like those scents called "blue linen" or "shower fresh," and she tries not to let his proximity rattle her. Cassidy moves her chair closer to him, a move she thinks is subtle, though it's really anything but. Leo gives her his kindest smile, and she flushes, panting before his eyes. "Are you going on the hike today, Leo?"

The casual way in which she says his name crashes into Penny, but she's used to women thinking they know Leo because they've seen him on the screen. And Leo, friendly to all his fans, grabs Cassidy's eyes in his. And that's the thing. The guy doesn't even have to try. His eyes just penetrate, seducing anyone in their path. It's not normal.

"Wouldn't miss it. You too?"

Which Cassidy mistakes for an invitation, and the zipper on her sweat jacket comes down a notch, revealing the breasts the group is already familiar with.

Penny stirs her coffee, refraining from dousing Leo and Cassidy in hot liquid.

Footsteps sound, and Henry and Sienna descend the stairs. Henry heads toward Lucy, and Sienna plops herself on her husband's lap. Now this makes sense. The high school cheerleader and her handsome football star. These two radiate. The sun and the moon.

Sienna reminds Penny of Claire. Claire Leonardo. Even her name made her and Leo kindreds. She was the one who finally wore Leo down, the one who had him breaking their vows. Claire with her California beach beauty, legs that stretch for miles, and chiseled features. Penny's eyes land on Leo, who's also appraising Sienna, and when he turns and catches her eye, it's too late. Penny's been caught staring at him. And instead of gloating, he simply smiles, bringing his coffee to his lips.

That's when she notices the platinum ring. There's no mistaking it: Leo's wearing the band she placed on his finger all those years ago. She doesn't remember if he was wearing it yesterday, but she'd like to think she would have noticed something that monumental, because in a few days, they'll be revisiting that memory.

Sienna asks them if they've been on this hike before, and Leo tells her that not only have they been on the hike but that's where he proposed. Cassidy gushes how cute that is, even though she clearly doesn't mean a word of it.

An awkward silence follows, no one really sure of what to say.

"So does this mean you're back together?" Sienna asks. "This nonsense about Claire Leonardo is just your typical celebrity gossip, right?"

"You can't believe everything you read on the internet," Leo says.

"I tell my clients there's no such thing as bad PR," Adam adds.

Sienna elbows him in the ribs, which halts further discussion. She meets Penny's eyes and guesses the woman sees her hurt. Sienna directs her next question to her friend. "Luce, can we get out our calendars and plan a Hamptons weekend this summer? You haven't been to New York in over a year."

Lucy's biting into a croissant when Henry answers, "That long?"

"Before we leave, we need to lock it in. The kids miss each other. And next thing you know, it'll be preseason, and Adam starts traveling again."

"Yeah, guys," he says between bites of pineapple. "We need to step it up."

Cassidy asks how old their kids are. Penny knows full well they told everyone last night, but that's what happens at these dinners. You drink and forget things.

Sienna can't wait to reply. "Our Julia and their Harry are eight, and our Sammie and their Julius are six." She pulls out her phone and scrolls to a picture of the four kids. The girls are in soccer uniforms, and the boys are in khakis, dress shirts, and thick glasses.

A flicker of last night's conversation shoots through Penny's brain. They were discussing how the girls were athletes and the boys more academically inclined. She remembers one aspiring to be a neurosurgeon, the other president of the United States.

She glances at Leo. He's sipping his coffee. He won't eat—not for any other reason than he doesn't like breakfast. Cassidy makes her way to his side, and she peppers him with one question after another, and because Leo has an innate friendliness, he doesn't dismiss her, though small talk before noon has never been his strong suit. Rosalie and Jean-Paul disappear into the pantry, where he's selecting ingredients for their cooking lesson. When they return to the cooktop, the girl's eyes light up at the mention of a trip to the farmers' market.

Renée addresses them as they languidly sip tea and coffee, noshing on a variety of pastries and an assortment of fruits and granola. "Simone will drive you to Crab Orchard Falls. I suggest comfortable shoes, preferably hiking boots, and if you're inclined to take a dip in the water, which I recommend, pack a bathing suit and towel."

Cassidy cracks some joke about skinny-dipping, but the joke falls flat, and Renée continues, unfazed. "We have a lovely lunch packed. And some wine. Clothing is mandatory."

CHAPTER 17

ROSALIE

No, Rosalie isn't going on any hike with her mother. She has plans. Plans that don't include Cassidy. And even though she feels a smidgen of guilt as she watches the others board the van, Rosalie has lived with the torment of her mother for years. Now she's taking matters into her own hands.

Last night wasn't terrible—well, the parts that didn't involve Cassidy, anyway. She loved cooking, and Jean-Paul was a great teacher. Simone was nice, and they watched an episode of *The Bear* and talked for a bit after dinner.

"It must be cool living here. Meeting so many people."

"I love it," Simone said.

She asked Rosalie about school and her life in Chicago. "Do you have a boyfriend?"

"I'm not exactly my mother," she quipped.

"A girlfriend? It's an equal-opportunity question."

"No girlfriend. I like boys."

Simone slid back on the sofa as Jeremy Allen White dominated the screen with his piercing blue eyes. "I had the biggest crush on Leo Shay when I was a little kid," Simone said.

"Ew. He's so *old*."

"Tell that to my five-year-old self. I mean, he was in movies, on billboards!"

"What's the big deal about them being here?"

Simone eyed Rosalie suspiciously. "It's all over the news. You couldn't have missed it."

Rosalie stared at her blankly.

"Leo and Penny got married here. *Tante* Renée told me that on their wedding day, they promised each other to come back on their twenty-fifth anniversary, which is this week. Here's the thing: Leo recently got caught cheating with his costar—you know, Claire Leonardo? The pictures of them holding hands and kissing are all over the internet. The trolls are buzzing about it because Penny picked up and moved her and the kids to Miami last August, and no one knew why. So there's speculation about a divorce . . . an affair . . . all this drama."

Rosalie had no idea. "I don't really pay much attention to celebrity news."

"I'm sure you have more important things to think about," Simone says thoughtfully.

That's when Rosalie took her eyes off the screen and studied Simone. "How'd you end up here? Where are your parents?"

"It's just my mum. She's in London. Detests the States. My dad . . ." Her voice lowers. "He died when I was three. It's been me and Mum ever since, but I never loved London. Too rainy. Too noisy. Summers spent here were the highlight of my year. So as soon as I could, I moved here. It was supposed to be temporary, but I like it. And my aunt and uncle—he's Mum's brother—they've been—"

Simone stopped, because that's what people did when the subjects of fathers and family came up. They were careful and cautious about saying the wrong thing to Rosalie, but Rosalie pressed her to go on.

"*Tante* and *Oncle* are great. They're helping with my photography. At some point, I'm going to make a career out of it, but it's hard to leave this place. My uncle has been a dad to me in a lot of ways. And *Tante* Renée's a bonus mom."

Rosalie marveled at the girl's resiliency. Her luck.

"Do you have any sisters or brothers?" Rosalie asks.

"Just me." She smiled. "What about you?"

"No siblings. No pets. No dad."

Simone's eyes were kind. "I'm sorry. When did you lose him?"

Lose him, Rosalie had thought. *Such an ambiguous term.* It was probably too much to lay on a complete stranger. *My mother had a one-night stand. I don't know my father.* Rosalie chose her words carefully. "He doesn't know about me."

"Ohhhhh. I'm sorry. That's hard."

Rosalie brightened her expression, as she often did when trying to make the best of her mother. "There's nothing to be sorry about."

"Yeah. Your mom seems cool."

Simone was being nice. Cassidy Banks wasn't the easiest, or the most approachable (or likable) of mothers. Rosalie overheard how kids in their town talked about her. They commented on the low-cut blouses that showed off her fake boobs, and how Wendy Sweeney once riffled through Cassidy's medicine cabinet during a sleepover and reported on the boxes of Ex-Lax. They gossiped about how her mother overslept, leaving Rosalie to fend for herself—breakfast, a ride to school—and how if Cassidy did show up to car pool, she showed up frazzled.

Rosalie found relief that the whispers centered on their differences. The vanity gene was lost on Rosalie, and she liked her weight, which she called "just right." And she especially appreciated the individuality of her hair and makeup. The girls at St. Andrews looked like replicas of one another in Dyson waves and rolled-up skirts, an assembly line of mediocrity.

It didn't take a rocket scientist—or a table comprised of a therapist, a famous actor, and an astronomer—to figure out that Rosalie was rebelling. She knew. She had railed against Cassidy early on, and their differences only amplified as Rosalie assumed the role of the responsible adult and Cassidy the selfish child.

The last straw was when Cassidy admitted to lying about her father. Gene, her high school boyfriend turned husband, hadn't died as Cassidy professed. As quickly as that stupid story had materialized, it dissolved. Rosalie thought back to the day she'd written his sister a letter. And as if concocting the death story hadn't been enough, Cassidy had followed it up with the news that Rosalie was the result of a one-night stand. A one-night stand. If she hadn't felt awkward and different before, she certainly did now.

Which explains why they're here.

Rosalie is finally going to tell her mother her news. *Imagine her face.*

Jean-Paul interrupts the memory, dropping bags of flour and sugar on the counter. He's kind and patient, which gives her a boost of confidence. She knew from an early age that she wanted to work in a kitchen and surround herself in food and flavors. She could have never guessed she'd have this alone time with a professional, and for the first time in a while, she feels like she belongs. With the ways he describes his methods and how he brings his dishes to life, they speak a similar language. Though she has a propensity to measure out quantities, she's always instinctively known the right ingredients to spice up an omelet or enhance the flavor of a boring grilled cheese sandwich.

She asks Jean-Paul every single question she can think of. She's even written up a list, but she's too embarrassed to whip it out. When they finish preparing the beignet dough, he lets her assist with the marinade for tomorrow night's pork. "Some prep is behind the scenes, Rosalie. I don't give away all my secrets."

She studies how he shakes seasoning into a pan, measuring spoons nowhere in sight, and she wonders if his intuitiveness might rub off on her.

"Try it." He hands her a spatula. "What do you think it needs?"

She hesitantly takes it. "I might mess up dinner."

He doesn't reply, just watches as she raises the utensil to her lips.

"You're thinking."

"That's what people do."

"Trust your senses. Close your eyes, take in the flavor, the consistency, the smell."

She breathes it in. Takes another taste. Shuts her eyes. She sees the kids teasing her, broadcasting Cassidy's mishaps. She chases them away and focuses on impressing Jean-Paul. Her fingers tremble as she shakes more seasoning into the pan. When he takes a taste, he clucks his tongue and shakes his head.

"You're not trusting yourself, Rosalie."

She can't tell him that trust has never come easily. Not when she has a mother with a penchant for drama and an arsenal of lies. It was her mother's dishonesty that had ultimately led Rosalie to do what she did—her mother, and Diane Rodriguez, a classmate whose aunt's best friend's uncle had located a long-lost cousin on the internet. At first, Diane's story hadn't interested Rosalie. But once she realized she could use the same means to similarly track down long-lost relatives, the story interested her very much.

She wasn't scared when she signed up for the Ancestry site, lying about her age and using a fake email with the password *findmyfather*. She was ready to understand where she came from. Ready to find out why she and Cassidy were so unequivocally unmatched. She'd begun the search out of boredom, a way to pass the time, and then it turned into something obsessive and unstoppable. What did he look like? What was his profession? Was he married? Did Rosalie have a sister or a brother?

It was all she could think about.

She almost told Simone last night—she's been dying to tell someone—but she couldn't. She has to tell Cassidy first. She owes her that much.

Doesn't she?

This time she closes her eyes and breathes in the flavors. She loves creating; she loves playing with ingredients. A pinch here. A pinch there. And when Jean-Paul tries the marinade for a second time, she knows she's nailed it.

CHAPTER 18

JEAN-PAUL

Rosalie might not have the stamina for a hike, but she has plenty of vigor in the kitchen. He's impressed with how eager she is to identify flavors and discuss appropriate food pairings. She's hungry for information, but he supposes that's what happens when you have a mother like Cassidy.

As they head outdoors to the small garden of herbs and spices, he sees Renée on her way back from the mailbox. They hadn't retrieved the mail in a few days, neither of them interested in the demands from bill collectors, and he can tell from her face there are many. He rushes through his tutorial on basil and rosemary, but he's thankful for the distraction.

Rosalie seems exceptionally grateful for the lesson, unlike most teenagers, though he's no expert. When they return to the kitchen, he sees her big bag sitting on a stool. It's bright green with pink letters that read SUN DAY. "A rebel," he says.

She eyes him curiously.

"Today's Monday."

"Oh, that." She smiles, and it's the first time he notices her features. Behind the raccoon eyes and the dark lipstick that distracts from everything else, there's a person in there. She reaches inside her bag and she pulls out a book. "Do you read?" she asks.

"I don't."

Why does he get the sense she's disappointed in his answer? She sticks the book back in her bag. "Thank you for your time today," she says hurriedly, as though she needs to bury her nose in the pages.

"We'll do it again."

"I hope so."

And she's off. Her footsteps disappear up the stairs, and he tries to hold on to the kernel of joy he felt in sharing his passion with her, but the stack of bills waiting on his desk derails him. Renée is nowhere in sight, and he suspects that's on purpose.

He tears through the envelopes, each notice another weight strapped to his back. Then he pulls the leather ledger from a drawer, expenses and recent transactions, numbers that make him twitch.

They'd been doing just fine with their successful business, their idyllic home, and then the cards came tumbling down. The end began with a simple phone call four years ago. The man on the line introduced himself as a representative from Bluebird. He'd researched their business, Vis Ta Vie, and he thought they'd be interested in hearing about an investment that promised a high return.

"We need the money," he'd said to Renée that night over a glass of port. "This could solve our problems."

She was less convinced.

"It's just a meeting in Charlotte," he pressed. "Nothing to lose. We can stop at that antique shop you love on the way back."

A week later they drove south on Highway 321 for a meeting.

There was a reason they were in the business of food and hospitality. To them, finance and numbers were a foreign language, and when the Bluebird associate reiterated the sizable return—"Like nothing we've ever seen"—Jean-Paul trusted him. That night, after Renée placed the porcelain duck she'd bought at the antique shop on a shelf in their office, they'd lain in bed, legs entwined, and she tried to talk him out of it. "We'll get through this. It's just a rough patch."

But the list of necessary repairs and upgrades was long. The air-conditioning (which had started misbehaving around the time the call came from Bluebird) was a fraction of his concerns. They needed to refinish the floors and repaint the house. Appliances needed to be replaced, along with the linens and towels. She recommended raising their prices to cover a touch of lipstick and rouge, but he argued the dated property didn't warrant a rate increase. Jean-Paul loved the inn so much, he fought for a complete renovation. He listened to her pragmatic reasoning, but they had put repairs off as long as they could. They were bleeding problems, unable to withstand the competition.

They made the call that spring day just as the rhododendron had begun to bloom, and a week later, Renée's birthday, they invested their entire savings in Bluebird. Jean-Paul whisked Renée up in the air just as he had when they were kids, and they made the drive to Artisanal in Banner Elk for a festive dinner, where they fed each other pimento scones with pepper jelly and sipped cocktails by the streaming river. The owner sent over champagne to celebrate, and when Renée blew out the candle on the chocolate pear tart, they were certain more of their dreams would come true.

He had felt so appreciative that night. The decision meant he could take care of his wife and give her what she wanted. The investment was a new beginning, and they'd barely made it through the inn's door before he undressed her, his hands sliding up and down her skin. He carried her to their bed, kissing her first on her lips and traveling down her neck to her breasts and then her stomach and between her legs. She grabbed at his hair, the sensations blotting out their fears. Everything would be okay, he had told himself.

The balance on their latest statement snaps him into reality, and he bites back the betrayal. The morning he discovered that Bluebird had been a scam, and all their money was gone, Renée had returned from the market joyous over plump red tomatoes and bright yellow squash. He'd been sweeping pink glitter off the hardwood floors, remnants from the bachelorettes who had partied late into the night, when she came in. He was sickened over what he was about to tell her.

She stared at his face and then at the mess on the floor.

"Trickier than expected," he had said.

"Oh, honey," she exclaimed, dropping the paper bags on the countertop. "Let me help."

But his frustration had nothing to do with glitter, and when she wiped a few pieces off his chin, he backed away.

"Jean-Paul."

The broom slipped to the floor.

"Renée, we need to talk."

CHAPTER 19

CASSIDY

They're piled into a black minibus. Simone points out the scenery, the lush landscape, her favorite mountain views. A real snore galore.

Penny sits in a seat by herself; Leo's across the aisle.

The couples in the back of the bus are deep in discussion about last year's visit. From what Cassidy gleans, it rained the entire week, and with little else to do, they drank. One of them laughs. "Things got pretty wild that last night."

Another agrees, and Cassidy sneaks a glance over her shoulder. Ken and Barbie are giggling. Lucy and Henry are staring out the window, expressionless. Cassidy's radar detects the uneasiness that stretches across their faces.

"We were out of control," Ken continues.

"And how do you think we got that way?" Barbie responds.

Cassidy perks her ears up. She always enjoys a good tale.

Then Lucy, the team psychologist, says rather loudly, "Can we just forget that night? It gives me a headache."

To which the Ken doll responds, "I'll never forget."

Barbie breaks out into a full-toothed grin. "Come on, it was fun. So we drank too much. Got stupid. That's what we're supposed to do when we're on vacation and channeling our former selves."

"We were naked at a campfire," Henry counters.

Adam chuckles. "I almost roasted my balls."

"I thought those were mini marshmallows," Lucy quips.

They laugh, a shared camaraderie in poking fun at some private inside joke she's not a part of. But Cassidy, as the observer, the listener, the one standing outside the inner circle, has a sharp perspective from her vantage.

"Come on, you loved it," Adam says with a laugh. "You all loved it." More laughter, and Cassidy imagines being at the firepit naked and free.

When they pull into a church parking lot and exit the car, Simone motions them past the pastor's house bordering a meadow that leads to a path with a sign that reads CAUTION: BE ALERT FOR BEARS. Fantastic. She knew they should have gone to a spa.

They begin the trek, a lively, chatty group, fallen branches cracking beneath their shoes. Simone provides a brief overview of how the hike meanders before making a steep incline. "The payoff's on the other side. It's all downhill with a twisty, shaded path that leads to the stream. Be careful, though: the rocks get slippery."

Cassidy watches as Leo drops a baseball hat on his head; strands of hair nip the back of his neck. Penny's nearby, but they aren't really talking. Barbie and Ken are hand in hand waltzing ahead of everyone, Henry not far behind. Adam's mentioned no less than five times how they've done this trail seventeen times. *We get it. It's not your first rodeo.*

Lucy sidles up to Cassidy, making friendly small talk in Rosalie's absence. "I have friends in Chicago." Yes, she had mentioned them at the table last night. Then her line of questioning takes another turn. "Where's Rosalie's dad? It's nice the two of you have this special mother-daughter time."

Cassidy feels her heart quicken, the muscles in her jaw tightening. This is what happens when the subject of Rosalie's dad comes up. She inhales and manages to dodge the question by responding to the compliment. "We do this every year, alternating locations. This year's her turn to pick."

Lucy appears surprised. "Interesting that a girl her age would want to come here. Is there a reason?"

"Of course there is. This is typical Rosalie. If I want to go to the Hamptons, she'll pick Hampton, Tennessee. If I choose Vail, she insists on Vilas. I mean, it's obvious we have different tastes."

She waits for Lucy to argue, but Lucy only nods. This makes Cassidy nervous, and she starts talking aimlessly. "I don't know what it is with these young girls today. Rosalie's a beautiful young woman parading around Chicago in a Darth Vader getup. And don't get me started on the hair. Women pay a fortune for her rich, brown shade, and she's turned it into Madame Mim—"

Lucy nods. "Kids can test us. But in my experience, it's crucial they express their individuality. And for parents to learn to accept that individuality."

"You call that individuality?" Cassidy snorts. "I'm no shrink, but it's just rebellion. Directed at me." And when Lucy doesn't respond, Cassidy keeps going. "She loves to push every single one of my buttons. She chose this place, a destination centered on fattening meals, thinking she was fooling me. She knew there wasn't even a gym."

Lucy doesn't even wince, which impresses Cassidy.

"What's your ideal vacation?" she asks.

"A fat farm in Malibu, for one." This woman would never understand. "Just wait until your kids turn into combative teenagers. If you think it's tricky now, you're in for a surprise. Slammed doors. Drama. I'm not sure about boys, but there's no greater fury than a menstruating teenage girl with a hate-on for her mother."

Their pace accelerates as they get comfortable on the path, and Lucy predictably starts off her next bit of unwanted advice with "In my experience." It's followed by a soliloquy on teen girls and self-worth, the role a parent plays in their growth and development. "Is she like this with her father?"

Cassidy's no idiot. If Lucy thinks her probing into Rosalie's absent dad is subtle, it's not. Cassidy knows how to read a room, and she's well aware of Lucy's intentions, trying to figure her out, put the puzzle together. If Cassidy had a nickel for every therapist or teacher with an opinion about her, about Rosalie, about their relationship, or about (let's just call it what it is) Rosalie's daddy issue, she'd be far richer than she already is.

"I get that you're a shrink. It's commendable, really, but can we skip over the unsolicited analysis?" It's rude, but Cassidy's weary of the lectures and gratuitous opinions, and even though Lucy seems genuinely kind, her pedantic psychobabble grates on Cassidy's last nerve.

"It's offensive to refer to us as shrinks."

Cassidy casts a sidelong glance Lucy's way. She respects the woman's boldness. And the fact that she's managed to keep up with her without breaking a sweat.

They're far ahead of the others. She can feel the burn in her calves and hamstrings as they climb the steep incline, and their breaths become shorter. She loves knowing how each step sculpts her tight ass. The crisp, rustling sound of her sneakers against fallen leaves whispers in her ears, and Cassidy, with each exhale, relents a bit.

"Hey, I'm sorry." Her voice softens. "It's just that you're not the first to give us . . . me . . . an opinion. It gets monotonous."

"I imagine it's frustrating."

Cassidy's catching her breath. The words don't come easily. "I can't help her." They reach the top of the hill, pausing to wait for the others. And she doesn't know why she says it, maybe because she knows she'll never see these people again, but the words spill out. "She wants a dad. And I can't give her that. He was a one-night stand. Meant nothing to me."

Lucy pulls on the zipper of her jacket, unshaken. "In my experience—"

"Yes, we know. You've had many experiences."

Lucy starts over. "Teenage girls need to be heard. They need to be seen. It doesn't matter by whom. Mother. Father. Aunt. Uncle. They need a steady presence in their life. And they need to know they're loved."

"I'm pretty sure my daughter knows she's loved," Cassidy scoffs. This conversation shouldn't surprise her. This is why she's never fit in with the women in her life. Every time she's tried—acceptance is something she's always yearned for—she somehow managed to come across as confrontational and defensive. She silently counts to ten, adopting Rosalie's calming method, and checks on the others.

Gazing over her shoulder, she sees Leo climbing the hill, out of breath. Penny's beside him, scowling, and Henry and the dolls have almost caught up. Simone brings up the rear, holding a hiking stick in one hand, her camera slung around her neck. Barbie's in slim-fitting yoga pants with a top that shows off her perfectly flat stomach. She's casually popping M&M's in her mouth as she climbs. The nerve of the woman.

"You all right, honey?" Henry calls out to his wife.

Lucy smiles at him, and Cassidy catches her giving him a thumbs-up.

"Let me guess"—Henry directs this at her—"my wife's giving you therapy."

Barbie chimes in. "Everyone could benefit from therapy."

"Not me," Adam says, pulling her close to his side. "Right, babe?"

"She'll have you psychoanalyzed by the end of this trail," Henry says. "At a discounted fee."

They gather at the peak, chugging water and posing for pictures before setting off on the downhill path along a ravine. Cassidy takes off ahead of the others, ditching Lucy and her 1-800-Therapy. The sounds of the falls emptying into the humming stream have her quiet and introspective, considering Lucy's advice. Maybe repairing things with Rosie is a start to being welcomed into their circle.

She loves her daughter.

She loved her so much she fought to have her, recognizing how difficult it would be without a coparent. She loved Rosalie when she held her in her arms those first few nights, lulling her to sleep with a bottle and placing her in the bassinet beside her bed so she could watch her sleep. She'd stroked her tiny fingers and feet, amazed at what she'd created, imagining the life they'd have. There it was, all laid out, a winding road dotted with cheery destinations. She and little Rosalie at the playground, rocking back and forth on the swings. Summers on the lake, dipping their toes in the cool water. She had visions of being best friends, like she and her mother were. They'd be a mother-daughter duo, with matching outfits and manicures. They'd share their secrets and laugh at *I Love Lucy* reruns, recite the alphabet while twisting apple stems to find the first initial of a future boyfriend. The road curved and stretched, but she hadn't expected Rosalie's detour. Their differences were one thing, but the lie Cassidy constructed about her father was the harsh turn that led Rosalie away.

She stares down at the ground while an overwhelming regret winds through her chest. Who walked away first? Blaming Rosalie was a lot easier than blaming herself. She knew how she disappointed her daughter. She'd seen the embarrassment on Rosalie's face. Losing her own mother had devastated her. She didn't know how to be a better parent.

Leo nears, and the mirror Cassidy has avoided evaporates. His energy field reaches across the path, nipping at Cassidy, and over her shoulder Penny stares on with a blasé expression.

After Cassidy's early-morning jog around the property, she sat on her phone, googling the Shays and falling down a rabbit hole lined with speculation and juicy details. Leo and his costar, Claire Leonardo, caught at a café in Studio City holding hands under the table. And then the infamous kiss.

The picture was in every gossip rag and entertainment show. The press hunted Penny down at every turn as she picked up the kids from school, grocery shopped, exited the gym—hiding her watery eyes beneath a big, floppy hat until security was called in.

Penny and Leo's brief statement read:

It has recently come to our attention that there are images circulating that challenge the state of our marriage. We have not and will not make any comment about our private life or personal matters. We ask that you respect our family's privacy, especially that of our young children, during this difficult time.

Leo and Penny Shay

Typical Hollywood-speak. Offering no rebuttal, no denial. Leaving the public to swirl in rumors. Cassidy almost felt sorry for Leo. One fateful afternoon spurred the internet trolls to post countless sexy images of Leo and Claire taken from their movies and press junkets, blurring the line between real and make-believe.

A Thousand Lives released, starring Leo and Claire Leonardo. The drama—loosely based on the imagined lives of John F. Kennedy Jr. and Carolyn Bessette-Kennedy, had they missed their plane—was filmed a few years before, and should have been one of the biggest films of Leo's career. Instead of smashing records, the film flopped. The public had made their opinions known, and there's nothing as persuasive as the court of public opinion. Leo may have single-handedly tanked his marriage, but the audiences had crushed him, stripped him of their loyalty. There was speculation of an imminent divorce. Production on Leo and Claire's next film came to a screeching halt.

Now here he is on a mountain path, smiling at Cassidy, the others pausing to photograph a passing deer. "I was on her therapy couch last night. Don't sweat it."

Leo Shay is comforting her, and she doesn't know if she should thank him or fuck him. She prefers the latter, but it would do her no good on her quest for acceptance. She settles on the former.

"Thanks. What's with you and Penny, anyway?"

He stumbles on a tree root and rights himself. "Are you a reporter?"

Cassidy laughs. "God no."

She sees a glint of vulnerability in his eyes, a weakness he's been holding in. He shrugs, seeming unsure of what to say.

"Are you getting back together? I won't tell anyone. It's not like I have a ton of friends."

He ponders his answer. But Cassidy sees the way his temples pulse, his acting skills failing. "I didn't do what they're saying."

Something about the forest and the sounds of the trickling water slips under Cassidy's skin and draws on her compassion. "Yeah, you really got caught with your pants down."

"I love her." He doesn't look up when he says this, his voice just above a whisper. "We hit a rough patch."

"If you love her, you fight for her," Cassidy says.

His cheeks redden, though she can't be sure if it's from her words or physical exertion. "Look who's doling out the advice now." Cassidy feels the slap as they reach the steps to the narrow footbridge. She stops. His eyes fix on hers.

"I didn't mean it like that," he says.

"It's okay. I know what you meant." She can't hide her disappointment.

"No. I was just referring to Lucy giving therapy—"

"It's fine. I get it all the time. The unmarried woman can't possibly understand relationships." She really doesn't. She just watches a lot of Hallmark Channel.

He stops. "I really didn't mean it like that."

"It's fine. Really." And she flashes him a smile, done trying to be nice. "If it doesn't work out . . . I'm just down the hall."

The others catch up, and they line up single file on the steps and cross the rickety bridge to the tumbling falls. There they disperse, some climbing the rocks around the shallow swimming hole, others stripping off their shoes and socks. Simone directs them in front of the falls for a group shot. Leo stands between Cassidy and Penny. It's tense, and she thinks she might faint from his nearness. She's not imagining how Leo's body stiffens.

The air is warm and breezy when Adam slips off his shirt and wades into the cool water. The others follow, and soon they're kicking and splashing while Simone documents every detail. Adam grabs Sienna's hand, and they climb a set of boulders to another waterfall. Lucy and Henry are stuck in deep conversation, which leaves Cassidy with Penny and Leo.

Penny's struggling with a knot in her shoelace, and Leo's determined to help. He drops down on one knee as Penny's eyes fix on Cassidy's. She feels a drop of shame for what she said to Leo earlier, realizing Leo isn't interested in her at all.

She smiles awkwardly at them. "Good times."

CHAPTER 20

HENRY

Henry's happy to be out of the van and away from the conversation. Breathing fresh air relaxes him, keeps him from thinking back to that rainy night at the inn last year. He doesn't enjoy the foggy memory, the sketchy details, or the jumble of regret. When they returned home, no one discussed their drunken behavior. Maybe things had gone too far, or maybe they were too intoxicated to care. Since then, Henry can't bear the smell of tequila, turning to the smooth comfort of bourbon. But now they're back, and it's hard to ignore how their routine stay had become overshadowed by a tangled memory.

Today he feels similar discomfort as he crosses over twisted tree roots. Maybe it's because Lucy keeps repeating, "I should've stopped after the third shot." Or how Adam crudely comments that they should do it again—causing Henry's skin to itch, making him wonder if he touched poison ivy. And Sienna, Sienna just giggles, her bronzed cheeks turning pink.

Henry didn't need the guidance of the stars to predict that night wouldn't end well. The steady rains had been so abrasive that the other guests had cut their trip short, leaving the four friends indoors for most of the week. Their days began with Jean-Paul's home-baked muffins with bellinis and mimosas. Enjoying a morning buzz, they'd hunkered down for movies. If he remembered correctly, they watched *Castaway*, and the girls spent countless hours discussing the rainy kiss between Helen Hunt and Tom Hanks, wondering what might have happened had Helen hopped in that truck with Tom. Their debate dug into the layered complexities of relationships and fate's cruel hand. And of course, there was Adam being Adam: "It's a fucking movie." From there, they moved to the less provoking backgammon and checkers, puzzles and playing cards, while Jean-Paul fed them copious amounts of food.

Henry wonders, if the other guests had stayed, would the night have unraveled as it did? They were playing with a dangerous mix of alcohol, boredom, and secrets. Twice, Lucy urged him to tell their friends about his father, but he refused. Sienna kept asking why Henry was so quiet. Cooped up in a vacation house that felt like their own created a strange sense of belonging and bravado. Of course things would escalate. After they wolfed down plates of oysters, finishing them off with flaming bananas foster and a few bottles of Casamigos reposado they'd sneaked in—the inn served only wine—the rain had subsided, and with an almost manic case of cabin fever, they set out for the damp firepit, using some kindling to help get it started. The flames heated their bodies and sparked a dare. Which was how they ended up playing strip poker.

Henry shakes his head at the memory, shakes the vision of another man's bare-breasted wife out of his brain. He remembers checking the lunar calendar, but they hadn't even been close to a full moon.

In the months leading up to the trip, the stress over his father had taken its toll. Lucy pushed him to talk, to open up, but he resisted. They'd started to sleep apart and argue about the toothpaste cap and hair in the shower (ridiculous things), and that week her anger was palpable. His father's crimes had divided them, and after leaving the firepit, when they returned to their room, the anger and blame effortlessly poured out, ending with a sensational blowup of shoes and clothes thrown across the room. That night, he slept in *Le Beau*.

It turned out they weren't the only ones feeling the pressures of marriage. Sienna had confided in Lucy her frustration over Adam's excessive travel. Lucy had remarked to Henry about the tiny chink in their golden armor, "Maybe they're not so perfect after all."

At the falls, Lucy interrupts the memory by nudging him toward Adam and Sienna. He hesitates, the dampness and their half-naked bodies an unwelcome reminder of that night. He breaks into a light sweat.

She tugs on his arm. "Let's get a picture."

Why she feels the need to document the end of their marriage, he'll never understand, and that's what he's whispering to her when Simone points toward another fall, a slick plume of water jutting from the stacked boulders. "It's a short walk," she says as Lucy glides past, and he reluctantly follows. The sunlight dances along her black workout pants, and the memory of her naked in bed flashes through his mind before he can extinguish it.

They're walking single file, carefully stepping along the path, when Lucy slips. At first, it seems harmless, but when Henry gets closer, he sees her ankle has contorted unnaturally, and she's wailing. Penny and Leo, Simone, and Cassidy circle around while Henry kneels on the slippery rock beside her. This isn't good. Lucy's a strong woman, two natural labors with hardly a whimper. Yet here she is writhing, squirming under his touch. He whispers in her hair, "I'm here."

Penny's on the other side, stroking Lucy's back. Cassidy's searching in her bag for something, finally pulling out a pill bottle. "You're going to need one of these."

Leo snatches it and reads the label. "Whoa."

Adam shows up, Sienna not far behind, maneuvering the rocks with an ease that emphasizes the others' clumsiness. Adam shoves Henry out of the way—not Penny. "I've seen every injury on the field. Let me take a look." Standing on the NFL sidelines is the furthest thing from being a doctor, but Adam tries, somewhat convincingly, to assume the role of one. Henry, a doctor by degree, though not in medicine, fumes. He can tend to his wife. But Adam's being Adam, and he sweeps his irritation aside to watch as Adam pokes and prods, his fingers running up and down Lucy's calf. She's borderline hysterical, screaming at Adam not to touch her when Adam recommends she take the pill Cassidy offers.

"It's definitely broken."

"How am I supposed to get back?" Lucy squeals.

And it wouldn't be Adam if he didn't throw in a story about the famous linebacker he helped to the sidelines at a recent practice. "You're a lot lighter than him."

They help Lucy stand up, her arms over both Henry's and Adam's shoulders. Henry's annoyed. When they get Lucy to the bridge, he's confident he can take care of his wife, and he scoops her in his arms and carries her along the trail. They eyeball him in disbelief. Who's he kidding, and why the sudden urge to stake his claim? There isn't a chance in hell he can carry her the entire way.

CHAPTER 21

PENNY

This thing with Lucy happened fast. One minute they're careening down the windy path, and the next she's fallen and crying out for help. Penny can't help but notice how the two couples look after each other, and it reminds her of when she and Leo spent every waking moment with their former best friends, Alara and Buckley.

God, she misses them. But she can't think about that now.

Simone encourages them to stay put and enjoy the afternoon. "*Tante* Renée is meeting us at the hospital. One of us will come back for you." But the mood has shifted. Sienna won't leave her best friend, and Cassidy's carrying Lucy's backpack, edging closer to their bubble. Penny knows she and Leo should go back. She knows the rules of hiking: the group stays together, but Simone is already handing her their lunches, and between her moans, Lucy breathlessly tells them there's no reason for their day to be spoiled. Penny can't help but think this is some sort of ploy, as though the gang is pushing Leo and her together.

And maybe it's the sound of the rippling water, or the sparkle that catches the sunlight and turns the forest a vibrant green, but she remembers how she once loved being here. And she once loved being here with Leo. She's caught between the group already crossing the narrow bridge and the tug of Leo wandering toward the stream. Against her better judgment, she places one hesitant foot in front of the other and makes her way downstream. And it is decided.

The sounds behind her fade away, and she follows Leo along the water's edge, keeping a safe, reasonable distance. She studies the shape of his shoulders, his confident gait. Leo. Is it really him, or is it his alter ego, movie star Leo? Because that's what she wondered when the picture of him and Claire Leonardo popped up on her phone. She felt duped.

In Penny and Leo's world, every move had to be calculated and meticulously thought out. You couldn't risk lunch with a platonic friend unless you wanted to end up splattered across Page Six with some shocking accusation. The press could make up bold, splashy lies with headlines, but despite the cliché, pictures don't lie. Leo had been on set, at that point the distance between them more than physical miles, and she had just dropped the kids off at school when her mother texted the photo of her husband and Claire holding hands under the table at Marie et Cie, their favorite coffee shop.

To say her world came crashing down that day is an understatement. There's no phrase powerful enough for that gut-punch, the visceral ache that spread through her bloodstream. Penny felt the heat rise in her chest, the nausea closing in. She would always remember that moment, her sweet Cody turning around before she entered the school building, smiling and giving her a wave, her cheeks dimpled, the French braid falling down her shoulder. She'd smiled back, though this would mark the moment their lives irrevocably changed. It had all been leading to this, the sad patch of grass they couldn't skip over.

A cold sweat paints her skin, and she stops. *I can't do this.* If she turns back now, she can catch up with the others, so she spins around, her heart thumping loudly, and she tries to escape before Leo sees her. She can't do this. She can't get stuck inside the memories and forget the pain. But he's fast. She hears him approach behind her, and then she feels his hands on her shoulders. Firm. Too firm.

"Don't go," he says, out of breath.

His hands move down her arms. Close. Closer than he deserves to be. Closer than she should allow.

"Stay." He says it again, reminding her they're alone in the place that holds their history. She slowly turns to face him. His eyes are their brilliant blue and brown, and she loves that about them—their differences, the contrast, how he can be so many things at once, though she hates it too, because it's the same reason she lost him.

His hands, soft and smooth, slide to her fingers, and she doesn't have to look to see the scar on his left thumb from when Buckley's German shepherd bit him when they were seventeen. She memorized his hands long ago.

"Come with me."

He grabs hold of her hand and leads her down the path. With each step, warnings blare, but her legs mechanically follow. This is what happens when they're cut off from "breaking news" and *Entertainment Weekly*. Once, their relationship was entirely theirs, a private arena where no one got through. She tells herself this is merely a walk along their favorite trail, but the charge radiating from their palms says otherwise.

He stops to face her as they reach the boulder. And this is no ordinary boulder. This is the boulder where he took her hand in his, got down on one knee, and asked her that question people ask when they're in love.

He's staring, and she can't turn away. She sees all the hurt and pain and regret. She knows. It mirrors her own.

"What are you doing, Leo?"

He sits on the boulder, and she resists following but gives up and takes a seat near the edge. The stream hurries by, and she imagines sticking her hand in to make it stop. To make him stop. She doesn't want to dredge up the past. She doesn't want to remember all the events that led to this. Ellie died. Does he think reminding her of the promises they made will change that? Love does wild things to a person, and theirs made them careless. Now their goddaughter is dead, and Alara and Buckley are gone from their life too.

"Maybe if we talked about it last summer, we could've worked through it. Maybe you would've stayed—"

"And what?" She can't help herself. "You wouldn't have fucked Claire Leonardo?"

This is what she does when the subject of Ellie comes up. Seething rage falls from her tongue.

"You know I didn't fuck Claire, but if that makes it easier for you . . . to blame me . . ." He pauses to let that soak in, but all she feels is the spray of water from the flume. Much like that day in Palm Springs. Six tan kids splashing in a shimmery pool.

The public had no idea why Penny picked up the kids and moved back home. But in Hollywood there's always speculation. So when the picture of Leo and Claire surfaced months later, the media shaped and molded their story to fit a trashy magazine's narrative.

"I got the divorce papers," he finally says. "Is this really what you want?"

Their love once burned big and bright, their passion deeply sensual. But how could she stay in a marriage when his touch reminded her of that day? When his lips and hands are tied to regret? When something marks a marriage so deeply, it's hard to find your way back. A silence takes over, and the crack widens.

She inhales, stuffing Ellie back into a dark crevice in her head and finding her strength. "I filed. Of course it's what I want."

He stares down at the platinum band on his finger, refusing her eyes. "I don't believe you."

"I'm not the liar, Leo."

He ducks from a bee floating by, but it could've been her words.

When the picture landed on her phone, the relationship was already broken. He tried explaining, but she had seen enough. Nothing he could say would change her mind. And he tried. He'd said it was Ellie's birthday, that he and Claire had gone off the lot for lunch. She had no idea the restaurant was Penny and Leo's place. There'd been some production delays; the director was "unimpressed" with Leo's performance.

He and Claire had always been able to work through any on-set tension, but this time they couldn't.

"I told her about Ellie."

"You crossed a line."

"I was broken, Penny," he says. "She held my hand to comfort me. And it did comfort me. For a minute. But Claire misread, and she leaned in for a kiss." He stops. "I turned away. The paparazzi were fast."

She remembers how she laughed when he tried to explain at the time, her emotions numb and hardened. "Your own Me Too moment."

Leo doesn't find it funny. "She assumed we were having problems . . ."

Spite spills from her mouth. "No one could ever refuse you, Leo. Do you want a prize?"

Claire had called her to explain, but the damage was done. They'd been friendly, as friendly as any wife could be with the sexy actress who spends more waking hours with her husband, mostly in compromising positions. Her statement was weak, the apology flimsy. Claire's gift was acting. How could anyone believe her? Penny had seen the way Leo looked at Claire. The two got caught, and now they were playing cleanup.

"Come on, Leo." Penny snaps back to reality. "Now you're free to do all the things a family held you back from."

He looks as though she's beaten him with a stick, and it should make her feel better, but it doesn't. "I love my family. And the only woman I've ever wanted was you."

It sure doesn't feel that way.

He drops his head. "I think we abandoned each other." He unlaces his shoes and takes off his shirt. "But I didn't cross any line." Edging closer to the tumbling water, he slips a foot in.

"I didn't need to come here to rehash all this, Leo. I've lived it every day."

"Then why did you come?"

She's still asking herself that question. The girls come to mind—a plausible excuse—and by taking this leap, she'll be a hero in their eyes, but there's more. There always is. Maybe somewhere deep inside, somewhere she's kept caged and guarded, is the desire to go back to the beginning. That simple place before fame and red carpets.

"I'm not sure, Leo."

"I think you do."

She feels his eyes travel up and down her skin.

"Come in the water."

"I'm not going in the water."

"Come in the water."

And before she knows what's happening, he's dragging her by the ankles, ripping her shoes and socks off, carrying her into the falls. Their bodies are slick and wet, and she feels her nipples against his bare chest. The rush of the water is cold, but instead of chilling her, she feels a warm longing.

"Please don't, Leo." She backs away, steadying herself on the slippery rocks lining the riverbed.

"Don't what?" His eyes bore into hers. "Pretend that I'm not feeling everything you're feeling? You think it was easy to come here knowing what I'm up against? To go down the memory lane of this horror show, to see myself in the mirror of your eyes knowing how badly I hurt you? That maybe you wouldn't even show up?" He stops to take a breath. "I love you. I love you fucking madly. Whole heart, full stop. Finally, every love song makes perfect sense."

"Are you fucking kidding me, Leo? You think I didn't see you on that sappy holiday special with whatever her name is using that exact same line?"

He splashes her when he says this: "I knew you watched."

"Your daughter watched. I was hovering nearby."

"You let her watch? Don't you think that's confusing for her?"

"Not as confusing as seeing you and Claire plastered all over the news."

He ignores the swipe. "But you watched."

She splashes him back. "All of America has used that line. Almost worse than that *hello* line Tom Cruise used on Renée Zellweger."

"*You had me at frog dissection* is much better." He bows his head. "But it's true. It's how I feel."

"Why'd you have to go and ruin everything?"

"I didn't ruin anything. I'm not lying. I would never lie to you. Ask yourself why you're fighting it, why it's easier for you to believe I cheated. I know we agreed we wouldn't speak to the press, but I will if I have to. I'm not with Claire, and that kiss . . . it wasn't even a kiss."

She swallows hard, running her fingers through the water. "There's someone else, Leo."

This gets his attention. "I know when you're lying. If there were someone else, you wouldn't be here."

A gaggle of screaming kids comes tumbling down the bank, and soon they're jumping into the narrow pool. Their parents aren't far behind when one of them spots Leo. Their whispers bounce off the trees. *Is that who I think it is? Oh my God, Leo Shay!* This is the part of their relationship that has often given Penny an out, an excuse to duck down and leave Leo with his fans while she slips away.

"Don't go," he says.

"That's the thing, Leo, I'm already gone."

CHAPTER 22

SIENNA

They're walking down the mountain toward the parking lot, and she's worried. She's worried about Lucy. And she's worried about the gnawing in her gut that has her analyzing Adam, which in and of itself is troubling because that's always been Lucy's job.

Her husband is handsome. That's a given. Charming. Always the life of the party. Devoted. But something's off. She hears the niggling doubt that she's been trying to quiet. Fine. So maybe it was the conversation in the van about last summer. She thought they were all on the same page, that they'd continue to act as though it didn't happen. Maybe they should have discussed it at some point. Instead, they're all skipping around some land mine that feels like it's about to blow.

She knows her best friend. Lucy's been distant, noticeably passive-aggressive with Adam. And isn't she acting just as uncomfortable around Henry? They all have their roles. Lucy with her psychobabble. Henry and his sensibilities, always even-keeled and pragmatic. Adam being the overly friendly extrovert. And then there's her. The pretender. And it's getting exhausting.

Or maybe it's the darkness.

She didn't sleep last night. The minute Adam shut off the light, her heart raced, and she panicked, a heaviness smothering her chest. She gasped for breath and had to turn the light back on, which sparked an argument. He demanded answers; she didn't have any.

She knew what everyone said about them. She used to relish the praise. *I wish I had a husband who loved me like that. You guys are perfect. You're so lucky.* Because she once felt that way, until she didn't. She doesn't want to blame it on the money, but as soon as Adam started making the kind of living that set them apart from the rest of the world, he changed. She tells herself that because she can't imagine she would have chosen this. Chosen *this* Adam: the entertainer. Adam who pours on the PDA when they're in a crowd, bragging, flaunting his elite connections and exclusive access to the very best perks.

At first, she enjoyed being able to breathe a little easier without the financial pressure, and she'd be lying if she said she didn't love their large Colonial, with its sprawling backyard and pool. They'd christened the pool house that first night, sipping champagne while he explored her body. They'd been so happy.

She's not sure when she started to notice the subtleties that turned into big blots on their marital screen, but now she can't unsee them. The affectionate Adam who's all over her in public, bragging about his "hot wife," disappears as soon as they're out of range. He'll drop her hand and bury his face in his phone. The rejection magnified the rumblings she'd already overheard at cocktail parties and sporting events.

"What a douche."

The first time she'd heard someone call her husband that word, it was at the annual ESPN Christmas party. Handsy Adam had been showing her off to anyone he could. She'd smiled on cue, careful to make the right impression, but even so she'd cringed when she heard that word, *douche*, whispered in their wake. Adam wasn't a douche—she thought—until they got in the car to go home, and he fell silent away from an audience. His mood spilled over when they got into bed. Rote and performative. The passion and desire diminished. The disconnect carried over the next morning after she carted the kids off to school. She caught him before he holed up in his office, trying her best to explain how he made her feel. And that's the thing. There was nothing left to feel. Not when someone treated you as though your entire being was predicated upon glossy hair and a tight ass.

Now here's Adam, on the phone with someone as he works his way down the mountain. She and Henry support a whimpering Lucy; the pill Cassidy gave her hasn't kicked in yet. They all stare at Adam, screaming into the speakerphone as though he's cordoned off in his private office. Lucy glares the hardest.

Her conversation with Lucy will have to wait. She hates feeling at odds with her closest friend, their little family scooting through life with a broken wing. They've relied on one another for so much, their first steps toward independence and adulthood taken side by side at college. They were a team, a package deal, and they coasted through those years with the assurance and understanding that they had each other's back, a loyalty that strengthened with time.

So why does it feel as though their team has broken up?

CHAPTER 23

JEAN-PAUL

Jean-Paul's back in the kitchen, and for a fleeting moment the laughter and conversation have him believing that everything will right itself again. *That talk* with Renée on the morning she found him sweeping up the glitter was catastrophic. Their investment. Their savings. All of it. Wiped out.

After the initial shock wore off, Renée's accusatory eyes had found his. "You can't be serious?" Her skin was as white as the paper with the incriminating numbers.

"How could this happen?" Her voice trembled. "How could you let—"

He hadn't heard the rest. *You.* She had blamed him, something they swore to each other they'd never do. At some point, she threw the antique duck they purchased the day they made the investment against the wall, missing his head by an inch, the pieces scattering across the floor. And he lived with that guilt, because even though they'd made the decision together, and even though Bluebird had royally screwed them, he was supposed to protect her from something like this.

And just as they'd dealt with disappointment in the past, they forged ahead. Renée pointed her finger at Bluebird and its employees, and he pointed his finger at himself.

He preheats the deep fryer for the beignets. The lesson with the young girl has him thinking about life after the inn. If he had a kitchen full of students as eager and interested as she, he could make a lucrative business out of it. He reminds himself to share the idea with Renée.

The water on the stovetop begins to boil, as he chops eggplant for the ratatouille. Lucy sits at the head of the table, her leg elevated as the doctor ordered. The ankle is broken, and she'll have a cast for the next six weeks. Despite the injury, she insisted they stay, and she appears to be in decent spirits while she sips a club soda.

There are few secrets at the De La Rues' table. By the time the first glass of wine was poured, whispers were circulating about Cassidy Banks's bottle of oxy.

He's glad to see that despite Lucy's fall, the group is in a festive mood. They returned from the hike refreshed and hungry, though Rosalie and her mother remain at odds. The girl he was with earlier today doesn't resemble the one seated at the table tonight. She still wears the dark, broody look, straight out of the Addams Family, but the girl who asserted herself in the kitchen, tasting, focusing on flavor, was in her element. She glowed. The girl seated at his table beside her mother does not.

Tonight, Rosalie has the seat adjacent to the cooktop, and her eyes follow his hands as he punches out the centers of the beignet dough they prepared earlier. When he asks her to slice the green apples to stuff inside the dough to fry, she jumps up.

"Careful with that," Penny warns. Cassidy barely notices her daughter wielding a sharp knife. She plunks her empty wineglass on the table for Renée to refill, but his wife takes her time, and when she reaches Cassidy's side, he watches as she makes her signature move, dropping a handful of ice cubes in her glass.

"Did you just put ice in my glass, Ms. De La Rue?"

All heads turn, and there is no sound except for the sizzling of the beignets, their sweet aroma filtering through the air. Jean-Paul guesses

Cassidy wants the wine more than she wants an argument, so she lifts the glass to her lips.

The quiet breaks up after Cassidy gulps down her not-yet-watered-down wine in one single swig, and Lucy, trained in navigating awkward lulls, directs an innocuous line of questioning at Leo. "What's the most fabulous destination you ever visited?"

He peers at Penny. "French Polynesia."

"Bucket list," says Sienna. "Tahiti and Bora Bora are a dream."

"It's beautiful," Penny flatly answers.

He listens in, Rosalie by his side. Simone plates the crispy filled dough.

Leo grabs his phone off the table and slides through his gallery, flipping through pictures of what Jean-Paul imagines is a turquoise ocean, thatch-roof bungalows, and close-ups of the couple smiling into the camera. The picture he holds up for them all to see is just that. Jean-Paul steals a glance at Penny and Leo smiling for the camera, their tan bodies blended together in a tight hug.

"I saw that picture!" exclaims Lucy. "It was on the cover of *People*."

Leo drops his head, as though he's embarrassed by the attention.

"My players have made multiple covers," Adam brags.

Jean-Paul turns to Rosalie, gesturing at the table. "See how they're talking and eating and enjoying themselves? We've created this. You've created this. Now go sit and enjoy yourself too."

She smiles. No, actually, she beams.

"What do you think is behind our fascination with celebrities?" Sienna asks.

"It's this ideal people hold themselves to." Lucy lifts her glass of water for a sip. "And we're fascinated because we're innately curious and want to connect with people who appear to have these perfect, better lives."

"It's a myth," Penny says.

The table quiets. Jean-Paul isn't surprised at Penny's candor. It's a quality he admires about her.

"We're just like everyone else," she adds.

"She's going to tell you I fart and poop like the rest of you," Leo jokes, taking a bite of the beignet. "This is incredible, Jean-Paul."

"Thank my assistant. She had a hand in it too." He smiles in Rosalie's direction.

"It's a lot more exciting to fart in a luxury suite in Bora Bora than the suburbs of New York," Adam says.

"That's never stopped you before," Sienna says, playfully poking Adam.

"When it comes to celebrities," Lucy says, "think about it. You have these larger-than-life people. We watch them take over screens . . . we fall in love with them a little bit. Then we put them on these pedestals. So it makes sense to want to get beneath the surface, to bring them down to earth . . . our earth . . . so they're more like us."

"Then why the backlash when people find out we're just like them?" Leo asks. "That we're human . . . and we make mistakes. It seems unfair that I should get ruined in the tabloids for a mistake my costar made."

Penny sets her glass down, resting her chin on her hands.

"You're a public figure, Leo, so you're held to a higher standard," Lucy replies. "When you chose that life, you knew the expectations and the consequences to bad behavior."

"Okay." Penny brings a napkin to her lips. "I think we get it."

Leo argues, "I think this is an important conversation." And then he addresses Lucy. "You just said people want to humanize us. Didn't you just say that? And then we become human, and we're still the enemy? If I'm so relatable now, why did my last movie bomb?"

"Leo, you can't choose this life and then parse out the parts you don't want people to see," Penny says. "And so we're clear, since we're all obviously invested in this story . . ." *True,* Jean-Paul agrees, because no one moves. No one says a word. They all stare with pitiful, probing looks on their faces. "This happened to me," Penny continues. "I didn't ask for our personal life to be plastered in the news for every gossip-monger and hater to feast upon. I didn't ask for any of it, not even the ridiculous perks." She eyes Leo when she says this. "Because they're meaningless, and they change people. The people you love. The people you once trusted."

Jean-Paul feels the tension rise and fall. You could hear a pin drop as Penny speaks, and he notices how Leo stares at his plate. He doesn't miss the look that passes between Lucy and Henry either. It's the first time the two seem aligned since arriving, a private *uh-huh* moment that has him convinced he's witnessed something big.

Penny continues, "Our kids didn't ask for it either. And none of you know what happened. None of you can ever understand the scrutiny we're under . . . what we've been through. There's so much more to us than what you see in the news.

"And you . . ." Penny gestures toward Leo. *Poor Leo,* Jean-Paul thinks. "I can't sit here while you play victim, as though losing fans hurts worse than losing me." She then surprises Jean-Paul and the rest of them by hopping off the stool and storming from the room. He thinks he might be the only one who sees the giant tear that slips down her cheek.

"You should go after her," Cassidy says.

"I think she needs some time to sit with her feelings," Lucy says. She looks at Leo. "You both do."

"Isn't that the point of throwing a tantrum?" Adam asks. "For attention? For someone to chase after you?"

"You know nothing about Penny," Leo snaps at Adam.

"It could be about attention," Lucy begins. "When you're pursued, there's momentary validation, but it doesn't get to the core of the issue, the void that needs filling. And to be fair, I don't think this is what Penny's doing." She turns to Leo. "I think Penny's genuinely hurt. I think she's been holding it in for some time."

The knife slips from Jean-Paul's hands and clangs as it hits the floor. Bending to pick it up, he hears the regret in Leo's voice. "Nothing hurt worse than losing Penny."

Jean-Paul signals Renée and Simone to assist him in serving the beef Wellington. The tender meat is garnished with greens and lathered in a mushroom mousse. He's proud of his work. He hopes the flavor adds some comfort to the uncomfortable conversation.

"Do therapists have their own therapists?" Cassidy asks Lucy.

Lucy chuckles. "Some do, but the rest of us like to think we're flawless specimens."

Which initiates chortles and a discussion on Harrison Ford in *Shrinking*. He and Renée watched the show and enjoyed it.

"In my experience," begins Adam, his arm resting on the back of Sienna's chair, "therapists are more fucked-up than some of their patients."

Jean-Paul looks to Lucy for her reaction, and he's happy to see she waits to reply until she finishes chewing. He just saved a choker last week. "That's a broad generalization," she says. "What are you basing that on?" Then she apparently changes her mind. "Actually, don't answer that."

"Hey. He's only kidding, Luce," says Sienna. "Right, babe?" She twists in her seat and places a palm on Adam's scruff.

"I wasn't kidding."

Sienna tilts her head and whispers something Jean-Paul assumes is a reprimand. He knows how to multitask. He could prepare a four-course meal while picking up on every nuance. The vibrations that mean a lively evening, the whispers that spin a fine tale. Renée joins his side, asking if he thinks she should check on Penny. He cautions against it. From what they know of Penny, she needs time to sort this through. He whispers, "Being here with him can't be easy."

"I agree." And then: "And by the way, my intuition about last summer is correct."

"Shh," he replies.

She brushes him off with a wave. "They can't hear me over all the chatter. Something's going to boil over this week, and it's nothing in your pot."

"Don't let your imagination get the better of you."

"Imagination pagination."

He hands her his glass of wine, and she takes a sip.

"Maybe we're getting too old for this."

The defeat in her eyes stops him. She passes him the glass.

Swallowing the worry, they step back and watch the show. Henry's describing the universe as a metaphor for life, how we're all made of stars and an energy that pulls us near and far, how the *final frontier* means possibility, facing the unknown. Leo looks as though he's trying to make sense of the idea, as if any of it will bring Penny back. "The sky is a canvas for our imagination," Henry continues. "The stars are dreams and goals, and the constellations are the connections that shape our story. When the universe speaks, you need to listen."

Jean-Paul falls inside Henry's words. Aren't they all just dreamers? Aren't they all just people yearning for sunshine, to touch a piece of the moon?

But then he adds, "Unfortunately, there are disruptions. Like comets. And supernovas. You heard about the Tasmanian devil, right?"

They shake their heads.

"It's a star that died in a rare, intense blue-light explosion, and instead of fading away, it re-energized, baffling astronomers by shooting flares into the sky. They had never seen anything like it before. The point is, we don't always know what's heading our way. Or"—Henry dips his head—"if we've lost something for good." He turns to Jean-Paul. "We should have dinner under the stars."

"You're cute when you get all romantic," Adam teases his friend.

Jean-Paul likes the idea. They don't dine on the patio enough, and this group might need the sky to guide them.

"I don't much follow the stars and planets, but I do enjoy a sexy show on Netflix. Has anyone seen *Sex/Life*?" Cassidy asks.

At the mention of the steamy show (likened to mommy porn, featuring Adam Demos's oversize appendage), Rosalie gets to her feet. "Mother! Why?"

"Rosie, you need to lighten up. I watch *Modern Family* and *Grey's Anatomy* too."

Renée catches Jean-Paul's eye, and he wipes his hands on the dish-towel and comes around from behind the island.

"Renée and I watched *Sex/Life*. We rather liked it."

He isn't sure what he's doing, intervening, but Rosalie backs down.

"Really?" she asks, surprised and somewhat pleased to know that her mother isn't the only freak in the room. He makes sure Rosalie can read his expression: *You should go a little easier on your mother.*

Rosalie's eyes search the floor, and "Sorry" falls off her tongue, as though the word is the enemy, a word she wants to dispose of but is unsure how.

The momentary lapse in conversation comes to an end with Renée replenishing Adam's wine as he name-drops some famous athletes in one sentence. Henry doesn't comment, but Jean-Paul swears his face reads, *Here we go again.*

And when Adam sees that he's got everyone's attention, he throws back another gulp of wine and shamelessly crows about his chumminess with these athletes. How they play golf together. How he was invited to a certain someone's fiftieth birthday party in Vegas, then took a jaunt on a 150-foot yacht in Miami.

Jean-Paul has learned to tune people like Adam out. And he believes the rest of the table has tuned him out too. Sienna sits perfectly still beside him with a static look he can't decipher. She's smiling, as she often is, but when he peers closer, the vacant eyes are a giveaway. She's either cringing inside or dazed by her husband's mind-numbing self-importance.

"Where'd you go to college?" Rosalie asks Adam.

Adam drops his fork and knife. "You don't need college, Marilyn."

"My name's Rosalie." Then she stops. "Wait. Did you just refer to me as Marilyn Manson?"

"Who's Marilyn Manson?" Cassidy asks.

"College is for amateurs," Adam responds.

"Adam," Lucy begins. "That's not at all true."

"Where did you go?" Rosalie asks again, a little more confidently.

Jean-Paul has to hand it to her. She knows which button to push with the man who dropped out of college.

"Do you know who I am?" he asks, staring directly into Rosalie's eyes.

"I don't really care who you are, but I can vouch for your pretentiousness, and I'm guessing it's your deep-seated insecurity that makes you act like one of the biggest blowhards I've ever met in my entire life. And I'm not even sixteen."

Jean-Paul bites back a laugh. He feels like a proud uncle watching Rosalie come to life.

"Rosalie Banks!" Cassidy shouts.

She turns to her mother. "You're all thinking it. I'm the only one brave enough to say it."

Jean-Paul waits for someone to argue. Nobody does. They just drink and wipe crumbs from their lips that aren't there. Except Cassidy. She's managed to push her food around the plate, faux eating, not taking a bite.

Adam turns to Cassidy. "You let your daughter talk to adults like that?"

"Show me the adult," Rosalie says.

Renée approaches Rosalie and drops a hand on her shoulder. Jean-Paul notices the young girl's body slacken with her touch.

Adam can't help himself. "You know something, Rosalie—"

Jean-Paul can't let this go on in his kitchen. "That's enough, Adam."

"Let me finish." He turns to Rosalie, and Jean-Paul waits, prepared to pounce. Adam tells a story of how he grew up with nothing and worked his way through school. "Heck, I didn't even know my mother. And when I got to college, all those kids were partying and playing and cheating their way through exams and finals—"

"I wasn't doing any of that," Henry says.

Adam ignores him. "I was passionate about sports. About players. I dug around. I made contacts. And maybe I finessed a bit to get what I wanted . . ." He turns to Henry. "Stars and constellations, you said it yourself. I made up a few stories, because I had a goal. And I was focused. And I worked harder than any of those frat boys collecting degrees they'd never use. I made sure I was in the right place at the right time. And guess what? I didn't need college because I'd already succeeded. I had a job, and I was supporting myself."

Sienna beams with pride.

Rosalie gulps her soda.

They all look on, perhaps seeing Adam in a different light. "So if I want to flaunt that success"—he pauses for effect—"I've earned the right."

Rosalie claps. "Pompous. With a side of motivational speaker. I'm impressed. But just so you know, when you drop names like that, it reeks of insecurity. Just my observation."

"Okay." Jean-Paul claps. "Enough entertainment. Time for dessert."

Renée joins him as they take the Grand Marnier soufflé out of the oven, noting its golden crust and melted chocolate middle. She whispers in his ear, "Hard shells and soft centers. You know how to match the menu to the guests. I love that about you."

He squeezes her bottom in response. "And I love this about you."

TUESDAY
Day 3

First Course: Avocado, shrimp, feta, and lime tostado

Second Course: Soupe à l'oignon

Main Course: Alléno rack of pork, fennel, raisins, and saffron

Dessert: Carrot cake with cream cheese icing, salted caramel bourbon sauce with pretzels, pecans, and pralines

Cloudy Bay sauvignon blanc

Orin Swift Palermo cabernet sauvignon

CHAPTER 24

PENNY

A dull morning rain taps at the window as Penny buries her head under the covers. Her body's tired; she didn't sleep. She's upset—at Leo, at her outburst at the table—and she thinks she may have reached her boiling point. Being around Leo is breaking her in ways she doesn't want to admit, and his nearness on the other side of the wall doesn't help.

She reaches for the cell phone beside the bed and sees three notifications from her kids. Nothing from Leo. She half expected teary apologies clogging up her messages, but there are none, not a single missed call.

She quickly checks in on the girls and hops out of bed.

The rain echoes her mood, and she embraces the idea of wrapping herself in a blanket and curling up by the fire. Only the fantasy comes to a screeching halt because of Leo.

Throwing on her favorite sweatshirt and sweatpants, she pulls her hair back into a long ponytail and drops a baseball cap on her head. And even though she doesn't need sunglasses on this sunless day, she grabs her Ray-Bans to hide the truth spilling from her eyes.

Stepping into the kitchen, Penny sees Rosalie standing over a limp Cassidy, feeding her salted crackers, a can of ginger ale nearby. She dashes toward the coffee when Leo descends the stairs. His eyes are also puffy from what's likely lack of sleep. She quickly turns away because she can't bear to see him.

"Good morning, ladies."

"Speak for yourself," Cassidy mumbles.

Penny pours cream into her mug as Leo watches.

"I thought you take your coffee black."

She stares at the cloud that forms in the center of the dark liquid, savoring that first sip. "I guess things change, Leo." And she moves past him toward the array of colorful breakfast foods arranged on the table.

"Rainy days call for blankets and a warm fire," Leo says as Penny takes the seat farthest from him.

Sienna and Adam step down into the room. Adam's laughing. "Another rainy day at the inn." He winks at Sienna.

"Don't get any ideas," she says.

"Please don't mention alcohol." Cassidy picks her head up, her voice gravelly.

"That bad?" Sienna asks.

Rosalie answers, "The usual."

Penny catches the sarcasm.

Jean-Paul enters with a head of damp hair, Renée not far behind.

"Lucy's in a lot of pain," she says. "We're going to bring breakfast to their room."

"Breakfast in bed sounds like the perfect morning," Leo chimes.

Her mind silences him, but her body argues. It doesn't make a bit of sense. She's mastered avoiding him, perfecting the wall between them. She filed for divorce! But something about his eyes, the way he pleaded with her yesterday, weakens her. The bedhead. His smell. She needs him to disappear, and she glares at him behind her glasses before pushing her plate of eggs and fresh brioche away. Moments ago, she was famished.

Jean-Paul scribbles notes on a piece of paper, and Rosalie rises to join him, peering over his shoulder with interest. Penny notices he's a lefty, because she's also a lefty, and Rosalie figures it out, because she's soon mentioning how she's a southpaw too. The revelation is the perfect distraction—anything to get off the subject of snuggling under the covers and sharing room service with Leo. Cassidy pats the seat beside her for Rosalie to come back, but Penny doesn't have the heart to tell her that her daughter is far more interested in cooking than nursing her hangover.

"Can I help with the menu for tonight?" Rosalie asks Jean-Paul.

Penny appraises the mother-daughter dynamic. The young girl's indifference is hard to miss. On one hand, she wants to be anywhere but in Cassidy's presence, and on the other, she tends to her every need like a parent might a child. Mothering a daughter is tricky. She knows. She has three. How could Cassidy be so blind to what's happening?

She can't worry about the strange dynamic between those two. She has enough problems of her own. Maybe she should talk to that Lucy woman. Now that she's laid up, perhaps she wouldn't mind giving her some advice.

A thunderous roar claps through the room, clanking the china in the nearby cabinets and flickering the lights. Sienna lets out a yelp. It's cute.

"I love days like this," Penny says.

"Not me," Sienna says.

Penny proceeds to describe one of her favorite childhood memories: playing cards and board games with her brother by flashlight. "I loved the simplicity of those days. The innocence."

"There was nothing innocent about last year's rainstorm," Adam says with a laugh.

"You have us intrigued," Leo says. "You keep talking about last year. Who's going to spill?"

"It was nothing," Sienna says, popping a lemon raspberry scone into her mouth. "He loves to repeat himself. The strip poker. He thinks that by repeating himself it'll spark a do-over, and that's definitely not happening. We were so hungover. It was brutal."

"Rosie, baby. I need more ginger ale," Cassidy says.

Another boom rattles the windows, and Sienna grips the table, her eyes widening. "Do you think they have a generator here?"

Adam cozies up to her and plants a kiss on her lips. "You're going to be fine." But she seems doubtful. Adam has the boyish good looks of a younger Leo. He could've been a movie star with that pearly grin and that chiseled dimple. Their tableside kiss is awkward. Leo turns away. PDA makes him uncomfortable. She knows him. He does that thing with his lips, licking the top and then the bottom.

"Can we go somewhere and talk? About last night?"

They can all hear him. The kitchen is small, and without the sizzling sounds of Jean-Paul frying bacon, they don't pretend otherwise.

Adam, ever the charmer, raises his hand in the air. "How many lefties think Penny should give Leo a chance to explain?"

The room goes quiet, everyone careful not to overstep. Rosalie's hand flies up. Jean-Paul's too.

Hopefulness marks the girl's eyes, and it hits Penny in that soft, tender spot that believes in happy endings.

Before Adam has a chance to ask the righties in the room for their vote, Penny slides off the stool and heads up the stairs with Leo trailing behind.

CHAPTER 25

ROSALIE

Jean-Paul has her stirring a concoction of raspberry jam and horseradish for a dip they'll serve at lunch. Inside, Rosalie boils.

Today.

Today she had planned to tell Cassidy about what she'd done, about the search and what she'd learned. But no. In classic Cassidy form, she had to go ahead and ruin everything. Rosalie had waited for the right time to ease into the conversation, giving her mother a chance to acclimate to the peace and calm of the inn, but nothing ever goes as planned when Cassidy is involved. Appointments with teachers. Shuttling her to driving lessons (because no one in their right mind would take a driving lesson from the woman who's racked up more tickets than Taylor Swift's Eras tour). She was perpetually late. Frazzled. A no-show.

News flash. They all know her mother's a mess. It's not as though Cassidy's trying to hide the hangover, the bobbing head, or the glaze in her eyes. Rosalie was foolish to think it would be any different in a picturesque mountain inn, that the peacefulness would make her announcement any easier. She considers the irony. How the one thing she thought might bring some order and consistency to her life is a total shit show.

At dawn, after listening to her mother retch in the bathroom, Rosalie wandered off to the library to escape the sounds. Simone was there, and at first, Rosalie was reluctant to join her on the couch, but Simone patted the empty seat beside her. "I wondered what took you so long."

"You heard?"

"My room's directly above hers. She must have her window open."

"Sorry."

"Don't be silly. She's the one who's sorry."

The wind thumps against the windows, storm clouds rolling across the sky.

Simone played with her camera, peering through the lens, training it on Rosalie.

At that hour, Rosalie's face was scrubbed clean, and she knew what Simone was thinking, because she'd heard it before. And it wasn't a few seconds before she said it. "I like how you do your makeup and all. I like your technique, but girl, you don't need all that stuff."

Rosalie took it in. But it wasn't easy.

She wasn't overtly feminine like her mother. The kids her age preferred that type, and she'd spent the last fifteen years wishing her mother would eat a Dorito.

Rosalie quickly changed the subject, holding her palm up to the lens. "What do you do with all these pictures?"

Simone tucked her knees beneath her and pointed to a bookshelf. "Every week at the inn is featured in one of those albums."

Rosalie stood, craning her neck to read the spines.

"I've been capturing memories since I moved here."

She glanced back at Simone. "Did anyone ever tell you that you look like Natalie Portman?"

"I hope not *Beautiful Girls* Natalie Portman."

"I was thinking more like *The Other Boleyn Girl*."

"Haven't seen it."

Rosalie picked up one of the albums and started flipping through the pages. "Your aunt and uncle look so different."

"That was the pre-beard stage. I kinda like it on him."

Rosalie studied the couple, smiling at the table with eight guests surrounding them. Then she returned the album to its place and chose another one. Each book opened with the menu for the week and the first night's photo of the guests on the stairs. Then candids. Laughter and food and beautiful scenery. She admired what the De La Rues had created.

"How'd you guys choose this place?" Simone asked.

Rosalie returned to the couch, covering herself with a blanket.

"Every year, Cassidy and I alternate. This was my year to pick, and to be honest, I chose self-preservation."

"Tell me about it. It's so peaceful here. It's like breathing clouds."

Rosalie smiled. "You must see a lot of interesting things."

"You have no idea. I see it all." Simone stared past Rosalie, a faraway look in her eyes. "What do you make of this group?"

Rosalie shrugged, unsure of what Simone was getting at.

"Don't bother. I'll fill you in. Something's going down. Something big."

Rosalie's intrigued. "How do you know?"

"It's easy. When you've been doing this as long as I have, you know. You get a sense of people."

Rosalie's stomach tightened. *Did she know?* She stopped short of counting aloud, tapping her fingers under the blanket instead.

"So when I tell you something's going to blow this week, trust me."

"Can you be more specific?"

"Just mark my words, there's going to be . . . like that thing Henry talked about . . ."

"A comet?"

"A comet . . . a blowup . . . like that Tasmanian devil . . . something . . . some type of . . . I don't know."

Simone's premonition made Rosalie quake inside. She wasn't a psychic—lots of people got vibes about things—but it still freaked her out. Rosalie was used to being a step ahead, minimizing danger.

"Does it have to do with me?" Her words came out with a tremble.

Simone finally recognized she had put the fear of God in Rosalie.

"Oh, gosh, I'm sorry. I didn't mean to frighten you. It's nothing like that, I don't think. It's Lucy and Henry and Adam and Sienna. There's something brewing, and it has to do with last year. Something went down. They're hiding something. It's so obvious. Even my *tante* Renée thinks so. I heard her talking to Jean-Paul." She leaned back on the couch. "I know. You think I'm weird."

"I don't think you're weird."

Rosalie should have relaxed, but what Simone said only amped up her anxiety. She had her own secrets.

The house creaked, the sounds of life hitting the floors.

"I better get going," Simone finally said. "I have to help with breakfast. But maybe when I'm done, we can take a ride to Boone. There's cool shops there—my favorite is Lucky Penny—and we can get tacos at the Black Cat."

"Jean-Paul said I can have another cooking lesson, so maybe after that." Rosalie liked the idea of spending time with Simone. Even if she scared the daylights out of her.

"It's cute you have a little crush on him."

Rosalie grimaced. "I wouldn't call it a crush. He's kinda old."

"I loved Leo when I was five. He was twenty-nine. Okay. Gotta run. See you later. And let's keep this conversation to ourselves."

And that's what she's been doing since she entered the kitchen. She should have argued that the idea of having a crush on Jean-Paul is gross, but she was too fixated on the imminent drama Simone predicted. That and Cassidy showing up to breakfast hungover was a lot for her at once.

No, she wouldn't tell Cassidy the news right now. But soon.

CHAPTER 26

HENRY

Lucy's seated by the window in their room with her foot elevated while Henry tries to ignore the missiles attacking his phone. His father has his cell phone back, and he wants to talk. Henry has no fewer than thirteen missed calls and seventeen texts. He silenced his phone, but he didn't have to. The thunder outside would have drowned out the noise.

The texts begin with Son . . . we need to talk, followed by a series of question marks. Then he tries another tactic. I'm sorry.

He looks to Lucy, ready to ask for her sage advice, but changes his mind. Then a thunderous clap resounds, and the lights flicker off. They're left on edge in the gray light from the window.

A knock at the door startles them, and Renée brings in a heaping tray of fruit, pancakes, omelets—and is that crème brûlée French toast he spies? A small ceramic vase sits at the center with a single pale rose. A notecard reads, *Happy Everything*.

He had almost forgotten. But then, so had Lucy. Ridiculous when they booked the same trip year after year. His birthday. Their umpteen years of friendship with the Kravitzes. But life had gotten in the way, and then Lucy fell. Their eyes meet when they recognize their mistake.

"Thank you, Renée," Lucy says. "You always spoil us."

She places the tray on the nearby table. "Not the party you had imagined, but there's still much to celebrate."

Weakly, they smile, and she reminds them to check out the games and books in the library. "Jean-Paul will provide you with endless snacks, and I'll be there with wine—or champagne, because it is a special occasion." She pauses, walking toward the window and drawing the curtains wider for some light. "Or stay here. It's a perfect day to remember and reflect."

The message scrawled across the thick, creamy card pricks at Henry's skin, and they patiently wait for Renée to exit before they acknowledge what's right there in front of them. The door closes, and Lucy sits upright.

"I think she has a touch of psychic in her . . . like she knows what we're thinking."

They haven't agreed on much lately, but they agree on this.

"What does he want?" she asks.

He had forgotten about his father. "You're the psychic one."

She sighs. "You think I don't know who's been calling and texting? I know you've worked hard to free yourself from him . . . but are you sure that's a good thing? Now that he's out, how long do you think you can keep this up?"

Henry thinks about this, though he'd rather be studying the sky, tracking the lights outside their window so he can prepare himself for what comes next.

Henry prides himself on being a private man. He avoids social media, rarely engages in that six degrees of separation game everyone likes to play, and he does his best to avoid drawing attention to himself. It's why he feels so comfortable behind his telescope staring at the sky. He feels as protected as the planets orbiting the sun.

Henry has wonderful memories of his childhood in Charleston. They were a close family. When they moved cross-country after he left for college, their bond remained, the distance a minor setback. But then his dad switched jobs and started working in a fast-paced world.

A world that changed him. And years later, when he was arrested and sent to the Federal Detention Center, SeaTac, Henry made the choice to cut him off. The man he had worshipped, the man who had carried him on his shoulders, a man he had been proud to call his father was gone like a fallen star.

Henry never made it to the hearings. He never visited him in prison. His disappointment was so powerful it blinded him, kept him from using his telescope for almost a year. How could the man he admired, the man with whom he shared blood and an uncanny close-ness, do what he'd done? Witnessing his father's downfall and the awful aftermath had tested Henry's faith in their relationship. Even if he had looked through his lens after his father was convicted, there was nothing for him to see.

"Henry?"

"Lucy?"

"Don't you think it's time to face this?"

He sighs. He couldn't face it back then when his father's crimes hit the Seattle news, or when victims came forth and cursed the day they'd met him, calling out his "flagrant irresponsibility." Even though Henry hadn't technically been conned, he felt as though he had. His love and adoration for his father were once immeasurable, his fall from grace, cataclysmic. It was time. The denial had seeped into their marriage. Collateral damage.

"I think . . ." But then she stops. "Hear me out. This is me. Your wife. Not a therapist. All this distance . . . it's made it impossible to work through the emotions. You never had a chance to express your feelings . . . manage your disappointment."

He sits on the bed and drops his head in his hands. He thinks about the investors who lost all their money, the couple who felt they had no other choice but to end their lives. "People lost everything, Luce. Because of him. How can I reconcile with someone who's proven to be a monster? How do you forgive someone like that?"

She tries to raise herself from the chair but falls back.

"Don't," he says. The last thing he needs is more pity.

The conversation makes him sick, much like the smells coming from the breakfast tray. A collection of words forms in his mind. Shame. Humiliation. How could he have been so blind? His lips purse, and if he taps into the emotions, he won't be able to stop the flow. He'll break under the pressure, drown in the flood.

He doesn't have to look up to see the disappointment cross her face. He has felt it for some time. Their distance has more to do with him. He closed her out, so what did he expect when she became distant herself?

"You're not the only one this has affected. He was like a father to me. I lost him too. And so did the kids."

"I know." It comes out a whisper.

"You can feel two things at once. You can love him and hate him. They're not mutually exclusive."

"Do you mean like us?"

The lights flicker, but they remain in the dark.

CHAPTER 27

CASSIDY

They're gathered in the library under blankets in the semidarkness. The gray, dreary day casts a veil over the inn, and rain patters against the rooftop. She's still nauseated and a little dizzy from last night's drinking, but she ate an entire piece of toast with jelly, and she's thinking about splurging on another.

Simone and Rosalie went to Boone for some shopping and girl time, and Cassidy feels relieved her daughter is finally out of the kitchen. Lucy and Henry haven't left their room, and Leo and Penny went off somewhere to talk, which leaves her with Sienna and Adam.

As much as she'd like to dislike Sienna—the unearthly beauty, an enviable figure (despite eating M&M's at any given moment)—the woman doesn't make it easy. After a few competitive games of Connect Four and Sorry!, Cassidy finds her witty, and she likes the way she asks questions and listens to the answers.

Adam buries his face in his phone while half listening and half watching an episode of *Billions* on his iPad. There's a peacefulness to the afternoon that surprises Cassidy, and she wonders if this was Rosalie's intent when she picked this place, for the two of them to become a part of something—to make friends. A surrogate family.

After they tire of the games, Sienna squishes beside Adam on the puffy sofa, and Lucy hobbles into the room beside Henry. Adam sets his phone down and fills them in on what's happening on the episode.

The storm outside seems to pick up steam, and a clap of thunder shakes the building.

"Does anyone know if the power's coming back anytime soon?" Sienna asks.

"You'd think they'd have a generator," Cassidy replies, turning her phone off to conserve power. She catches Sienna watching her. She looks afraid.

"Do they have candles?" Sienna asks. "We're going to have to light candles."

"No candles." Lucy waves a finger. "Ever since a candle burned that cabin down a few miles away, Renée has a no-candle policy."

"I don't remember that," Henry says.

"That woman and her husband. Near Roan Mountain. I think she was pregnant. The husband died."

Cassidy feels awful about that.

"They must have something for light!" Sienna lowers the bag of M&M's. "We can't sit here in the dark."

Her high-pitched squeal gets Cassidy's attention. Is Sienna shaking? Cassidy wants to ask her if she's okay, but she's not sure they've reached that level of friendship. "I'm sure the power will come back on soon."

"But what if it doesn't?"

Adam (the guy's a dimwit, she's decided) finally notices his wife's discomfort. "Hon, we're not doing this night-light stuff again, are we?"

Lucy's intrigued. "What night-light stuff?"

Sienna glares at Adam.

"Sienna, what's going on?" Lucy asks.

Sienna turns to her friend, her voice shaky. "I was planning on talking to you about this."

"We have to sleep with a night-light," Adam says, talking over her. "Something about the dark."

"What do you mean, Sienna?" Lucy asks. "What's he talking about?"

Sienna's face turns beet red, and she stares at her hands clasped in her lap. Everyone in the room notices her fingers trembling.

"It's true," she stutters. "Something happens—"

Lucy pushes, asking her to explain.

"I can't explain." She's knotted like a pretzel. "I just freak out."

"How long has this been going on?" Lucy asks.

She shrugs, and she looks like she's about to cry. "But it's gotten worse the last few months. And we literally just got Julia to sleep in her own bed without a night-light."

"Now we have a Nemo lamp in the room," Adam says. "It's very romantic."

Lucy sneers at Adam. "This is important, Sienna."

She looks up, her eyes brimming with tears. "I've wanted to talk to you, but you haven't been the easiest to reach."

Lightning flares outside the windows, another clap of thunder. Sienna looks like she's on the verge of hysteria. "If we don't have power tonight, what am I supposed to do?"

Cassidy wants to help, but she's never been good at advice. People like her aren't taken seriously, and her advice is often ignored. So she reaches inside her bag and hands Sienna a prescription bottle. Sienna takes her time reading the label.

"Trust me. Two of those, and you'll sleep right through it."

CHAPTER 28

PENNY

"I still love you."

It's the second time Leo's said those words, but love was never their problem.

They've been holed up in his room for most of the day, discussing the kids, the inn, anything but their relationship. His familiar scent wafts off the sheets, and she's wondered, several times, what would happen if she dove inside the tangled white and pulled him on top of her. There'd be no turning back. She instead studies the rain falling outside the window, how the drops swathe the property in glittery diamonds and turn the trees an electric green. And she wonders how much of what Henry said—how they are all specks of stardust whose destinies and fates are controlled by something bigger—was true.

At some point, they ventured to the kitchen, where the De La Rues had set out sandwiches and salads, chips and a tangy raspberry dip. They fell easily into their rhythms, though guarded things left unsaid. It was a challenge to see who would give in first.

Now, it's almost time for dinner, and he's pacing at the foot of the bed in his faded blue jeans and a black T-shirt, his hands buried deep in his pockets. She paces too. They circle around each other like hungry wolves. They're going to have to address their problems. They have no other choice.

"I wish you wouldn't say that," she says.

"And I wish you'd say something."

Which is when Penny halts, and Leo halts too, and they stand face-to-face. Leo. Tall and *strapping*, they'd called him. A young Paul Newman. And God how she had loved Paul Newman. Would it matter if she just reached across and touched him? Ran her fingers up and down his smooth chest? She moves closer. She can see the birthmark on his shoulder; she can feel his body on top of hers, the two of them falling onto the bed, burying themselves in those tousled sheets.

He's breathing hard. His breath is on her cheeks, and she watches his chest move up and down, but then she spots something on the floor, poking out of his travel bag.

Penny backs up. It's a script. He's reading a new script. She lunges for it, and he tries to stop her, but she's quick. Another movie. With Claire Leonardo.

She shakes her head in disbelief. "You sit here professing your love and how you want to work through this, but you've agreed to do another movie with her?" She shoves the pages of *Love Me, Again* (seriously) in his face.

His hands act as a shield, and the pages float through the air, scattering on the floor, and she can't believe she ever questioned who he was: the cheater or the man she loves. He grabs her shoulders, and she drops what's left of the script. His eyes find hers. "Look at me."

"I'd rather punch you."

"Don't do that."

"It would be so much more satisfying." She lunges at him, but he's strong.

"You have it all wrong." They're stuck in a push-pull. "And you're wrong about me and Claire." And then there are those eyes. She wants to turn away, but he holds on. Blue. Brown. Why couldn't he just have one color like most people?

He doesn't say anything else. He just slowly slings one arm over her shoulder, and then the other. He takes his time, slowly pressing himself into her, slowly drawing her toward his chest. And she closes her eyes because she knows his body has never lied to her before. His heart beats wildly against hers, and she feels it. "The studio sent it. Once I saw it was with Claire, I told them it's a hard no."

She lets that sink in. Then he whispers in her ear. "What are you doing with someone else when you still feel this way about me?" She almost forgot about the little white lie she told him on their hike. Before she can pull away, he continues. "What are we doing when we both feel like this?"

She wriggles away from him, dropping on the bed. They've already wasted enough of the day. Someone has to be the grown-up.

"You know what hurt the most, Leo? Your hands. Seeing your hand in hers under that table. At *our* place."

He swipes at his eye with the back of his hand.

"No theatrics, Leo. What were you thinking?" She feels herself crumbling. They've always been careful about the paparazzi.

He stands in front of her and lifts her chin. "I was in a really bad place, Pen. *We* were in a bad place. You left for Miami, and I thought being on set would make it easier, but it made it worse. There were three of me. The person I was with you. The role I was playing. And the person who came after we lost Ellie."

The mention of her name slices the air. He runs a hand through his hair and finds her eyes. "You were in that bad place too. You know that. And Claire took my hand under that table. She comforted me. She listened. But that was it. She leaned in . . . she kissed me . . . I wasn't expecting it . . . and I turned, but it wasn't fast enough. Then it all blew up. Someone saw a story, and they ran with it."

She feels her eyes brim with tears. "I used to be the one you talked to. You used to get comfort from me."

His eyes brim too, and she can't look away. "It happened so fast, Pen. Every time we spoke, every time I looked at you, I saw Ellie. I saw how we failed. Then you moved . . . and Claire. I didn't want any of that." He fixes his gaze on her. "I never wanted that."

"You went back to set, and I relived that memory. Every single day. The girls were a mess. I was a mess."

He bows his head. "I should have stayed. I should have told the studio my family needed me."

Leo's lips are a deep red. They remind her of the hours they spent making out in her bedroom after school. His mouth against hers, demanding, his tongue parting her lips to get inside. She wishes she could go back to that place, but she knows how dangerous it is to be swept away by those feelings.

She sucks in her breath and steadies herself, terrified to feel that way again. "It's fine. George is a good guy. The guy I'm seeing. He's good to me. Just sign the papers, and we can move on."

"I don't want to imagine you with someone else."

George is a friend. They walk the dogs together. He doesn't need to know that.

The rain pounds hard against the window. Claire flashes in her mind, Claire laughing beside Leo at Marie et Cie, their hands clasped under the table. The infamous kiss. Claire and Leo all over the internet looking a lot like Penny and Leo once looked. Happy. In love.

She reaches in her back pocket for pictures she and George recently took at the dog park. "I can make it a little more real for you. Let you see how it feels."

His hand on hers forces her to stop.

"What did you expect me to do? Just never have sex again?" It's a small lie, but he deserves it.

Their virginity had long been a gift they'd given each other. The act itself hadn't been that monumental, a tangle of legs and arms knocking into each other, nothing like what you see in the movies. But it left them joined for life.

"I wish you'd understand . . ." He stops when a faint knock comes at the door. It's Rosalie, back from Boone, her hair and clothes soaked.

She's horrified to interrupt. "Renée said there might be some extra lanterns in your closet."

Leo opens the door wider to let her through. "Whatever you need," he says, waving an arm as she passes.

"It's okay," Penny says. "We don't bite."

"I don't want to bother you."

"You're not bothering us. *Promise.*" She emphasizes the word to prove a point, but something else catches her attention. Penny has been around enough movie sets and heavy makeup that masks secrets and scars, but the eyes always expose the truth. Penny's taken with Rosalie's eyes. She's surprised she didn't notice them before. They're big, beautiful eyes. Clear and blue like the ocean.

"Why are you looking at me like that?"

"Your eyes. There just . . . they're really pretty."

Rosalie smiles, unsure of what to say.

"Thank you. You just say *thank you*," Penny says.

Leo rummages through the closet for the lanterns.

"Hey, Rosalie," Penny begins. "Have you ever seen *Man on Fire*?"

Man on Fire was one of Leo's most popular movies.

Rosalie's eyes bounce between the two of them as though this is a trick question. Penny wonders how she'd react if one of their girls came home with dyed purple hair and lips painted inky black. She'd like to think she wouldn't judge, that she'd accept her daughter unconditionally. She reassures herself she would. She absolutely would.

Rosalie tries to muster a response, but nothing comes out.

Poor thing, Penny thinks. "It's okay. I'm just curious what you thought of the scene at the end."

Rosalie hesitates. "I'm sorry. I didn't see it. The movie. I don't really go to the movies that much. I prefer books."

"Wise woman," Penny says.

"There's just this one," Leo interrupts, holding out a lantern.

Rosalie moves toward him.

"Can I say something, Rosie?" Leo asks.

"It's Rosalie."

"Rosalie. It gets easier. It does. This stuff with your mom."

She stares at Leo, her face blank, and then she quickly grabs the lantern's handle, scurrying out of the room.

"What was that about?" Leo asks.

"I was engaging the girl in conversation."

"What was the purpose of mentioning the movie?"

"Engaging the girl in conversation."

His eyes widen. "I know what you were trying to do back there. Bringing up *Man on Fire*. You're not even subtle about it. A movie about a powerful CEO who had the world by the balls and lost everything when he got caught cheating with his cancer doctor. Lost the company. Lost the girl. Lost everything." He pauses. "I'm not that guy, Pen."

"You're right. You may be worse." She takes a seat across the room. "And I brought up that film because . . . shit, Leo . . . it's not always about you. There were other players. Do you remember the character in the movie? Libby? Little Libby Sommers? Her world imploded when you—"

"For fuck's sake, it wasn't me, Penny. You can't keep doing this. I'm not those characters."

"Yet you play them so well."

"That's unfair."

"Don't talk to me about fair." God, she misses the boy who was afraid to touch a fucking dead frog.

"You used to be so much sweeter."

"Hollywood changes people, Leo. You used to be more tolerable."

Outside, the rain intensifies, and she stares at the soaked property. The droplets gather on the window like tears. And she feels her own forming beneath her eyelids. She misses Leo. The younger Leo. The boy who climbed through her window so he could kiss her good night. The boy who always gave her the pizza crust because he knew it was her favorite part of the pie. It didn't matter that it was his favorite part too. When Hollywood came knocking—he was so innocent back then—he told her he wanted to be a star, and she smiled. "I want to be a star with you."

They'd had so many dreams, so many hopes for their future. And it had been so easy, and maybe that was the problem. Maybe it had come too easily for them. What had happened in the last year was proof that no one could have it all. Because for a time, she'd really believed they did.

He sits beside her, and they watch the splotches of rain.

"Remember Tina's party?" he asks.

She crosses her arms, sinking inside the sweatshirt. She should get up and leave, but she doesn't.

"We were so young. So stupid."

Tina lived in Pinecrest. Her parents had gone away for the weekend, and she invited the entire grade to her house for a summer pool party. The rain was mighty that day. They didn't care. One by one, they took turns jumping off Tina's second-floor balcony and cannonballing into the pool. Penny remembers the euphoria of the jump, cold rain mixing with pool water, but she'd kill her girls if they did something so dangerous. "We were invincible back then," he says.

"We were, weren't we? That's the thing about childhood. You believe you have the ability to fly."

Lost in the memory, they let nostalgia set in.

When it gets to be too much, she stands up and paces. She does that when she's nervous, when she overthinks things. "Look. I get this is strange. And for some reason, we're both here. Let's just skip the enemies-to-lovers trope. We can't salvage this. We need to let each other go."

"I can't do that, Penny."

She bows her head. "Yeah, why's that?"

"Because I love you. And I think you still love me too."

CHAPTER 29

SIENNA

By the time the power comes back on, Sienna has already worked herself into a frenzy imagining worst-case scenarios and what-ifs. What if night falls and leaves them in complete darkness? What if their phones die? What if the lanterns Renée promised would last through the night fail?

She's getting ready for dinner, her movements hindered by the dread that has climbed inside her arms and legs, when the room lights up and music pipes through the overhead speakers.

"Thank God," she whispers.

Adam doesn't notice her relief. He's only interested in plugging in his cell phone.

This fear that has plagued her the last however many months has steadily worsened. Almost as bad is the anticipatory anxiety. She can't pinpoint when exactly it started, but she remembers one night lying beside Adam after sex—good sex—when he rolled over, snoring within seconds. She felt a wave of indescribable fear, like something awful was about to happen, and her heart rate skyrocketed. The darkness took hold of her throat, smothering every breath, and she threw the covers off, running away from a feeling she couldn't define.

When she reached their bathroom and switched on the lights, a switch inside her flipped too. The light enveloped her. She could breathe again. Relief coursed through, and she brushed the fear off as an isolated incident. But then it happened again the next night. And the night after that. Until Adam went out of town, and she lay in their bed with the lights on, waiting for the fear to creep in, and it didn't. For the first time in a long while, with a light on, she slept.

That's when she googled *fear of the dark in adults*. This was a thing. This was real. Her first call was to Lucy, but after several attempts, Lucy didn't answer. Then she felt foolish. And then when it kept happening, she felt unbearable shame. For the most part, she could control the situation; she knew which scenarios to avoid. But the weeks leading to this trip have been difficult. Now here they are, her secret out in the open, and she needs her best friend.

She and Adam are the last to enter the kitchen and take the two empty seats. Jean-Paul's seasoning the pork and slicing avocado. Renée's reminiscing about past guests, the wife who sleepwalked into Renée and Jean-Paul's bed, a literal food fight among a group of lawyers when one criticized another for being vegan. And then there was the time when Mr. McDaniels admitted that he'd been talking to his dead wife. "She's sitting right there!" he had said, pointing at the vacant seat beside him. Her favorite story is about two guests in their seventies who thought they were strangers before they spent a week at the inn and realized they'd dated in high school. "They're back together again."

"Night three always sparks a change in the room," Renée says. Simone agrees, pouring water into glasses.

Tonight is night three, and as Sienna glances around the table, all she notices is how the rainy slog has dampened spirits. The table is mostly quiet. Simone's describing their day in Boone and how she and Rosalie had success shopping at Lucky Penny. Cassidy's somewhere between miffed and pleased. "I can never get her to shop with me."

Jean-Paul's going into detail about the feta cheese and lime for the tostado and how he marinated the pork overnight. Sienna's exhausted. Expending energy on the fear—fighting it, worrying about it, imagining those worst-case scenarios—sucked the life out of her. She stares at the yellow ranunculus in the center of the table, hearing every other word. Simone takes pictures of the food, the flowers.

Lucy leans over. "You okay?"

She is. For right now. But she knows that can quickly change.

"We'll talk later," Sienna says, and the relief puts her on the brink of tears.

Adam steps out of the room to take a call, and when he returns, Simone's lens is trained on Penny. Adam drops an arm over her shoulder and smiles. Penny pulls away, and Leo explodes: "Get your hand off my wife."

"Dude. Relax. It's a picture. And besides, she's too old for me anyway. No offense."

"Adam," Sienna says, embarrassed.

But Leo's mad. "I said, get your hand off my wife."

Adam laughs, and Leo's quick out of his chair, the stool crashing to the floor, and just as fast, Henry and Jean-Paul are between them, arms out, holding them back.

Sienna can tell Penny isn't happy, but about which part she's not sure. Penny swallows her wine in one gulp as Leo returns to his seat. Sienna guzzles hers too.

Renée approaches her niece and whispers something in her ear. Simone slinks away, setting her camera aside for now.

"What's wrong with everyone?" Rosalie asks.

Her mother pats her shoulder.

"We've been cooped up all day," Lucy says. "It happens."

"I was waiting for a repeat of last year," Cassidy jokes. "Sounded fun."

Rosalie rolls her eyes at her mother, and Sienna studies the girl. "You have beautiful eyes," she says.

"I thought the same thing," Penny joins in.

Rosalie blushes a deep pink.

"And I love that color lipstick on you," Sienna adds.

Tonight, Rosalie wears a magenta shade instead of the black she had on last night. "Thanks," she says, her eyes darting toward her mother. "I picked it up in town today."

"Next time the rain keeps us inside, we should do a glam squad," Lucy says. "We can give each other makeovers."

"That'd be fun!" Penny says.

Sienna slinks into her seat. She's hoping the bad weather is behind them.

"Maybe you'll have better luck than I've had," Cassidy scoffs.

"Are they expecting rain again tomorrow?" Sienna asks.

"It's supposed to be a gorgeous day," Renée says. "We have a hike planned for you on Beech Mountain. The views are spectacular, and the trail is a great workout."

"Excellent. Time to work off some of this food," Cassidy says, patting her concave stomach.

"I guess I'll stay back and finish my book," Lucy says, glancing at Henry.

Normally, Henry would insist on staying behind, but he's mute, and this strikes Sienna as odd.

"What's got you so quiet?" she asks him as he spoons a shrimp in his mouth. "Is there something going on up there that we need to know about?" She points to the ceiling, which prompts Renée to ask him about tonight's planetary show.

At the mention of the word *planet*, Henry's face lights up.

"I know you mentioned you're a planetary astronomer at the Fernbank Center, but what exactly do you do there?" Penny asks.

He explains how he runs the science programs. "My team coordinates the content—shows and speakers—and the curriculum for field trips and workshops. Next month we have a showcase on the possibility of life outside planet Earth and an exhibit on dark matter and dark energy."

"You said we're all made of stars."

"There's a lot of theories about that." He uses his hands when he speaks. "It's believed that the atoms in our bodies came from stars. You've heard of the big bang theory, yes?"

Penny nods. "Sure, but it's been a minute since science class."

He describes how billions of years ago, the universe began as dense, hot matter called a singularity. "With a big bang, the world ignited."

Penny looks fascinated.

"Gravity, stars, planets, and entire galaxies were formed. That matter made you."

"That's pretty cool," Rosalie says.

Sienna wants to pay attention. She's trying, but she can't get the canvas of black sky out of her brain. Even talking about the darkness has her jittery.

She notices Renée in the corner placing tiny candles on a cake. Simone has already set flutes in front of each guest, and Jean-Paul pours champagne. Renée carries the carrot cake to the table. It's drenched in cream cheese icing, pretzels, pecans, and pralines. She begins by thanking them for celebrating Henry's birthday and their friendship at the inn. She says, "It's been a real joy watching your two families grow and to see you so happy together." She raises a glass. "To many more."

They clink glasses, and Sienna sinks into the blissful moment. There's laughter, and Renée lights the candles. The flames remind Sienna of endurance. The couples gather and make their silent wishes.

"Dude," Leo says, staring straight at Adam. "Sorry about that little dustup."

Adam holds his champagne up to Leo. "It's fine, man. You love her. I get it."

"You've got a good one. Don't jeopardize it."

"Yeah." Sienna elbows him. "Don't."

Adam turns and kisses her full on the mouth, and she curls into him, letting his touch chase away her fears.

After Henry blows out the candles, the conversation about his profession continues. "Do astronomers make money?" Cassidy brazenly asks. Renée carries the tray with the cake toward the counter so she can slice it. She whispers to Simone about the salted caramel bourbon sauce.

Rosalie says, "You did not just ask that question."

Henry's face shows no sign of being appalled. "It's a fair question. And you're not the first to ask."

Adam's staring at his phone. "Not everyone can be as rich as those pricks at Bluebird, stealing millions from innocent, trusting people." He shoves the phone in Sienna's face. "Did you see one of them's been released?"

The clatter is loud, and their heads turn collectively toward the noise. Renée's standing, arms by her side, the tray of cake on the floor. Like the remnants of a toddler's birthday party, frosting mixes with pretzels and pecans.

"Oh dear," she says. "That was very clumsy of me."

CHAPTER 30

HENRY

Renée is probably upset that she dropped the tray, but it's a welcome distraction while he processes *Bluebird* coming out of Adam's mouth. Bluebird. The company that his father worked for. The company he had sold his soul to. He hadn't expected his release from federal prison to make national news. This is why his father has been calling and texting. This is why he has been resisting answering.

He doesn't feel much like celebrating. Lucy was right about shame—he feels it in his bones, spreading beneath his skin and now through his blood.

Today is his father's birthday too. His mother always bragged that Henry was the greatest gift. He draws on a memory. It's quick, a flash through his mind. The two of them in the backyard, his dad pushing him on a swing. The higher he went, the more afraid he became.

"I've got you," his father had said.

And then the cake slid out of Renée's hands, and something in him snapped. Jean-Paul rushed to her side, concern lining his face as he reassured the guests. "Everything's fine. I'll bring out some fresh fruit." But Henry's eyes meet Lucy's, and he's had enough of the charade.

Maybe Lucy isn't wrong about sharing their news, but they were both wrong in agreeing to come here. It was a mistake, and now he swigs his champagne, all sentiment lost. He clears his throat and stands.

"You don't have to do this, Henry," his wife says.

"But I do."

Henry stares at his wife. *His wife.* Knowing what he's about to say will change all that. "I can't do this anymore, Lucy. We need to be honest." His gaze moves from Lucy to the group gathered at the table. "Lucy and I are getting a divorce."

Sienna stands up, her long blond hair whipping around. "What?"

Lucy squints in disbelief. "I thought—"

He supposed she expected him to disclose the other secret, the one he's shamefully hidden from everyone. The one that has kept him awake at night, had him depressed and short-tempered, and left their marriage depleted and broken. They will deal with that one later, but for tonight, their dead-end relationship takes priority. He can't pretend any longer. He can't bear the kindness of complete strangers.

Jean-Paul announces the flaming Spanish coffee is ready.

"I think things are already heated enough, Chef." Adam says this while pouring himself another glass of wine.

Leo stares at Penny.

"You can't be serious," Sienna says.

"I wish I wasn't," Henry says, tasting the bitterness of defeat. "We're getting a divorce."

It sounds less strangled when he says it this time. It slides right off his tongue with the kind of ease that has him believing it's the right thing to do.

Sienna turns to her friend. "Lucy, how could you . . . Why didn't you say anything?"

Lucy stares down at her cast, fidgeting with something that's not there. "I guess I thought we'd share the news with you in private."

Cassidy's unmoved by the admission. "There's nothing private here, folks. The walls are paper thin . . . no offense, Jean-Paul and Renée. And all this truth serum"—here Cassidy holds up her empty glass—"doesn't help things."

"Really, Cassidy?" Penny asks. "What do you think you know? Enlighten us."

Henry sighs, relieved to have the attention momentarily off him and Lucy.

"'Cause I bet we can all attest to what's going on over there." Penny points to Cassidy and Rosalie.

"Okay," Henry begins, "it wasn't my intention to upset everyone. We've still got our friendship anniversary—"

"Henry," Lucy interrupts, "it's okay to talk about it." Then she adds to no one in particular, "This is one of our problems."

"You're a therapist," Sienna says, singling out Lucy. "You couldn't use your psychological prowess on your own husband?" Henry frowns. Sienna doesn't seem to care about their eighteen years of friendship. She stands tall, her back rigid. "No. You're not doing this. I won't let you. You love each other. You're the best two people."

Henry soaks in the way she fights for them, every word an attempt to hold them close.

"It's not going to work." Lucy reaches for her glass of champagne, but it's empty, and Renée has yet to replenish. Or maybe she's decided against it. "There's been too many—"

Adam cuts her off. "Whatever's going on, you two will work it out." He looks at Henry with imploring eyes, and Henry wonders what he's thinking. Does Adam know about his father? Has Lucy told Sienna, and has Sienna told Adam?

"You sound like you know something I don't," Henry says, genuinely curious.

Adam shakes his head. Tonight, his eyes look more green than blue, and the shameless way in which he gloats as though he's in the know—because he always is—makes Henry sick. "Come on, Henry. How long have we been friends?"

Henry catches a glimpse of the old Adam—their once easy friendship. Adam has changed, but so has Henry. His father's crimes made him a liar, omitting huge chunks of his life. But then an image of the four of them by the campfire last summer knocks into him, Lucy and Adam deep in conversation, and an uneasiness crawls down his spine. It passes quickly, and he spots the sheepish pride on Adam's face. Arrogance.

He turns to his almost ex-wife. "Does he know? Did you tell him?"

She balks. "Why would I do that?"

Anger coats his next words, and he regrets saying them before he has a chance to stop himself. "I know how you get when you drink."

Lucy gets up from the table, reaching for her crutches. Sienna stands too, angling around Lucy to make sure she doesn't fall. Lucy shoos her away, but Sienna's determined. That's what a best friend does, he thinks. She fights. Lucy's pissed, and if his wife's expression isn't enough, there's Adam, sitting there fiddling with his napkin.

Henry says, "I wish someone would tell me what's going on here."

CHAPTER 31

CASSIDY

She wouldn't necessarily call herself a mean girl, but she finds something cringeworthy and satisfying in watching these boastful, happy couples crumble before her eyes. Maybe it's insensitive, but she's been the brunt of jokes and pity stares for the last however many years because she embodies that godforsaken word: *single*. She knows. She's heard people talk even when they thought she couldn't. Muffled whispers with sharp daggers: *it would take a saint to put up with her* (that's why she is picky), *poor thing must get lonely* (that's what she has her rabbit for), or her favorite, *she's too set in her ways* (and she won't apologize for that). She won't apologize for any of it.

After Sienna follows fragile Lucy out of the room, a quiet descends on the table.

"Man, you just never know what people are going through," Leo says while Adam keeps filling and refilling his own glass.

"You didn't answer me," Henry says to Adam. "Is there something you need to tell me?"

"You okay?" Penny whispers to Rosalie. "I bet this isn't what you signed up for."

Rosalie shrugs. "I'm in high school. Drama is a required course."

They delve into a conversation about stereotypes and mean girls and bullies and cliques. "Stereotypes are dangerous," Penny says. "Wherever you sit."

It's a relief for Cassidy to see her daughter talking to someone other than Jean-Paul.

Henry and Adam have that macho, sword-wielding ego battle waging between them. Something weird is going down. She can read the cues.

Jean-Paul places a coffee with chocolate and cherry cream in front of Cassidy. She won't touch it. She's already met her daily quota for caloric intake, and because there's no gym and she can't jog in the rain, she's feeling stuffed and bloated. She grabs her wineglass and finishes the night off with a swig.

Adam notices her sitting there. "You must be enjoying this."

"Now why would you think that?"

Adam thinks they're on the same side. They're not.

"It must be hard to raise a child alone."

She snorts and lies. "Rosalie's always been an easy child."

"Does she have an uncle? A father figure? How's she going to learn about sports?"

Cassidy is used to guys like this and their sexist, antiquated minds.

"Wow. They let you say things like that in the twenty-first century? 'How's she going to learn about sports?'" She uses air quotes. She loves air quotes. "Sydney Leroux and Hope Solo, for starters."

This quiets Adam, and she thanks her lucky stars for Rosalie's curious mind and the paper she wrote for a class about female athletes raised by single moms. But she's going to need more than wine to make it through the rest of the week with a "man" of Adam's "brilliance." Her heart races, even though she put Adam in his place, and she feels around in her bag for her pills, wondering if anyone will notice if she pops one in her mouth.

The conversation continues around her. That Simone girl skittered out of the room with her camera in tow, and Leo Shay is trying desperately to join the conversation with Rosalie and his ex, which has shifted to Penny's describing Leo's high school insecurities. Penny bats him down, first with her eyes and then her words.

"You're talking about me in the third person," he says, "as if I'm not sitting right here."

Rosalie smiles at Leo. Penny continues unfazed.

Cassidy understands. She's been dumped and berated by girls her entire life. First, they made fun of her parents' divorce and her noticeably absent father. Then it was her chubby phase. While all the girls conquered puberty with swanlike necks and long, lean bodies, she packed on extra pounds. She saw how they snickered at her—the cool, popular girls who never had to think about what they put in their mouths, devouring endless streams of Fritos and Pop-Tarts at sleepovers that she was never invited to and only heard about in PE class on Monday mornings.

She thinks maybe this was where it all began, her obsessive desire to be thin. And she never wants to feel not good enough again. When she grew a few inches, and the extra pounds evened out across her body, her mother showered her with praise and new clothes. Being thin and pretty meant being loved.

She still misses her mother, but seeing the relationship between Lucy and Sienna, she wonders what it would be like to have that form of trust. She feels a twinge of regret. She doesn't have a best friend, a committed posse of loyal friends to usher her along life's winding roads. Do the girls in her SoulCycle class count?

CHAPTER 32

SIENNA

They're settled on the couch, Lucy's foot resting comfortably on the ottoman.

"I'm guessing this is why we haven't seen you this year . . . why you've been distant. How could you have kept this from us?"

Lucy's blue eyes are dull and dim. "Henry's been going through some stuff. It hasn't been an easy few years."

Sienna asks about counseling, a fix Lucy believed in.

"It's complicated."

"I thought we tell each other everything."

Lucy gazes out the window.

"Have I done something wrong? Did something happen between the kids?"

"No. It's nothing like that."

"Then why does it feel like you've been avoiding me? Why can't you talk to me?"

Lucy looks about to cry, her lip trembling. "It's been awful for a while . . . I didn't want to bother you."

Sienna tries to comfort her, but Lucy moves away.

"I'm your person. We tell each other everything."

"This is different. Embarrassing."

"More embarrassing than the time you walked out of the fraternity party with a panty liner stuck to your ass?"

This gets a scant laugh out of her friend.

"We shouldn't have come," Lucy says.

Sienna brushes the hair off her friend's face. "Talk to me."

That's when Lucy breaks down.

"We've been distant. I don't know what happened. I mean, I do . . . we just can't seem to connect."

Sienna doesn't know if Lucy's referring to herself and Henry, or the two of them.

"What happened, Luce?" She wants the answers to all of it. "You know you can tell me anything."

Lucy's eyes fill with tears. She's wrestling with something.

"This won't change things," Sienna assures her, wrapping her arms around her friend.

"You know how these things work, Sienna. People always take sides."

"Nothing can come between us. You're my sister from another mister. There's no one I trust more in the world."

This only makes Lucy cry harder and louder. Sienna finds her a tissue and squeezes her fingers. "It's going to be okay. We're going to get through this together. We got through losing Harry at the airport and Julius getting attacked by that horrible dog. We'll get through this."

Lucy's shaking her head, but Sienna reminds her of her strength, their collective strength.

Lucy whispers, "I'm sorry, Sienna. I'm sorry I fucked everything up."

WEDNESDAY
Day 4

First Course: Fig, prosciutto, and melon salad

Second Course: Pasta del Magnifico with shrimp, orange, and mint

Main Course: Bistecca alla Fiorentina with porcini

Dessert: Chocolate lava cake

Far Niente chardonnay

Torbreck The Factor shiraz

CHAPTER 33

JEAN-PAUL

"Don't beat yourself up," he says as they lie in bed, staring up at the ceiling. "It was a surprise to me too."

"What a spectacle . . . the cake!" She turns to face him. "How didn't we know about any releases? Why weren't we told?"

The heat rises inside him. "The prosecutors don't care about us anymore."

At the mention of Bluebird last night, his stomach tightened. The company and that wretched man had governed so much of his head-space, he couldn't untangle himself. As soon as they returned to their room after the fiasco, Renée powered up her laptop and searched for Michael Wall. His face on the screen filled Jean-Paul with venom—a fair-skinned man with a cap of short, dark hair and jewel-tone green eyes. The headlines confirmed his release. How he hated him.

"Do you think Adam and Sienna invested too?" she asked. "I hadn't realized he'd made such a name for himself."

"Don't go there, *mon amour*."

That's his job. The torment keeps him awake some nights. He feels he's to blame. He should have done more research; he should have protected them.

He should have protected her.

After the initial shock wore off, they stood on the same side. It didn't matter. He held enough regret for them both. She understood. But he can't harp on that now, not when they're on the cusp of selling, no other viable option in sight.

She curls into him, and his arm comes around her. "It's just not fair, JP."

He strokes her hair. He knows that better than most.

~

The next morning, he's in the kitchen with Rosalie, knee-deep in charcuterie boards. He's showing her how to fold thin slices of salami into a rose while she takes in every word. He ordinarily doesn't spend this much time with the guests because they're usually not interested in culinary skills, but he likes this Rosalie and the interest she takes in learning.

Renée pops in and out, updating him on Lucy, who's been holed up in the library.

Something seems different about Rosalie this morning, but he's not good with stuff like that. Her hair's still that strange purple color, but what does he know about teenage girls? She smiles at him when she holds up her completed board. It's impressive, with sliced oranges that look like stars, blue-cheese stuffed olives, and banana chips. She's included Manchego, honey, and assorted fruits. He notes the artistry in her display, and that's when the difference in the young girl registers. She's happy.

He can hear Renée in his ear going on about the inn working magic on its guests. That very morning, she'd said, "All Rosalie needs is a change in scenery and some attention. Then she would sprout."

Renée compliments their work, pouring cucumber-infused water into their empty glasses. And Jean-Paul notices that Rosalie is not only happy, she's chatty.

"Tell me how you two met."

He catches Renée's eye. She has always said he tells the story best, and even though he's shared it a thousand times, it never feels old. They love flashing back to their youth, to their time in France.

"We were staying at the same hotel in Paris. I wore a dark suit with red stitching on the back, bragging to my buddies how the red trim matched my tie. She didn't have the heart to tell me that the red threads were supposed to be cut before I wore the suit. Then she lost her sweater, and I lost my tie. We met in the lost and found." He smiles. "Didn't care very much about the tie. I found her."

"And I got to pull the red threads from his suit."

Rosalie's cheeks flame when he waltzes over and gives Renée a side hug, planting a kiss on her cheek.

"Where are your kids?"

Jean-Paul handles this question too.

"They're all over the world."

Rosalie's eyes dance at this idea. "They don't live here with you? It's so pretty."

"There's quite a lot of them. Not sure we'd have the room."

Rosalie's interest piques. "How many exactly?"

This tactic works on some, not all. And something in her eyes, her inquisitiveness, urges him on. "We don't have children of our own, Rosalie."

Rosalie's brows tighten; her lips press together. "I don't understand . . . You said . . ."

"Our guests are our children. It's like sleepaway camp here."

He feels the dread and regret in Renée's stare. He's being honest, but the question, for him, is always met with the same reaction: a flip in the stomach, a sting that emphasizes a dream they never got to realize. He's always put this positive spin on it, no sign of blame or fault, because Renée has punished herself enough. It devastated them to learn they couldn't conceive, but it was worse for her since she was the one with fertility issues.

"It's okay," Jean-Paul says. "We're okay with the hand we've been dealt—"

Rosalie lifts her head. "I just . . . I'm sorry. That was probably a rude question. Don't tell Cassidy. She'll be pissed. You two just seem like you'd be great parents."

Jean-Paul reins in his long-held feelings. It's an unusual conversation to have with someone so young, but no subject is off-limits. He sips from his glass, the cool flavor refreshing. "Having Simone here has been good for us. She's my sister's daughter. Her father passed away when she was young."

"I've always wanted siblings," Rosalie says, staring out the window to where one of the gardeners tends to the landscaping.

"You never know," Renée says. "Maybe your mom will meet someone and get married. You could end up with a little sister or brother."

Rosalie soaks it in, though she doesn't seem entirely convinced. Her eyes cloud with skepticism.

"You're lucky to have so many people in your lives," she says.

Her loneliness chips at him. He doesn't know what to do with it. "Eat up," he finally says.

Rosalie shrugs, admiring her plate. "I don't want to mess it up. It's perfect."

"What's the point of creating anything if not to enjoy it? Go on."

Tentatively, Rosalie lifts a piece of cheese to her lips. Jean-Paul joins, grabbing a handful of nuts. The three of them laugh, watching the masterpiece turn to crumbs and leftover jam. Rosalie's a good girl. And for a fleeting second, he lets himself imagine the children he'd wanted to have with Renée. What they'd look like. If they'd share a passion for cooking and the mountains. As quickly as the thoughts traipse through his brain, he brushes them into the small box in his heart he hides for what-could-have-beens.

CHAPTER 34

PENNY

Penny's nauseated from the curvy roads leading to the hike. She's listening to Simone explain where they are, pointing out landmarks. "On your left is the Grandfather Winery, which we might be able to make a pit stop at on our way back. They've got food trucks and a gorgeous stream running through the property. Live music." They travel a few more miles on a straight, flat road, and only then can Penny begin to collect her thoughts.

The news of the Rose-Walls' divorce hit her hard. Divorce always does. She's been up close and personal with it and knows how it can upend lives. She hates that she and Leo are headed in that direction. Hates that their children will have to face any challenges.

She glances out the window, Leo in the seat in front of her. The brown strands of his hair nip the back of his smooth neck, the soft skin, but she doesn't touch it. Last night, they came close to spending the night in his room. She'd followed him upstairs, and they'd opened the window and passed a joint back and forth. It reminded her of when they were teenagers, hanging out in his bedroom, having sex. So much sex. And it was that memory that tugged at her. That sensual pull that's ever present when Leo is near.

"Have you heard from Alara?"

She shook her head.

"You?" she asked. "Buckley?"

"Nothing. I think they need more time."

She inhaled, holding her breath before releasing. "There's no amount of time that will ever heal them."

The sobering reality sat between them, imagining the worst possible thing to happen to a family. She allowed the drug to flood her bloodstream, unable to process the magnitude of the loss.

"We should have been able to mourn together. *We* should have mourned together." He looked at her when he said this. "We could've been there for each other."

She went over that day in her head. She went over every decision, every choice. She thought about all the pieces that had to fit together to eventually blow them apart. She looked at him. And she hated what they'd become. Because she loved this. Being alone with him, just the two of them, the life they had away from the big screen.

"What was that about tonight?" She didn't have to elaborate.

"I told you I don't like seeing you with someone else."

"Ouch." She puffed, propping herself atop the window seat, dangling the joint out the open window. "As if I'd ever be interested in that jackass. Sienna's so cool. I don't get it." She inhaled, let out a cough. "Guess you never know the secret formula."

"Nothing's ever as it seems." The phrase came out simultaneously, and they laughed, stripping away some of the tension.

"I guess I see these couples," he began, "and I wonder, if we could go back, would we do it differently? Knowing what we know now." He sat beside her, and she thought about how easy it would be to give in.

"You feel it too, don't you?"

He latched on to her eyes with his. The brown and the blue held her in their stare.

Then he reached over to touch her face, his hands sliding along her cheeks. She leaned into him, smelling a mixture of weed, Leo's musky scent, and a whiff of the North Carolina mountains. She could never give his scent a suitable name, but it always reeled her in. She wouldn't lie. She had dreamed about this moment. Night after night, she had imagined Leo being hers again, and in the dream, there was no tragedy. How easy it would be to just move in closer and taste his lips, feel his mouth.

But the fear was too big. She couldn't lose herself again.

Or worse, let him in and lose him again.

"I should go," she had said.

"Please stay."

"I can't, Leo."

"But you want to."

"I do, but there's a million reasons I can't."

He dropped his head, and she kissed his hair, breathing every inch of him in.

~

She snaps back to the present as Simone points to the eyesore that is Sugar Mountain. The mountain itself is bold and lush, but the ten-story condominium at the top sits like a concrete figurine on a wedding cake, poking at the sky and marring the view.

They pass through the quaint town of Banner Elk, families crossing the two-lane street to get to the café or walking their dogs to the Barkery. The nausea returns as they make the turn to Beech Mountain. The switchbacks and narrow roads that hug the mountain are too close to the edge of the ridge for Penny's comfort.

This part of the area is new to her. Back when she and Leo were married at the inn, they rarely left the property. Not then, and not the few years that followed. They had sunk inside the cushiony rooms and peaceful forest and wrapped themselves in cottony white linens, rarely coming up for air. The reprieve gave them time to reconnect and recharge away from Hollywood's glare. But then the kids came along, and their schedules revolved around their togetherness, and their visits to the inn came to an end.

A faint hint of music filters through the van's overhead speakers, and she lightly sweeps her fingers across his skin as she hears the first few notes of Cyndi Lauper and Sarah McLachlan singing "Time After Time." It reminds her of those afternoons on Key Biscayne when the original song hummed through the breeze. Things were simple back then.

They had waded in the flat, turquoise water as the song danced around, and he promised her that their lives would never change. He kissed her lips, and she tasted the salt; his mouth opened wider to let her in. Now, with her hand grazing his neck, he doesn't turn around, but his hand finds hers, and if Penny weren't sick from the steep incline, she might have smiled.

Beside her, she catches Cassidy staring at them. Her expression is hard to read, a mixture of longing and approval. She's wearing a large floppy hat, and her lips are pressed together tightly. Henry's next to her, having left Lucy, at her insistence, to convalesce. Whether it's due to her broken ankle or her need to recover from their uncorked story, Lucy wants to be alone. Adam squawks into his cell phone. Rosalie's absent. The efforts to get her to join them failed. She prefers to be in the kitchen.

Penny thinks Cassidy has a right to be disappointed. It would bother Penny if her kids chose to be anywhere but with her. But she can't entirely blame Rosalie for opting out. Penny's ears pop as they ascend another switchback. The road flattens, and they pass a minigolf course and pizzeria. Her stomach grumbles. The song comes to an end, and they pass Fred's General Store and descend the backside of the mountain. The nausea kicks in again.

"You okay?" Cassidy asks. "You look a little green."

"I'm fine," she mumbles. "How much longer, Simone?"

And before the words come out of Simone's mouth, the tires screech, and the car veers off the road.

CHAPTER 35

HENRY

Henry dozed through most of the car ride to the Lower Pond hike, but he jolts awake when the car lurches and they're sent off the road. Beside him, Cassidy yelps, and his hand comes up to block her from hitting the seat in front of her. Adam and Sienna jerk forward, their screams mingling with the screech of the car's skid.

When they come to a complete stop, Leo turns to Penny to make sure she's okay.

Simone is rubbing her shoulder and hollers, "Everyone all right?"

A few cars have pulled up beside them. In the road, a family of deer casually crosses the street. The mother and her twin fawns are blissfully unaware how narrowly they missed a tragic end.

"Just came out of nowhere," Simone adds, visibly shaken.

Leo leans over and drops his hand on Penny's shoulder. "It's okay. We're okay."

They watch as the deer safely cross the road, and Simone switches the car into gear, resuming the drive at a slower pace. The road winds up and down, switchback after switchback, and Henry listens as Penny and Leo retell a story of a sweltering night. They were staying in Scarsdale at the home of a well-known producer. They'd driven into the city for dinner and a show, returning via dark, winding roads. Penny and Leo were in the back seat, the producer and his wife in the front. A deer shot out in front of them, and there was no time to stop. The unsuspecting animal smashed the hood of their car and ricocheted through the windshield. It was terrifying and gruesome. For weeks, Penny had visions of the deer's battered face and desperate eyes. It took her almost as long to get in a car again.

She says they were lucky, that it could have been worse. "Maxwell and his wife, Alec, were treated for cuts, a few minor stitches." Henry can see there's more that isn't said, the way Penny stares down at her hands, her eyes glazed. He bets she couldn't get the visions out of her head—how quickly everything can change, how life can be cut short.

Leo knows too. Henry sees him squeeze Penny's hand.

The van passes a handful of tennis courts, a pool, and nearby pickleball courts, then turns at the sign that reads LAKE COFFEY. There they travel down an unpaved, rocky stretch. Even Adam, who usually has something to say, is hushed, and they eventually park at the trailhead.

Henry takes his time getting out of the car. Maybe he shouldn't have come. Maybe he should have stayed back with Lucy so they could talk, but then he reconsiders. What more is there to discuss? Saying the words out loud provided finality, a bittersweet relief he hadn't felt the day before. There's nothing worse than the in-between, the purgatory of not moving in any direction.

Henry overhears Leo whisper to Penny, "It's going to be okay."

Anything Leo Shay says sounds convincing. He wishes someone would give him the same reassurance.

He and Lucy should have done a better job. Lucy had tried to reel him in, but he couldn't find his way. It didn't take a trained therapist to predict what would happen next. When you push someone away, they have no other choice but to leave.

∾

Simone leads them over a narrow footbridge, cascades of water streaming from both sides, and the sounds bolster him, washing away some of the gloom. He's never fully immersed himself in the ground beneath his feet; Henry's usually more interested in the sky. The land is a mystery, uneven and unpredictable, but he can already tell after a few steps that he's entering a wonderland. They cross natural ponds shaded by a canopy of lush green trees. It's mystical and damp, and yesterday's rain turned the docile stream into a roaring river. Every step provides a gorgeous view.

"Take it slowly," Simone warns. "And avoid the rocks. They're slippery. Especially the ones that are mossy. Grab on to a tree root or branch for support, and don't be ashamed to use a stick. That's what they're there for."

Shame. He could tell them a thing or two about shame.

Cassidy's already raced up ahead, showing off her strength and stamina. Adam's actually on another business call, and he mentions no less than ten times how much money he stands to make on some deal. It's better if Henry steers clear of him. He's not in the mood for an inquisition. Leave that to the women.

There's a tentativeness to their climb, and Henry does his best to silence the chatter in his brain, the creeping suspicion that there's something he's missing. Something Adam knows that he doesn't. But he files it away. He's the one with the secret, so he puts one foot in front of the other and enjoys the beauty and solitude.

The trail is narrow and scattered with mud and mulch. Someone's marked the trees with purple paint splotches that soon become Henry's guiding lights. He refuses to look down, searching upward as he's always done. Dark, shadowy holes appear in the surrounding boulders, and he imagines creatures hiding, waiting to pounce. He's tall, so he's forced to duck under low branches, but occasionally, he takes a lashing to the forehead. They're nothing compared to what the last few years have been like.

Simone captures pictures of the scenery, the flowing creek, the six of them in front of the falls, and what should have been an hour-long hike round trip becomes longer. They don't talk much. That's what the forest does to you. The greenery cradles you in its hands, leaving you no choice but to slip inside.

At one point, they veer off the path and wind through a thicket of trees until they reach a smooth boulder jutting into the stream. They sit on the rock, and a cascade sprays them with mist as Simone unloads sandwiches and snacks from her backpack.

Henry has no choice but to converse with the others.

"I don't believe it, Henry. I won't believe it," Sienna says in between bites of a turkey sandwich.

"Are you sure this is what you want?" Adam asks.

Henry eyes his friend curiously, wrestling with conflicting emotions. His feelings toward Adam have grown increasingly worse. Now his shady smile works Henry's every last nerve. He can no longer quiet the persistent doubts about his friend.

"Do you want to talk about it?" Leo asks.

Henry shrugs.

"Marriage is tough," Penny adds. "I'm sure you never heard that before."

Henry wonders if they're contemplating their own marriage and whether they should have tried harder too. Adam is unusually quiet. Typically, Adam would pull some stupid prank where he'd hide in the bushes, and as the others approached, he'd shake the tree branches or toss a rock, laughing as he sent them into a panic. This Adam is too quiet.

Now it's Sienna's turn. "You love each other. You're, like, the best couple we know. Who are we going to travel or spend our birthdays with?" She pauses, a look of horror crossing her smooth cheeks. "What about the kids? They're going to be devastated."

Cassidy lifts her head out of the sugar-free Chobani yogurt she'd wrapped in an ice pack. "They'll be fine. Don't make this about the kids, please. Kids are resilient."

Henry finds this amusing considering that she and her own daughter barely speak.

"Kids definitely factor into things," Penny begins, but Leo signals for her not to get involved.

After a short break, they pack up their leftovers and trash and make their way back to the trail. Henry is acutely aware of the pity stares, and they don't even know the entire truth.

Sienna finally gives up on her interrogation, and when they reach the end of the path, they turn around for the mostly uphill climb back. From this vantage, the views of the river and falls change. The stream that was previously on their left is now on their right. With the sun directly above, the leaves look greener, the water like glass. An entirely new perspective.

Cassidy has once again fled ahead, paying no mind to the others. The two couples follow, and Henry lags behind a short distance, with Simone bringing up the rear. He watches how Leo assists Penny through a web of tangled roots, offering his hand as he hoists her over a slippery rock. Henry envies the way that, even now, they take care of one another, how they understand that their vines are still connected. He sees in their eyes, in the way they handle each other, that there's still love. He wants to tell them that tonight is a sturgeon supermoon, a rare occurrence of a spectacular sky when the moon nears its closest point to Earth. Extraordinary things happen during supermoons; Earth's magnetic field has intense power.

Months ago, when Lucy mentioned the *D* word, it had been a supermoon. He told her she was being dramatic, blaming it on the sky, which only heightened her anger. "Why doesn't the supermoon work on you?" she had asked. "Why can't I get you to open up? To share the brunt of this with me?" And when he simply remained silent, making no effort, she added, "Let me help you."

It was a legitimate request, one he couldn't meet.

Maybe it was just too late.

Today, he finds it easier to focus on Leo and Penny. He'll tell them about the supermoon later. He isn't some kitschy clairvoyant, but he does understand the Earth and the moon and rotations and gravitational pulls. Penny is the Earth, and Leo, he's the moon. And there is no better time than now for them to right a wrong, to get back what they need most—each other.

He had needed Lucy for some time.

He was just too stubborn to admit it. Too angry and embarrassed and resentful.

He hears a loud squeal, and he looks up to see Leo lifting Penny. He's carrying her across the bridge, and they're laughing. And when he looks away, their happiness magnifies his sadness. Adam stares, questioning him with his eyes. Sienna runs ahead to meet Cassidy, leaving the two men alone.

"You okay, man?"

Henry nods.

Adam's cheeks are red, and he's out of breath from the incline. They both are.

"Did something happen between you and Lucy?" he asks. A branch snaps beneath his feet. "This just seems so sudden."

Henry thinks about his response. He started it. He's sure of it. He got stuck in his head, in his stifled emotions. He pushed Lucy away. And she tried. She tried so hard, the desperation in her eyes impossible to forget.

But he doesn't owe Adam shit.

"I don't know." It comes out just as they round a narrow, crooked corner and have to steady themselves on the mossy rocks. And something about the cold, slick stone on his palm shocks him, and he finds himself speaking, though he's not sure where the words come from. "It hasn't been the same since we were here last summer."

Adam hunches over to catch his breath, then straightens and takes a swig of water. "I barely remember last summer."

When they arrived home last year, Henry went on a monthslong drinking hiatus. By then, Lucy had stolen a move out of Henry's miserable playbook: avoiding him. Closing herself off. She had had enough. They politely danced around the kids and engaged in loud brawls when alone. Eventually, there was silence. The dissolution hissed like a balloon deflating and coasting off into the sky.

He had learned from Lucy and her many patients that indifference can often mean growth. When someone can't hurt you anymore, when you neither love nor hate, the intense emotions can be spirited away into a place of neutrality. But in this case, indifference signaled a dangerous problem. The emptiness sneaked up on him until it was too late to fix. He was fighting too many battles at once, and he didn't have the energy for all of them.

Henry feels winded and annoyed all over again. At the situation. At Adam's inquiries.

"It wasn't my idea to announce it here."

"Why'd you bother coming at all?"

All that comes to mind is *what a dick*. Instead he says, "Lucy loves you guys. This place means a lot to her. She wanted to tell you here. For all of us to be together."

"Yeah, but it kind of just ruins the whole mood, you know."

"I knew you'd say something stupid like that."

Henry knows how to get under Adam's skin: the fact that he didn't actually finish college, that he didn't attend their school but went to the "subpar" university down the street. Adam graduated summa cum laude with a degree of complete and utter bullshit, the gift of gab. Yet people love him for it, as though his words sprinkle them in sunshine.

"You really are a jackass sometimes," Henry says.

"Yeah, that's what I've heard."

"I can't expect you to understand real-world problems."

"Dude, my wife sleeps with a night-light. Did you see her freak out during the storm? It just wasn't the time to drop this news on all of us."

"It's always about you, Adam. I don't know what the hell happened to you." He knows he should stop. They've been friends for years. Adam was once like a brother.

"Whoa. Lighten up."

But Henry doesn't want to lighten up. Something in Adam's eyes has been taunting him for days, maybe longer. He gets in Adam's face. "Go fuck yourself."

And the two old friends hike back to the trailhead without speaking another word.

CHAPTER 36

CASSIDY

Cassidy's on edge.

She's felt this way most of her life, but it's gotten progressively worse in the last few days.

The hike on Beech Mountain is strenuous, even for her, but she feigns ease, breathing through muscle strain and forging ahead. The mood among the group has turned sour, she thinks to herself. So much drama. Who knew that an inn, peaceful as a puffy cloud, could hold so much weight? And she knows about weight.

There aren't any scales on-site, but before leaving Chicago, she threw hers in the trunk of the rental car. Sneaking out to retrieve it that morning, she was disgusted to see she'd tacked on three pounds since their arrival.

She hears the laughter. The names those girls in high school called her. Then her mother flashes in her mind. The extra weight she gained in her last years. Her unexpected death. Cassidy won't let that happen to her. So yeah, she would smile and sweat through it.

Her mind wanders to Rosalie, and she feels a pang of sadness about the little time they've spent together. Wherever Cassidy goes, Rosalie chooses to go somewhere else. She doesn't understand it, especially when she and her own mother were so close. Suddenly, Rosalie is taking advice from the inn owners and makeup tips from Simone, and she even looks different, though Cassidy can't put her finger on why.

Tonight, she'll try to have some alone time with her. And she'll wear the white dress to dinner, the one from Calypso St. Barth she picked up on Gilt. It is long and flowy with a sizable slit that runs from her hip to her ankle. She feels sexy in it, and that empowers her.

She can tell something has happened between Adam and Henry. One minute they were making their way through the forest together, and the next they were miles apart, not uttering a word. Adam has been eyeballing her the whole time. She can feel him staring at her tits and ass, not even bothering to try to hide it. Penny saw it too. She rolled her eyes in that way that signaled girl code. Something about that guy rubs her the wrong way.

The lightheadedness comes on fast. She counts her morning calories and her special pills and wonders if her body is defying her. She stops, grabs hold of a tree, and steadies herself. The last thing she needs is for anyone to see her slowing down. She takes a swig from her water bottle and lets the cool water stream through her body.

When she hears the others about to catch up, she inhales and forges ahead. She doesn't care if it kills her. Being first to finish the trail is worth it.

CHAPTER 37

ROSALIE

Rosalie's sprawled across her mother's bed, watching her put on makeup. She studies her as she applies moisturizer and foundation, a hint of blush. She's yammering on about the hike, complaining about their limited time together.

"You know, Rosie, this summer trip was meant to bond us, and all you've done is avoid me."

Rosalie doesn't want to fight, so she doesn't bring up her mother's drinking. She thinks maybe now might be the best time to tell her. She's sober, for one. But first, she checks her email. Nothing. Her father still hasn't written back. She doesn't even know if he got her message. She opens the Ancestry app just to be sure she hasn't made a mistake, which is ridiculous, because she's checked at least a hundred times already. He's still there. Still 50.2 percent of her DNA.

"What are you so immersed in?" Cassidy asks.

Tell her. Tell her.

Instead, she counts and then says, "Nothing."

If her father responds, she thinks it might be easier to tell Cassidy. Then she wouldn't be in this alone. But then she has another thought. Maybe he got her email and isn't interested in having a daughter. She banishes the notion, tells herself that he didn't get the message. If he did, he would have written her back.

CHAPTER 38

PENNY

When Penny boards the van for the drive home, she's hot and sweaty, and she's sure Leo notices her breasts pressed through her white T-shirt. This time, he takes the seat directly beside her and drops a hand on her thigh. The warmth dissipates, replaced by a cool thrill, and he spots the goose bumps floating down her leg. He takes his time, sliding his palm along her skin.

His nearness excites her, and she can't deny what's building between them, what never died. Hiking beside him felt normal. Effortless. They didn't have to talk; proximity was plenty. She spots Henry out of the corner of her eye. The irony isn't lost on her. One marriage ends, another begins again.

She mulls this over as they enter the kitchen. Tonight's menu has some of her favorites, fig and prosciutto, pasta with shrimp and orange and mint. The chocolate lava cake sounds like they're in for a festive evening.

She wonders how things will play out between Henry and Lucy. She's surprised they're still here. But not as surprised to see Cassidy waltzing down the kitchen steps, her hand plucking the seam of the attention-grabbing slit in her skirt. Leo doesn't seem to notice the effort in her grand entrance. If only his on-screen image didn't contradict his true persona. *Fan expectations,* his publicist, Lucinda, had called it. She'd begged him to learn to flirt, to work the room with more than those eyes. But he didn't know how. He blamed it on Penny. *You did this to me.*

Renée offers her a glass of wine, and Penny swigs it back. Leo sidles over and takes the empty seat beside her. Cassidy deflates, and the table quietly fills. Adam and Sienna. Lucy hobbling on her crutches, Henry in tow. Rosalie.

They gather and do what they do. They reminisce about their day, talking over one another. Someone's describing the hike, the twisty trail surrounded by tumbling water. Someone brings up a comparable hike in Colorado. Another compliments the wine. Henry ties everything into a lesson about the sky and stars. They talk about travel disasters and the dangers of the internet and the type of alcohol they can never drink again. Henry and Lucy seem less on edge now that their secret's out in the open. Like they've made peace with their truth.

Jean-Paul's quiet. Something's weighing on his mind. Renée too. She ordinarily scurries around the table, but tonight she huddles over her phone intently reading. Penny knows the concerns surrounding the inn. They all do. She wonders if there's a way they could help.

Cassidy's on her second, maybe third drink, and her words begin to slur. Penny spots the worried look Rosalie shoots her way, but it doesn't make a dent in Cassidy. She gulps her wine in one swallow and holds the glass up for Renée to fill. That's when Rosalie's hand shoots up.

Good for her. Simone preserves the moment on her camera.

CHAPTER 39

SIENNA

As soon as Renée sets the wine bottle down, Cassidy rises from her seat and fills her glass herself. No one seems more upset than Rosalie. Sienna fights the urge to intervene when Adam asks about a particular snowy day on campus.

"Do I remember?" Lucy asks. "It's my favorite memory of college."

"I thought I was your favorite memory," Sienna says.

Henry's silent, even though that's the day he and Adam became "brothers," stripping naked in the snow-covered mall for some ritual for Henry's fraternity. He doesn't mention it. Maybe his silence has to do with the fact that she saw Henry walk up to Adam and tell him to *fuck off* on the hike. Henry doesn't usually get provoked that easily, and when she asked Adam about it on the way home, he brushed her off with a wave. She hates when he does that. Keeping her at arm's length and in the dark.

Lucy's retelling the story of their first snow day together and how they spent the morning at the campus bar, The Vous. "That was the first and last time I ever funneled beer."

Sienna struggles with whether to dive in. Something has transpired between the men, but then Lucy details Adam and Henry trudging through the snow, the naked climb up the steps to Testudo, the turtle statue situated at the front of the library.

Adam laughs. "It's a good thing smartphones didn't exist back then."

Sienna can't help herself. "I still have to look at that picture every time I walk into Adam's office."

"What picture?" Penny asks.

"Oh, just these two clowns posing naked with the turtle. The gift that keeps on giving."

This garners a round of laughter, and someone pops a joke about a certain shriveled part of the anatomy, and for a moment, they're sent back in time, down a memory lane paved in tailgates, lecture halls, and all-nighters.

"Life was so much easier back then," Sienna says. "Remind me why we were in such a rush to grow up?"

"Youth is definitely wasted on the young," Leo says.

"Right?" Sienna agrees. "We had no way of knowing we were living our best years."

"I'm living my best years now," Adam says, smiling at her.

"You know what I mean. The innocence. No major responsibilities. Our world was small and insulated. Our biggest problems were getting to class on time . . . passing Theater 110."

"I hated that class," Henry joins in. "That was my only D."

"I took a theater class in college," Leo says. "Got an F."

They collectively laugh, traveling back in time.

They reminisce about a road trip to the Jersey Shore when they ran out of gas on I-95, and the year they went to Sienna's house for Thanksgiving and played football with her brothers, and the exact moment they knew they'd become lifelong friends: the beginning of sophomore year, when Adam dropped out of school altogether.

Adam reaches for his phone, and Keyshia Cole's "Heaven Sent" fills the air.

"Wow. That one takes me back," Lucy says. "Formal. Baltimore Harbor."

Penny and Leo meet each other's eyes. "Different memory. Same nostalgia," Leo says. "We had just had our daughter Amelia. The song was playing when we brought her home from the hospital."

"You remember that?" Penny asks.

"How could I forget?"

"I miss that time in our lives." Sienna hears the melancholy in her voice. She certainly didn't have any strange phobias back then.

"You're not that old," Renée offers as she clears another round of plates.

They're engrossed in conversation, noshing on pasta with shrimp and a basket of artisanal breads with sweet raspberry butter. Dishes are served and taken away; the table has a festive rhythm. Jean-Paul every so often interrupts with some interesting fact about meal prep. Sienna takes the first bite of the Italian steak, and the flavor melts in her mouth. The others follow with their praise. She notices Cassidy cutting the meat and moving it around her plate, but nothing reaches her mouth except the garnish, which has the nutritional value of a grain of sand.

Someone mentions COVID, who had it, who didn't.

"I never had it either," says Henry.

"How's that possible?" Penny asks. "Leo and I . . ." She stops. "I had it three times."

"Same." Leo raises his hand.

"I couldn't taste anything for a month," Sienna says. "It was scary. And strange."

"I should only be so lucky," Cassidy slurs.

Rosalie jabs her mother.

They talk about who should perform at the next Super Bowl half-time show, and whether Ozempic is a wonder drug or a danger. The table is loud and lively, and Sienna's glad to see that Henry and Adam have resumed speaking, that whatever happened has passed. She watches the interactions between Henry and Lucy and wonders if maybe they'll change their minds about the divorce. It doesn't make sense to her. They seem perfectly normal together.

One turn of her head and she might have missed it, but she spots Renée by the sink, her eyes wide as she angrily whispers into Jean-Paul's ear. The room is noisy with the conversation and clattering of silverware, and Jean-Paul shakes his head as though he can't hear. And when Renée repeats it, her voice echoes loudly through the room: "They should have never let Michael Wall out of jail."

CHAPTER 40

HENRY

And like that, the night splits in two.

If he thought his impending divorce was a plot spoiler, the words *Michael Wall* sliding off Renée De La Rue's tongue is the twist he didn't see coming. The table resumes conversation, paying no mind to his father and his trail of deceit. But he stares at Renée and Jean-Paul, racking his brain, asking himself why Renée would care about Michael Wall. His father lived on the other side of the country. He's sure their paths haven't crossed. If so, they would have connected the dots by now. Had he inadvertently mentioned his father to Renée and Jean-Paul? Or vice versa? He can't remember, and the fear slides up his throat. It's as if his dad has taken a seat at the table.

Leo Shay notices that Renée and Jean-Paul have gone quiet, and Henry eyes him as he strides in their direction, whispering, "He's the one with Bluebird? The one you invested with?"

Henry can't breathe. A brick has just lodged in his chest. This can't be. This can't be happening. The tray slipping from Renée's hands last night was no accident. She recognized the name Bluebird. She knows his father.

He bends his ear, trying to hear Renée's response, but it's impossi-ble to make out what she's saying. Lucy stiffens; her hand lands on her chest. He shrugs and silently pleads with her to stay quiet. He needs to process this. Had Renée and Jean-Paul invested in his father's bogus company? Had he bilked them out of their money, their life savings? He buries his head in his hands as a throbbing ache climbs through his temples.

The whispers and hushed silences begin to make sense. Renée and Jean-Paul selling the inn. Renée and Jean-Paul facing financial ruin.

The guilt travels through his body, and he's sure they all can see it. He's as hot as a star's core nearing the end of its life cycle—which makes perfect sense as he dangles from the sky in his own private hell. A cold sweat dots his skin, and no amount of wine can allay his fears. This is as surprising as the Tasmanian devil.

Michael Wall. His father. Married to Dominique Rose-Wall. His family. And now Michael's a stranger, someone he detests, loathes—yes, that might be a better word. He's the shadow he can't escape, the man he loves and hates.

Not even Adam and Sienna have pieced it together. Most people didn't. His mother had called Henry a *gift* because he was born on his father's birthday, but the real gift was his mother's brilliant hyphenation, Rose-Wall, an early decision that saved him from being directly associated with Michael Wall. That and homes on opposite coasts and different skin colors make it tricky to connect the dots between Henry and his father. When his parents left Henry's childhood home in Charleston for Seattle, they never returned, and when Michael was indicted, it was as though their familial bond had never existed.

Whenever Henry mentioned his father, he eliminated his last name. He was vague, rarely discussing Michael's financial success (he'd made a lot of money), and to many, he seemed like an ordinary dad, a man Henry adored. Henry used to light up when he detailed his childhood. They were once as thick as thieves. Michael Wall raised Henry in a loving home with proper values and respect. So when the news broke of Michael Wall bilking all those hopeful, trusting people, Henry was grateful that his father's arrest in Seattle hadn't made it to the East Coast, and that their last names didn't match. His crimes weren't Madoff level, but they were enough for Henry to cut the familial cord that had tied them together. Henry iced his father out.

Michael Wall tried dozens of times—phone calls at all hours (he never did pay attention to the time difference), long rambling letters and emails where he vacillated between defending himself (*I did this for you, I did this for us*) and sheer remorse. And then came the flurry of texts when he got released. So disruptive, so confusing, so erratic. Lucy tried to guide him through it all, to help manage the range of emotions, but he wasn't sure if he was angry, ashamed, or facing a collision of contradiction, because he loved his father. It felt like the man he once knew had died, and how do you grieve for someone who's still alive? He was his North Star. Present. Unreachable. How could he so selfishly and callously take from innocent people?

Henry fought hard to understand. Lucy warned him the answer wasn't in his telescope, but he naturally kept looking, searching for a sign. Because they shared DNA, so what did that say about him?

On the one occasion he visited Charleston since the arrest, he found that his father had left his stench. A sprinkling of townsfolk had picked up the story and whispered in hushed voices. They didn't think Henry could hear; they didn't think he noticed them pointing, their repulsion. Henry couldn't help but feel guilt by association. He hadn't been back to Charleston since, and he held on to the illusion of the privacy and protection they had in Atlanta.

He regrets not telling Adam and Sienna. As close as they were, he couldn't bring himself to relive the story. Was a sin of omission unforgivable? People omitted things all the time, conveniently forgetting to mention an uncle who did time, or a daughter being thrown out of summer camp for smoking pot.

He just stopped mentioning his dad. And then there he was, arraigned in Seattle, begging Henry to fly out and support him. His father, who blew up their lives in one fell swoop. Henry could never escape him or their shared history. And now he finds out that his father, the person he counted on the most and who betrayed him in the worst possible way, had infiltrated the inn.

He grabs hold of the marble tabletop to stave off the dizziness.

Leo rests a hand on Renée's shoulder and reassures her they'll help in any way they can. Henry sees an emptiness in her eyes. This is something Leo's megawatt smile can't fix. Renée straightens, and instead of returning to the table, she exits the back door, Simone in her wake. Jean-Paul steps out from behind the cooktop and grabs the bottle of wine she left behind. He mentions something about Renée needing fresh air and resumes refilling glasses. It happens fast. Fate and circumstance smacking into one another. Jean-Paul tops off Lucy's glass when Henry's phone blares, Michael Wall's name flashing across the screen. He'd changed his contact name from *Dad* long ago.

He has no time to conceal it. No time to reject the call or hide what Jean-Paul sees. Henry grabs the bottle out of Jean-Paul's shaky hand to prevent it from slipping to the floor.

"Henry," Jean-Paul says calmly. "Why on earth is Michael Wall calling you?"

CHAPTER 41

JEAN-PAUL

Few things have the power to shock Jean-Paul, but seeing Michael Wall's name stretched across Henry's phone knocks the wind right out of him. Sure, there could be another Michael Wall in the world; his isn't such an uncommon name. But there is no denying the accompanying picture, and Jean-Paul knows that face, has memorized every feature.

Michael Wall.

On Henry Rose-Wall's phone.

A foreboding chill snakes down his back, and they stare into each other's eyes as Henry sets the bottle on the table. Cassidy scoops it up and gives herself a generous pour, blathering on about her Peloton and how when she returns to Chicago, she's going in for a neck consultation with her plastic surgeon.

Renée appears when the phone rings again, and Jean-Paul points to the screen. Her hazel eyes stab at Henry. "Is this how he got to us? You know him?"

Lucy moves in closer to Henry and drops a hand on his.

"Did you tell him about us?" Jean-Paul asks. "About the couple who owns the struggling inn? Did you see a profit? Do you get a cut?"

Henry gives a resounding no, and Lucy shakes her head.

"Henry would never do something like that."

Jean-Paul doesn't know what to make of this. Renée crosses her arms.

Michael Wall and all he represents would make a normally even-tempered man furious. He'd dug deep inside Jean-Paul and twisted him into knots, knots that had grown and bulged over time. He's keenly aware the table has grown bored of Cassidy's mind-numbing jabber and how everyone's eyes are fixed on him. Renée grabs the crook of his arm. "Let's not do this here, *mon amour.*" But he can't help himself. His rage for the man is palpable. He can't hold back.

"What's going on over there?" someone asks. He doesn't know who. Maybe Sienna. Maybe Penny.

But he notices how Henry doesn't flinch, and how Cassidy pops a pill in her mouth, sucking it down with a gulp of wine. She's the only one moving in the room except for Simone, who's plating chocolate lava cakes. Renée tells him to walk away, but he can't. His legs won't move, and he's tired of being powerless.

"Did you tell him about us?" he repeats. "Did you . . ."

Henry looks him in the eye, torment mixed with something unreadable. "Michael Wall is my father."

To which Jean-Paul delivers a swift punch to Henry's face.

The other men are on their feet.

"Jean-Paul!" Renée shouts.

But there's no ensuing fight to break up. Henry merely brushes his red cheek with his palm, almost as though he deserves it. Lucy reaches for her crutches, but Henry stops her.

The punch should feel good. The release of months, maybe years, of pent-up aggression. Jean-Paul has waited so long for this, waited to feel something other than helpless regret.

Renée tries leading him away from Henry while Adam and Leo sit back down. Jean-Paul catches the stricken look on her face. The punch was a miscalculation, reckless behavior in front of guests. He recognizes that, but Michael Wall made a terrible mistake when he targeted and crossed them. He doesn't care about Yelp or how one-star reviews might highlight an outburst from the inn's once-gracious owner.

Jean-Paul scans the table, his chocolate lava cakes deflating, the warm centers turning icy cold. Leo and Penny twirl their spoons around their plates, mixing the vanilla and chocolate like finger paint. Sienna and Adam appear as surprised as anyone at the identity of Henry's father. Cassidy reaches inside her bag for another pill, and Rosalie, poor Rosalie. He wishes he could shield her from this.

"Why don't we go somewhere and talk?" Henry says.

But Jean-Paul's not thinking rationally. That Michael's flesh and blood inhabits their home, charming them all with his cosmic observations, makes him shake. How could Henry have failed to mention his father?

"Jean-Paul." He stares him in the eyes. "I had no idea. This comes as much as a shock to me—"

"That your father is a fucking thief?"

Henry ducks his head. "That you invested. I have no idea how he found you."

The phone rings again, and Jean-Paul's fast. "Let me talk to him. Let me tell him how he's ruined people." But Henry's faster.

Renée's voice quavers, her fist comes up in the air. "He's the reason we have to sell . . . he's ruined us!"

Henry lowers his eyes. "I am so sorry."

"You're sorry? That's all you have to say?"

Lucy stands, balancing herself on her crutches. "You can't blame Henry for this. He has nothing to do with his father's crimes. This broke him. And it broke us."

Jean-Paul tries to assess the situation, but he can't think straight. Renée's soft curls frame her heated face. She's been described as tough on the outside and warm and soft on the inside, but there is nothing warm and soft about her now. Like the mess on their plates, all her rage blends into something unrecognizable.

"I'll handle this, *mon amour*," he says.

"I can't. I can't sit here . . ." she says. Her eyes train on Lucy, and he hears the vengeful spite crawling through his wife's lips. "How can you sit here? How can all of you sit here? Professing to be best friends . . . to love each other . . . when all you have are lies?"

"I'm not proud, Renée," Henry replies.

Lucy's anger intensifies. "You have no idea what this has done to him. It's not something he enjoys talking about. With anyone. Hate the situation, but not Henry. He adores you and Jean-Paul. He would have never put you in this position."

"Don't act like you don't know what I'm talking about, Lucy," Renée says.

"I don't—"

"You know exactly what I'm talking about."

Renée's sinister tone is hard to miss. Lucy's face flattens.

"But of course you're going to defend your husband. It's the least you can do. Right?"

"Renée," Jean-Paul says, trying to prevent her from doing something awful.

"What is she talking about?" Henry asks, glancing at his wife, then Sienna and Adam.

The words tumble from Renée's lips. "You think I don't know? I know everything that happens under our roof."

"Renée!"

"No. No. No. Keep going," Cassidy slurs, shuffling her palms together.

"Enough, Cassidy," Penny yells.

"Renée," Jean-Paul says, "you need to stop."

But she can't.

"I know what you did last summer." She points in the direction of Lucy when she says this.

Water shoots from Rosalie's nose, and she hides her face in a napkin.

"Did she just quote that movie, Rosie?" Cassidy asks.

"I don't know what you're talking about," Henry nervously answers.

Jean-Paul can't believe Renée has chosen now to disclose her nagging hunch.

"You want us to feel sorry for you?" Renée asks. "You want us to feel bad for Henry shutting you out? Is that how you live with yourself?"

Lucy's cheeks flush, her eyes narrow, and she calmly speaks. "I'm not sure what you're getting at, Renée. I know you're upset—"

Renée cackles while Jean-Paul steps out of the way to let a drunken Cassidy pass through on the way up the stairs to the bathroom. "Come on, Lucy, you know exactly what I'm getting at. Isn't this the reason for the divorce? Henry shut you out, so you found attention somewhere else?"

Lucy's visibly shaking. "Renée, you're upset. I don't think—"

"Sienna." Renée turns to face her. "Is she really your best friend? She's kept so many things from you. The divorce. Her father-in-law, the criminal."

"Renée!" This time, it's Adam. He looks pissed. "That's enough!"

What on earth is my wife doing? Jean-Paul wonders.

Sienna looks at her husband and then Lucy. "What the fuck is going on here?"

"Tell her, Lucy. Tell her about last summer. Tell her what you did." Renée points at Adam. "With him."

The words silence the entire table. You can hear a pin drop. Sienna's lip trembles as she hops out of her seat and races for the door. Adam's out of his chair, close behind. Leo Shay rests a palm on Penny's hand and squeezes. Henry. Poor Henry. He's in shock. His face pales. His eyes widen in disbelief.

And that's when they hear a loud thud.

CHAPTER 42

ROSALIE

The startling noise causes a commotion, and their eyes land on a figure at the foot of the stairs. It's her mother. Rosalie jumps up, scratching the stool on the floor. Cassidy's lying motionless, her white dress swirled around her like frosting. Rosalie reaches her side and drops beside her. Her hands shake, and she can't even manage to count to calm herself.

"Mom! Mom!" she shouts while Leo comes up beside her, warning her not to move her, something about the angle of her head and neck. "We need to do something!" she's screaming. Penny's dialing 911 while Rosalie leans over Cassidy, her voice soft and whimpering. "Please don't do this to me."

Penny makes her way over when Leo shouts, "I don't feel a pulse."

The couple exchange nervous looks as they begin CPR. They take turns. First Penny, then Leo. They count breaths and compressions in sync as though they've done this before. Rosalie sits motionless, her heart screaming inside her chest. *How could this happen?* Renée is across the room, arms down by her sides, her face laden with regret. Jean-Paul goes to Rosalie, and her tear-streaked eyes gaze up at him. He places a hand on her shoulder and draws her to his side. "I'm here for you."

She's waited a long time for someone to offer those words, and she sinks into his embrace. Her body trembles as she sobs uncontrollably.

She tries counting along with Leo and Penny as the paramedics rush through the door. There's a scramble in the kitchen; Simone wipes down spills and crumbs. Lucy and Henry stand apart from one another, lost in thought. A door slams upstairs.

The EMTs load Cassidy onto a stretcher, and as she's carried out, she takes the air in the room with her. Penny threads an arm through Rosalie's, offering to take her to the hospital. Jean-Paul and Renée step back, dazed and upset. And before Penny and Rosalie are out the door, Renée approaches with Cassidy's bag. "Penny."

Penny spins around.

"You're going to need this."

~

Rosalie rides shotgun in Leo's rented Mustang as Penny drives to the hospital.

It's one thing to be angry with your mother 90 percent of the time, but it's another to be on the precipice of losing her. That's when the 10 percent kicks in, and the dislike begins to diminish. Suddenly, Rosalie can't recall cleaning up her mother's messes, the embarrassment she feels at her neglect, or how Cassidy despises the color of her hair and lipstick.

Penny adjusts the radio and tries to convince her that everything's going to be okay, but Rosalie asks her how she knows that. Too often, people offer sentiments and platitudes without knowing the outcome.

"I don't know," Penny says. "But it's worth mentioning."

Penny's trying to be nice, and Rosalie should go easy on her, but she doesn't feel like talking, so she just nods at whatever else Penny's saying and hopes she'll get the hint. She simply wants to hang her head out the window and rewind the last few weeks. Go back. Agree to go to the Sonoran Desert. Maybe deactivate her Ancestry account.

"We're here." Penny pulls into a parking spot near the emergency room entrance. Rosalie wants to snap at her, tell her that the brightly lit building's huge Watauga Medical Center sign is a giveaway, but she commends herself for her self-control. Then she spots her mother's purse in Penny's lap, and their eyes meet.

Rosalie's not stupid. She knows what they'll find in her mother's bag. Most people carry lipstick or breath mints. Cassidy Banks carries a pharmacy of pills. "They're going to need her insurance card," Penny offers.

They both know she's being kind.

They move quickly through the parking lot and hospital doors. Penny takes charge, which is a relief to Rosalie, and they learn her mother is in triage.

"Can I see her?"

A man in green scrubs approaches. "The doctors are with her right now. It's best for you to wait out here. We'll find you when we know more."

Rosalie's desperate, her voice wobbly. "I'm her daughter."

The man repeats himself, and Penny ushers her toward a dingy sofa in a corner, where they sit without talking. Rosalie can't shake the feeling that this is her fault—that somehow she's being punished for deceiving Cassidy, for going behind her back and finding her father.

CHAPTER 43

HENRY

Henry lets out a breath.

He can't think.

They're in *Blanc D'Ivoire* with the door slammed shut, though he can hear Adam's and Sienna's voices through the flimsy walls. He doesn't know which betrayal to wade through first. They're all distraught about Cassidy Banks and what this means for her poor daughter, and then there's the revelation involving his father. That he stole from the De La Rues infuriates Henry, but first he must tend to his wife. His soon-to-be ex-wife.

She's across from him in the sitting area, a small round table between them. Her skin is splotchy from crying, and she can't meet his eyes. She stares into her coffee mug, spooning circles in the liquid.

"Renée's upset," he says. "She's lashing out."

Lucy places the cup on the table, and her head falls into her hands.

A thundering clap jostles the room. There's blackness outside the window. He's never felt more adrift in his life.

Adam.

Lucy loves Adam. The way a sister loves her annoying little brother. She has no problem calling him out on his highfalutin nonsense, the entitlement, his grating self-importance. She's been his conscience for years, planting his feet on the ground when his head reared danger-ously close to the sky. Unlike Henry, he doesn't understand the sky, and maybe that's what connected him to Lucy. The thought makes him sick.

He shakes his head, refusing to believe it. Renée is wrong. But what if? He's not bothered by what Lucy's said: it's what she hasn't said. He understands the sin of omission. She hasn't denied anything. Is that the same as a confession? For the last three years, he's closed himself off, built walls, and squeezed Lucy out. Did he unknowingly push her too far?

And fucking Adam?

"It's not what you think."

"Honestly, Lucy, I don't know what to think."

The floor feels like it's given out from beneath him. He understands the issues in their marriage, but Sienna and Adam are in love. No cracks, no fissures, no meteor shooting through their orbit. And Lucy would have known if something was wrong. She has a nose for failure seeping through shiny veneers.

"It was a stupid mistake."

He couldn't let it in before, but the memory of last summer grips him and squeezes. The alcohol. The weed. The naked bodies by the firepit.

"Henry."

The idea, the memory, it sickens him, and he sees it spotting an already stormy sky. "I can't deal with this right now."

"We need to deal with it, Henry. That's been our problem."

He stands up. He's good at this—avoiding. The injured expression on her face isn't new, and before he turns from her, he says, "This is why you wanted the divorce, isn't it?"

She bows her head. "I hated myself. And I knew you'd never forgive me. I'll never forgive myself."

She isn't wrong. He can't look at her. He strides across the room and flings open the door, making his way toward the sunroom and a better view of the moon, when a figure seated in the living room stops him.

Jean-Paul.

"Not now, Henry," he says.

"Just hear me out." Henry takes a seat across the room, but it's close enough to see Jean-Paul's pained expression. "I had no clue what my father was up to. He never discussed his business dealings with me."

"How do you suppose he found us?"

Henry racks his brain, trying to piece that together. He had mentioned the inn in Vilas, a summer destination they shared with their best friends, but he never mentioned the owners by name. His father must have done his own research. Vis Ta Vie. He was a smart man. Resourceful and cunning. And Henry can't help but feel responsible.

"My father was once a good man, Jean-Paul. I can't expect you to understand that." Remembering the way it used to be hurts. The sadness washes over him like the rain tapping outside. He's held in the anger for so long, he feels like a dam about to burst. "When I try to reconcile that person with the man he is today . . . Lucy's right. My father died. I don't know the man in his place. I never brought it up because I was embarrassed and ashamed. You think I would have shown up here had I known? What kind of person does that?"

Jean-Paul uncrosses and crosses his legs. His voice is flat. "We trusted him, and he took everything from us. We have nothing now."

Henry squeezes his eyes shut. *God damn that man.*

He thinks about trust, how it's given and taken so freely.

"I'm not my father." Another clap of thunder jolts the house. "How much did you lose, Jean-Paul?"

Jean-Paul fiddles with his wedding band. "Do the numbers matter? Everything we had, we gave to him. Our families have tried to help, but it's been too much of a burden. You know how this works. The settlements take time." Jean-Paul is dejected when he says, "Renée trusted me. I vowed to take care of her."

Henry tastes the fig and melon coming up. He's going to be sick.

He tells him how sorry he is. He tells him he understands if Jean-Paul and Renée want them to leave. "We can pack up tonight."

"It might be for the best. Renée is awfully upset."

And before they can say anything more, the lights flicker, and the conversation comes to an end.

CHAPTER 44

SIENNA

"You need to leave."

"Sienna, you're being ridiculous. No offense, but I wouldn't fuck Lucy."

She hurls a shoe at him and misses. "I can't do this, Adam."

"Do what? Why are you being so dramatic?"

She unbuttons her shirt, too royally pissed to wash her face or brush her teeth, and slides into her pajama bottoms. "I honestly can't listen to you." She heads toward the door and flings it open, dropping F-bombs that ricochet off the walls. "Get out."

He's undressing, oblivious to the finality in her tone. And that's always been their problem. Nothing she says computes in his tiny brain. This is the lowest of the low. Adam has always been about one person: Adam. And now he's destroyed her and Lucy's long-standing friendship.

"You need to get out of my sight," she says.

"Sienna, it was nothing."

"How dare you? How dare you say it's nothing when it involves my best friend? How could you take the one person who mattered to me more than anyone else?"

"Lucy's always had this frisky side to her. It was hardly—"

"You're disgusting."

Frenetic, she opens drawers and starts flinging his shorts and T-shirts into the hallway. When that doesn't satisfy her, she heads to the closet and rips his shirts and pants from their hangers, tossing them through the open doorway.

"Hey! Those are expensive."

"Get out, Adam. Get the fuck out. I don't want to look at you."

This is when she realizes the bold move she's about to make. How has she not seen it? She's going to leave him. She *has* to leave him. She can't bear to be in his presence. It has slowly been building, but tonight is the last straw.

"Just go. Take your shit with you."

"Where am I supposed to go, Sienna? You're being ridiculous."

"You're right. Putting up with your bullshit all these years is ridiculous. I don't even know who you are anymore. Do you know what people say behind your back?" She doesn't wait for an answer. "'Adam Kravitz is a douche.' They call you a fucking douche. They laugh at you. They think you're pompous and pretentious. And grating. They call you a sniveling, little, insecure dick, because you have to be lacking any shred of confidence to put on these shows all the time to impress people wherever you go. Well, I'm not impressed. Get out."

And with one small shove, he's on the other side of the threshold, and she's slammed the door, locking it behind her. She backs up to it, shaking, and slowly drops to the floor to hug her knees. She's been so caught up in her rage she didn't realize how the weather had taken a turn. Outside, the lightning bathes the property in light. Thunder dances along the roof. *Shit.*

"I need my toothbrush," he yells.

"Hygiene is the least of your problems," she shouts back.

The rain picks up, and the thunder vibrates the walls and windows.

"The power's going to go out tonight, Sienna. Then what are you going to do?"

She tries to tune him out, but she feels the tick of her heart.

Lucy. Her best friend. Her sister.

She hugs her knees tighter, and the lights flicker.

"Hello, darkness," she says to herself. *You are not going to break me.*

THURSDAY
Day 5

First Course: Watermelon salad with feta and mint

Second Course: Jumbo lump crab cake

Main Course: Prime meat loaf with whipped potatoes

Dessert: Apple pie à la mode

Gabrielle Vivien Chablis Premier Cru Vaillons

Clos des Papes Châteauneuf-du-Pape

CHAPTER 45

PENNY

One eye pops open, and then the other. Despite the drama last night, she feels more rested than she has in weeks.

The news about Cassidy hadn't been good. Upon arriving at the hospital, Rosalie and Penny learned that Cassidy regained consciousness in the ambulance, vomiting all over herself before losing consciousness again. Her heart had stopped and started multiple times. They had to revive her twice. The doctors working on her didn't know if she'd pull through. It was a tense couple of hours until she stabilized. At some point, Penny rummaged through Cassidy's purse like a thief, searching for evidence of life outside the inn, a family member, emergency contact. One of the administrators asked for her signature, even after Penny told her she'd only just met the mother and daughter a few days ago, tacking on that taking a few hikes and eating dinner together hardly made them friends. She quickly regretted the insensitivity.

It occurred to Penny that fifteen-year-old Rosalie was Cassidy's only relative, and she later held the girl's cold hand when they told her as delicately as they could that her mother needed brain surgery. The young girl cried. Then she began counting to herself.

Penny held Rosalie close. She tried to smooth away the worry, as did Dr. Benck, the doctor who worked on Cassidy. She explained how the surgery would relieve the pressure on her brain, and when she offered details about the procedure, she did it with her palm resting along the girl's shoulder. The doctor's brown eyes were hopeful.

Then Dr. Benck pulled Penny aside. She spoke candidly and without apology. "In addition to the blow to Ms. Banks's head, we found a combination of diet pills, alcohol, and Xanax in her system." Dr. Benck's findings didn't come as a surprise. "You said she fell coming down the stairs—"

"There was some commotion at the dinner table . . . She had gone to the bathroom . . . I wasn't paying much attention. She couldn't have been gone for more than a few minutes—"

Dr. Benck starts off slowly. "It's my medical opinion that Cassidy may have been vomiting—"

"You think she ate something bad?" Penny asks. "No one else got sick."

"I believe it was intentional. She was brought in severely dehydrated, and you may have noticed her cheeks are swollen."

She had, but all this time Penny had thought the swelling was due to the Restylane that Cassidy had injected into her face.

"Her low electrolyte levels and potassium deficiency, coupled with mouth sores and her thin frame, are consistent with someone who has an eating disorder."

Penny leaned back in the chair, catching Rosalie out of the corner of her eye. What it must be like to live with a woman this deeply troubled.

"I'm guessing her condition caught up with her. She might have been dizzy, unable to manage the stairs. We'll know more later. We have our best team working on her."

Dr. Benck walked Penny back to Rosalie, and Penny wasn't sure if the anguish on her face was for her mother's secret or for the possibility of losing her only living relative.

"I'll check back as soon as we have more information. Right now, they're prepping her for surgery. It's going to be several hours before she's cleared. I suggest you go home and get some rest."

Home. Where was home?

Reluctantly, they left the hospital. Rosalie spent most of the thirty-minute drive back to the inn staring out into the darkness. "Is she going to die?"

Penny couldn't lie. There had already been too many. She'd learned from experience that the truth was best in these situations. Besides, at fifteen, Rosalie wasn't a child. "I don't know. But I know the doctors are doing all they can."

"I know about the pills. And I knew she was making herself sick . . ." She stared straight ahead, focused blankly on the windshield. "I tried to get her to stop." Penny waited for her to continue. "She made me the adult, and then she refused to respect me." Her face turned sullen. "That's why I did what I did."

Penny squirmed in her seat. "Did what?"

Silence.

"Rosalie, what did you do?"

"You'll see."

∼

When they returned to the inn, most of the lights were out. The earlier storm had cleared the sky for a dazzling display of stars. The house was still and quiet, and she'd walked Rosalie to her room, tripping over what looked like men's pants in the hallway. Penny remembered the blowup leading to Cassidy's fall, how Henry's dad was involved with Bluebird, and how Renée and Jean-Paul lost everything. Renée screamed at Henry before blurting out some cryptic secret from last summer. The table had veered into a tense spiral, then a deafening quiet. Penny figured everyone must be locked in their rooms wading through the shrapnel.

"Get some rest," she told Rosalie, pulling her into a deep hug.

Leo sat waiting for her on the back porch. The cicadas were buzzing, the lightning bugs, showing off their shine. "Hey."

She fell into his arms, burying her face in his chest. Home.

He knew she was reacting to more than Cassidy's collapse.

There was a reason Leo and Penny had handled CPR magically in tune with one another. How precise their tempo and beat had been, as though they'd had practice.

She tried to block the memories out when she pressed on Cassidy's chest and Leo counted in measure, but it was impossible. She closed her eyes, and she saw little Ellie's lifeless body on the patio. She forced her eyes open. *This isn't Ellie.*

Penny shook, her body trembling. "I can't go through this again."

He brushed her hair from her face. "This isn't the same thing, Pen." Then he lowered his head and kissed her forehead. His lips were feathery soft. "I promise."

She let herself fall into the feel of her hands in his, his lips grazing her cheeks. She didn't fight him. She needed this. Needed him. It had been a long time since she felt safe. She wasn't sure who pulled away first, but they parted, and Leo led her inside to the kitchen.

He opened the freezer and took out a carton of ice cream. Pistachio. Her favorite. Riffling through drawers, he found a spoon, and they sat at the pristine table, no evidence of what had transpired earlier. The moon cast a glow on their faces. He sank the spoon into the carton and slowly brought it to her mouth, the cold sweetness awakening her senses.

"I can't stop thinking about her."

His eyes shifted downward, and she ran her fingers through his hair. "Me too."

The loss sat in her belly, creeping up toward her chest. She'd held it in so long. "We did everything we could, right?" she asked. It was a question she'd never asked aloud.

He set the spoon down, lifted her with both hands, and dropped her on the table in front of him. He stepped closer, and she spread her legs to let him in.

Her eyes filled with tears.

"They called it," he whispered. "She was under the water too long."

She relived the anguish of the young EMT who had to physically pull her off Ellie. Alara screamed beside her, a bloodcurdling wail that haunted every one of Penny's dreams. Buckley, out golfing when his daughter took her last breath, had to be carried off the green. Like a horror show, the reel played, and she shook her head, tried to shake it away, but she couldn't any longer.

Ellie died. And then came the shameful what-ifs and could've-beens that had left them in a puddle of regret.

It had all happened so fast. The snack bowls on the poolside table were empty. The cooler in need of more juice. She'd shot up from the lounger to restock, and Leo tagged along. He held her hand as they walked inside. The kitchen was cold compared to the desert heat, and as soon as the door closed behind them, he pressed her against the wall, nothing between them but his damp bathing suit and her string bikini. He kissed her hard on the mouth, and she ran her hands ɔ and down his skin. The busyness of their lives meant opportunities like this were fleeting. She inhaled his sunscreen and grabbed at his hair. He kissed her neck, shoved the triangle top aside, and grazed his pink tongue along her nipple. She closed her eyes and disappeared in the throbbing between her legs. At one point she reminded him they had a job to do. He laughed, and covered her mouth with his lips.

They returned with the snacks and juices. Alara had her nose deep in her book, and the kids were horsing around on the giant blow-up raft when Penny did what she always did: took a head count.

"Ellie." It came out as a whisper but then turned into a scream. "Where's Ellie?"

Alara shot up out of her chair, the kids halted their activity, and Leo, Leo jumped into the pool, disappearing under the giant float. When he came to the surface, he had Ellie's limp body in his arms. Alara was incoherent. Screaming. Crying. Dialing 911 and shouting at the operator.

"Get the girls in the house," Leo shouted at Kayla, their oldest daughter, as he laid Ellie down and began CPR. Penny pressed and blew, and he frantically counted. They took turns when she became winded. She kept going over how long they'd been in the kitchen, trying to calculate the minutes between life and death, all while keeping in sync with Leo. If Ellie had gotten stuck under that raft when they left for the kitchen, it had to have been six or seven minutes. She couldn't be sure. She would regret that decision to linger in the kitchen for the rest of her life.

"There wasn't more we could've done," he said, drawing her out of the memory.

But there was. They could have done what they were supposed to: gone inside for snacks and come right back. It didn't matter to either one of them that Alara was out there. They were all responsible that day, and she finally had the chance to say what she had never been able to say before. "We shouldn't have left Alara alone . . . those minutes . . . three sets of eyes might have prevented it . . ." Her voice drifted, and his head fell.

After Ellie, their golden life turned bleak. His heart no longer beat in tune with hers. That day by the pool, they wanted each other so much—maybe too much—and maybe the force of that love was what ultimately broke them apart. That moment in the kitchen was the last time she remembered being happy together.

They did their best to manage the girls and their grief. And the questions. So many questions. How could they respond when there weren't any answers? Closure was impossible when Alara and Buckley disappeared, slamming the door on their friendship. Leo returned to set. Actors are seasoned at compartmentalizing. She envied his ability to assume another role, to disappear from the ache that crawled inside. Tending to the girls was her escape.

What happened that summer buried itself deep beneath her skin. Beneath his skin. They were already miles apart when she and the girls moved to Miami.

~

They sat like that. In the dark. Sweet pistachio on their lips. Their mistakes closing in.

They had been so bruised. It was no wonder they couldn't talk. Instead, they held their separate grief, and relationships don't work if you don't fight demons together. They couldn't hide from it anymore. She knew that now. The very thing that had pulled them apart was luring them back together. Ellie's being gone would forever be an ocean of sorrow. Penny hadn't understood deep water until she was drowning in it. People don't like to talk about death, especially the death of a child. But avoiding it is another death.

And just as he had always been able to read her, Leo knew what he had to do. He lifted her and carried her up the stairs and through the maze of the house. His footsteps sounded insistent against the wood floor, and even though it was dark, he knew where he was going.

He opened the door to her room and laid her on the bed. He didn't try to touch her any more than he had already. He pulled up a chair and grabbed a blanket from the closet. She felt herself forgiving him because he knew what she needed and what she wasn't yet ready for.

And that's why, even after last night's chaos, she feels more rested than she has in months.

Leo's beside the bed, curled in an uncomfortable tangle, lightly snoring.

CHAPTER 46

JEAN-PAUL

Jean-Paul's lost in thought, recounting last night's dustup. As he cracks eggs into a pan, Renée pours fresh orange juice into a tall glass pitcher.

When he returned to their room last night, remnants of the storm remained, and she hid beneath the covers.

"I made a mistake," she said when he slipped in beside her.

Agreeing would only make it worse. They'd dealt with blame before, and saying nothing was far more productive. She knew she shouldn't have mentioned the supposed transgression between Lucy and Adam; he didn't need to tell her that. She was angry. Shocked. And after his talk with Henry, he knew exactly what they needed to address.

"The person you're mad at is me," he says. She didn't answer. "I brought the deal to the table. I introduced you to Bluebird."

She turned to face him. "We made the decision together. We've made all our decisions together."

He was surprised by this. Pleased. A little guilty too. Guilty because they hadn't made all their decisions together. Some were beyond their control. "Henry said he didn't know. I believe him."

Sienna's voice plowed through the building: *How could you do this to your best friend? To me?*

To which Renée mumbled, "Henry can't stand Adam, Sienna."

"I didn't sleep with her."

The slamming of a door.

If she heard what he had said about Henry's innocence, she didn't respond. The inn quieted, and that quiet lingered as Jean-Paul turned away from Renée and fell asleep.

~

Today, he's not sure what to expect.

He's furious at Michael Wall.

She's furious at Henry.

He's furious at himself.

He can't imagine Lucy, Henry, Adam, and Sienna sitting at any table together.

A guest hospitalized.

Maybe they are getting too old for this.

Maybe selling isn't a bad idea.

They enter the kitchen like a line of delinquents walking into the principal's office. He's guessing no one got much sleep.

Sienna arrives first, her normally fresh face blotched in red, her eyes puffy from crying.

Henry's next. His head dips low, his lip swollen. He refuses to meet anyone's eyes.

Lucy hobbles in, doing her best to maintain some semblance of control, but it's not easy to balance both crutches and betrayal. Dark sunglasses hide most of her face. She and Sienna keep a reasonable distance, and Jean-Paul knows this isn't going to work. He and Renée might as well send them all home now. Adam shuffles in with a nice shiner on his left eye, and their home is officially a clinic.

"It wasn't me," Sienna says. "And believe me, I tried."

"That end table by the couch is a hazard," Adam says. "Do you have Tylenol, Renée?"

"He's leaving today," Sienna answers. "I'll be damned if I let him ruin my one vacation."

They race toward the coffee as though caffeine is the fix.

Lucy asks about Cassidy.

"Nothing yet," Renée replies.

"And Rosalie?"

She says this as Rosalie traipses in. One of them sets their coffee mug on the table loud enough for the others to stop talking. They stare at Rosalie curiously.

It's Rosalie. There's no doubt. But the girl is different.

For starters, she's not wearing black. Not that Jean-Paul's one to notice teenage girls' styles, but it's jarring to see her so drastically changed. She's wearing a white T-shirt and jeans.

Jean-Paul studies her carefully. Her eyes are a stunning blue. They're big, and they're sad, and he's inexplicably drawn to them.

Penny and Leo descend the stairs, and Penny shares another update. "The hospital just called."

Rosalie rushes to her side. "What did they say?"

"Your mom's out of surgery. She'll be in recovery for a few hours, and then you can visit."

Jean-Paul sees the relief wash over her cheeks. "Did they say anything else?" she asks.

Jean-Paul focuses on the scrambled eggs and omelets, but he can't miss Rosalie's worry. She means, *Is my mother going to die?* And something about that cracks him open, unearths that place he buried.

"You can come with me for a quick stop at the market, and by then she should be ready for visitors," he offers.

She nods, and he feels a small victory.

Henry makes his way over, and Jean-Paul circles back to their conversation last night. He told him to leave, but today he's not sure if that's the answer.

"We're working on getting a flight out of here as soon as possible," Henry says.

And Jean-Paul doesn't dissuade him.

"We're headed on another hike this afternoon if anyone needs fresh air," Leo says, bringing his coffee to his lips.

"Is there a cliff?" Sienna asks, taking a bite of her bagel, chewing madly.

Adam smiles. He thinks this whole thing is funny, digging into his eggs with an offensive gusto. Henry sips his coffee, skipping breakfast altogether.

Rosalie excuses herself from the table, telling Jean-Paul she'll meet him out front, and as soon as she's out of earshot, Lucy whispers to Sienna, "I'm glad Cassidy's out of surgery."

Sienna gives her a look. "You're not really trying to make small talk with me right now, are you?"

Lucy folds her hands in front of her and stares into her coffee.

"Are we going to sit here and act as though you didn't fuck my husband?"

"I did not have sexual relations with that woman," Adam says.

"That's not remotely funny." Sienna throws back a swig of orange juice. "How can we even be having this conversation? You're supposed to be my best friend." Her voice begins to crack.

Adam looks everywhere but at Sienna. Leo and Penny slink away from the table.

"Those two definitely had sexual relations last night," Adam says.

"Still not funny," Sienna replies.

"It was a mistake," Lucy says. "A stupid mistake that shouldn't have happened. We were drunk. Stoned. Henry—" She stops herself. "All this stuff with his dad . . . it's been horrible—"

Sienna's unmoved.

Renée gives Jean-Paul the signal that they need to disappear, and they do.

CHAPTER 47

HENRY

The four of them stare blankly at each other, wondering who's going to speak first.

Sienna shakes her head. "Tell me I just woke up from a miserable fucking nightmare, because—"

And she stops herself. The reality too shocking to repeat.

Adam stands and heads toward the open wine from last night, and even though it's not even nine, he pours himself a drink. Henry studies his movements, remembering a time when they were like brothers. Remembering how they managed college together, held each other's firstborns, but today his squinty blue eyes and short-cropped hair irritate him. His smug mouth, always in some dickish smirk. He restrains himself from slugging Adam in the other eye.

"Someone needs to explain to me what happened last summer," Sienna says.

Lucy tried to explain the night before, but Henry turned his back on her when she climbed into bed. Henry isn't one to overreact. He collects data and sorts it out in his head, sifting through facts to make informed decisions. Science has served him well, but this time, the answers are out of reach.

They probably should have the conversation in their room or take it outside. They could hurl insults into the open air, hurl their disappointment across the murky pond. But Henry feels beaten. First his father and the De La Rues, and now this. These were his people. And even though Adam has changed in ways he doesn't understand, their history glues them together. They've always been there for each other.

He catches Sienna's pitiful stare across the table. "Is anyone going to answer me?" she asks.

Anger rises in his chest. The swell started as a simmer, but then it grew. How long it's been growing, he's not sure. He hasn't felt awake or alive in a while, drowning in resentment. This thing with Lucy and Adam, it's tipped him over. Like the dying stars he studies, he's crashing at an inordinate speed. If he can't get himself under control, he too will burst. His voice is calm, but fury bleeds through. He repeats Sienna's question. "How did this happen?"

"What do you want, Henry? A fucking play-by-play?" Adam doesn't even attempt to disguise his arrogance.

"Don't make me have this conversation with my fist," Henry says casually. "How the fuck did you end up screwing my wife?"

"I told you," Adam says. "We didn't have sex."

We. Henry tries to wrap his head around the word that ties his best friend to his wife, the mother of his children.

The table is silent, and the only sound comes from a faucet nearby with a tentative drip.

Lucy's hunched over with her face buried in her hands. Sienna waits.

"Let's not do this," Lucy says into her palms.

Sienna doesn't flinch. "We're doing this." Disgust falls from her tongue. "And when I get up from this table, I'm done." She directs her gaze at Adam. "So this is your last chance to tell me this didn't happen. That this is some sick joke."

"It's not a joke." It comes out in barely a whisper, and when Lucy lifts her head, tears stain her face.

Sienna's forehead crinkles as if she's misunderstood. She shakes her head and takes a deep swallow. "Lucy." Her face crumples. "You can't . . . you can't be serious . . . it's me . . . it's us . . ." Her voice shakes. "We shared everything." Henry can't help but think it's a fact that doesn't age well, but there's no time to point it out because Sienna's bombarding Lucy with questions. "Were you having an affair? Has this been going on—"

Lucy stares straight ahead—not at Henry, not at Sienna. She talks robotically, her words dull and practiced. Henry doesn't understand how she held them in this long. How she kept this secret as they lay next to each other in bed night after night. "We were all really fucked-up last year." As if that's a valid excuse, but she keeps going. "Henry . . . this thing with his father . . . we were hanging on by a thread."

He glares at his wife, this woman he once knew intimately, the one who's now a stranger. "Please don't blame this on me."

"Why didn't you tell me?" Sienna implores her friend, as though adultery weren't enough of a crime. He will never understand the mystery of female friendships. Her voice is shrill. "How could you keep something like this from me?"

Lucy's voice rises; her hand gestures at Sienna. "Look at your life. It's damn near perfect. How could I tell you? It was humiliating."

Henry cowers.

Sienna nods. "I get that." And then she stops. "I mean, the part about it being difficult. But Adam and I . . . so, you hook up with him? Why? For what?"

"I don't know!" Lucy yells, raising her hands in question. "I was in a dark place. I was scared. I was lonely. And alone."

Sienna eyes her questioningly. "With all your training . . . all the advice you've given me over the years . . . you were my person . . . my vault . . . I trusted you!"

Lucy can't face her. It's tough for Henry to watch.

"What happened?" Sienna asks. "You need to tell me. I deserve answers." Then, as if she's afraid of those same answers, she lets out a sob. "I don't get it. Adam throws some attention your way and you . . . did you even think about our friendship? About our kids?"

Lucy shrinks into the stool, and she answers plainly, "No. In that moment, I did not."

Adam mutters under his breath, but they all hear. "There wasn't much time to think."

Sienna swings around, her hair smacking her face. "Shut. The. Fuck. Up," she says. "Really. Just shut up."

And Henry can't help himself. "Adam." He fixes on his friend. "Have you really forgotten who you once were? Who we were? All of us? The shit we've been through?" Adam's face remains unchanged. "I've made excuses to justify your bullshit. But you can really be offensive." He can't think of a better word. "To be honest, I haven't liked you in recent years. I've tolerated you at best, out of respect for Sienna and Lucy's friendship. But you're not even close to the guy you used to be. You've turned into one of the most pretentious, self-important people I've ever met, and as embarrassing as it is to have Michael Wall as my father, your obnoxious entitlement may be worse. I don't doubt for a second you made this happen."

Sienna screams for them to stop. She's crying, tears bursting from her eyes as she swipes at them with the back of her hand.

"If we're going to do this here," Lucy begins, "let's just get it over with."

Lucy's undeterred. He can tell by the way she sits up, how her hands clasp together, the determined expression in her eyes. She trains those same eyes on Henry. Only him. And she talks to him freely, as though no one else is in the room. She sobs, intermittently, then briefly composes herself. It breaks his heart to listen. "I've loved only you, Henry. There's never been anyone else. But you won't let me in. You've built your wall so high, I can't climb it. Since the story broke about your father, you've disappeared. Staring up at those stars, living in another world. Away from me. Away from the kids."

She isn't wrong. She's trained to pick up on couples shutting each other out.

His eyes wander over to Adam, who's playing with his expensive watch.

"You and I were both complicit last summer," Lucy says.

"Except I didn't try to fuck your best friend." Henry detests the words falling from his tongue.

"I didn't sleep with Adam." She's a little more indignant this time. "I don't know how much of that night you remember, but I came back to the room. I tried to get close to you . . . and it wasn't the first time. It had been months since we—"

He shakes his head. Great. More fodder for Adam to use. "You had no idea what it was like."

"No, I didn't. And you didn't give me a chance to help." Now she focuses on Adam, dismantling his ego with her stare. "I went outside. Adam was there. He poured me another drink . . . the last thing I needed." She doesn't break the stare, forcing him to turn away. "Maybe I was starving for something. Affection. Attention. I don't know. I wasn't thinking. And I wasn't in my right mind. I never drink like that. With pot. We were sitting in the grass . . . he was . . ."

Sienna stands up and heads toward the sink. "I can't listen to this." She proceeds to vomit in the steel basin.

"We didn't have sex."

"Just stop," Sienna says, wiping her lips. She drinks directly from the tap.

"No. You need to hear this. We all need to hear this. Then there'll be nothing left to the imagination." She rakes a hand through her hair. "I can't hold on to the ugliness any longer." She sits back. "We fell back on the grass. Sloppy. Incoherent. And it happened. One minute we were laughing about old times, and the next . . . he was on me . . . we kissed . . . that was it."

"On you?" Sienna's hands cover her face.

"It was just a kiss."

"A kiss?" Sienna asks. "Like a friendly lip thing? But he was on you?"

Adam stirs his coffee.

"Adam?" Sienna prods.

Their eyes prance around the room. Henry's disgusted.

"It wasn't a friendly lip thing," Adam admits.

"Tongue?" Sienna paces around the table.

"Tongue was involved."

"How long?"

"Fuck, Sienna," Adam begins. "You want to know how long? I don't know. I was plastered."

"Actually, I do want to know, because there's a big difference between your tongue mistakenly finding its way inside my best friend's mouth and a full-blown make-out session."

"No blowing was involved."

"Why is this a joke to you?" Sienna asks.

"He may have grabbed my . . ." Lucy's palm lands on her chest.

Henry clenches his cup and throws back some ice water. Adam is working his every last nerve.

"I don't think I did," Adam says.

Lucy holds his eyes in hers. "You did."

The images plant themselves in Henry's brain. Adam sticking his tongue down Lucy's throat, clutching at her breasts.

"You have everything you want," he says. "You had to have Lucy too?"

Lucy gazes at Henry, tears spilling over. "I'm sorry." And then she turns toward Sienna. "I know our friendship is over, but you have to know, I'd give anything to go back and change that night. It was a mistake. And I'm sorry."

Sienna stares out the window, her back to the table.

"It was me who asked for the divorce," Lucy continues. "Even when I knew I loved Henry . . . I knew how big of a mistake it was . . . I couldn't face him with this secret between us. Hating myself felt better than having all of you hate me."

Adam's annoyed. He crosses his arms at his chest. "Why exactly are you doing this, Lucy? It's not helping, but at least you'll have a clear conscience, right?"

She holds her chin up when she speaks. "I'm nothing like you, Adam."

After Henry has a moment to dissolve the image of Adam doing whatever he did in the grass with his wife, he considers his wife's courage. He could never have done that. He kept his dirty secret hidden, let it crawl inside and wreak havoc.

Lucy would tell him it takes two to break up a marriage, and he knows he's been an active participant in this. He has been a silent partner. He shut her out. But he can't admit that yet. The anger is too raw. But the fact that she stood at this table and confessed, knowing how much it would destroy, is more than he has ever done. He is a coward. And his lies hurt the people he loves most.

"There's something else," Lucy says.

Adam's eyes narrow in on hers.

"There's something else I want to say. If we're being honest here." And she gazes squarely at Sienna. "There's something you need to know."

Adam's face twitches, a mix of fear and desperation. "Come on, Lucy. That's enough."

"She's my best friend."

"Don't be stupid," he says.

Which is all the trigger she needs. But then Penny waltzes in the room, beelining for the fridge.

CHAPTER 48

ROSALIE

Rosalie's drifting through the farmers' market in a daze, checking and rechecking her phone for the time. There's no sense in rushing. They said her mother would be in recovery for a while. Jean-Paul's up ahead, testing the firmness of the squash and avocados, but she hangs back, not really in the mood to squeeze vegetables. *What would she do without her mother?* The question kept her up late into the night, sleep a futile effort with her mother's room empty across the hall. She hadn't expected to feel such loneliness, but there she was, back in their Chicago apartment, waiting for Cassidy to wake up from a drunken slumber. She'd been alone (and afraid) for some time.

And now she has a name. A face. A living, breathing human being with her DNA.

Jean-Paul finds her sulking by the fresh flowers. Her head feels so foggy that the bright petals and stems blur together.

"Let's grab a bunch for your mom," Jean-Paul says.

Jean-Paul is always so nice to her. She isn't sure why. Not when she's grumpy and standoffish and pissed at the world. But lately, she hasn't been feeling that way. In fact, she feels a change, a subtle shift, as though her steps are lighter. Something about Vis Ta Vie softened her. Maybe the bright surroundings and pale hues have reached inside her.

Or maybe it's something else. Henry said they are all made of stars, and despite worrying about her mom, she's beginning to feel a tiny glow.

Jean-Paul pays for the flowers, and Rosalie offers him the emergency twenty in her pocket. She may be the youngest one at the table, but she's not an idiot. She heard how the De La Rues lost a lot of money to Henry's father. This is why, when she gave up on sleep, she researched Michael Wall on the internet, browsing through pages of his offenses, apologies, and later his incarceration. Rosalie doesn't know anyone who's gone to jail, but she suspects—well, she knows—that Henry's embarrassed to be related to someone so awful. She understands. They've both lost parents in some regard. And she shakes the negativity from her head because she has this idea that doing so will prevent her mother from dying. *Positive thoughts.*

After researching Michael Wall, she did what she told herself she wouldn't: she googled brain injuries. And what she read terrified her. Sure, her relationship with her mother is tenuous, but she doesn't want her dead. And if she does live, what if she wakes up a different person? What if she doesn't remember Rosalie and their life together? The possibilities are terrifying.

"Put your money away, Rosie."

She'd forgotten she was holding the bill in her hand, and she stuffs it in her pocket.

"Only my closest friends call me that."

"Haven't we become friends?"

She looks up at him. "Do you always do this . . . Are you always this nice to guests?"

He laughs. It's a deep laugh, and she wonders what it would have been like to grow up at the inn with people like him and Renée, Jean-Paul's happy laugh dancing through her ears. She likes that about him.

"I wouldn't call punching Henry nice."

She can't stop what comes out of her mouth next. "Why didn't you and Renée have kids, Jean-Paul?"

"Ah, the million-dollar question, Rosie."

"Is that a terrible thing to ask?"

"Sometimes. Sometimes the question makes people sad." And then he adds, "But asking questions is good. It shows you're curious about people. Too many people only talk about themselves." He runs a free hand along his beard and shakes his head.

She thinks about her own recent search and the way Henry described family, like planets floating around the sun. She wants the entire sky and all the stars. "I just think you would've been great parents." She feels the blush crawl up her cheeks when she says it.

"That's nice of you to say, Rosie." He knocks into her. "I think this makes us officially good friends."

The woman at the flower stand hands Rosalie ranunculus wrapped in brown paper and a raffia ribbon, and Jean-Paul hoists the bags of fruits and vegetables. It begins to drizzle as they walk to the car, and Rosalie raises her head up to the sky to let the cool liquid tap her cheeks.

"Not everyone is meant to be a parent . . . to have children." His lips press together in a tight line.

"Does that make you sad?"

"For some, it's a personal choice."

"Was that yours?"

He nods. But she doesn't believe him.

"Our guests become our children. And their children too. What we do requires tremendous responsibility. It's a mere week, but they entrust themselves to us." He unlocks the car, and Rosalie settles in the passenger seat, the flowers on her lap. They're pale pink. Her mother will hate them. She likes bright hues, jewel tones.

She watches his hands maneuver the steering wheel, and he catches her staring. "You must have your learner's permit by now, right? You're fifteen."

She slinks back into the seat. "I have my permit, but I don't get a lot of practice."

Outside the window, the pastures and farmhouses fall away, and Jean-Paul says, "I'll tell you what, if you're feeling up to it . . . and your mom's okay . . . I'll take you for a lesson."

She brightens. The offer makes her weepy. And the words spill out. "Jean-Paul, I found my father."

She wishes he'd say something, but he doesn't. In the last few days, she's begun to read his expressions. He's thinking. Intently. So unlike Cassidy. But she again banishes the negativity and bad karma. Luke Combs plays softly on the radio, and Jean-Paul tightens his grip on the wheel, waiting for her to continue.

"I made contact. Through one of those ancestry sites." She pauses, picking at a nail. It felt good to say it. "Cassidy said it was a one-night stand, you know. I thought maybe I could find him." Her voice trails off. "There he was: a 50.2 percent match."

She studies his nose, the salt-and-pepper beard, when he replies, "Does your mother know about this?"

"Not yet. But my plan was to tell her this week."

"That's quite a bit of grown-up stuff to tackle alone."

"I'm used to being alone." She peers out the window. "And a grown-up."

He finally asks, "Did you hear back from him?"

"Not yet." And then: "But I'm patient."

She's caught between these two worlds—the one where she may gain a father, and another where she risks losing her mother. She's holding on to both, unwilling to give up either.

"Cassidy and I . . . we've just never seen eye to eye. But I'm scared, you know. What if he doesn't want to know me? What if he doesn't like me?"

They're at a stop sign, the bright red blaring a message. He turns to her. "How could anyone not like you, Rosie?"

She doesn't know how to respond, and she wants to say more, but she doesn't trust herself. So she whispers, "Thank you," but he can't hear it over the song playing on the radio. "When she told me . . . I was only ten . . . I really didn't understand . . . one-night stand."

"Tricky. But that means he never knew you. Because if he did—"

"What if this isn't what he wants? What if he's not interested in me?"

"What is it you're looking for, Rosie?"

She sniffs at the flowers. "I don't really know. I just feel displaced. Like there's this missing piece."

"Oh, Rosie. That's what it means to be a teenager. Everyone has felt that way, even the ones who seem to have it all." He continues, "You have to tell your mother. This isn't something you can manage on your own."

"I've done so many things on my own, Jean-Paul."

"That doesn't mean it's right. Or that it should continue."

And then she finally says it: "What if she dies? What if she doesn't wake up?" And with each question, she feels her mouth go drier. "Or what if she wakes up and she's someone else? I'll have to tell him. I'll have to do it on my own."

"That's not going to happen. Your mom is going to come out of this stronger than before, and you'll talk to her. You can't just show up on someone's doorstep declaring you're a long-lost child. That can be traumatic for someone your age. And for your father."

But she's not listening. They're at the hospital, and everything he's saying is wrong.

CHAPTER 49

PENNY

She can't help herself. She's nosy. What woman isn't?

The four of them at the table, hashing it out: it's better than any reality TV. And she's not entirely heartless and cruel. She's curious. She knows what it's like to lose a best friend, and she wonders how these four friends will master infidelity.

She was almost at the landing to the kitchen, a quick detour to grab water for her hike with Leo, when she heard their raised voices. No fewer than three *fuck*s per sentence. At least they weren't in public, with eyes on their every move. They wouldn't be trolled and trashed in cheap magazines, fodder for strangers to ridicule. But betraying a best friend, the person you trust most in the world, that's a colossal mistake.

She admires Lucy's candor—and strength—as she confesses her loneliness, her inherent need for Henry's attention. She lets it sink in. They've all experienced their own forms of betrayal. Cheating isn't just being unfaithful. The room falls silent, and Penny takes the steps one by one, and just as she crosses the threshold, Lucy says, "There's something you need to know," and Adam says, "Come on, Lucy. That's enough." And she thinks that she should turn around, but she tells herself she'll be fast.

Having shared the last however many days together means she's justified in stepping through their web. Vis Ta Vie has bonded them, provided sustenance and stability. She's had her own stint in betrayal hell, and she's no stranger to it.

They watch her make her way toward the refrigerator.

Penny's actually surprised at Lucy's transgression—with Adam, of all people. From day one, she knew Adam had the makings of a lying cheat. She caught him leering at Cassidy on the hike; he didn't even try to hide it. The quintessential braggart. He and Sienna are that couple that reeks of perfection and gushy affection, but Penny knows how those relationships play out. That shiny facade disguises secrets and problems—because there's no such thing as a perfect marriage.

People like Sienna and Adam value the look of their relationship more than the relationship itself, priding themselves on a curated social media feed highlighting their best parts. Lucy is the therapist. She had to know what lurked beneath the surface. And while Sienna is nothing but friendly and funny, she has a poor defense. She chose Adam as a partner. One didn't need a degree to figure it out: if you have to constantly brag about your money and success, you're compensating for something.

She should take her Smartwater and gracefully exit, but she decides against it. She stands at the table, the couples on either side. She tucks away her judgments, opinions, and most of her distaste for Adam as she interferes: "I'm going to offer some advice. Don't blame. It's a waste of time. You somehow got here . . . and everything you're feeling is real and fucking raw. It's understandable. You've got kids, people who rely on you, model you, and love you, so don't make this just about you. Think about them." She pauses to unscrew the cap on the bottle for a sip. "Give yourself time. And if there's one thing you should focus on, it's not whether you love this person, because the answer is yes. It's always yes. It's a reflex. The real question is, can I live without this person? Legitimately gone. Think about it. Loving someone's easy. Living without them—that's what you need to figure out. And if you can't live without them, then do everything in your power to fix this."

She twists the cap back on the bottle and slips out of the room. And it's only then she realizes she's been holding her breath. Because she loves Leo. That has never been a question. And as for living without him, she isn't sure she can do that anymore.

CHAPTER 50

HENRY

Penny exits the kitchen, leaving them with her sage advice. They're quiet, staring at each other, soaking in her words. He needs to stop asking himself how they got here because he knows. Most people do. You look deep and long enough, and you see the signs. The silences. The hand not held. The shape of your lover's shoulders as she turns away. The trail is obvious and long. You don't need a special lens to see it.

But could he live without Lucy?

"Are you attracted to my husband?" Sienna asks Lucy.

"God no," Lucy replies. Adam rolls his eyes. Adam believes that anyone with two X chromosomes wants him. "I was in a weak moment."

Henry studies her carefully. "It's no excuse," Lucy continues. "I wasn't myself. I was weak. He filled a hole."

Henry is about to say, *He sure as shit did*, but he stops himself.

Sienna and Lucy have always been able to read each other. They're halves of a whole, their phone conversations spilling late into the night. Henry rarely had to guess who was on the other end of the line.

"You should've come to me. Why didn't you?" Sienna says, tilting her head toward Lucy. This betrayal is bigger than a marriage. Henry thinks of dominoes lined up. One push and all the tiles topple over.

Lucy's face is lined with regret; dark circles frame her eyes. "I never intended to hurt you. And I understand if you never want to talk to me again."

"It was just a kiss," Adam tries to explain. "And a little boob. What's the big deal?"

"You seriously need to stop," Sienna shouts. "Your stupidity isn't helping anything."

"It's never *just*," Lucy begins, unable to say his name. "It's always more."

Henry's surprised at his reaction to his wife. He knows he should feel every ounce of bitterness. He should be finger pointing and blaming, the visual of Adam on top of her repelling him, but he feels something else as he watches Lucy come clean. He loves her. He loves her honesty, how she admits how she's failed. *It was just a kiss.* Penny and Leo weren't the only ones. *Just a kiss* had broken up a million marriages. And he wonders, if any of the scorned had taken the time to focus on the real problem, the circumstances leading to the kiss, would the couples be together today?

He loves Lucy. And he's unexpectedly afraid to lose her, desperate to keep her. And he feels a tidal wave of regret for pushing her away.

"What were you about to say?" Sienna asks Lucy. "Before Penny walked in?"

"Guess you thought you were off the hook." Lucy directs this at Adam.

"I'm outta here." Adam stands, addressing Sienna: "I don't even get why we're having this private conversation here. With them."

But Lucy is unwavering. She stands too.

"Private." Sienna laughs. "You opened us up to this. This is on you." She turns back to Lucy, and Henry can't imagine what she's about to do.

"Adam called me Suzy," Lucy says.

Sienna's cheeks burn crimson, and she grabs on to the table.

"Suzy?" Sienna shouts. "Who the fuck is Suzy?"

"He said it more than once," Lucy adds.

"I knew it. You're so predictable." Sienna stands and points at the door. "Get out. You need to get the fuck out of here. And out of my life."

And Adam surprises them by heading for the door and leaving them speechless.

CHAPTER 51

PENNY

He's waiting for her in the Mustang. She studies his profile as she approaches, the sunlight streaming along his face—the golden boy brighter than she remembered, or maybe she sees him with fresh eyes. He turns toward her, just as she opens the door, his smile wide and welcoming. She tosses him the extra water and straps on her seatbelt.

"Are you ready?" he asks.

She leans back in her seat. "Let's do this."

They're barely a mile through the Profile Trail when Penny realizes they might have made a mistake. The climb is steep, and the sunny sky is turning gray. A raindrop pelts her cheek. Leo isn't as outdoorsy as he professes. She's the one who coerced him to climb mountains, roam through thickets and trees. He had done it for her; he had done a lot of things for her. But now he's out of breath, and she can sense the worry on his face, especially when the last batch of hikers warned about a bear in the area. "Maybe we should go back," he says.

"I'll protect you," she teases.

A group of teenagers passes by, showing off their speed and stamina. They don't recognize Leo because they're too young, or maybe because his yellow ski hat and oversize glasses hide his most recognizable features. But then a group of college coeds in ASU gear catches up to them just as Leo slinks behind a tree to pee. One of them spots Penny, and she screams, "OMG! Penny Shay!" She's youthful and dewy in head-to-toe Lululemon. "You're even prettier in person!"

The four girls hover around as Penny takes a backward glance at Leo, who holds a single finger up to his lips.

"You can't hike Profile alone!" another one shouts. This one has kinky curls and enormous blue eyes. "Come with us!"

Penny smiles. "I'm good. My friend's on a bathroom break."

They gaze behind her, unimpressed.

"Penny," begins the one in head-to-toe Lululemon, adopting her first name as though they're lifelong friends. "Thank God you moved on from that prick, Leo. What an asshole."

And once they get started, they don't stop.

"I'll never see another movie of his again," says Vanessa, introducing herself and offering her hand.

"I don't think he's making any more movies. I think he's been blackballed." This comes from the girl dressed in sweatpants and a white tank top that shows her nipples thrusting against the thin fabric.

Penny catches Leo hiding behind the tree listening in. He must hate this.

"What about Claire Leonardo?" Nipples asks. "She should be ashamed of herself."

"You can't blame Claire," Vanessa says. "Leo's a grown man. He was the married one."

"He didn't deserve you, Penny," Lulu says.

Nothing about the conversation feels good. They don't know Leo. Or her. They don't know about Ellie and the grief that swallowed them whole. How water had filled their lungs and drowned them too. She wishes they hadn't agreed to the vague public statement, but Leo's publicist insisted, "You don't pander to gossip." But if Leo had come out with the truth, then she wouldn't be standing here defenseless on this mountain.

"His loss," Lulu adds.

Then they ask if they can pose for a selfie, and she relents—that Penny, always the pleaser. They stand together, their lithe bodies crammed next to hers, and one of them laughs. "All together: 'Fuck off, Leo Shay.'"

Penny fake smiles, and it's weirdly unsatisfying—their outrage at Leo. She feels Leo's eyes on her. And when she hears the crackling of leaves and sees his shadowy figure approaching, she braces for a showdown.

The girls, moments before cackling with energy and insults, go mute when they spot Leo removing his hat and propping his sunglasses on top of his messy hair. A light film of sweat covers his cheeks and neck, and Leo's no dummy. He knows exactly how to shift the narrative, make people—women—speechless. Leo, with his annoying good looks, is even more handsome when he's "mussed" up. If you typed *mussed hair* in Google, Leo Shay would appear first in the search results. He's the Jen Aniston of man glam. This isn't lost on Penny, who just ran her fingers through that hair.

"Leo Fucking Shay," Lulu announces. "Should've known you'd be lurking around, ashamed to show your face."

Leo flashes his high-voltage smile. "And who do I have the pleasure of meeting?"

Leo's upset. This won't end well.

"Come on, Tracey," says Nipples, the quiet one. "Let's get out of here." The poor girl can't keep her eyes off Leo. Another one holds up her phone.

Leo manages to avoid Nipples's nipples. "Hello, Tracey," he says, offering her his hand, and she wastes less than zero seconds before taking it into hers. And her smile. It's cloyingly sweet and immediately gets under Penny's skin.

But then this Tracey moves in and points. "What the hell's wrong with you, Leo Shay? You had the world by the balls! Look at this woman . . . Now, granted, Claire Leonardo is beautiful too, but she's no Penny. Your wife. The mum to your kids."

Leo crosses his arms close to his chest and listens, innocently giving Miss Tracey his famous starry-eyed gaze.

"You are everything that's wrong with men today. You're the reason marriage has become a hopeless ideal. And you broke the trust. Look at us." She gestures to her pack of friends, staring in disbelief. "You and Penny . . . you were everything we wanted. Everything we dreamed about as little girls. And not just because you're Leo Fucking Shay. We idolized you two. We watched you hold doors for Penny. Piggyback your daughter through the Oscars. You were macho, but you were sensitive and sexy and unflinchingly loyal. You made us believe that happily ever after just might exist."

Penny thinks this Tracey might begin to cry.

"I love Penny," Leo says softly, not nearly as loud and insistent as Tracey. "I still love Penny."

Penny breathes in his words as a pulse of lightning illuminates the sky, a telling sign that they should end this madness and turn back.

"If you loved her, you wouldn't have embarrassed her publicly. That's the problem with you stars, with your egos and entitlement. You think relationships are disposable. Then you sideswipe her with a divorce—"

Penny interrupts. "I think I may have been the one to file."

She smiles at Penny, this Tracey. "You know what I mean. Tomato. To-mah-to."

"No, actually, I don't know what you mean. I had a say in this. It wasn't only Leo."

"You wouldn't have had to file had he not let that other head of his do the thinking."

She's wrong. They're all wrong. It's taken her some time, and maybe she's been unfairly stubborn, avoiding the bigger issue but she knows

Leo didn't cheat. Leo didn't lie. But why are they arguing with this woman? "Leo," she says, "let's go."

Tracey raises her voice. "If you love her, Leo, you need to prove it."

Penny waves a hand in the air. "This is ridiculous."

Leo's losing patience. She sees it in his eyes.

"I'm not engaging in this lunacy," Penny says, louder than she should. She grabs Leo's hand, and that's all the girls need to start snapping with their phones. Tomorrow's headlines will blare, "Are They or Aren't They?" And "Is the IT Couple Back Together?"

They form a human blockade, preventing Leo and Penny from passing.

"Look at you, Leo. Pathetic." Then they shift to Penny. "It's abusive to stay in a relationship like this, Penny. Didn't your mother ever teach you about self-respect?"

This is the point when Leo loses self-control, dropping Penny's hand.

"Don't you dare talk about Penny like that."

"There he is. Our little action hero. Come on, Leo, show us what you got."

"I'm really getting tired of this, Tracey."

"Come on, Leo," Penny says. "Let's go."

Then Leo turns back to Tracey. "You don't know me. You don't know Penny. You think you know us because we're on magazine covers, or you saw me on some screen, and you thought I was talking to you. I wasn't. I wasn't talking to you, and you can't just come here—"

"Actually, I can come here. This is a state park."

Penny tugs on Leo's arm, but something in him snaps.

"Tracey, you want to know what happened? You're so self-important you think you know everything. You don't. Here's something for your little TikTok show—"

"Leo! Enough!"

But Leo can't stop. "You can insult me all you want, but Penny's off-limits. Do you get that? My wife . . ." He gazes at her, and Penny can't let him do this. She can't let him shoulder the blame because it's hers too.

"Leo, please don't."

But he's too far gone. "I hope you never experience what we went through. Long before that day. Long before you thought you saw me cheating. The two of us . . . I am not a cheater!"

For fuck's sake, what is he doing?

"We lost someone we loved . . . she was just a child . . . and man, it's messed everything up. Is that what you want to hear? You want to know how we screwed up, that there was an accident? A mistake we'll live with for the rest of our lives? You want to know how it tore us apart, tore up our family?

"But you . . ." He motions toward the girls. "You saw what you wanted to see. Claire. Me. Because for some reason, you're so damaged you can't imagine anyone else being happy . . . because you don't know how to trust and have probably never been loved the way I love Penny. You just created your own story . . . like you always do."

"Guess that's the price you pay for being Leo Shay," Tracey says.

"I'll pay that price, but my wife, my children, and the people who didn't ask for this are off-limits. You need to back the fuck off."

Leo turns to Penny. All the pain and hurt there in his two-tone eyes.

"You have no idea what you've just done," she says.

"I won't let them disrespect you."

She breaks free and starts heading down the mountain. The rain has descended, pebble-size splotches slapping the ground, slapping her face.

She doesn't know how much time passes before she hears his voice: "Penny, wait." The desperation in his tone stops her, the wind scattering leaves in the air. When he gets close, she searches his eyes for answers, wondering how the hell they'll manage this. How long until the press finds Alara and Buckley.

"You can't say those things to strangers, Leo—"

The realization hits him, and he hides his face with both hands.

The girls aren't far behind. Rain coats their hair, and Tracey's phone is perched in the air recording everything.

"You sure got them to back off."

The forest is dark and stormy, and they move as quickly as they can until they lose the girls. "What were you thinking? You just gave them more to talk about. We made a promise. This will wreck Alara and Buckley."

"I'm giving them the truth, Pen."

As another loud boom cracks through the sky, she stomps along the slick, muddied ground. It's the fallout that scares her. What he's just done courses through her veins and sends her down the mountain at an alarming speed. The last thing she hears is Leo behind her shouting, "Penny!"

CHAPTER 52

HENRY

Lucy and Henry return to their room, processing what she just shared. She hops through the door on her crutches and makes her way over to the window seat. He sits in a nearby chair.

"That wasn't easy."

"Imagine being the one saying it." She sets the crutches aside and presses her nose against the window. "I'm sure this makes it easier . . . for you to walk away."

There's a vindictive side to him, a scared, angry side that wants her out of his life. They can move on, split up their expenses, the children, their lives, but something stops him. Letting her go would be easier than forgiving her. "I don't want to walk away."

"Good," she says. "I don't want that either."

He leans in closer.

"I've hated myself for some time," she says. "Don't feel sorry for me."

"I hate myself," he replies, "knowing I contributed to this."

She's twisting her fingers in her hands, and he wants to make her stop, but instead, he watches the ducks playing in the pond. "I wish it wasn't Adam of all people, but I mostly wish we didn't get to this point."

Her eyes are red from crying, and he thumbs away the tear that slips down her cheek.

"I am so sorry," she says. "I was trapped in the black hole. I couldn't get out."

He likes that she's speaking his language. "I was there too."

"And I'll live with this forever. But I'm going to look for the light . . . for the stars."

"They're there."

"They're worth fighting for," she says. "We're worth fighting for."

"I'm sorry I didn't try harder," Henry says. "I'm sorry I shut you out."

"Does that mean you're going to join me here on Earth? Or will I find you hiding up in the sky?"

"Maybe we can meet in the middle."

"You know what you have to do first."

He nods, takes her hand in his. "I'll handle it. I promise."

She backs up, dabs at her eyes. "I have to get ready for an emergency Zoom with a client."

"I'm going to go for a jog, and then we have to book those tickets home. Jean-Paul and Renée want us to leave."

Once downstairs, Henry considers forgoing a stop in the kitchen when he spots Renée at the table poring through a file, but it's too late. She sees him. He makes his way toward the fridge. "I'm just grabbing some water for a quick run, then I'll be out of your way."

She takes a generous bite out of a chocolate éclair. "Your being here isn't good for me, Henry, but I suppose neither are these éclairs."

He keeps a safe distance, waiting for her to continue.

Her hand rests on a folder. "This is the file on your father. On Bluebird. Why I've held on to it this long, I don't know. I take it out from time to time, imagining we could have done something differently." She holds up a sheet of paper. "Take a look."

His legs are defiant, heavy, but they lead him to her side.

"Here are our signatures on the document agreeing to terms." She points as though he can't see it for himself. "And there's Michael Wall's name. My mother always told me that if something sounded too good to be true, it probably was. But you know how it goes." She holds up her fingers in air quotes before closing the folder. "'The return was nothing they had ever seen before.' Michael brazenly took our money. Even when we told him it was everything we had. He still did it, knowing full well what would happen. Without a shred of remorse or decency." She takes on his father's tone when she quotes him. "'We're investing wisely. You'll have more money than you ever dreamed of.'"

The pit in Henry's stomach grew.

"He promised us a few months . . . less than a year to triple our investment. It was all we needed to complete our renovation. I'm guessing you already knew this?"

"I didn't know."

She looks down at the folder. "Throwing this file away feels like forgiveness, and I just don't know if I'm ready for that."

There is nothing he can say to right this wrong. "I'm sorry, Renée. We're going to fly out tonight."

The sunny day has turned dreary, and by the time he returns from his jog, the skies are dark and menacing to the south, the smell of rain on the horizon. Maybe it can wash away their messes. He stops to stretch his legs at a wooden fence when he spots Renée again. She's tending to the flowers, twin butterflies fluttering around her. He could take a second loop and avoid another confrontation, but he has something to say.

"Renée," he begins, "do you have a minute?"

She doesn't respond. Instead, she pulls at weeds, dropping them into a plastic bag. He takes it as a sign to continue.

"I had no idea his reach came this far. If I had known . . . I swear . . . I would have never shown up here."

She reaches for her shears to cut a stubborn root.

"Please say something," he says.

She waits before she stands, peering out from underneath her visor. "I see him in your eyes."

"Something other than that."

"Something other than that." She's thinking, shifting her weight, tackling a new section of the flower bed. "I feel sorry for you, Henry. You're caught in the fallout. We never had an opportunity to tell those Bluebird people how they've destroyed us. How could we not take out our rage on you?"

He stands against the old sugar maple, his hands tucked inside his pockets.

She touches on every nerve. This is the reason he kept things to himself. The reason he shut Lucy out.

"I have his blood, but I'm not him."

She takes off her hat and wipes sweat from her brow. The wind whips her curls. "I know it's foolish to blame you. To blame anyone but him, but this is what people do."

He blinks. "I understand blame."

She sizes him up. "I know you do."

His gaze lands on the inn, searching for the right words. "I've learned a lot since we arrived. Sometimes our anger gets displaced."

The door swings open and out flies Adam, dragging his suitcase. A car travels up the drive and stops. The door opens again, and this time it's Sienna. She chases after him, gets right in his face.

Years of anguish fall from her tongue. Obscenities, words Henry didn't know she knew. "I gave up my career for you." She lunges. Points. "I hate you. I hate what you've done to me. I hate who you've become, and I hate that I let myself believe we were happy. You made a career out of fucking other women. Fucking *Suzy*. Were you ever faithful?" she hisses, ripping off her wedding band and throwing it at him. Adam scrambles into the back seat, and as the car hightails it out of the driveway, dirt flies through the air. "To answer the question," she screams,

"I damn well can live without you!" Then she drops to the ground and weeps.

Henry feels sorry for her, but he knows not to get involved. Lucy's at the doorway, leaning on her crutches. Sienna's the only person she'd step off a client call for. No one moves until Sienna gathers herself and pushes through the doorway, Lucy hopping behind her. Which leaves him and Renée.

"I don't think that was displaced anger," Renée says, turning and taking in the tired building. "You love it here, don't you?"

"You know we do."

She shifts from one foot to the other. "I was foolish."

"You're anything but. You were duped. And I'm sorry for that. You didn't deserve it. None of those people did."

She mulls on this. "Henry, you were always too kind. When was the last time you spoke to him?"

She doesn't mention him by name.

"I cut him off around the time the indictments were brought down."

She pauses, looking like she's thinking long and hard about her response. "That had to be tough. For you. Your mom."

The rain begins to fall, splotches landing on Henry's head. He sees his reflection in the windows, the dampness washing over him.

"What will you do, Henry?"

"I don't know, Renée."

She knots up the bag full of leaves and weeds and dumps it in the nearby trash. They walk back inside. "I used to find answers up there." He points to the sky. "Not so much anymore. He keeps calling. I've yet to pick up the phone. I love him. The man he used to be. But I hate him too. I hate what he did. And I'm sorry if that upsets you, but—"

She nods. "I can accept that."

They end up back in the kitchen, as guests so often do. She shifts into action and pours them some iced tea. Despite the turmoil that's thrown the inn out of whack, the De La Rues continue to take great care of their guests. The table holds an array of comfort foods: peanut butter and banana sandwiches cut into triangles, mac 'n' cheese in shot glasses, and mini cheeseburgers and french fries. Mindless snacks that suggest better days.

"How can I make it up to you, Renée? What can we do?"

She almost breaks out into laughter. "I'd say you have your hands full."

"We want to help. I want to help."

She thinks about her response. "Forgive me for what I said last night. About Lucy . . . Displaced anger and all. And stay. If you want. Look at it as one of those meteors or comets dotting our very dark canvas, right?"

He smiles, knowing stars can't shine without darkness.

She shuffles around the kitchen, putting dishes away and checking on tonight's menu. Henry watches as she picks up a notebook resting on one of the chairs. "Rosalie must have left this behind." She stuffs it in her bag. "I've got to get to the hospital and relieve Jean-Paul, or we won't have dinner tonight. I'm glad we talked, Henry. I'm sorry. For you. And for us. But I hope you'll stay."

CHAPTER 53

SIENNA

Adam's gone, and she doesn't care.

She's collapsed on the driveway, hyperventilating, wiping snot from her nose. Could the demise of their marriage be that swift? Who's she kidding? She's been feeling this way for a while. Suzy was just one in a long line of women. She's finally had enough.

When Adam left the table, she wasn't entirely sure he'd understood. When she heard his suitcase rolling down the hall, she followed him, running outside, getting in his face. She didn't care who heard. Renée. Henry. Let them bear witness. She was blazing with fire. Let it rip through the forest.

Out of the corner of her eye, she sees a figure standing at the door, waiting. She has never loathed and needed a person more, and she yells at her best friend to go away. Picking herself up off the ground, she runs. She runs past Henry's and Renée's shocked faces, and she runs past Lucy. Lucy. Her person. She makes it through the open doorway, into the house, and down the stairs. It's a maze of doors and hallways, and she runs and runs, believing the answers might appear. Deep in the house, she lands in front of the wine cellar, and before she knows it, she's crossed the darkened hallway.

CHAPTER 54

ROSALIE

Cassidy would be royally pissed if she saw herself in a mirror. Her hair, what's left of it, is matted against her scalp. They've shaved her head. Oh my. Her mother would not be very happy about that, and her skin is makeup-free. She looks even thinner than usual, which is alarming, and she has a large purple bruise centered above her eye. Rosalie tries to ignore the apparatus helping her breathe.

Moving in for a closer look, she spots a black hair jutting from her mother's chin. Oh dear. This would ruin her. She makes a note to ask the nurse for scissors. Cassidy had made Rosalie promise to cut unruly hairs that would sprout along her mother's chin when she got old. "Always cut. Never tweeze," she'd said. "Tweezing makes them grow back quicker and coarser." Rosalie wants to yank it out, but she draws back.

Her mother made it out of surgery, but she's unresponsive, unconscious, un-everything. Dr. Benck had met her and Jean-Paul in the hallway after the surgery and tried several times to explain, but nothing computed. "There's a bruise on your mother's brain," she finally said. "The bruise has blood collected around it, which is pressing on the brain. We inserted a shunt, a medical device, to relieve the pressure. While that's in place, we have a ventilator breathing for her."

Rosalie maintained a modicum of calm by quietly counting. "Are you saying . . . without it . . . she'll die?"

Dr. Benck looked to Jean-Paul. "We're doing everything to keep your mother alive."

Jean-Paul had slipped a hand on Rosalie's shoulder. She liked that he didn't say things like, "It's going to be okay," because none of them knew. She found it sincere.

"There's not much to do here," Dr. Benck had said. "Except wait."

Rosalie mustered the courage to ask, "How long?"

"We don't know. But your mom's a fighter."

Damn right, she was a fighter. All the times she fought her when Rosalie tried to wake her up to drive her to school or tried to get her to cover up her boobs in public.

"Can I sit with her a few minutes?" she asked.

"Of course. Take your time."

Which is why she's now seated beside her mother, angling to rip a hair from her chin while Jean-Paul sits in the waiting room.

"Mom," she finally says, the words sounding strange on her lips. "You need to fight." She's thinking about all the times Cassidy left her alone, left her to take care of herself. This is worse. "I know our relationship isn't ideal. But I need you to come back." She feels the tears pressing against her eyes. "There's something I need to tell you."

She waits for her mom to answer, to say something, to signal that Rosalie should keep her news to herself, but Cassidy says nothing.

She knows what she needs to do.

She knows if Cassidy dies, it will matter.

So she proceeds to explain about Diane Rodriguez . . . how she stumbled across the sites—Ancestry.com, 23andMe. "Sure, there were age restrictions and certain requirements, but I found a way," she says, and she leans in closer, "even though I may land in a federal prison for falsifying information. But I found him: your one-night stand. The site didn't provide much information, but I got his name. And I googled him. And I think I understand why you liked him . . . even for that brief moment. He seems nice. And he's not ugly.

"The thing is, I'm super curious how you met . . . how your paths crossed . . . because . . . well, I guess I imagined you having a type, and this guy . . . well, he's not it. So maybe that's why it was a one-night thing."

She doesn't tell her that she's as surprised that he chose her.

She's interrupted by the nurse who comes in to check Cassidy's IV and dispense more medication. "I'll be a few minutes," she says. She changes the bandages, and Rosalie waits patiently. She's already waited long enough.

CHAPTER 55

JEAN-PAUL

He's seated in the waiting area, watching women arguing on a TV screen when Renée finds him.

"*Housewives*, Jean-Paul?"

He throws his hands up. "I don't understand, *mon amour*."

She laughs. "Me neither. How is she?"

"Not so good."

"And Rosalie?"

"She's okay. I think she's conflicted."

She reaches over and takes his hand into hers. "How are you holding up?"

He leans back in the chair, resting his head against the wall. "This hasn't been the extraordinary week I had imagined."

She recaps her conversation with Henry, and he thinks of the lingering effect of decisions, how every choice has an impact, guides you on an individual course. Henry wasn't wrong. We're stars, circling the sky, trying to find our way. We're light and dark, and sometimes our shine hurts. Some of us fly high, others fall to Earth.

"What's that?" he asks, pointing at a bright green notebook sticking out of her denim messenger bag. It's hard to miss.

"Rosalie left it in the kitchen. I thought she might want it."

"She's an interesting young girl," he says.

"She is, isn't she?"

"I see a difference in her since she arrived."

"You've taken a liking to her," she says. "I think it's mutual. I'm not sure she has many adult figures in her life."

The conversation touches on their deepest pain, nears the fringes.

"See this?" She points to the faded photo of the inn sticking out from the notebook. "She did her research. Her mother said she's always been a curious girl. It's sweet."

She stuffs the notebook back in her bag, and he's not sure if he's supposed to repeat what Rosalie revealed to him, but Renée's his wife. "She told me on the way over here that she went looking for her father."

"Are you serious?"

"She went on one of those ancestry sites and found a match."

"The one-night stand?"

He laughs, though there's nothing funny about it.

"She's certain she found him. A 50.2 percent DNA match, to be exact."

"Does Cassidy know?"

He shakes his head.

"Shit." And then: "What if she doesn't wake up, Jean-Paul? The girl has no other family."

"According to some report, she does."

"Has she reached out to him? Does he know? Does he have a family?"

"I know nothing other than she found him. I think she may have made contact. Emailed him through the site. I'm not sure how these things work."

"Goodness. This is something."

"She said she needed to find him . . . to understand where she came from. I'm not sure what else she wanted, but Cassidy's condition changes things."

"That poor girl."

He leans back in the chair and watches the women on TV shouting at each other across a table. He wonders if Renée's thinking the same things he is. About the miscarriages. How badly they had wanted a child, until the doctors told her she couldn't have one, and the disappointment that spread wide. Soon after, they bought the inn, and the guests became their family.

"We should help her," she says, interrupting his thoughts.

"I'm not sure what we can do, *mon amour*."

"We help her find him. That's what we do."

"We barely know the girl."

"She trusts you. Why else would she confide in you?"

He shakes his head. "I don't think we should get involved."

She's thinking. "Maybe. I just thought it would be nice to do something for her. She's all alone."

He feels something swell inside him. They'd been helpless once, but now they had a chance to help. "We know nothing about this person," he says. "He could be a monster."

"Or he could be kind—"

"That doesn't mean he wants the responsibility of a teenage girl. He may already have a family. I don't know . . . I think we stay out of it."

"You're probably right. But she's lost so much. And she stands to lose more."

His arm comes up around her. "She's gotten to you too."

She sinks into him.

"Let's not get ahead of ourselves. Cassidy can very well pull through," he says.

She untangles herself from his embrace. "I'm going to find a nurse and see if they can give us some updates." Which gives him time to stretch his legs. The hospital buzzes with activity, and as he passes the nurses' station and patients' rooms, he hears Rosalie's voice through the open door.

"Thanks for taking care of her, and for the charger. She'll want her phone when she wakes up." The nurse exits the room, nodding in his direction, while Rosalie keeps talking. "I don't know why you can't have an iPhone like most normal people. Anyway, so I really hadn't imagined telling you like this. It's never been the right time, but you need to know."

There's a short pause before Rosalie continues.

"I don't even know if you can hear me, but maybe you can. I'm hoping some of this makes it through to you because . . . because . . . I'm going to tell him. I hope that's okay. Especially now . . . with you here . . . there's no one else. I hope you're not mad, but how could you be? It'll make things easier for us, right?"

Two doctors stroll by, and he strains to hear more.

"I guess what I'm trying to say is that you have some explaining to do, because I'm going to tell him. I'm going to tell Jean-Paul he's my father."

CHAPTER 56

JEAN-PAUL

He's sure he heard incorrectly.

Did Rosalie just say Jean-Paul is her father? That *he* is her father?

No. The girl is confused. He misunderstood.

He had never met Cassidy. He would know. He would remember something like that. And he has never cheated on Renée. But the dots are beginning to connect, and they're painting a heart-thumping picture. He backs up, banishing the idea. It's too implausible, outlandish. Something that those women on the television screen would squabble over.

Rosalie is oblivious to his presence, and he darts down the hall to find Renée, to forget what he's just heard. He repeats to himself that he misunderstood, and by the time he returns to the waiting room, he almost believes it. Renée's not there, but her bag sits tucked beneath the seat, Rosalie's green notebook peering up at him. He could take a quick look. It wouldn't hurt. And before he chickens out, he snatches the notebook, pretending his heart isn't hammering against his chest.

He finds pages and pages of photos and articles about the inn and about them that Rosalie must have printed off the internet. Then he spots the form. It's crinkled, as though she has handled it over and over. Or had she crumpled it up and tossed it in the trash with second thoughts at some point? He picks it up with both hands, his fingers trembling.

Explore Your Match!

Jean-Paul De La Rue. 50.2% shared DNA: 3700 cM across 23 segments

He grabs the armrest of the chair when the room begins to spin. He doesn't yet understand what he's reading, but something tells him that everything has led to this. Rosalie. His daughter. How is this possible? He flips to the next page, and there it is. Indelible black ink. *Explore your match*, followed by loaded questions with life-altering results: How are you and Jean-Paul De La Rue related? Parent-child relationship.

He tells himself there must be another Jean-Paul De La Rue. That's it. Rosalie merely mixed up the two. This is a glaring mistake. But the secret he holds taps on that memory he's long tried to bury. And hadn't he noticed the similarities? When Rosalie walked in that morning without her makeup, hadn't those eyes called out to him? Rosalie hadn't researched the inn for vacation purposes. The inn was secondary. She had researched Jean-Paul. And she had been clever enough to lure her mother into turning it into their summer trip.

He can't think. What had she planned to do? Announce it at the table? Instead of asking him to pass the pepper, did she plan to announce her paternity? He can't imagine what this will do to Renée. To them. He stares at the pages, feeling a headache coming on. It's slow moving and packs a punch. An ominous shiver slips down his back. What the fuck did he do?

Out of the corner of his eye, he spots a figure approaching. Rosalie. And the only thing he notices is the translucent blue peeking out from her long lashes. Her eyes are so striking it's hard to pin down an exact shade. But the resemblance is unmistakable. They're his eyes.

"That's mine," she says, reaching for the notebook, but it's too late. She spots the paper sitting face up on his lap. Jean-Paul's name. The percentage that ties them together.

"Why are you looking through my stuff?" She's upset, her cheeks red.

He stands, and the contents of the notebook fall to the floor. "You left it behind. Renée thought . . ." He trips over his words, suddenly aware that this person could be his child. His flesh and blood. She will remember everything about this moment.

Rosalie stares down at the floor, soundless, slowly dropping to her knees to pick up the papers. She may be crying. He can't be sure.

"I didn't want you to find out this way, Jean-Paul."

"What is this, Rosalie?"

"I'm sorry. I'm so sorry." Rosalie's eyes fill up with tears, and her voice cracks. "I planned to tell you . . . but first I needed to tell my mom. You have no idea what it's been like."

As confused and shocked as he is, he fights the urge to pull this lonely, terrified girl into his arms. "I'm trying my best to understand, Rosalie. But this is—"

She holds up the paper with his name. "I know what this means, but you have to believe my mom had no idea. And she didn't recognize you. I watched." She stops. "She said you looked like a chubby George Clooney."

This doesn't make him feel better.

"I'm guessing neither of you remembers."

He's trying his best to grasp what she's saying, to roll the pieces around until they make sense. She's referring to the one-night stand Cassidy told her about. He places his hands on his head. This is bad. This is very, very bad.

"I know how these things go," she says.

"I didn't cheat on my wife," he says.

She lets that sink in. "Sixteen years is a long time."

He's still wrapping his head around the fact that he's talking to his daughter, that Rosalie Banks could very well be his child. "So this is why you're here? This is why you chose the inn?"

Her lip trembles when she speaks. "I emailed you through the registry. You didn't answer."

He never got an email, and he looks up to see Renée approaching. "Are you going to tell her?" she asks.

He exhales. "She's my wife. Of course I'm going to tell her."

"I can't find anyone around here to give me answers," Renée says, noticing she possibly interrupted something. "What's going on?" She doesn't wait for a reply, which is good because he doesn't know how to break the news to her. He should have never kept this from her in the first place. "I'm going to the bathroom, Jean-Paul. Wait for me to get back before heading out. Oh good." She turns to Rosalie. "You got your notebook."

They wait until she turns the corner. Jean-Paul is tense, jumpy. The person he needs to talk to is unconscious. The only person who can verify that he didn't sleep with Cassidy is Cassidy. And the other minor detail—the hasty, complicated decision he made a lifetime ago—is a boulder about to roll down their little mountain.

Rosalie sighs. "Do you think it's a mistake?"

"I don't know what to think. Maybe?" He tries to sound convincing. "Could it be the immaculate conception? Probably not."

He's too stunned to formulate words. His mind swirls with possibilities, and none of them will end well. "Are you sure your mother said she had a one-night stand?"

She crosses her arms. "I wasn't in the room, if that's what you mean."

He needs to talk to Cassidy.

"I did everything right. I followed the directions, provided a sample. How could it be a mistake?"

"I don't know what to think, Rosalie. You shove a piece of paper with a statistical probability that I'm your father . . . What am I supposed to think?"

"I didn't exactly shove it."

"Right." But it felt that way. He stares at her, soaking her in and pushing her away. "I heard you talking to your mom."

Rosalie sits in the seat, her shoulders hunched over. "I had to tell her. What if she doesn't make it?"

He opens his mouth, but nothing comes out. She sees a parent in him. Whatever he says matters. He wonders what Renée would say. "You need to be positive. She feels your energy."

"Henry said big things were about to happen. A supermoon. And I knew I found you for a reason. And when Mom fell . . . the stars . . . they aligned. They're aligning now."

He wants to believe her, but he's doubtful. She sees an alignment; he sees the stars colliding. A big burst of chaos about to rip through their sky. He thinks back to the conversation he had with Renée moments ago. He suggested they leave it alone, to steer clear of Rosalie's search for her father. She was the one willing to interfere to help Rosalie. He wonders what she'd think of her plan now. How could they have known that the person Rosalie was trying to find was him?

"I see myself in you," she whispers. Her eyelashes flutter when she says this. He's embarrassed to be staring, but how can he not? He may have had something to do with those eyelashes.

Renée's heading their way, and he feels himself shrinking in her presence. He doesn't know how long he can maintain control.

"Are you going to tell her?" she asks again.

He musters what minuscule rationale he has left. "Not here, Rosalie." He guesses by the way she ducks her head that she takes this as rejection, denying her of what she believes is hers. He swallows back the emotions, and Rosalie grabs her notebook and holds it close to her chest. Renée smiles at them, and he can't bear being witness to how everything is about to change.

He should have seen this coming. Energy. The universe. All of us magnets. He focuses on Rosalie. Her cheeks. Her hands. Her fingertips.

He thinks before he leaves, *I see myself in you too.*

CHAPTER 57

PENNY

They drive home in the pouring rain. As soon as they pull up to the inn, Penny gets out and slams the car door behind her. He tried to get her to talk along the way, but she wasn't interested. She knows the video will go viral, and not only did they promise to protect their friends but they have their kids to consider too. Her daughters have just stopped having nightmares, and now the leeches will unearth the drama, blast it all over the news.

"What do you want from me, Pen?" he'd asked her as he drove.

"I want you to be quiet!" she had said, pulling her jacket tighter around her.

"I'll never apologize for protecting you."

The winding roads were slick and steep on the drive back, and while he concentrated on the wheel, she sank inside the tapping of the rain along the roof.

Penny hurries to her room, the conversation with the young women on the trail pedaling back and forth through her mind. *If you love her, prove it.*

Was that what he was trying to do?

CHAPTER 58

SIENNA

She races deeper inside the cellar, her eyes adjusting to the near darkness as she passes bottles of wine lined up from floor to ceiling. She runs until she can't run anymore, and only then does she trip upon the dark brown leather chair in the corner. It's musty and cold, and she curls into a tight ball and cries. It's a few minutes before she hears the metal clicking of crutches.

"Go away," she shouts.

The shape of her friend approaches; she's carrying something in her hands. She shuffles closer, and Sienna's glad she can't make out her face. Lucy knows not to speak. Not yet. She tosses a blanket at Sienna, but Sienna swats it away, and the blanket lands at their feet. Lucy, undeterred, leaves it there as she manages to abandon her crutches and sit on the cold floor. The only sound is their breaths.

Sienna's shivering, and she eyes the warm throw.

"Go away," she says.

"I'm not leaving."

She screams. Not at Lucy, but at the ceiling, the walls, the rows of wine. The echoes bounce, hitting their ears. The release feels good, and she punches at the armrest and the seat, and when she's done screaming, she grabs the blanket and wraps it around herself. Lucy doesn't say a word. She waits. She listens.

And then Sienna cries. A guttural cry that travels from her stomach up to her chest.

"I don't know how to forgive you," she finally says. "Our friendship was one of the few things I trusted . . . you took that trust . . ."

"I know. I'm sorry."

Their history plays in her mind. All the times she leaned on her friend, how they depended on each other. Lucy knows her deepest secrets. How she stuttered as a kid. How she battled postpartum depression with both her children. Why didn't she feel she could tell her about Henry's father? If she had, maybe they could have avoided all this.

Sienna knows all about humiliation. She heard what people said about Adam. She'd witnessed how the money and prestige changed him. It didn't matter how hard he worked for it. The effort didn't mean anything with all the name-drops and grandstanding. And with status came entitlement. Adam believed he could have anyone or anything he wanted, regardless of the cost.

They were out of their right minds last summer. Drunk. Stoned. Lucy didn't stand a chance. It's not an excuse but an explanation. Sienna will have to decide if she hates Lucy as much as she hates her husband.

"I don't expect you to forgive me," Lucy says, her voice a whisper. "I can barely forgive myself. Henry and I . . . we just haven't been the same since his dad's arrest. I lost Henry, and I lost Michael too. He thinks it just happened to him. But I was terrified for us, especially the kids. We were getting death threats. How could I tell you?" She pauses. "We were miles apart last summer. And I made a grave mistake."

Her honesty strikes a chord in Sienna. They've shared a lot, but hasn't she held back too? "I knew there were other women," Sienna admits, dabbing her eyes. "I'd smell them on his clothes, found the occasional lipstick on a collar. I turned a blind eye for the kids—for what I thought would give me peace. I was too embarrassed to tell you. I figured you knew. That was even more humiliating." For this, she lowers her head and sucks in a breath. "I'm going to need some time. But I think I understand. I mean, look at Leo and Penny. We all thought he was the biggest cheating asshole, but he's kind of nice. And he definitely loves her. Adam took advantage of you. That's what he does. He did it to me too."

Lucy doesn't entirely agree, maintaining she played a part, but Sienna doesn't want to think about it. The blanket warms her, and she feels the air around them shifting.

"Sienna," Lucy begins, a lilt in her voice that wasn't there before. "You know it's really dark in here."

Her instinct is to steady herself, evaluate her surroundings. She hasn't been able to breathe in a dark room for the last year, let alone sit in one for this long. Her heart begins to clang in her chest, and fear climbs up her skin. "Okay," she exhales. "This is weird."

"Do you want to go upstairs?"

She thinks about it. "No. I'd rather live amongst wine forever." She laughs. "What is happening here?"

"Psychologically?"

"I think I'm owed a free session, don't you think?"

"I think you've been holding in a lot of your feelings. And when we hold on to feelings, they manifest in strange ways."

"You think my fear of the dark is because of some hysterical feelings?"

"Maybe you've felt 'in the dark'"—she uses finger quotes—"with Adam. Even me, maybe."

"That's ridiculous."

"Then explain why you're in the dark right now and not having a full-blown panic attack."

She's waiting for it to happen. Waiting for the terror to clamp down and squeeze. But it doesn't. And she doesn't know what to make of it. And she doesn't want to tell Lucy that maybe it's because her best friend is beside her. "This. Is. So. Strange," she says, enunciating each word slowly.

"You've said some powerful things in the last twenty-four hours. Shouted, I should say. Stood up for yourself. Told Adam to leave. Felt the anger. Let sadness in."

Lucy isn't wrong. In fact, Sienna feels braver than she's felt in a while.

"Holy shit."

Lucy's features are fuzzy, but Sienna detects a smile.

There's residual fear, a token reminder that she still has feelings to work through. But for now, she feels hopeful. She wants to hug Lucy, but she can't. Not yet.

"I'm sorry," Lucy says again.

"I know."

"I'll understand if you let me go too. I will. What I did was awful. But just know, to answer Penny's question, I can't imagine my life without you in it."

Sienna drops to the floor beside her friend, and Lucy's arms automatically go around her. She falls into her, mumbling something about hating her but hating Adam more.

Footsteps approach, and Henry appears, almost stepping on them. "I'll never understand you two," he says. But Sienna understands their ability to swim through murky water and find clarity in an embrace. He drops a bag of M&M's in her lap before walking away, and she eagerly pops a handful in her mouth, suddenly hungry.

"Adam's a shitty kisser, right? Way too much tongue."

And they laugh.

CHAPTER 59

HENRY

Henry's seated at the table, waiting for the others to arrive. He's thinking about all that's transpired, knowing that when they walk out these doors, they'll have decisions to make, mistakes to confront. The table acted as an intermediary, but reality is closing in.

Lucy and Sienna don't know he heard part of their conversation. He followed them downstairs, standing behind a wall of wines to make sure nothing escalated, and when Sienna mentioned how Adam took advantage of Lucy, Henry released a breath he hadn't realized he held in. The relief washed over him, the anger morphing into a forgiveness he clung to with both hands.

~

"Henry?" Simone says it twice before he hears her. "Are you okay?"

She holds a bottle of red in one hand and white in the other, and he catches the smell of whipped potatoes as he stares at the wine. He wants something stronger, but he chooses the red Clos des Papes Châteauneuf-du-Pape. Jean-Paul had boasted about the full-bodied blend produced in France's Rhône Valley. The first swig goes down smooth and velvety.

A car pulls up the drive, and in walk Rosalie and Renée. The young girl's eyes look sunken into her face; her purple hair is pulled back. She looks peaceful, despite her somber mood.

"How's Cassidy?" Simone asks.

"No change," Renée answers.

Rosalie drops into a chair and lets her face fall into her hands. The ringing of Henry's phone breaks the silence, and his father's name and face cover the screen. Filling Rosalie's glass with water, Renée says, "Maybe you should answer," but he hits "Decline."

He'll have to deal with his father at some point.

He hears them before he sees Sienna and Lucy step into the room. Lucy's managing the crutches, able to keep pace with her friend.

They crowd around Rosalie, concern for Cassidy spilling over, and Rosalie shares her monosyllabic responses. They don't promise her it will work out. They don't make baseless platitudes. They reassure her that they're there for her, which is the one thing they can control.

Henry reaches for his phone. His father leaves another voice message, one that he may or may not listen to, and he sees a notification from the Night Sky app about what's in store for them tonight. He wants to delete it. Come down to Earth. He knows the answers he needs aren't there, but the possibility used to give him a small comfort.

"Where's Adam?" Rosalie asks.

"Adam left," Sienna says.

"He went home?"

"It's over," Sienna says, unflinching.

"Shoot," Rosalie says. "Wait. So you're all getting divorced?"

Sienna adds, "We got to the root of our problem, I suppose. You can always count on this place to give you the truth."

"We promise to peel onions, literal and figurative, while creating connection and reflection." Renée half smiles. "I think we've accomplished that."

Jean-Paul doesn't look amused.

Their voices flurry around the table, but Henry is cautiously eyeing Lucy, curious about the question Rosalie posed, the one they had all ignored.

"It's better this way," Sienna begins. "I'm better off. The kids are at my mom's, and he's going to pack his stuff." Renée rounds the corner and offers her wine. "I'm strangely okay," she adds. "It's like this relief washing over me . . . I mean . . . I stayed with him too long . . . It's time." She points to the white wine. Renée serves a generous pour, and Sienna takes a taste.

"I know you're all staring at me as if I've lost my mind. My best friend and my husband . . . well, it could have been worse." She downs another swig. "We weren't as perfect as people assumed. We were barely holding on."

Henry lets her finish.

She holds Lucy's eyes in hers. "Adam never ever saw me. We've been living in the dark for a while."

"To a lot of us, it looked like he worshipped you," Henry says.

"That's what he did. That's his gift. He puts on an act when people are around. The affection, the compliments, the adoration. That bright light. But he never really saw me. It was an eclipse." She takes another sip. "How could I complain about someone who worshipped me, right?"

She rambles on, not the least bit concerned about who's overhearing the tawdry details of their life. "When we were alone, he was different. Aloof. Distant. And don't get me started on our sex life."

"Hold on," Henry says, motioning at Rosalie.

"I'm almost sixteen, Henry. I know about sex."

"You've had sex?" Renée asks, which sends three sets of eyes spinning in her direction.

"You guys are weird," Rosalie says. "You're starting to creep me out."

"If we're going full-on creepy," Henry begins, directing the observation to Sienna, "we thought you and Adam were like bunnies—always all over each other."

"Oh, that," Sienna says. "Part of the show. Let people think he's this ideal husband with an insatiable appetite. For me." She shakes her head.

"We all want to feel beautiful and wanted," Lucy finally says.

Sienna blinks away tears. "I never felt those things with him. I felt like an impostor. A body." She inhales, tucks the sadness away, and puts on a brave face. "Henry."

He's half listening, half reading the update on his phone about tonight's sky. "Sienna."

"I'm sorry for his behavior. I hope you'll find a way to forgive Lucy—"

"That's really cool, Sienna," Rosalie interrupts. "I'm not sure I'd be as forgiving."

"You will. When you know what matters, you figure out a way. And it's good for you to know that not everything's as it seems, and that we're all just . . . what do you call us, Henry?"

"Atoms. Energy."

"We're just people with flaws and faults."

They're interrupted when Leo walks in looking like he's been beaten up.

"Hey, gang."

A chorus of muffled greetings follows.

Renée comes around with the wine, offering Leo the red. "Is Penny joining us?"

"She's got a headache. Probably not."

Sienna holds the glass up to him. "To solidarity." And they clink glasses.

"How's everyone doing?" Leo asks.

They all gulp simultaneously.

"I didn't have sex with Adam," Lucy says, "if that's what you're thinking."

"I'd never think that. He's way too big of a jerk for you."

"Thank you, Leo," Sienna scoffs. "I'll take the compliment."

"Where is he?" Leo asks.

"You didn't hear him take off?"

"I was dealing with my own shitstorm."

"Full moon," Henry says.

Jean-Paul comes around with a tray of crab cakes.

They eat in silence, lost in their thoughts. The table feels smaller, as though it's shrinking beneath their troubles. Simone circles around, taking photos of the food, a close-up of the yellow calendula adorning the apple pie.

Henry's the only one who notices that Jean-Paul hasn't said a word the entire meal.

FRIDAY
Day 6

First Course: Moules marinières à la crème

Second Course: Salade Niçoise

Main Course: Poulet rôti au jus de citron with haricots verts

Dessert: Crème brûlée

Domaines Ott Château de Selle rosé

Ramey Wine Cellars cabernet sauvignon

CHAPTER 60

PENNY

It's morning, and Penny's eyes open, adjusting to the darkness. She had drawn the curtains and blinds thinking she could shut yesterday out along with the rising sun. She slept fitfully, the memory of the video taken on the Profile hike a punch to the gut. The girls and their stupid selfies, Tracey's stirring up a hornet's nest. She's terrified to turn on her phone. Jean-Paul had been kind enough to prepare a tray for her, but hiding in her room signaled defeat.

Her foot grazes against something, and she startles. A body. And then she remembers. Rosalie. Afraid to wake her, she remains still. It had taken Rosalie a while to fall asleep, and only when her breaths had smoothed into a steady rhythm did Penny attempt to sleep herself.

Last night, she caught Rosalie with her suitcase coming out of her room, thinking she could slip outside unnoticed. Something about the girl struck a chord in her—*someone else's child.*

"Where are you going?" Penny asked.

"I can't stay here." Penny was pretty sure she'd been crying. "I've ruined everything."

Her maternal instincts kicked in, and she managed to coerce Rosalie to come inside to talk. "It's late. Where do you think you're going at this hour?"

Rosalie didn't argue. The ease with which she dumped her bag and plopped on Penny's bed suggested she'd been looking for someone to mother her, and through the dim light, Penny noticed she was back in her dark T-shirt and jeans.

"What's going on?" Penny asked.

Rosalie folded her head in her hands. "I made a mistake, and I can't take it back. And it'll just be better if I leave. I'll go stay in a hotel or somewhere near the hospital."

Penny sat beside her on the bed. "You're not leaving. Do you want to tell me about it?"

"Not really, but I'm guessing you're not going to take no for an answer."

"I'm not."

Her backpack sat on the floor beside her suitcase, and Rosalie leaned over and pulled something out. She handed Penny a green notebook. "Open it."

She leafed through the papers one by one when something caught her eye. It was hard to miss. Jean-Paul's name in bold black letters.

She grabbed her glasses from the end table, certain she had misread.

"Rosalie."

"Penny."

"You know what this means."

"Yes. I just detonated Jean-Paul and Renée's marriage."

Penny was stunned, and she tried to keep it contained.

"I came here because of him. I didn't think it through. I wanted to meet him. I thought it was such a great plan." Her hands came up to her hair and clenched.

"Jean-Paul was Cassidy's one-night stand?"

"I can't think about that. It's gross. And Jean-Paul swears he didn't sleep with my mother, but I have this document that, well, kind of says he did. Now he's going to tell Renée, and everything is ruined, and it's all my fault." She buried her face in her palms and began to cry.

Jean-Paul? And Cassidy? Was it possible there was another Jean-Paul De La Rue? She scooted closer to Rosalie and wrapped an arm around her shoulder. She tried reassuring her everything would work out, but she wasn't convinced herself. A meteor was heading their way. First Henry's father made off with the De La Rues' savings, and now Renée was about to find out her husband has a daughter with another woman. What could she possibly say that would help?

"I should have never lied and gone on that stupid website. I'm an idiot."

"You're not an idiot. You've lost out on a lot. It made sense for you to go after what you needed."

"But I cheated. Just like him."

"It's a little premature for that, Rosalie." But the parallels were clear. "We are not our mistakes. We are not our parents' mistakes. Or our loved ones'."

"I should go," she said.

Penny didn't want to let Rosalie go. She wanted to hide her in her room and protect her from all that was about to blow. "We've all made mistakes, Rosalie."

"I'm sure you haven't."

"Oh, I've made some big ones."

She thinks about Ellie. And Tracey harassing Leo. Leo spilling everything. What it all meant.

"Sometimes mistakes change us in ways we'd never expect. I made a mistake once." Listening, Rosalie fell back on the bed. Penny didn't know where she was going with this, but she kept talking, desperately wanting to help, to fix what she couldn't before. "Don't pull away from the people you love, or want to love, out of fear. You deserve to be loved. Let's be patient and see how this unfolds. I bet you'll be surprised."

"As surprised as Renée?"

"Renée's an adult. And I'm sure there's an explanation of some kind." What that explanation was, Penny couldn't even begin to fathom.

"Can I say something without you thinking I'm the most awful person in the world?" Rosalie asked.

"You're not the most awful person in the world. There are several people with that honor. You're not one of them."

Rosalie smiled, and Penny's heart ticked in her chest. She wasn't ruined after all.

"I don't want Cassidy to die. I swear—"

"Of course you don't."

"But I'm mad at her. And it's confusing."

"Go on."

"You sound like Lucy."

"Moms are ad hoc therapists."

"That's the thing. I'm not sure how to say this . . . I've never felt that with Cassidy."

"Felt what?"

She stared at the ceiling when she replied. "It's always been the other way around. Cassidy's never felt like a mother to me."

Penny let it sink in, the burden Rosalie carried.

"And I think I'm angry. I *know* I'm angry." Her voice broke. "Like, why couldn't she be like the other mothers?" She rolled over on her side to face Penny. "Why couldn't she be like you? Or Lucy and Sienna?"

Penny took her time in answering. She didn't want to get this wrong. "Some people are just limited. That's all. It doesn't mean there's no love. It just means they're incapable of more." Penny inched closer. "It shouldn't be like this, and I understand being angry. You want a mother. And the one you have isn't there."

"She was never really there." It came out hushed.

Penny stroked her hair, wondering how that had to feel for a young girl. What it must feel like to need a grown-up, having to make decisions on her own. She couldn't imagine her daughters taking on such responsibilities. This explained a lot. Rosalie hiding herself away, assuming the role of parent.

"That had to be . . . has to be very difficult for you."

She buried her face in her hands again. "In some ways . . . I think . . . maybe it would be easier if . . ."

"Don't."

"It's true." She was talking to her palms, tears spilling through her fingers. "I've been prepared for this day. *She* prepared me. Do you know how many times I went to sleep wondering if she'd be there in the morning? And if she was, which Cassidy would I get? I told you I'm a horrible person. But it's how I feel. And I feel like if I don't say it . . . I don't know what'll happen."

Penny thought about calling Lucy in. She didn't want to make another mistake. She'd lived with her own long enough. She reminded herself she was a good mother, a good person. "Come here." She leaned closer, pulling Rosalie into her arms. She hugged her hard, as though she could give her the comfort she'd been denied. At first, Rosalie resisted, but then she slowly succumbed, her body falling into Penny's, letting somebody love her, take care of her.

The next thing Penny knew, Rosalie was asleep.

This morning, Penny watches Rosalie's breathing, aware how precious it is. There's a lot to sift through, but they'll figure it out. Before falling asleep herself, she'd stayed up, thinking about their talk. Thinking about the events over the last week. The girl had no idea what she'd given Penny last night. She'd given her courage.

Her cell phone rings, and she grabs it before it wakes up Rosalie. It's the hospital. Cassidy's awake. She's relieved to hear the news, and she hangs up as someone knocks on the door.

"I came to tell you the good news," Renée says.

And before Penny answers, Renée pokes her head through the doorway. "What's Rosalie doing here?"

CHAPTER 61

JEAN-PAUL

Jean-Paul sleepwalked through dinner, distracted and jumpy. Every so often, he stole a glance at Rosalie. *His supposed daughter, Rosalie. He has a daughter. Rosalie is his daughter.* He played with the phrase as though it would change the outcome. All night long he kept telling himself it was a mistake. One-night stand. *One-night stand.* The more he railed against it, the more he knew it was a pointless battle. He knew what he had done.

When they returned to their room, Renée asked him what was wrong. He stepped into his pajamas, avoiding her stare, telling her everything was fine. She believed him. Why wouldn't she? If she had pressed, he had an arsenal of responses, none of which were *I've betrayed you in the very worst possible way.*

She chattered on about Henry. About forgiveness. About Sienna and Lucy. All her notions about apologies and imperfect people worthy of a second chance would float right out the window when it came to his own secret. He hated knowing he was about to upend their lives, that something worse was closing in.

After an empty kiss, she quickly fell asleep. He watched her features soften, listening to the steadiness of her breath. He envied the ease with which she slipped away from him, and he wondered if she was already preparing herself.

The call from the hospital comes at dawn, and Renée is up and out the door to let the others know. He's already decided that when she returns, he'll tell her. There's no other way. He should have never made a decision like that without her.

"That was strange." She steps through the door, closing it behind her. "Rosalie slept in Penny's room last night. I guess this thing with her mother has her upset. Penny's going to take her to the hospital. Why don't we take a walk after breakfast?"

He's already lacing up his sneakers. "Why don't we take a walk now?"

They're strolling down the gravel driveway, the birds chirping, the morning dew dotting the foliage. She's in good spirits, better than he'd expected despite all that's transpired. She's a lot more forgiving than he is, and he's banking on that compassion to save them. He imagines this is what it's like when your life flashes before your eyes. He can't bear to disappoint her. The sinking feeling hits him like a brick, and his heart thumps wildly against his chest.

"Renée."

She's staring up at the cloudless, blue sky. "I love days like this."

He refuses to look up, focusing on the path in front of him.

"Can we switch the fondue for the crème brûlée tonight?" she asks.

"Renée. We need to talk."

"It's just a simple switch—"

"We need to talk about Rosalie."

"That girl. My heart breaks for her. Has she said anything else about her father?"

"We need to talk about Rosalie's notebook."

"The green one. What about it? She carries it with her everywhere, all her research on the inn."

"The research is about me."

"Why would she be researching you?" They're in front of the gazebo, and she stops. "Jean-Paul?"

His head drops.

She starts to say something, but freezes: "No."

He saves her the indignity. "I've never cheated on you."

She tilts her head as though she can't make out what he's saying.

He reaches for her hand, but she snatches it away. "Rosalie told you she found her father." She shakes her head, the information not processing. "I don't understand. You either slept with that woman or you didn't."

Every ounce of courage has dissolved. He tells himself maybe the data isn't accurate. There has to be an explanation better than the one he's about to give. One that won't hurt as much.

"I understand," he begins with a whisper. "What transpired this week . . . it's made you doubtful about fidelity, and I'd never jeopardize what we have . . ."

"But . . ."

"But. There's something you need to know." He can't bear the agony on her face. "I fucked up."

"Fucking up is sleeping with that woman."

"I didn't. I'd never."

She stares at the ground, anywhere but at him.

"When we couldn't get pregnant . . . when they told us . . . I was devastated . . . I did something . . ."

"Just say it, Jean-Paul."

"I donated to a sperm bank."

"You did what?" She gives him the courtesy of not having to repeat himself. "Why would you do that?"

He didn't know then, and he knows less so now. He was angry. Bitter. He wanted children, and she refused to adopt. Refused surrogacy.

But how could he tell her that? His head falls in his hands. "I don't know, Renée. I should have told you. We should have considered other ways to have a child together." He wasn't lying. "I felt helpless. And I had to do something that didn't make me feel so weak and small. There were other couples . . ."

"What were you thinking?" she asked, her tone bathed in the desperate need to understand.

"I don't know. I wasn't thinking, I was just young and stupid . . . thinking maybe I could give . . ."

She exhales, all the air and tranquility leaving her body. "You did this . . . you did this huge thing without telling me?"

"I meant to. I wanted to tell you. But you were so upset . . . they told us we couldn't have kids . . ."

"*I* couldn't have kids."

She turns her back to him, and he realizes what he's done.

"So your sperm somehow ended up . . ." She touches a hand to her forehead, her words laced in spite. "This is some one-night stand, Jean-Paul."

"How else could I be a DNA match with Rosalie?"

"Maybe it's a mistake. Another Jean-Paul De La Rue."

"It's possible. I don't know."

"Do you have any idea what this means? There can be more of you. Sons. Daughters. We have no idea how many are out there . . . who else will come out of the woodwork. Did you even think about this when you made the donation?"

He lowers his head again. "I didn't."

"How could you keep something like this from me?" The betrayal seeps through. "We aren't those people. We don't lie to each other . . . we don't keep secrets. What are we supposed to do now?"

He tries to maintain a semblance of calm, but he's already disappointed her too much. He knows that face. The one of regret, where her eyes cloud with longing and shame. He knew the ache she carried, unable to give them what they both desperately wanted.

A tear slides down her cheek. "I hate that Cassidy Banks shares something with you that I never can."

"Let's find out if Cassidy went through a registry." And then he moves closer, gazing down at her. "Renée, I know you're upset. I know this isn't how we intended things to happen . . . At the time, it was in the abstract. I never imagined someone finding me. I didn't realize when one of our past guests had us all sign up for that ancestry site a few years back . . . I didn't know what I was opening myself up to. I frankly forgot about it."

He watches the way her eyes follow him, the ache spreading wider.

"But we're here. And Rosalie . . . she's been . . . a delight. And I know how unfair this is to you, but . . . I think I'm a father . . . I'm Rosalie's father . . . and I know you're hurt, and I know I should have told you, but I need you. I don't know how to be a father without you."

CHAPTER 62

ROSALIE

A sound wakes her from a deep, peaceful sleep, and the dread returns when she remembers where she is. Penny's standing beside the bed tossing a sweatshirt over her head.

"I have good news!" she says. Unless she tells her she's just woken up from a bad dream, she doesn't want to hear it. "Your mom's awake. Get up and get ready. I'm taking you to the hospital."

Rosalie's conflicted. She feels relief skipping through her body, but another emotion looms nearby. She can't shake it, but she powers on as she's always done. It doesn't matter that she wears the same clothes as the night before. She bolts upright and grabs her sneakers with an urgency to move she can't yet understand.

When Rosalie exits the inn, Penny's waiting for her in the Mustang. The sky is bright, and she squints to avoid the glare. Penny hands her a muffin and tells her to eat, but she can't think about food at a time like this. She wonders if Jean-Paul told Renée. She wonders if they're fighting. She wonders if they're going to throw her out of the inn. Her worries clench her throat, preventing anything from going down. But she thanks Penny, this woman who is nothing but kind.

As they wind down the driveway, she spots Jean-Paul and Renée in the distance sitting on the wooden fence. The conversation looks serious. She can tell by their faces that Renée is sad; her hands hang by her sides. And Rosalie hates that it's most likely her fault.

~

Six days. That's all it's been, but she knew. She knew the minute she laid eyes on Jean-Paul that the report wasn't wrong. Could never be wrong. Jean-Paul was the father she had dreamed about: kind and easygoing, thoughtful and patient. The similarities were obvious. The eyes, the way they both loved to cook, the fact they were both lefties.

She only now understands what this news means for the De La Rues. If Cassidy had had a one-night stand, and Jean-Paul was her biological father as per the ancestry report, that could only mean one thing: Jean-Paul had cheated on Renée. This doesn't bode well for Rosalie finally having a father. Not when his wife, her potential stepmother, would have reason to resent her.

Penny parks the car, and Rosalie thanks her for the ride. "You don't need to come up. I won't be long."

"I'll wait downstairs."

Rosalie hops out of the car and skips toward the entrance. Passing through the sliding doors, she smiles at the front desk security and they wave her in.

Rosalie's heart clatters when she reaches her mother's door and Dr. Benck walks out.

"Rosalie." She smiles. "She'll be happy to see you."

"How is she?"

Dr. Benck extends a hand toward the open doorway. "I'll let her tell you herself."

She hesitates. "Does this mean . . . is she going to be okay?"

But Dr. Benck doesn't answer because Cassidy's voice carries through the hallway. "Rosie, baby. Come give me a hug."

It's her mother's voice, but Cassidy sounds awfully weak. Rosalie wants to ask Dr. Benck for reassurance, but the doctor's already gone, and Rosalie feels herself being drawn in by Cassidy's energy. That's what her mother did. A tiny woman with a mighty pull.

"Rosie." She says it again.

Rosalie sucks in her breath. "Hey, Mom."

She approaches, stopping short of the metal bed rail separating them.

"Come closer."

Rosalie takes another step.

Her mother looks pale, the skin beneath her eyes dark and sunken. The purple bruise on her forehead has faded to a smudged yellow.

"Rosie . . . baby. You look . . . pretty."

Cassidy's fingers reach through the guardrail, and Rosalie knows she should offer her hand, but there's a hesitance she can't combat. The anger at Cassidy that has simmered beneath the surface has swiftly reemerged. What's wrong with her? She should be happy to see Cassidy awake.

A nurse walks in and adjusts the IV bags on the pole next to her bed. Fluid flows down a tube into Cassidy's arm. The nurse makes some cheery remarks about Cassidy's being awake, what good news this is, and how pleased Rosalie must be, but Rosalie can't form a response. She manages a thin smile.

She isn't as grateful as a daughter pulled from the precipice of being orphaned should be. She's furious. At her mother's carelessness, her selfishness.

The nurse fusses with the guardrail until the metal latch slides down, and Cassidy pats the empty space for Rosalie to sit. Cassidy's restless. She impatiently waits for the nurse to leave, but Rosalie silently wills her to stay. Gone is the desperation she felt when she unloaded at her mother's bedside the day before.

"Can you . . . can you give us a few minutes?" Cassidy breathes to the nurse.

Their eyes follow the nurse out of the room, leaving a dense quiet that smothers Rosalie. She can't breathe, and now it makes sense. The anxiety. The constriction in her chest. The anger.

She starts to count, pinching the skin between her thumb and pointer finger.

Rosalie glances down at her mother, taking in her appearance. She's always been small, but today she's especially so. Her skin is pasty, her eyes ringed in red. Rosalie sits on the edge of the bed, imagining dashing out of the room. *What is that smell?* She doesn't bring it up; she doesn't want to upset Cassidy. No. What she wants to do is far worse than upset her. What she wants is to shake her, remind her what she put them through, what she put her through. She wants to scream at her, tell her how irresponsible she is for all of it: the pills, the dieting, the recklessness. But wasn't she always like this? Rosalie doesn't remember it any other way. Rosalie cleaning up Cassidy's messes. Rosalie cooking dinner for the two of them. Rosalie covering Cassidy with a blanket when she fell asleep on the sofa fully clothed after a day spent drinking.

This woman denied her a childhood.

Stop. Breathe. Count.

"I'm sorry, baby."

She's always sorry.

"I didn't mean to scare you . . . I guess I had too much to drink."

"You almost died."

"I'm here."

"You promised me you'd stop . . . you said . . ."

Cassidy whispers, "I'm sorry."

"You're sorry?" Rosalie raises her voice. "That's all you have to say?"

"I'm going to get help this time, I promise."

She wants to believe her, but how can she? Cassidy's disappointed her too many times.

"Do you remember anything?"

"I remember having a grand old time that night—"

"Here. Did you hear me talking to you?"

She stares blankly.

"I told you something."

"Rosie, baby, I was unconscious."

"Can you just focus for a minute?"

She clasps her hands together. "Focused."

"I found my father."

Cassidy's face twists; an eerie shadow clouds her eyes.

"They're pumping way too many drugs in me," she croaks. "I thought you just said you found your father."

"I did." She hesitates. "That's exactly what I said."

Cassidy sinks deeper into the bed. "Why would you do that?"

"Come on. Really?"

"How? How'd you find him?"

"It wasn't that hard. There's registries for these kinds of things."

"Wait." She shakes her head in disbelief. "You went on a site searching for your dad?" Then she does something Rosalie doesn't understand. She chuckles.

Rosalie's voice trembles. "I made a profile . . . had to make up some stuff . . . sign things that may ruin my chances of going to college, but I managed to find him. We're a 50.2 percent match."

Cassidy laughs again. "That's nothing."

Rosalie winces. It's ridiculous she has to explain these things. "There are two biological parents, so 50.2 is a pretty good percentage."

But she keeps laughing, a raspy laugh. "You went through all that trouble? I knew you were resourceful."

She drinks in the compliment.

"I could've made it easier for you." Cassidy sighs.

Rosalie barely registers her point. There has never been a time when she made things easier for her.

"You're old enough . . . I should have told you the truth a long time ago . . ."

"Oh God, Mom, I don't want to hear about your one-night stand with Jean-Paul."

Cassidy freezes. "What did you just say?"

"I don't want to hear about you and Jean-Paul."

Cassidy's face, already pale, drains of all color.

"I guess you two didn't recognize each other. Maybe that's what happens in those situations."

Cassidy reaches for Rosalie's hand. "You think Jean-Paul and I—"

"You don't have to cover for him. That would mean he cheated on Renée, which . . . gosh . . . that's terrible—"

"Oh goodness . . . Jean-Paul. That's impossible. Listen to me—"

"You listen to me. I have the report."

Cassidy shakes her head. "I know those inn people are nice and all, taking you under their wing, but that man is not your dad. I'd know it."

Rosalie deflates, all the joy exiting her body. A cruel disappointment takes its place.

"Besides, and no offense, but Jean-Paul's really not my type."

"You're gross."

Cassidy drops her head back on the pillow. She's drawing on strength when she speaks. "What I was trying to say before you cut me off is that it wasn't exactly a one-night stand—"

Rosalie feels a familiar annoyance bubbling within. "How can you stand yourself? Is anything you say the truth?"

"It's semantics, Rosalie Jae. It wasn't the kind of one-night stand you'd imagine."

"I never imagine those things."

"My egg and Addison Fitch's sperm, well, they had a rendez-vous . . . one day . . . one night . . . whatever you want to call it. Technically it was a one-night stand, but not the typical kind."

Rosalie is thoroughly convinced that the blow to her mother's head knocked something loose. "You're not making any sense. Who's Addison Fitch?"

"No. This is the one thing . . . the one single thing in my life I'm not confused about. I wanted you. Desperately. And when I hit a certain age, I thought, if I could do this, make one positive decision, it would be to have you."

Rosalie watches her mother carefully, waiting for the other shoe to drop.

"For someone so gifted, do I have to spell it out for you, Rosie?" her mother whispers. "I went to a clinic, sweet girl. A place where they provide sperm."

Rosalie can't believe what she's hearing. There was no one-night stand. Her mother had lied. Again.

"Biogenics. They do these things. I looked through a catalog. It was like shopping for the perfect donor. I chose everything from his hair color to his eyes, his height and his weight. I saw baby pictures! He had to be the man I'd always wished for myself. And he had to have a certain pedigree, the right gene pool. They don't provide names, but now that you're older, I've always thought of him as Addison Fitch. You know, like the guy in the book you love so much. *To Kill a Songbird.*"

"It's *To Kill a Mockingbird.* And it's Atticus Finch. His name is Atticus Finch."

"Whatever." Cassidy waves a hand in the air. "I knew back then I wanted a man of understanding and empathy. Surprising, even for me, I suppose. I picked him out. He checked every box."

The wheels in Rosalie's brain begin to spin. And the fact that Cassidy doesn't see it is alarming. "Jean-Paul must have donated, right? If he's a match, he must be in the registry?"

"Please." Cassidy waves a hand in the air. "I saw a picture of the man as an adult. He was *not* Jean-Paul."

"But the report—"

"How long have I been telling you that you can't trust technology?" She raises a hand to her chin, lingering on the hair Rosalie forgot to cut. "This is why you chose this awful place."

And before she has time to respond, the nurse returns to announce that visiting hours are over.

"Despite what you think, I wanted you, Rosalie. You."

Which is funny, because in hearing her describe Addison Fitch, it sounded like she'd wanted him.

~

Rosalie's back in Penny's car, and she's peppering her with questions, but Rosalie doesn't hear. She has her own questions swirling and most lack answers. Cassidy saw a picture. It wasn't Jean-Paul. Rosalie doesn't want to admit she was wrong, that the Ancestry site was wrong, and she feels the loss creep inside. She has found her father only to lose him.

"Rosalie?"

"I'm sorry. It's just . . ."

"I know. It's difficult to see your mother like that."

"It's not that."

"What is it?"

She wishes she could tell her, but she's too upset.

Penny maneuvers the steering wheel with both hands. "Whatever it is, I'm here."

She knows that. But instead, she stares out the window, already missing the holidays she'll never have with her father.

CHAPTER 63

SIENNA

Simone places a tray of warm paninis on the table—turkey and brie, roast beef and horseradish. Sienna grabs the turkey, and the first bite explodes with the rich flavor of goat cheese and avocado. She hadn't realized how hungry she was. They're gathered in the kitchen—she, Lucy, Henry, and Leo—after a lazy morning flipping through magazines and playing mindless board games.

"Does anyone want to go to Grandfather Winery?" Leo asks.

"We were thinking about a movie in Boone," Lucy suggests.

They're quiet, and Sienna, setting aside the disbelief that her marriage is over, muses about sitting around a table with Leo Shay making coffee and plans like it's completely normal. The more she's gotten to know him, the more she's rooting for Penny and him. *It was just a kiss.* She is well versed on that subject. But unlike Adam, Leo just might be capable of love.

Tomorrow is their last day, and knowing that spreads melancholy through the room. She always felt this way after a week at the inn. It's like when sleepaway camp comes to an end, and you have to tuck the memories away and step back into regular life. But the thing is, you're changed. Everything looks different.

"Has anyone seen Renée and Jean-Paul?" Henry asks.

"They went for a walk," Simone says.

They look around the table, meeting each other's eyes.

Leo asks Sienna how she's doing.

"I'm okay."

"You seem okay."

"Is it that obvious?"

"You just seem happy."

"There's some sadness, but mostly for the kids. You know when you make a decision, and you know it's the right one? It's just easier."

"Like when you dropped advanced calculus in college and slummed with me in regular calc?" Lucy says.

They laugh, holding on to how far they've come.

"You could have told us about your father," Sienna says to Henry. "Why do we keep secrets from the people we're closest to?"

Lucy twirls the spoon in her coffee. "I have this idea that we think everyone else's life is better than ours. To admit to any shortcomings or problems drives the point home."

"Seems as though relationships would be a lot less complicated if we were honest and transparent," Sienna says.

Lucy disagrees. "I think there are some things that should be kept between two people. It doesn't mean you value a friend any less. Privacy's important in a marriage."

Leo and Henry are deep in a discussion about the four kids found alive near the Amazon after surviving a plane crash. Lucy and Sienna pull their chairs closer together and lower their voices. "Have you two worked things out?" Sienna asks.

"Me and Henry. Henry and me. I think we took the first step toward fixing things. We admitted we're not good at this living-without-each-other thing." Lucy takes a bite of her panini. "But Henry needs to make peace with this thing with his father. He's carrying around a lot of feelings and—"

"Shame," Sienna says.

"Shame," she repeats. "First families dictate a lot of our relationship patterns. He has to fix that one first."

"You're a wise woman."

Lucy reminds Sienna that she swapped spit with her husband. "That wasn't wise. That whole self-sabotaging thing . . . it wasn't my best moment . . . but it's like those stars Henry talks about all the time. How they arrange themselves . . . not in the best position, but in the one that makes the most sense at the time. If this thing with his dad hadn't happened, he wouldn't have shut me out, and I wouldn't have spiraled, and we wouldn't be here." She reaches for Sienna's hand. "Thank you for understanding. For seeing the whole picture and not judging me for one foolish mistake."

Sienna thinks about this. "You don't have to tell me about self-sabotage. It was an Olympic sport for me. I understand how we got here."

They exchange smiles, and it lightens the mood. Sienna promises herself she'll hold on to the good.

Simone approaches with a tray of lemon water and an array of fresh fruit cut into intricate shapes.

"Any word from Rosalie?" Lucy asks.

"She's awake. Penny and Rosalie should be back soon."

"Amazing," she and Lucy say in unison.

They hear Jean-Paul's and Renée's voices come through the front door, but then the sounds quickly disappear.

"What do you think's up with those two?"

CHAPTER 64

JEAN-PAUL

The extraordinary week has turned into an extraordinary challenge.

Jean-Paul and Renée aren't typically the ones to have the drama, but it's found them, and Jean-Paul's having a difficult time juggling. Renée's expression as they walk back to the house breaks his heart, but he knows his wife. She needs facts. They skip checking on the group and head for their office.

"Do you remember the password to your Ancestry account?"

He shrugs. "I haven't been on there in a while. I sent a sample of some sort, if I recall. They ended up sending an inordinate number of emails . . . I deleted the app."

She thinks about this. "You didn't cancel the account?"

"I deleted it. Isn't that the same thing?"

"We need to log in to your account." She hesitates. "Maybe it's a different Jean-Paul De La Rue. Let's see if you got the same email."

He doesn't argue.

He doesn't question.

Things always go smoother when she is in charge.

He reaches for his phone and nervously taps the screen. "I registered with an old email address. I don't remember the password."

They're quiet, the sunlight casting a shadow against the wall. His fingers shake as he resets his password and logs in.

Her eyes drop to the phone when a symphony of notifications clutters the screen.

"There was no way for anyone to reach you," she says.

"Who would want to reach me?"

"There. Click over there."

He clicks on the link that says he's matched with someone on the site.

It's her name.

Rosalie Banks.

Renée's face falls. "She would want to reach you."

He doesn't know what to say. She scrolls through the notifications, looking for more surprises.

"I'm so sorry, Renée."

"I'm the one who's sorry," she says. "I couldn't give you what you wanted."

"Don't say that. You've given me everything I've ever wanted."

There's a deep-seated sadness between them.

"Renée? Please talk to me."

She rubs at her eyes. "You just gave birth to a fifteen-year-old. I need a minute to catch up." And when she looks up at him, he sees something in her eyes he doesn't yet understand.

"What is it?" he asks.

"I don't know." She pauses. "I'm confused. And mad. And I'm terrified."

"I'll deactivate the account. I should have done that a long time ago. I didn't intend to be a dad. I just—"

"What?"

"I wanted some control back. I wanted . . . I don't know. I wanted to help someone."

She reaches up and touches his face. He presses his cheek into her palm.

"I was stubborn," she begins. "I refused a surrogate. And adoption. I left you with no other choice."

He shakes his head. "Don't do this. This is on me. I should've told you."

"Jean-Paul."

He braces himself for the fallout.

"It would be so easy to hate you right now. But I know you too well. I know that big heart of yours."

The noises from the table reach their ears.

"We have to go out there. I'm not sure how to do it," she says.

He places his hands on her shoulders; she looks ready to cry. "We're going to go out there and do what we've always done, because you're the strongest woman I know, and I'm going to be right there beside you."

CHAPTER 65

ROSALIE

The car winds up the driveway, and she jumps out before Penny has a chance to cut off the engine. Tears blur her eyes, and she tries to make it through the door without breaking down. She sees them in the kitchen. Jean-Paul. Renée. Lucy. Henry. Leo. And they see her, calling out for her to join them. She wants to run upstairs and bury her head in her pillow. She wants to run another ancestry test and find her father, even though she hasn't fully mourned the loss of this one. She was so certain Jean-Paul was her dad. Certain that they shared more than DNA. The realization that she was wrong devastates her.

She tries sneaking up the back stairwell, but Lucy and Sienna head her way, bombarding her with questions.

She brushes them off with excuses that she's tired, but then Penny walks in, and the three of them whisper something Rosalie can't hear. Her head throbs, and somehow she finds herself following them into the kitchen. She's greeted by Renée, who's pouring wine even though it's the middle of the day. Jean-Paul doesn't notice she's there. And that's the way it's been all her life. Fighting to be noticed. Seen.

She counts. That's the one thing she can control. Her lips quiver, and she's sure everyone's staring at her like she's come undone. Because she has. And as though she's on autopilot, the words tumble out of her mouth. They're talking around her, but one by one they stop. They've finally noticed her.

"I came here for a reason," she begins. "This was my year to choose our vacation destination, and I chose this place because . . ." Her eyes dart around the room. "Because there was someone I needed to meet."

Penny sidles up to her, but Rosalie shoos her away.

She clears her throat. The more she says, the stronger she sounds. "There was a test. I took it. And Jean-Paul was the answer. His DNA matched mine."

Their jaws drop in shock. She sees the way they shift in their seats.

"Rosalie." Jean-Paul stops whatever it is he's doing.

"He welcomed me in without knowing our connection. He was the first person who saw me for me. He was patient . . . and kind . . . and I know what you're thinking. Cassidy had a one-night stand, and I guess I didn't think it through. I didn't think about the innocent people involved." She catches Renée's eyes in hers.

Jean-Paul takes a few steps her way.

"Stop!" Her hand comes up. "You don't have to do this. You're not my father. Cassidy told me she went through some registry. Biogenics. She picked my father out from a bunch of donors . . ." Her voice cracks, and she's crying when she says the rest. "She had a picture of him. She named him Addison Fitch because she knew I loved the book. Atticus Finch. Whatever. It wasn't Jean-Paul." She catches his eyes. "He wasn't you.

"I'm sorry I dragged you into this, Jean-Paul." She pauses to look at Renée. "And I'm sorry for"—she doesn't know how to put it—"any hurt this caused." She wipes her cheek with her palm. "The registry says there's a one percent chance for error. I guess we were that one percent.

"But more than anything, I'm sad you're not my family, because you were the kind I dreamed of having."

Nobody moves. She's not an idiot. She just blew the roof off the house. But she's not sorry. Better to see the moon and the stars than this.

"I'm sorry, Jean-Paul."

He's leaning against the stove; his fingers rub his beard. She doesn't know what she expects from him, but what she never anticipated was Renée's walking toward her. She sets her wine on the table and curls Rosalie in her arms, stroking her hair. It comes out a whisper, but she hears it as clear as the sky: "You are Jean-Paul's daughter."

The way Renée says it makes Rosalie cry harder. "You're kind," Rosalie says. "You've always been kind to me, but you don't have to say those things."

Renée says it again, this time a little more forcefully.

"Jean-Paul." Renée waves him over.

Rosalie steps back. Her eyes shift from Renée to Jean-Paul.

Jean-Paul stops to grab something. It's a folder. He reaches her side and opens it. He pulls out his baby picture. And another of him around thirty. A thinner, beard-free Jean-Paul, named in accompanying documents as Biogenics donor #051738.

It takes half a second for it to compute.

She stammers, "I—I emailed you—"

He must realize that they're doing this very publicly, and he suggests they take it to another room, but she shakes her head, searching their faces, liking what she sees, feeling their support.

"I didn't get your email because it went to an account I don't use, and I had deleted the app. But"—he turns to Renée—"we logged in. Your email was there. Your mother chose me to be your father."

Someone's crying. She hears sniffling. Someone hands someone a napkin.

Rosalie's too afraid to believe what she hears. She's too afraid to trust the man with the eyes that so resemble hers, but she can't quiet her heart or the way it feels something big in his presence.

"I'm your father," he says, stepping closer. "You're 50.2 percent of me."

Her lip trembles. "Is this a joke?"

"I'd never joke about something like this."

"Wait," Lucy says. "He's the one-night stand?"

Rosalie laughs. "Sperm donor one-night stand."

"No way!" The group gathers around them; everyone has something important to say. They're cheerful and smiling.

Simone hugs her the hardest. "We're cousins!" And then she hands someone her camera for a picture.

"How did this happen?" Lucy asks.

"It's a long, complicated story," Rosalie says.

Penny assures her that's part of having a family.

Somebody claps, and they're hugging her, congratulating, crying. Rosalie can't help but think she's gained a lot more than a father.

Henry says it's the most beautiful meteor shower he's ever seen.

CHAPTER 66

HENRY

He wasn't wrong. He'd seen the sky show off before, but never like what he witnessed earlier in the kitchen. Jean-Paul and Rosalie. He didn't see that coming. With most shooting stars, you don't. Renée handled it beautifully, and he told her so, pulling her aside before they left for their rooms.

"We can't hold on to the things we can't control, Henry," she said. "We can only find the lesson and a way to move on."

Witnessing Rosalie find her father struck a chord in him. As much as he hated to admit it, it was there. Deep inside the piles of rage, there was longing. It was becoming harder and harder to deny it.

It's six o'clock, and they're gathered at the table. No one comes out and says it, but it's a celebration. Rosalie is front and center, beaming. The news about her mother is positive. They're cautiously optimistic Cassidy will make a full recovery, and there's relief on Rosalie's face when she assists Jean-Paul at the cooktop. They have a synergy, humming as they slice lemons, chop garlic. He offers directions, and she follows with ease. Brushing the chicken with flavorful seasoning, adding cream to the mussels. Sienna picks up one of the edible flowers and tucks it behind Rosalie's ear. Her face is clean of makeup. The girl has never looked happier.

"I bet you were an amazing lawyer," Rosalie says.

Sienna nods. "I was pretty good."

"Do you think you'll ever go back?"

Sienna shifts in her seat. "Maybe. Right now, I have to focus on the girls."

Lucy leans over to Henry. "I'm going to take the rest of the summer off. We need to spend more time together. We have a lot of catching up to do. As a family."

He likes what she's getting at.

Leo's spotted some conversation cards on a shelf, and he passes a few around as the first course arrives. They used to play a game like this at dinner parties in Buckhead, cards with thought-provoking questions. *What one thing would you like to know about the future? If you could change your name, what would it be?* The game was a great conversation starter, a clever way to get to know someone, and they'd had their share of laughs amid some soul-crushing conversations. But didn't they already know enough about each other?

And then Henry's phone rings.

Michael Wall's name lights up the screen, and like a reflex, he taps "Decline." Soon afterward, a text appears. You can't ignore me forever.

He types back: Yes, I can.

"What is it?" Lucy leans toward him, popping a mussel into her mouth.

Another text comes through. I'm at your door.

The irony. He laughs.

"What?" she asks again.

"My dad's at our door."

She presses a napkin against her pink lips. "He's at the house?"

He opens the Ring app and shows the screen to her. "It appears that way."

"He's really trying."

"He'll figure it out soon enough."

"He went all the way to Atlanta?" Sienna asks, but he's watching Jean-Paul and Renée for a reaction.

He doesn't care if Michael Wall sits there all night. He hopes it's muggy hot, and he hopes the termites from the infestation they haven't yet gotten under control are swarming around his ears. "Okay, I'll start," he says, reading one of the cards. "Have you ever lied about your age?"

Rosalie's hand shoots up. "Me!"

"I've been twenty-nine for six years," Sienna says, pulling a card from the pile. "Who in the room has a tattoo?"

Leo, Penny, and Sienna raise their hands and roll up sleeves and pants to show off their various emblems. Sienna has a tiny butterfly on her ankle. Leo has his kids' names on the inside of his wrist. Penny's tattoo matches Leo's.

"New Orleans," Penny says while she stares at her wrist and then her husband.

"That was a good trip," he replies.

Lucy picks the next card. "What song would you sing at karaoke?"

"We need a karaoke machine here, Jean-Paul and Renée!" Sienna calls out.

"'Cat's in the Cradle,'" Henry says. Lucy rolls her eyes at the song about an estranged father and son.

"'Dancing Queen,'" Sienna says.

"'Wonderwall,'" Leo says.

"I can't think of one," Penny says. "Maybe 'Shake It Off'?"

∼

When it's Penny's turn, she draws a card and reads, "'Is there only one soulmate for every person?'"

The table quiets.

"Can I pick another question?" She doesn't wait for an answer, flipping through the stack and selecting another. "This is just not my night. 'What mistake is most unforgivable?'"

"Yeah," Leo says. "Next."

"'What was the best TV commercial of all time?'" Penny quickly answers, "Mean Joe Greene's Coca-Cola ad."

Sienna says, "Who watches commercials anymore?"

Another text lands on Henry's screen.

I'll bang until I knock the whole house down, Henry. You can't hide from me forever.

Henry's watching the camera from his phone; Michael Wall presses his doorbell. Henry steps out of the kitchen, crafting a text in his mind. His dad appears smaller, but maybe it's the video quality. He looks closer. No. He's definitely slighter. Fragile. Weak.

Please, he writes again. You're my son.

And Henry flashes to Jean-Paul telling Rosalie he's her dad. The look that said he loved her. Already. And his father continues: I've lost everything. I won't lose you too. The phone rings again. This time, Henry picks up.

"Henry." His father's voice is rough, no longer warm and smooth— no longer the man who used to read him to sleep. "I just need you to hear me out—"

"How did you find them?" Henry stops him. "Renée and Jean-Paul De La Rue?"

Silence. And then: "You talked about that place a lot."

"They're good, hardworking people. They didn't deserve this."

His father doesn't answer.

"They think I gave you their names."

"I'm so sorry."

His father's standing on Henry's front porch, holding the phone to his ear. Henry stares as the sight of his thin frame pulls him back through time. He wishes he could stop it. But he can't. He's felt only half-alive without him. Seeing him makes him feel almost whole again.

"Beans." That's the endearing name Michael gave him. Henry Beans. He feels himself falling under his spell.

"That's not going to fix this, Dad."

"I know. But I won't give up trying. You don't give up on the people you love."

"You should have thought of that before you destroyed us."

"Listen to me. I wasn't the mastermind behind Bluebird—"

"Please don't. Please don't try to rewrite history. We all know how you bilked innocent people out of their life savings . . . their livelihood. How can you live with yourself?"

"I know that's what you've heard, and what you believe, but I'm telling you that I was duped also."

This gets Henry's attention.

"I was lied to. And to make a long, excruciatingly painful and embarrassing story short, I've turned state's evidence against the partners."

"Why should I believe you?"

"Because I'm your father. And you know me better than anyone."

"I thought I knew you."

"Why do you think they let me out early? It's going to come out soon. Some *Vanity Fair* article. *Dateline* special. Pick. I made mistakes. I turned a blind eye when I shouldn't have, and I put my faith in someone who didn't deserve it."

"People killed themselves. Because of you."

Henry sees the slackening of his father's shoulders when he says this. His head drops. "I know. And I will forever live with that. But I need you to understand. I need you to hear me out."

Henry stares down at his shoes. "I can't. You've given me no choice."

"There's always a choice. Family protects each other."

"Who was protecting Mom and me?"

His father raises his voice, and Henry spots his fist in the air. "I went to prison, Henry. I never gave up on you and Mom. How can you do this?"

He doesn't feel bad for what he says next: "A lot of people want you to answer that same question. I don't think you understand the extent to which you hurt people or how humiliating it's been for me. I can never go back to Charleston."

His father faces the door, and Henry's glad he can't see his eyes. "I swear to you, I had no way of knowing."

Henry considers this. Considers his father. He's a bright man. He had to have known. Right? But was he really a master fraudster? Henry can't be sure. Now he has a criminal record, a mark stuck to him for the rest of his life. People despise him. He wouldn't be surprised if the death threats come back. And yet, Henry sees him, and he sees his childhood. He sees them tossing a football in the backyard, Michael teaching him to tie a tie. Reflexively, he reaches for his neck. His father. His best friend and confidant. The man who openly cried when Henry walked down the aisle to marry Lucy.

God, he misses him.

God, he hates him.

"I'm sorry, Henry."

All of them have experienced betrayal. Leo and Penny. Lucy and Henry. Even Rosalie and Cassidy. All flawed people trying to sift through the messes and find the parts to love.

Henry has to get back to the table. He's said what he needed to say. "Go home, Dad."

He closes the Ring app and imagines his dad walking toward his car when he speaks. "I made a mistake, Henry. I used poor judgment. But I'm not a bad person. If I could go back and change all of it . . . I would. You have to believe me."

He doesn't have his telescope, but he doesn't need it, because suddenly everything becomes clear. They have all made mistakes, poor decisions that lacked good judgment. The choices weren't made in a vacuum. There were variables and circumstances—much like in the sky and the constellations—that made events happen. Some resulted in explosions, others resulted in falling stars. He realizes that people aren't always bad, but some decisions are.

The father he knew was sensible and kind.

The father he knew had loved him fiercely and protectively.

He will find a way to hold on to that man.

This isn't entirely about forgiveness. It's about understanding that sometimes the stars align, and sometimes they fly off course and learn to coexist.

"Bye, Dad," he finally says.

CHAPTER 67

PENNY

"'What's your best excuse when you're pulled over for speeding?'"

They all shout, "Diarrhea!"

Leo says, "My wife's having a baby."

She remembers the day Leo got a police escort to the hospital for the birth of their third child.

"'What don't women want?'" Sienna reads aloud. "Where do we start, ladies?"

They're elbow to elbow, picking cards and laughing at the answers. They're spilling stories about life and relationships and kids.

"Our oldest tried to make waffles for his brother by pouring the dry mix directly onto the griddle," Lucy says.

"I was at a friend's house and helped myself to a bowl of grapes on the table. They were plastic!" Penny says.

They're laughing so hard, she's sure wine shoots from their noses. Her belly hurts from the memory. It feels good, but then her and Leo's phones ping simultaneously. They pick them up at the same time. A text from his publicist with a link.

Have you lost your mind? it reads.

She's surprised it took this long. She had just begun to wriggle away from the awful memory, praying those girls wouldn't be so foolish as to post photos from the Profile hike. She was wrong. This is TMZ gold.

She slams her phone down on the table, but she can hear the girls' voices from the video streaming from Leo's phone. Henry passes Leo on the way to his seat beside Lucy, and the room quiets as Tracey's voice booms through the speaker: "You are everything that's wrong with men today."

"Is that you, Leo?" Henry asks, leaning in for a better look.

Curiosity is piqued. The others get up from their chairs and stand over Leo.

Penny's trying to avoid Leo's eyes. Leo's not watching the film. He's watching her.

"You and Penny . . . you were everything we wanted. Everything we dreamed about as little girls. And not just because you're Leo Fucking Shay. We idolized you two. We watched you hold doors for Penny. Piggyback your daughter through the Oscars. You were macho, but you were sensitive and sexy and unflinchingly loyal. You made us believe that happily ever after just might exist."

The first time Tracey said it, she looked tearful. Now, with Tracey's careful editing, Penny is the one who feels like crying.

Tracey added music to the scene—Morgan Fucking Wallen—and the camera shines on Leo's handsome face. "I love Penny. I still love Penny."

Penny feels the table eyeballing her, studying her for a reaction.

"If you love her, Leo, you need to prove it."

"Please shut it off," Penny says.

But he won't. The video has the appeal of Taylor Swift's "All Too Well," except she knows this won't end all that well.

And the video rolls on. Leo losing his temper. Leo divulging to these strangers, and now the world, what happened that day in August. How much they lost and how they couldn't come back from it. She feels their eyes on her, on him. What will this do to Alara and Buckley?

"Please, Leo."

They're at the part when Penny broke free and headed down the mountain. She should get up from the table and go, but where? A part of her wants to know the end, a different end from the one they have. And that's when Leo finally presses pause.

Lucy is the first to say something. "I am so terribly sorry."

Sienna wipes her eyes. "That's the saddest thing I've ever heard. I am so sorry you had to go through that."

Henry takes a swig of wine.

"I told you this would happen," Penny says. "You gave those vultures everything they wanted."

Then he stands up.

"Penny."

"Leo, don't."

"Penny," he says, talking over her. "I did it for us. I did it for you."

"You think this is going to help us? Spilling our private life in the news for anyone to dissect and distort? How is this going to help Alara and Buckley? Or the kids?"

"They asked me to prove myself. They attacked you. I won't let them do that anymore. We've spent so much time protecting our privacy and keeping things secret that we succeeded in burying our very real feelings. We cut ourselves off from each other."

"Not now, Leo." Her heart beats wildly.

"Now, Penny."

He looks around the table. "We rented a house in Palm Springs with our best friends from high school. Normal people not in the business. Buckley was out golfing. Alara was with us at the pool, watching the kids." He pauses; it's not an easy story to share. "The kids were all good swimmers . . ."

"You don't have to do this," Penny says.

"I do."

"You don't have to share every detail. Some things can be ours."

"You're right, but I think we need to talk about it. Me and you. Because if we don't, we'll never find a way back to each other. I think you want that, and I do too." He keeps going. "The kids had been in the pool the whole day. Penny said she'd go inside for more drinks and snacks. I told her I'd help. I followed her inside. She looked so beautiful, my wife." He stops. Unable to say more.

Penny's back in the moment, back in the torment of that day. They didn't have sex, but they'd wanted to. He came up to her and pressed her against the wall. His thumb traced her lip, and they molded into one, he shirtless, she in a bikini. And he kissed her as though it had been months, and it almost had been. He'd been on a shoot, and she'd lost track. She felt his entire body against hers, and they got carried away. But she also told him to stop. She told him six kids were too many for Alara to watch. She told him they had a job to do, but he kissed her harder and reached for her nipple under the thin fabric. She let out a soft moan, but she managed to wriggle away.

"I kissed my wife." His voice breaks up the memory. "I wanted her. I loved her. And I kissed her longer than I should have. By the time we got the drinks and snacks and made our way outside . . ."

Nobody speaks.

"If we'd been there . . . if there had been more eyes . . . maybe . . ."

The memory of that day and all it signified broke them. Their marriage. Their kids. Their lifelong friendship with Buckley and Alara.

"We gave Ellie CPR, but it was too late. She got stuck under the float. No one saw. When we got to her, there was nothing more we could do." Leo is full-on crying, tears streaming down his cheeks. "Do you know how many times I've gone over it in my head? Do you know how many times I wondered what would have happened if Penny had gone in there alone? If I hadn't followed her? If I hadn't touched her?"

The anguish in his face is tough to watch. It's no wonder they tried to banish the memory.

"We lost more than Ellie that day. We lost our best friends too. They didn't say it, but they wanted to know why it had to happen to their kid and not ours. Alara had to be hospitalized for months from the grief. We only heard from them once. In the days that followed, they begged us to keep it private, begged us to protect their children. And we did." His bloodshot eyes look up. "But we took it too far. We shut each other out.

"Penny eventually moved back to Miami. We were hardly talking. Our desire . . . our passion . . . everything was tied to grief and mourning. And mistakes. I couldn't touch my wife. I couldn't hold her. That day at the café with Claire, I was having problems connecting on-screen, and somehow the incident got brought up. She took my hand under the table to console me. I was falling apart. The pain and guilt and grief were eating me alive. And she kissed me. It was unexpected, and it took me a second to process what she was doing, but I turned my head. It just wasn't fast enough. The pictures spoke a thousand words. And sometimes they get it right, but in this case, they got it wrong."

Seeing Leo with Claire confirmed what Penny already knew. They'd made a mistake, and the hatred she felt for herself turned on him. By then they were too far apart to find their way back.

"Leo. Penny." It's Lucy. "What you've been through, and what your friends have been through, is every parent's nightmare." She waits to see if they're okay with her continuing, and when neither of them protests, she says, "I know this is going to be hard to hear: you've spent a lot of time blaming yourselves, but this wasn't your fault."

His eyes narrow in on Lucy.

"What if we hadn't—"

"What-if thinking is a useless spiral. Your love didn't cause this. That kiss didn't cause this. Imagine how Alara must feel. The grief she carries. I bet the raft was big. Her daughter was a good swimmer. There were others in the pool at the time—"

"They weren't responsible for Ellie," Penny interrupts.

"Sometimes in life, things happen that we will never, ever understand. Losing a child is one of those things. It's incomprehensible. And blame and regret won't help you heal. It will tear you apart and keep you from ever finding peace again. You two probably single-handedly saved Cassidy."

Penny sighs. "It's brought it all back."

They've returned to their seats, and the mood becomes somber.

"I'm sorry. We wish you didn't have to go through this. We're sorry for your friends. You never get over that kind of loss," Lucy says.

Jean-Paul and Renée plate the crème brûlée, but no one seems to have an appetite. Penny's phone pings; so does Leo's. Everyone wants to know what happened. Everyone wants a peek behind the curtain. TMZ picked it up. E! News. *The New York Post.* Notifications pile up on their phones, and even though they're not mentioned by name, she waits for the video to reach Alara and Buckley.

"Penny," Rosalie says, "I'm not sure this is going to help, but when I needed you, you were there. You saved me the other night. I felt like somebody cared. You did that for me. Maybe you don't remember, but I do."

"Give some of that love to Leo," Renée says, joining in. "We've all seen how he looks at you. How he loves you." She stops and motions to Henry. "I know you call Sienna 'Sirius,' but Penny is the sun." She finds Penny's eyes again. "You have every right to shine."

Now Penny's sobbing, and Rosalie comes over and offers a hug. Penny takes her in, lets her in close.

"I didn't mean to ruin the night by bringing this up," Leo says. "I just needed to share this part of us." He looks at Penny when he finishes. "Because it's true. None of us at this table is exactly who we seem or expect—"

"Except Adam," Sienna jokes.

"There's more to the video," Leo adds.

"It doesn't matter," Henry says. "You got what you needed from it."

317

But Leo is Leo, and he presses play, and Tracey comes back on the screen.

"If there was something you could say to bring Penny back, would you say it?"

Penny's confused. This she hadn't heard.

He turns the screen toward her. "I love you, Penny Silverman Shay. I never stopped. And I'm sorry we let grief and guilt pull us apart, because I hate living life without you."

He turns to her and shuts off his phone. "Pen, if we can just get this piece right, I think we can fix this."

This isn't a line from a movie. This is Leo. Her Leo.

They watch her, waiting for her response.

She closes her eyes, and this time she doesn't see little Ellie's face or her tiny lifeless body; she sees Leo. Leo and her picking blueberries in Malibu. Leo walking the girls to school with three pink backpacks slung on his shoulder. Leo and her rehearsing lines together, laughing until their bellies ache.

She doesn't know how they'll do it, but she knows she wants to try. And she doesn't make her way over to him, but she nods. At first it's tentative, but then it's absolute. A singular gesture that means she's in. And she catches his two-tone eyes and gives him a thumbs-up. She doesn't imagine it. There's a collective sigh. "Okay, I need more wine," she says.

"Drinks are on me tonight," he says with a smile.

SATURDAY

Day 7

~~First Course: Oysters Rockefeller~~

~~Second Course: Hearts of palm, lemon, truffle vinaigrette~~

~~Main Course: Filet of beef, scalloped potatoes, brussels sprouts~~

~~Dessert: Wild blueberry cobbler~~

~~Champagne Billecart-Salmon Brut rosé champagne~~

~~Château Lynch-Bages Pauillac~~

Your presence is requested on the south lawn at 4:00 p.m. for a surprise celebration.

CHAPTER 68

JEAN-PAUL

Glitter. Again.

He's sweeping little pink and purple stars into colorful piles. After he and Renée slipped away, they could hear the group late into the morning hours. They'd gone to bed drunk on wine, giggly on gossip. It had moved him to watch Leo express himself as he had. To see the pair face their demons.

When guests came and went, they left pieces of themselves in the porous marble or in the cracks in the hardwood floors. Cassidy had left them with something they couldn't quantify, something he and Renée were still wading through. But watching his daughter—*his daughter*, he likes repeating to himself—come out of her shell to comfort Penny has made it clear that this particular group of guests has formed an inexplicable bond. An *extraordinary* bond.

He reaches for the dustpan and sweeps the memories into the metal. The inn has provided so much. All the revelations, secrets, and truths circling like stars. The choices made, the doors that swung open. He knows these experiences should grant him the grace to let Vis Ta Vie go. They have compiled enough moments for a lifetime, and now they have Rosalie.

Before he and Renée had drifted to sleep, they talked late into the night. He could sense her lingering doubt. She vacillated, wanting to fight and scold him for deceiving her before changing her mind. Jean-Paul wasn't a fighter. He let her argue, and when she broke down and cried, he pulled her toward him, and she let him squeeze away the pain.

There were many unanswered questions. And maybe that was the crux of life. Sometimes there weren't any answers, and you just had to figure out a way to move forward. He wondered what she was thinking as she lay beside him. Was she imagining what their lives might have been like had they had a child back then? Maybe. But this was the path they were meant to take. Rosalie was meant to be theirs when they were ready for her.

Jean-Paul made it crystal clear, as clear as Rosalie's eyes, that he wanted to be a part of his daughter's life. Needed her to be a part of their life. He called it a privilege. As the conversation deepened, Renée's upset waned.

"I'm sorry," he said. "I don't expect you to forgive me . . . but . . . is it possible I already love her?"

And the last lock slid open. "I think I just might love her too," Renée said.

And even though they knew what they had to do, they weren't entirely certain until they woke up in each other's arms. She lay against his chest, her fingers tracing his skin. "A man loving a child . . . there's nothing more beautiful. Except a man who fights for his child."

$$\sim$$

After finishing up the sweeping and wiping and straightening, the kitchen looks almost returned to her pristine condition. It's an optical illusion, because each week she lives a different story. She's never the same, touched by many different fingerprints. Today they'll begin a new chapter.

An hour later at the hospital, he and Renée enter Cassidy Banks's room while Rosalie waits her turn down the hall.

"Cassidy," he begins. "You're looking well."

"My apologies for the mess I've caused. The two of you have been so kind to Rosalie. That means a lot."

"We're glad you're on the upswing," Jean-Paul says. "You scared us there for a bit."

Her eyes trail downward, refusing to meet theirs. "My daughter has some imagination . . . She thought she was your daughter."

He hadn't been entirely sure how they'd start the conversation, but Cassidy led them right in.

"It wasn't a one-night stand . . . I'm sure she told you. I went through a registry, and believe me, I made sure to pick . . . no offense . . . Chef's handsome and all, but Addison Fitch, he's the donor."

They let her go on.

"Perfect pedigree . . . no known medical history . . . I checked."

It would almost be amusing if the truth weren't going to be such a mind blow. "Cassidy," Jean-Paul interrupts.

She's rambling on about the baby picture, Addison Fitch's physique. But when she hears her name and feels their stares, she stops talking.

"Addison Fitch isn't her father," he continues. "Unless you're prepared to address me as Mr. Fitch."

Cassidy pretends not to hear. "It's such a cute name."

"Cassidy, I'm not sure how to say this, but I'm just going to give it a try. I donated to Biogenics. It's sweet you named the donor, but the donor was me. I'm Rosalie's biological father."

Cassidy's face drains of color. "What did you just say?"

"I'm donor #051738. And if you check your files, you'll see you chose me."

"That's impossible. I saw a picture. Definitely wasn't you."

"It's him," Renée says. "He was quite the looker." She gazes at him. "Still is, in my opinion."

"I'd love it if we could figure out a way to coexist, because as much as you probably wanted Rosalie when you searched for a donor, that's how much I'd like to be part of her life now." He hears the crack in his voice, and Renée grabs his hand. "Your daughter is a brilliant, thoughtful young woman."

The tubes and lights blink and dance around Cassidy, but they can't protect her from the truth. They can't change the fate that's brought them together. She sinks farther inside the bed until the blanket swallows her up. "I don't believe you. You can't come in here and tell me a reputable company screwed up my order. I selected . . . someone else. A gorgeous hunk . . ."

"Yes, and that was me."

She's shaking her head. "No. No. No. That's like substituting green goddess dressing for . . ."—she flings a hand in his direction—"French. No one likes French dressing."

Jean-Paul can't believe his ears. "It's a DNA match at fifty percent, Cassidy. It doesn't get more precise than that."

He's losing patience.

"Look," he says, "I think we all agree that Rosalie's best interests are paramount to everything else."

Cassidy begins to register something. "Are you trying to take her away from me? You can't do that!"

"We're not going to take her away from you," he says, "but we'd like to have some sort of plan that's beneficial for all of us. Respectfully, we have one request."

"I can't wait to hear this."

"You scared the life out of that girl. You need to do better. That's why you should get help."

She rolls her eyes at them.

"Check into a facility; there's actually one not far from the inn. You need to get your mind and your health under control. Renée and I will do whatever we can to help Rosalie and be there for her, but if you love your daughter, you can't keep putting her through this. It's not fair to her. She's a teenager. She needs her mother."

Cassidy's limited in her movement due to the tubes connecting her to the IV, but she manages a weak smile. "I'll think about it."

Jean-Paul nods. "Good. I think it'll benefit Rosalie long-term. In the meantime, she can stay with us. We can get to know her."

"I said I'll think about it," Cassidy says, but she's staring at them with defeat in her eyes.

CHAPTER 69

PENNY

Penny wriggles in the bed beside Leo, memorizing the previous night.

It hadn't been like one of those rom-coms, where there's some big reveal and the couple has this hot sex and lives happily ever after. Leo hadn't proposed again. He didn't make any sweeping announcements. It wasn't the movies.

Instead, they'd sat on the porch in the old rockers, talking late into the night. They discussed that afternoon in Palm Springs and the parts that hurt the most. The way their bodies led them astray, the remorse that plagued their dreams the months thereafter. Ellie's tiny body, lifeless on the ground, as they pumped air into her. How they let Alara and Buckley down. How they let each other down. (Though no one beat themselves up as much as Alara.) They talked about their kids, assuring them that what happened to Ellie wouldn't happen to them. When you board a plane, and the flight attendants go over the safety demonstration, they tell you to put the oxygen mask on yourself before your child because if you run out of oxygen, you can't help anyone else. Leo and Penny had run out of oxygen.

Last night, they may have separately imagined running off into the woods and tumbling in the grass. But they saw how passion could overtake things, and they were being careful. When they finally returned to her room, they were sober and clearheaded.

She asked him to stay.

He said he would.

They didn't get undressed. They lay clothed beneath the covers, the moon casting a ray of light across the duvet.

She rested her head on his chest, and he stroked her hair.

He told her how much he had missed her.

She had missed him too.

When they had almost fallen asleep, their phones dinged.

He told her to let it go, but she worried it might be the kids.

She rolled over and tapped the screen with her finger. Abruptly, she sat up.

"Who is it?"

He didn't wait for her answer.

He leaned over and grabbed his phone.

She read the text several times, slowly letting it sink in.

He did too.

We won't ever get over losing our daughter. We've had to find a way to live in a dark, cruel world. But we're doing it. For her. For us. And you need to do it too.

She read it over and over, memorizing it when another text came through.

It was not your fault.

Penny burst into tears, releasing a flood of emotions she couldn't rein in as Alara gave her grace. Leo held her tighter, stroking her hair. Her gut instinct was to reply, *I don't deserve it,* but she held it in. The loss was too big. It would live inside them forever.

She missed Alara. She'd been racked with guilt. Stuck. Scared. Her fingers hovered over the keyboard because there was so much she wanted to say, to apologize for again, to bridge the distance, but she needed time.

She had no doubt they saw the video. She would call Alara when she got home. She would be there for her friend.

A third text came through, making her jump. Thank you for not mentioning her name.

They lay knotted together, his body wrapped around hers like a second skin. And sometime during the night, by the light of the moon streaming in, she watched Leo breathe. Something inside her came alive, and she kissed his cheek, slowly stroked his hair. He was in a deep sleep, and it took him a minute to stir at her touch. But when he did, he peered deep inside her eyes, rolling on top of her, peeling off their clothes. There was an urgency, but they took their time, and their bodies found the rhythm that first brought them together. She told him to stay inside her forever.

When they finished, he gathered her from behind, their naked bodies pressed against each other like shells. "I love you," he whispered in her ear.

"I love you."

"Is what's his name going to be upset?"

George. She had forgotten about that small fib.

"I trust he'll survive."

"Do you trust me?" he asked. "It's important you do."

She thought about it. The answer was unequivocally yes. "I do."

This is how they started their anniversary day, repeating the words they promised all those years ago

CHAPTER 70

CASSIDY

How dare Jean-Paul De La Rue come in here and make demands involving *her child*? He's known Rosie all of five minutes; he's no expert on her well-being. Which is almost a bit of a joke coming from Cassidy.

They don't make a move to leave, so she says it again. "I'll think about it."

Her head throbs, and she presses the button for the nurse. When she arrives, the couple finally gets the hint and leaves, but Cassidy's head still spins at Jean-Paul's words. *You scared the life out of that girl. You need to do better.*

The nurse administers an extra dose of pain meds in her IV when the door swings open, and Rosalie appears. Cassidy waves her in, and her daughter pulls up a chair. They sit in silence before Rosalie asks, "Did they say when you're getting out of here?"

Cassidy shakes her head. She's studying Rosalie. It's not her make-up-free face. It's something less obvious. She looks relieved. Happy even. Jean-Paul's voice strums and strums in her ear—*You need to do better*—and she remembers when her own mother got sick. How traumatic it felt to lose her. And how it changed her life.

"What's wrong?" Cassidy asks.

Rosalie shakes her head, though Cassidy sees through it. Her daughter then reaches inside her bag and hands Cassidy a cream envelope. "This was under my door this morning."

It's an invitation of some sort, requesting her presence on the lawn at 4:00 p.m. "I'm not sure what it is," Rosalie says. "Everyone got one."

Cassidy isn't interested in the card. "We should talk."

Rosalie licks her lips nervously, stuffs the card back in her bag. "I'm sorry for what I did . . . behind your back . . . but I'm not sorry for finding him. They're kind. It's like . . ."

"Family." They say it at the same time.

The medicine kicks in. Cassidy feels weak and regretful. "I understand." Then she pats the space beside her.

"I'm not staying long," Rosalie says, fumbling with a ring on her pointer finger and twisting it around.

"You got your wish."

"What's that supposed to mean?"

"Jean-Paul." She lowers her head. "I wanted you to have Addison Fitch. How was I supposed to know that man donated sperm and sent in a picture that made him look like a hot stud?"

"Mother, it's Atticus—"

She smiles. "I know. Atticus Finch."

"He's not real."

"He's also someone I'd never have to worry about taking you away from me."

"Jean-Paul said that?"

Cassidy doesn't answer. "So you concocted this whole plan to come to this fabulous inn because you knew. I don't know why I'm surprised. You've always been ridiculously smart."

"Is that a compliment?" Rosalie half jokes.

"I still think he doctored his picture."

The monitors beep.

"Was it really that bad?" Cassidy doesn't wait for an answer. "That you had to go find him?"

Tears well in Rosalie's eyes. The crystal-blue eyes she inherited from the man in the hallway. She nods.

"I can't imagine what it must have been like for you to see me on that floor."

Rosalie doesn't look up. She simply stares at her ring. So many disappointments in that head of hers.

"I wasn't always like this." When this doesn't get her daughter's attention, she raises her voice. "I'm talking to you."

Rosalie's eyes shift upward. "I tried talking to you too."

The accusation feels like a dart in her skin. Or maybe it's the pain from her fall. Cassidy feels lightheaded and afraid. Jean-Paul's request that she get treatment knocked something loose, and she steps outside herself. All the effort she spent trying to live was actually killing her. And she was taking Rosalie along with her.

"Your grandmother—"

"I don't want to hear how close you and Grandma Ann were."

The comment stings. But Rosie is right. She's told Rosalie about their closeness, but she didn't tell her how awful it was without her. In the beginning, she may have blamed Rosalie. Like it was an exchange somehow. She couldn't have both. Maybe she resented Rosie. Maybe she was terrified she'd become like her mother. Sick. It's all a jumble in her broken brain.

"I'm sorry, Rosalie."

She eyes her suspiciously. "For what exactly?"

"For all of it?"

After Rosalie leaves, the nurse returns with an enormous bouquet of flowers. She hands the card to Cassidy, who tears the envelope open.

Cassidy,
Your Vis Ta Vie family is rooting for your speedy
recovery. We're here for you, and we're here for Rosalie.
You're our family now.

Sienna, Lucy, Henry, Penny, and Leo

It takes less than three seconds for Cassidy to break into tears.

CHAPTER 71

ROSALIE

Her mom sounded confused and sad, and she didn't make much sense, but even in that state, Rosalie sensed something else. Maybe when the surgeons went inside her head, maybe they tapped on something, struck a synapse. Something shifted.

Jean-Paul's driving them home from the hospital. She wants to ask him what all this means. She wants to know if she'll see him again. Will they speak on the phone? She'll have to get his cell number. She could text him things girls text their dads about. And she realizes there's so much about him she doesn't know.

And as if reading his mind, they pull up the drive, and Renée hops out of the car.

"You stay," Jean-Paul says.

Rosalie's confused.

"I'm going to help you practice driving."

CHAPTER 72

PENNY

"What's this?" Penny asks when she finds the cream envelope slipped beneath their door. She opens it and reads. "Our presence is requested on the south lawn at 4:00 p.m." He's sprawled across the bed, and she sinks in beside him. "South lawn. Sounds so fancy."

"Does this mean we have to get out of bed?" His bottom lip drops in a frown.

"What do you think it could be?"

"Whatever it is, it can't be better than this."

"I've been thinking," she says.

He laughs. "That's dangerous."

She gently pokes him in the shoulder.

"I have an idea."

CHAPTER 73

JEAN-PAUL

She's skittish at first. Who wouldn't be?

But he takes her to the parking lot by the Mast General Store and explains gears and brakes and acceleration. They set the mirrors and seats. She's attentive and interested and asks the right questions. When she sits behind the wheel, she has a confidence that surprises him. And when she starts the car, shifts into drive, and manages to steer flawlessly around the lot without jerking them forward, he bursts with a new form of pride.

"That was good!" He beams.

"Jean-Paul."

"Yes, Rosalie?"

"I can't lie to you."

And before she says it, he knows. The innate connection they share. "You've had more practice than you led me to believe."

She nods. "There were a few times I had no choice. Groceries. That sort of thing. Let's just say, I'm a natural."

She continues to surprise him, but he warns her she can't drive without an adult in the car. His heart feels like it's no longer his when he adds, "Promise me you won't do that again."

And she smiles at him, because she understands.

They park the car and head off on foot to the Valle Crucis Community Park.

"There's a lot we have to figure out. It won't happen overnight. Renée and I will have more time when we sell the inn. It'll give us a chance to get to know each other better."

"Why'd you do it?" she asks.

They're on a path surrounded by babies in strollers, joggers, and laughter. He stares out at the beauty of their home. The looming trees, the grass, a burst of green. "Renée and I couldn't have children."

He doesn't wait for her to respond.

"For whatever the reason, it wasn't in the cards, and it was hard. I'm not sure why I did it. At the time, it was impulsive, and I probably didn't think it through. Maybe it gave me some power, knowing I could help someone else. I wasn't open with Renée, and that cost us. But you have to know, she felt it too. Early on. Even before I knew it was me. When I told her you found your father, she was the one who wanted to help. So whatever the reason I had for doing what I did all those years ago, it gave me you. And I don't regret that for a second."

They walk around the loop, and Rosalie shares some of her best memories. He already knew the worst. She asks him how this will work moving forward, and he doesn't tell her that he's already thinking about the future. About visitation and shared custody. Could he adopt her? He's getting ahead of himself. They will take it one day at a time. Much depends on Cassidy.

And the first step is getting through today.

He takes her hand in his and squeezes.

At five minutes to four, the guests begin to file out the front door. When he and Rosalie returned from their driving lesson, there was work to do. He had moved the wooden benches from the campfire over to the lawn by the oak tree, its branches fanned across the sky. Renée and

Simone set a table with flowers and an assortment of cheeses, fruit, and fig spreads. Another table has a plain white tablecloth. The setting is simple, but that's the best backdrop for the best memories. Above clouds chase each other, scattering along the sky directionless. *Go away,* he whispers.

Sienna, Lucy, and Henry arrive first, and Simone hands them each a glass of champagne. They're curious, but they're happy. Refreshed.

Henry asks, "Are you going to tell us what's happening?"

Renée waves him off. "What's the fun in that? More importantly, what's with the weather?"

"The sky is unpredictable."

That's when Lucy fits herself beneath his arm and grabs him around the waist. "Kind of like life. I like it that way."

They kiss, and Jean-Paul catches Renée basking in the healing power of their home.

Rosalie's next. She strolls toward them with her head held high, a deep smile across her cheeks. "Hi," she says shyly to the group.

"How's your mom?" Lucy asks, moving in for a hug.

"She's good. Better."

"How are you?"

Rosalie thinks about her answer before offering a slow-moving nod. "I'm good. I'm really good."

The inn's door swings open, and Leo and Penny waltz out. She's a vision in a sundress showing off her bare shoulders.

They toast and drink, gathered on the gorgeous property when Renée and Simone approach, pushing a cart stacked with boxes. One by one, they place them on the bare table, and Simone removes the contents from the cardboard. They're cakes. A lot of cakes.

CHAPTER 74

HENRY

He's admiring the petite-size cakes.

Eighteen in total.

Who on earth would need all this dessert? The table is a mix of color and decoration. Chocolate. Vanilla. Red velvet. Pink frosting. Blue frosting. Flowers. Balloons. Strawberries. Simone drops folded cards in front of each dessert, and the guests disperse, sauntering around the table, reading the inscriptions.

Renée pulls Simone close to her side. "We had a busy day, but we wanted to do this."

"Oh my gosh," Rosalie exclaims as she moves from one cake to the next.

"They're for every birthday of yours that I missed," Jean-Paul says.

"We missed," Renée corrects him.

Henry stops in front of a chocolate cake with his name surrounded in fondant stars, a sun, and moon, and Renée explains. "We owed you a replacement birthday cake, considering I dropped the one from the other night."

He turns to her. "I'm the one who owes you. Lucy and I have been discussing it, and we'd like to help you out with the inn. We can't let you give this place up."

Leo overhears and saunters over. "Did you see your cake?" Renée asks. "There's an anniversary cake for you and Penny. Today's the day. We didn't forget."

"We have an announcement to make ourselves," he says.

"Another wedding?" Renée holds her hands together in prayer.

Leo picks up a spoon and taps his glass.

CHAPTER 75

PENNY

She stands beside Leo, proud of their decision.

"I just overheard Henry make a generous offer to save the inn." Leo glances at Penny, his arm around her waist. "We'd also like to invest. We can't let you give up this place either. It's too important. It holds too many memories. It's our second home. We're family."

Leo gazes into Penny's eyes. Blue. Brown. She has never loved those eyes more. The differences. The then and now. All they possess. All they have seen.

Renée looks about to cry. Jean-Paul hugs her close. "We can't let you do that," she says to Leo.

"Yes, you can. It's time you let us give you what you've given to us."

"We'll discuss it," Jean-Paul says. "After we make some wishes. After we have some cake."

And one by one, they light the candles. Rosalie, hand in hand with her cousin, Simone, skips past each cake with a smile and a wish. Henry smudges his name with a finger, and Leo and Penny blow out the candle beside a bride and groom. And that leaves Sienna and her cake. There's a star—a big bright sun—and M&M's strewn about like little planets. The inscription reads: *Anything is possible. Wish big.*

Penny feels a joy she hasn't felt in months. She turns to Leo, flashing back to their bodies in bed. "You were wrong earlier. This is better."

CHAPTER 76

SIENNA

She feels a raindrop on her forehead and turns toward the sky.

She's scared. The decision she made is huge. But she's not scared to be alone. She will get used to the dark. As she continues to work through what's happened and what's to come, she watches Lucy and Henry, and she knows they'll be okay too. What she's scared of is the possibility that this might be her last time here.

Lucy makes her way over. She always knows when Sienna needs her.

"This isn't the end. You're coming with us every year. As long as that's what you want."

"I do. I do!"

Simone's snapping pictures, capturing the moment, and it's a good one: the two women embrace, years of memories stretched through their arms. The skies open up, but no one moves. They dance to Van Morrison and Kacey Musgraves. Leo scoops Penny in his arms and twirls her around. She's smiling, but she could also be crying; the rain drips down her face, and it's hard to tell. They're surrounded by so much love. And Sienna raises her hands up to the sky. She's ready for it.

CHAPTER 77

ROSALIE

The rain continues at a steady pace until they're soaked; the remnants of the cakes dissolve into pastel puddles. But they don't care. They're happy together, making magic and memories. Once she might have held back, but she remembers Jean-Paul's advice: *What's the point of creating something if not to enjoy it?* He encouraged her to get off the sidelines and jump in. So she jumps in, raising her hands in the air and swaying to the music and the rain.

Her phone buzzes in her pocket, but she's not interested. She feels free and light. It buzzes again. And again. It's a series of texts from Cassidy.

Rosie. I'm sitting here in this darn hospital bed thinking about you. Lucy once said we should write when we feel overwhelmed or afraid. She said we didn't have to actually give it to the person, but we could "explore" our feelings, get them on the page. I admit, I laughed when she said it like that. But she said sometimes it helps. Maybe I'll send this. Maybe I won't.

I'm sorry I'm here and you're there. I'm sorry I'm not with you. Though I don't know if I was ever really with you in the way that you needed. I wish I could say that I tried, but I didn't, not in the way a mother should. Jean-Paul's right. That man gave me a nice kick in the ass this morning, and I deserved it. I've been selfish, and I've put my needs before yours. And as awful as that sounds, and as shameful as it is for me to write, I want you to have this small part of me, because it's probably the most real I've ever been. With you. With myself.

Love never came easily to me. And I'm going to skip over the parts about my own father issues, because in hindsight, we can't blame our parents for everything. Remember that, okay? I was given choices, over and over. Me. And I was an adult when I made those choices. And perhaps my decisions were shortsighted or just plain wrong. But when I lost your grandmother, I was terrified that what happened to her would happen to me. That I would get sick. That I would die. And somewhere in there, things got jumbled. I had to be thin. Healthy. It was the one single thing I could control. Being thin made me feel good. Having people praise my body made me feel good. It became an obsession. And I thought you had to be like me. As my child, you were an extension of me. I thought for you to feel good, you had to live your life the way I did. I was wrong.

But I'll get to the piece that I know has been weighing on you.

You.

I know I said this earlier, but it's worth repeating. I wanted you. If there's anything you glean from this story, I hope it's that. And maybe I should have told you sooner about the sperm donor, but I was stupid. Who wants to talk about sperm? No one ever accused me of being easy. The reason I'm sharing this is because I know you, Rosalie. I've witnessed your quest to understand, your thirst for knowledge. Renée and Jean-Paul came to me this morning. They want to be in your life. And because of that, I'm going to get myself better. If it's what you want, stay with them and get to know them. Then when I'm done getting better, we'll figure it out. I'll heal quicker knowing you're being taken care of.

I hope he gives you the answers you've been looking for, and I hope he embraces you in ways I could not. And if he can't, I hope you find the strength within yourself to know that it's not you. But something tells me he's going to be good at this. And you deserve it.

Trust yourself as you always have.

I love you, baby girl.

Oh shoot. I hit send.

Oh. I really did this.

I'm going to do this.

Sorry for all the texts.

You know I hate these things.

Rosalie cracks a smile. Cassidy. She pulled through in the end.
She had given her so little.
This was all she ever needed.
She makes her way over to Jean-Paul. Her father. She's not ready to call him that out loud. Yet. But she will, in time.
She passes him her phone. Renée slides her glasses on and reads over his shoulder.

"You know what this means?" Renée asks.

Rosalie knows.

But it feels nice to hear Renée say it. "It means she loves you. Very much."

They collide like stars: she and Jean-Paul and Renée. There are lots of tears.

CHAPTER 78

ROSALIE

Departure Morning

The guests stand in front of the inn with their suitcases stacked and waiting. They move in slow motion, delaying the inevitable, stepping into the other world. They take turns hugging Rosalie goodbye before getting into the SUV that's taking them to the airport. Penny and Leo's Mustang sits nearby.

"You take care of yourself," Sienna says. "I'll see you next summer."

Henry's next. "Don't forget what I've told you about everything up there." He points to the sky.

She tells him she'll never forget.

"I'm here if you need anything, Rosie. You have my number," says Lucy.

Penny's openly crying. "I'm really going to miss you. But you'll visit. The girls will love you."

Leo makes her laugh. "Remember, those characters in the movies aren't me. They're never me."

"I know. You're one of the good guys."

He hugs her, and she thinks about all the girls in her high school who would kill to be in her shoes. He's an ordinary guy. Together, they're extraordinary people.

Tears prick her eyes, and she waves as the cars pull out of the driveway. The cloud that has been hovering disperses, and the sunlight reflects on the windows. Simone locks her arm in Rosalie's. "Look at this." It's a picture from the first night. Rosalie takes it in her hand, studies their faces, their posture, how so much has changed in a week. Simone squeezes her hand in hers. "All my *oncle* wanted was an extraordinary week, Rosalie. You gave it to him."

She chose the inn to find her father, and what she got was a family. Eight strangers circling around like planets orbiting the sun, guiding each other through light and dark. She closes her eyes and lets the warm breeze brush her cheeks. They will leave a lot richer than when they came, belonging to something greater than themselves.

Henry's right. *We are all made of stars.*

And when you raise your head toward the sky, you find the magic.

ACKNOWLEDGMENTS

First and foremost, thank you, Danielle Marshall. Not only have you been my editor, but you are a great source of comfort and support, a champion for your authors, and someone who has talked me off numerous ledges. Thank you for wearing all the hats, and especially the ones you didn't sign up for. You have been the one constant in this business, and I am grateful.

Thank you to my agent, Jane Dystel, and the team at Dystel, Goderich & Bourret for believing in this story.

This one I call the *bad boyfriend*. He came on strong and challenged me in a big way. There were times I loved him and equally hated him. Behold the big guns for setting him straight: Jodi Warshaw; my new BFF Angela Elson, who had me literally laughing out loud at her hilarious, eagle-eyed copyedits; Kellie Osborne; cover designer Lisa Amoroso, etc. This story is better and stronger because of your talented contributions.

Thank you, Gaye and Frank Luaces (and Grey), for sharing the Inn at Little Pond Farm with us. Our favorite memories have been under your roof sharing incredible meals and connections. Michael and Yvonne Coury, and Gaye Luaces for the menus and wine pairings. Drs. Richard and Ron Berger for anything medical related.

Early readers, in my opinion, are the most nerve-racking of all readers, but I couldn't send this baby into the world without passing it first through these thoughtful hands. Thank you, Andy Okun, Merle

Saferstein, Amy Berger, and Sam Woodruff, for your time, edits, and honesty.

Lisa Barr, Andrea Katz, Sam Woodruff, Kerry Lonsdale, Allison Winn, Camille Pagán, Emily Bleeker, Tracey Garvis Graves, Jamie Rosenblit, Sally Koslow, Alison Greenberg, Lauren Margolin, Jessica Jonap, Merle Saferstein, Annabel Monaghan, Camille Di Maio, Lynda Loigman, Rebecca Warner, Jackie Friedland, Elyssa Friedland, and Liz Fenton, thank you for your friendship and brilliant minds. Your input, advice, and support during every stage of my career have been invaluable.

Thank you, authors, reviewers, bloggers, and bookstagrammers who have read my work, shared with their followers, became friends, supported, blurbed, lifted me up, shared advice, or opened a door. So many of you have given your time and kindnesses to me, and at the risk of leaving someone out, please accept my sincerest gratitude—you all know who you are. Special thanks to Zibby Owens, Ann-Marie Nieves, Heather Sadlemire, Barbara Bos, Renee Weingarten, and Annissa Armstrong.

Which brings me to you, readers. I'm grateful every single day that I'm able to do what I love to do (most of the time), and that I'm able to share that love with you. Every review, every email, every share is a reminder of how lucky I am. Books have the power to change the world. And right now, the world needs that kind of love.

Thank you to my girlfriends for accepting my quirkiness, my anti-social introverted-extroverted ways, and the many times I couldn't talk. I love you all.

Thank you, RB5, Bergers, Weinsteins, and WeinBergGoldSonPowell, for the love, support, and always providing the best fodder. My stories wouldn't be complete without you.

Mom. Even though you're no longer with us, I feel you on every page. You introduced me to the mountains of North Carolina when I was four and gave me a place to always call home.

Steven, Jordan, and Brandon, this is the eighth acknowledgment, and it remains unchanged: you are my heart, my home, and every single star.

ABOUT THE AUTHOR

Photo © 2018 Hester Esquenazi

Rochelle B. Weinstein is the *USA Today* and Amazon bestselling author of eight women's fiction novels, including *What You Do to Me*, *When We Let Go*, *This Is Not How It Ends*, and *Somebody's Daughter*. A former entertainment industry executive, she splits her time between sunny South Florida and the mountains of North Carolina. Rochelle is the monthly book contributor for NBC's *South Florida Live*, Miami's *AQUA Magazine*, and *Women Writers, Women's Books* and teaches publishing workshops at Nova Southeastern University. She is currently working on her ninth novel. For more information, visit www.rochelleweinstein.com.